From country bumpkin down south, to Chicago citified pimp, to coveted Evanston resident, Wayne Hunter always searches for more through his own lust and greed. As we enter the characters of Wimbey's Corner, David Covin spins a fascinating coming of age tale of one Black man's search for his larger than life aspirations.

Linda Goodrich, Chair and Professor, Department of Theater and Dance, CSU, Sacramento

WIMBEY'S CORNER

Also by David Covin

Black Politics After the Civil Rights Movement:
Activity and Beliefs in Sacramento, 1979 - 2000

The Unified Black Movement in Brail, 1978 - 2000

The African Race in California, Darkness Visible

Brown Sky (a novel)

To Edward, Dorothy, Myrtle, and Lela, who knew life
in a place very like Wimbey's Corner

Copyright by David L. Covin. All rights reserved.
Library of Congress Cataloguing in Publication Data.

Covin, David, 1940 -
Wimbey's Corner

1. World War II 2. Chicago/Evanston 1939 - 1945 - fiction

I. Title

ISBN - 13: 978-0-9844350-3-6

Published by Blue Nile Press
PO Box 188213
Sacramento, CA 95818-8213

An Imprint of Path Press, Chicago

Cover Art by John F. King

Cover design by Marshall D. Bailey

Manufactured in the United States of America

TABLE OF CONTENTS

WAYNE'S STORY

1

Wayne Hunter never would have been touched by the twentieth century had it not been for the selective service act of 1940. After its passage, someone found the way out three miles past the nearest road, down the winding trail, through the woods, across the cleared ground the Hunter family worked, and up to the canvass-covered doorway of the colorless, faded, wooden quarters they occupied. There the stranger wrote down the names of the male Hunter children who were of the correct ages and told them to report to the post office in Bardwell for instructions.

They went to Bardwell. From there they were bussed to Mayfield where they took the test. The day they arrived in Bardwell was the first time Wayne had seen the Illinois Central tracks. He never got over it. They all failed the test since none of them could read or write. The other men laughed at them and laughed at their country ways.

Wayne decided as they walked home he was going to learn how to read. After Penny, that is. Because as soon as he got back he went straight to her. He had to see somebody who made him feel like a man.

Penny was pretty. She was not only pretty, she was cute, so cute Wayne could not keep his eyes off her. Penny's mother had named her because she had been pretty even when she was born. "Pretty as a penny," she had said. So she named her Penny. Wayne had heard her tell that story at least 715 times. He never tired of it. Because she was. Pretty as a penny. She had the cutest little shape, round, soft, sweet titties, just large enough to fall outside his big hands so that he could not quite hold all of them, a smooth stomach, a big, juicy, round butt so soft for squeezing, and sweet, black thighs, full and tasty, sweet as baby's milk. He could not keep his hands off her. That is why they had Bobo. He was a good baby and smart as a whip, talking up a blue streak and only three years old. He had been talking since he was one.

When Wayne returned and went to Penny she did make him feel like a man. They were together all night and she made him feel so much like a man he stayed three days and three nights before he went back home. When he got home he searched out Uncle Remington and told him he wanted to learn how to read. Uncle Remington read the Bible six hours a day. He could read fine. But he had never tried to teach anybody to read. He had never even thought about it. He soon learned it was not easy.

Wayne loved fishing. He had caught Mr. Big when he was ten years old and he had never recovered from it. The only other person he knew who had caught Mr. Big was Algonquin Brown. Algonquin had taught him how to fish. Algonquin was so old when you looked into his eyes all you could see was darkness. His skin looked as if spiders had made webs in it and then someone had hung it on his bones in folds. But he moved quick and smooth and if you ever saw him going off through the trees at a distance you would think he was a boy of thirteen. He was very small.

Algonquin told Wayne about Mr. Big. He told him that every body of water held a Mr. Big. Whether it's a lake or a creek or a pond or a slough or a bayou or a river, each has its own Mr. Big. He is the biggest, oldest, and wisest fish in that body of water. He's the biggest and the oldest because he's the wisest. He's almost impossible to catch. Only a master fisherman can catch him, and then only with steadfast patience and a piece of luck. The bigger the water, the bigger Mr. Big. Mr. Big was always much larger than anyone imagined because people were used to ordinary fish. Mr. Big was not ordinary. He laughed at baits regular fishermen threw into his waters, and when the younger fish were not too full of pride and arrogance, he taught them to avoid baited hooks. Though he was master of the waters, one could count on the fingers of both hands the people who were aware of his existence.

Anyone who ever saw Mr. Big knew it because there would be nothing in that watershed which even approached him in size. Years before Algonquin had caught Mr. Big out of the Tennessee River. He was the biggest Mr. Big ever caught. The kind of fish Mr. Big was varied, depending on where he lived, but the Mr. Big Algonquin caught was some kind of fish nobody had ever seen. His back, not counting the dorsal fin, rose a full foot above the top of Algonquin's head when he stood next to the fish as it lay stretched out along the bank. Algonquin could easily have walked into the fish's open mouth. Algonquin's heart had broken when he had finally beached him. He never caught another Mr. Big. He had hooked several - in sloughs and bayous and creeks and ponds - but when he realized it was Mr. Big, he always cut the line. Some of them were very big - nothing like that Tennessee River fish, but monsters nonetheless.

When Wayne was ten years old he caught Mr. Big out of Bois Slough. It was like looking on the face of God.

Afterwards, every time his line broke the surface tension he knew he stood at the vault of creation, that he might bear witness to the mystery of mysteries ascending from the deep, that the secrets of heaven and earth might open before his eyes.

One half of Wayne's life was spent on the water. That did not change even after Remington started teaching him to read. Wayne took his lessons fishing with him.

Sometimes he fished from the bank. Sometimes he used a pirogue. It all depended on the water he was fishing and the time of day and the weather and what he was after. Wherever he fished he was alone. Even when he went to a heavily fished body of water he went where no one else would go. Because that's where the big fish were.

His world was Spanish moss and cypress trees, water lilies and cattails, quiet sounds. An oar dipping into still water. Frogs thrugging in the saw grass. The humming of flies, mosquitoes, and bees. The flitting light buzz of dragon flies. He heard the patter-patter of heron feet trailing through the water and the flapping of their great wings as they lifted themselves in flight.

It was a green world, green and the silver-blue sheen of water, reflecting sky and clouds and trees, leafy and dark. The woods and bayous were places of mystery, enigmas shrouded by dark water. Wayne was so much a part of them that when he left they clung to him, as if a piece of swamp or river bank walked across the fields and in through the front door.

One year after the army had called him, Wayne walked back to Bardwell.   He had sworn he would not stare, but he did. He stared at the automobiles, the trucks, the poles with wires stringing them together, everybody wearing shoes, and such clothes as he had seen only once before in his life. He looked at the stores and wondered where they found glass so big for the windows.

Involuntarily his mouth popped into a grin. A sign on top of a pole said, "Main Street." Another said, "Stop." There were signs everywhere. "Filbert's General Store." He started laughing. He could read every damn one. He fell down in the street laughing.

When Wayne came to himself, he had gathered a crowd - all white. They stood around him, looking down at him lying on the ground, on his back. A lot of them were laughing. Some pointed their fingers at him.   They made fun of his bare feet. "Country nigger," one said.

Wayne wanted to hide. He wanted to go right back home. He wanted to turn around, walk down the street until it turned into a road, stay on the road until it met the mule-track. From there he would run the rest of the way home. That's what he wanted to do.

Just a country nigger, he thought. That's all I is. Popeyed at everything. Fallin' out in the street like some kind of fool.

He raised his eyes. The first thing he saw was writing on a plate glass window that said, "Gumpstead's Hardware."

He could read.

He was country. But he could read. He could read sure 'nuff and it didn't have to be no Bible neither.

He stood up.

He was still country, but he was a different man than he had been last year.

The sign in the bakery window was what he had been looking for. It said: HELP WANTED.

Wayne looked above the hand-printed sign. Words were stenciled across the glass: Mueller's Bakery.

Wayne went in the door. He liked the way the place smelled. Fresh bread. Warm. Sweet-smelling. Hungry-making. His stomach growled and saliva ran in his mouth. Behind the corner stood a man of generous flesh, moderately tall, his face touched with splotches of red. He wore a white shirt, an apron, and a tall, white hat shaped like a mushroom.

"Well, there, boy, do you want something," were the words the man said, but he said them so strangely that it took several seconds for Wayne to realize what they meant.

"Oh, yes, yessir," he said, "I s-s-s-seen yo sign in the w-w-w-wi-window and I b-b-been lookin' fo work, sir."

"Work is it," said the man. "If this war keeps up and America gets in it, with a name like Mueller and the accent I've got, *I'll* be looking for work. When can you start?"

"Right n-n–now, sir.

"Okay. You got a job."

Wayne could not believe his luck! He not only had a job, but a job where even breathing the air was sweet. Grinning and salivating he followed Mr. Mueller into the back of the shop.

Joe Harrison came to Bardwell. He lived in Mayfield where his father was the sole proprietor of the Real Chicken Barbecue and Grill and the biggest Negro in the county. Joe had learned of a used car for sale in Bardwell and he had driven over in his father's pickup to see if he could meet the terms. He brought Emery Wilson with him.

The man wanted too much money for the car. Disappointed, Joe hung around downtown Bardwell with Emery, drinking one of the distillates for which Kentucky is famous concealed in a brown, paper bag.

Wayne, Penny, and Bobo walked by, within ten feet.

"Damn, Emery," Joe's voice was loud. "Did you see the shape on that little woman? Ooooh-oooowee!"

Penny, unable to make out the words, turned her head to see who was making so much noise.

"Look, Emery. Pretty, too - pretty as she wanta be!

"Hey, sweet thang!"

Wayne was unaccustomed to such situations, but he knew men. "Don't pay no mind," he said to Penny. "Just turn 'round and let them be."

But Joe would not let her be. He had too much corn squeezins in him and she looked too good. He had not expected to see someone so fine in a little, hick place like Bardwell.

"Say, good-lookin'," he called.

"We just gon' keep walkin'," said Wayne.

Joe ran after them. "Don't you hear me talkin' t'you," he shouted.

Emery stumbled after him. "Hey, Joe," he mumbled. "Hey, Joe, leave 'em alone. They just a couple o' country niggas. What does they know? Leave 'em be."

Joe caught up with Wayne, Penny, and Bobo, ran past them, and turned around to face them. "Hey! I'm talkin' to **YOU**!"

He stared directly at Penny, a grim expression on his face. It melted, at first imperceptibly, into a giant smile.

"Hey, little mama," he said. "I just want t'talk t'you. You so cute." He grinned.

"Pardon," said Wayne. "Would you get out the way. She don't wanta talk t'you, and you is blockin' the way."

Joe looked up at Wayne as if realizing for the first time that

7

he existed.

"Pardon me, big man," he said, "but I wasn't talkin' t'you."

At six feet, two inches and 200 pounds, Joe was no little man, but Wayne's physical presence overawed his.

Emery caught up with Joe, "Come on, man, let's go," he said. "Let's get out o' this stinkin' little town. We got yo Daddy's truck. Let's get out t'Three Mile Inn. We can have us a good time befo' the rooster crow."

"What about that," said Joe, looking dead at Penny. "With you, baby, we could make that joint jump - oh, hot damn!"

Wayne stepped between Joe and Penny. "Why don't you do like yo friend say and get out o'town."

"Look, big nigga, I'm gettin' tired o' yo ass," said Joe.

"Come on, man, leave this country nigga alone," said Emery. "These backwoods boys never knows how t'act noway. Let's go, man."

"Step back, Emery," said Joe. "I don't want t'hurt you, too. This nigga been in my way just too damn long."

Emery put his hands on Joe's shoulders to pull him away.

Joe shrugged his shoulders. "Don't do that, Emery." His voice was cold.

"Wayne, don't," said Penny. She tugged at his shirt sleeve.

Wayne turned to her.

With Wayne turned at an angle away from him, in one quick movement Joe brought the bottle high into the air then smashed it down with all his strength on Wayne's head.

Glass, blood, and whiskey exploded in a spray. The force of Joe's downward stroke drove Wayne to his knees.

Triumph radiated in Joe's face.

"Wayne!" Penny screamed. She threw her arms protectively around his head and shielded it with her own.

Bobo let out a loud, terrified wail.

Very gently but so quickly he could not be seen, Wayne

was out of Penny's shielding embrace. He came up so fast Joe's alcohol-numbed motor responses had no chance to react. Only his face showed the appropriate changes - gloating, incomprehension, fear. Wink. Wink. In the wink of an eye.

Wayne's great hands grabbed Joe, one on his throat and one on his knee. Wink. He had him in the air over his head. Wink. Wink. He drove him down to the concrete, head first. Wink. Blood flew. With a snap, a pop, a sound that turned goose pimples on all five of them, a vertebra snapped. Wink. Joe's head turned at an inconceivable angle.

"Oh, no," hollered Emery.

Penny screamed in terror.

3

When Wayne got off the train in Chicago his jumbled thoughts and stretched emotions were stunned by the numbers, the absolute numbers of people leaving the train. So many were colored, colored from the South like him.

Outside on the sidewalk people rushed by in streams. Where were they all going? Where were they all going, so many, so fast? Cars honked and screeched up and down the streets. People hurtled by - two wide lines of them going in opposite directions.

Wayne was saved by a shoe-shine man on a corner. The shoe-shine man saw the drowning in Wayne's face, in the slump of his shoulders, the hopeless way his huge body drifted along in the crowd. He reached over and fished him out. Drew him onto shore.

For a long time, Wayne stood there - on the bank - saying nothing, thinking nothing. Reviving. Reviving. Coming back to life. He realized he was not dead. If he were in hell, it was a hell on earth, not an afterlife. He began to breathe deeply, and to orient himself to his surroundings. He looked, finally, at the man who had rescued him, and thanked him.

From the shoe-shine man, Jersey-Blue, Wayne learned where he could spend the night, directions on how to get there, and how to look for a job.

He went as Jersey-Blue directed him, to the South Side: twenty-third and Indiana. It was not far from the Twelfth Street Station. Not a long walk at all with Jersey's directions. Wayne got a room and a newspaper and sat in his window and marveled.

This is where the train takes peoples, he thought. I's here. At the end of the line.

Niggers was everywhere. The streets were full of them.

They were loud, talking and shouting all up and down the street. They marched and strutted. They slinked and slanked. They stood on the corners. They leaned against the walls. He saw some doing what he was doing, looking out the window. Some called down to people on the street. Others yelled across to other people in windows. Some just watched. There were people dressed fancy, and people in undershirts, people in countrified clothes like his. Some sat or leaned on the stairs in front of doorways. He smelled cooking. Fish and chicken and ribs and cornbread. Beans and pork.

City. City life. He was still staring out the window as dark came. He jumped when the streetlights turned on. He did not know what happened. Who turned them on? He kept watching them, wondering if they would go away. Before long, groups of men and groups of boys began to cluster around streetlights. He stood transfixed, until he could hold his eyes open no longer.

A familiar sound woke him in the morning. Horses' hooves. He ran to the window. A horse pulled a tall, white, enclosed wagon down the street. The driver was dressed in white, wearing a little white hat.

For the first time Wayne laughed.

I's here. In Chicago.

Before the sun was fully up he was out and down in the street. He walked to Jersey-Blue's stand. The city felt oddly fresh and quiet in the morning. As Wayne walked he smelled water, a great deal of water. He wondered what it was.

Jersey-Blue let Wayne help with the shoes and paid him a little change. They talked all day as they worked and Jersey Blue said if Wayne were really a baker by trade he was sure he could help him find work. A lot of businesses were losing their young men to the war and they were desperate for help.

He was as good as his word.

Hansen's Bakery was on the south side of the loop, with a

11

very steady trade, and badly in need of help. In three months they had lost four men to the service. They had never hired colored, but if they reduced their production, their customers would go elsewhere. The men who stayed were overworked and over-tired. They gave Wayne a try out and hired him on the spot. The work was hard, steady, with a lot of overtime.

Every week when Wayne got paid he bought a money order. He had a nice stack of them. He planned to send them to Penny, but he did not know how to do it and for a long time he did not think about how to do it because he did not want to remember.

He did not go out after dark. All the Negroes in Chicago were crazy. They were not only crazy, they were bad. Mean. Would kill you in a minute. Slash - cut. Some even carried guns.

The other thing Wayne noticed was there were more niggers it seemed like everyday. They never stopped coming. It seemed to him they were starting to fill up the cracks in the sidewalks and the chinks in the walls. Everywhere. They were pouring in all over the place. They were filling up all the space. He started feeling as he had when he first got off the train. People were mashed up against him. There was no where to turn, no where to breathe.

As frightened as Wayne was of those bad, Chicago niggers, they fascinated him. He had not known there were so many Negroes in the world. The only time he saw white people was when he went to the Loop. On the South Side all he ever saw were his own people. Their variety thrilled him. Colors cream and bitter chocolate, café au lait and cinnamon, colors pecan and sandalwood, mahogany and rosewood; colors of summer dawns and ocean sands, midnight and golden noon. How he loved to look at them - hair that bunched itself in wooly crowds, or separated in rings on the scalp, hair that ran in flowing waves or straight like a piece of string. Hair black and brown and copper and grey, even naturally blonde and red. He never tired of seeing his people. Terrified of them though he was. He was amazed at them, too, because they did everything.

They gambled, drank, fought, cussed. They were smoking reefer and stabbing each other. They were shooting and stomping. Niggers eatin' barbecue and chittlin's. Niggers shootin' craps and playin' cards. Niggers doin' everything. They were in gyms, boxing. They were on the streets playing baseball, and football, and basketball. There were schools full of them. Negroes read newspapers. Negroes went to libraries. They drove jitneys and busses, and cabs. Negroes were policemen. Negroes were mailmen. They taught school. They wore suits to work. They played in jazz bands and danced on the stage. They owned stores and theaters and shops and funeral parlors. They were doctors and lawyers. They owned banks and insurance companies and their own newspapers. Niggers did everything.

The storm struck the last week of November. The hawk dove down the streets and through the walls. Even in bed, wrapped in blankets, there was no escape. The hawk leaped into the elevated trains and raked the people in their seats. He swooped into the downtown bakery and chilled men working in front of ovens. In two days two feet of snow fell, the forty-five mile an hour wind blew drifts six feet high, and the temperature staggered down to fifteen degrees.

The day the first snow stopped, Wayne departed from his normal route home. He went to the Illinois Central station and picked up schedules for all the trains going through Western Kentucky. When he got back to his room there was no relief from the hawk but he warmed himself by reading the schedules again and again. He was convinced it was impossible to live through the winter in Chicago.

13

It was cold and then the wind. It ripped through your clothes. Tore at your face. Dragged tears out of your eyes.

It would be all right if you could get warm. But Wayne never could. His toes and his fingers, especially, never warmed up.

They had to be lying. It could not last until April.

It even hurt to breathe the air. When he was outside his face got so stiff he could not move his mouth. Couldn't talk - at least not so anyone could understand him.

It got cold at home in the winter. It even snowed. But the cold was not like this. You could live in it. You could get warm.

4

Huddled under his blankets in the dark, Wayne heard a knock on his door.

No one ever knocked.

He stared into the darkness.

Who could it be?

Wayne exhaled.

Maybe they'll go away if I just lies here and breathes quiet so they don't hear me. Maybe they'll think I ain't home.

Wayne became terribly aware of his own breathing. Suddenly he realized he did not know how to breathe anymore. Cold as he was, sweat slid down his body, icy.

He was going to die because he could not remember how to breathe.

The knocking was much louder.

O Jesus. Sweet Jesus. Help me.

He clenched his teeth and waited.

The knock came again.

Without any intent on Wayne's part, his mouth blurted out, "Just a minute!"

Wayne heard the sound as if it had come from someone else. He could not believe it.

The exaggerated noise of everything - his renewed breathing, the blood pumping through his veins, the floorboards creaking in the cold - told him it was true. He actually had said it.

His will, his resistance, deserted him. He wrapped a blanket around him as he walked without sensation, without thought, across the room. His body moved of its own volition. He watched his arm as it raised his hand to the latch and the door knob. He watched his hand as it worked the fixtures and swung the door open.

The man was framed by the light in the hallway. Wayne could not see his features, only the bulk of a man's frame in the doorway.

"I see I got you up," said the man. "I'm sorry. I'm Delgado Taylor. I live down the hall in 311. I came now because nobody ever knows when you're at home - we never see you around, but somebody seen you come in tonight. So, I said, 'now or never.' We having a little Christmas party next week. We want everybody on the floor to share a little holiday spirit. We hoping you will come by."

The Christmas party was friendly and cheerful. Wayne began to come out of his shell. He liked the people. They were Chicago niggers, those bad Chicago niggers, those crazy Chicago niggers, but he liked them.

With friends the winter became endurable. There were times - fleeting only - but times when he did not feel the cold.

After Wayne made his peace with the weather, after he accepted the proposition that it was going to stay, he even found a way to profit from it. His boss had him shovel snow in front of the bakery. At first he did not know how and made a mess of the walk. But after his boss threw a fit, one of the other bakers showed him how to do it. Wayne became good at it. He bought his own shovel and made spending change shoveling the walks of nearby shops. He also took his shovel home and walked around the neighborhood near his room, hustling jobs, clearing sidewalks for three-flats, churches, and small businesses.

The extra money left him free to tag along with his neighbors in the building when they went out. Since he put most of his earnings into money orders for Penny, before snow shoveling, he had lived on the slimmest of margins. But

16

afterwards he found himself going out with his friends once a week.

Wayne did not run after Chicago women. He was not married to Penny, but she was his woman. He felt she was his wife. Many times he saw women who flared his nostrils and sent blood surging through his body, but he accepted the feelings for what they were and did not try to act on them. Besides, he recognized after a few times out with Delgado and his partners that most of the women seemed to prefer men who looked nothing at all like himself. Their ideal man seemed to be one who was almost white in complexion, with narrow, straight features, and wavy brown hair. Anyone who saw those men would have to say they were pretty. Pretty men. Most men did not look like that, but the closer they were to that ideal, the more acceptable they were to a larger number of women. Wayne was the opposite of the ideal.

The stranger was sitting across the room at a table by himself, staring through the smoke and moving bodies and the sounds of laughter straight at Wayne. Wayne probably would not have remembered him except that before he went to bed that night he happened to look down at the cold spring rain falling on the pavement, and there staring up at his window stood the man from the cabaret.

Wayne did not mention him to anyone, not even when coming home from work the next Monday evening he saw him standing across the street from his building. Only the next weekend when Wayne saw the stranger standing in a shadowy corner of the nightclub he and Delgado had attended, the direction of his gaze unmistakable, was he sure, absolutely certain, that the

17

stranger was after him.

Thinking over everything he had done since he had come to Chicago, Wayne knew he had not offended anyone. He had not made any enemies. Until he had started going around with Delgado and the men in the building, he had not gone out at all except to work and shovel snow. Now, when he did go out, to clubs, he went with the same group of men. He stayed with them and did not even talk to anyone else. There was no reason for anyone to be following him.

Unless the stranger did not come from Chicago. Unless he came from Kentucky.

The police.

Wayne knew he was going to have to find out what was going on in Kentucky. He was going to have to find out who they had sent after him. He composed a letter to Penny and sent it off via Remington.

Three days later he saw the stranger on the El, moving towards him. Wayne got off quickly at the next stop and disappeared in some streets he had never heard of. He was scared to go home. He spent the night at a transient hotel for fifty cents and took busses to work instead of using the El. For a week he stayed in hotels, a different one each night and rode busses. On the weekend he did not go out but sat in a hotel room alone in the dark and watched the street below.

Wayne realized he could move. The thought had never entered his mind that he could stay in Chicago, keep his job, but just move to another location.

It clicked. He not only *could* move. He *would* move. The question was where?

He kept his ears open. He began to listen to what people were saying when they talked about places. He dropped by Jersey-Blue's stand and talked to him and listened to people who came by. In all the conversations he heard "Evanston" mentioned here and there.

He wondered about it.

"You sure colored lives in that there Evanston," he asked Jersey-Blue.

"You heard me say it, boy."

"I - I uh didn't mean no offense, uh, uh, Jersey. But what I mean like I done heard that's up on the North Side and don't nothin' but rich folks live up that way. Uh, uh, I ..."

"You ever heard of rich folks doin' they own laundry, and cookin' and chauferrin' theyselves around, and housecleanin', and yard work, and baby settin', and all such?"

"No, sir. Uh, no, sir. That make sense."

"You durn tootin' it make sense, you country fool. Now stop botherin' me 'bout Evanston. It's plenty of colored what lives out there."

Wayne had to see for himself. He believed. But he had to see.

Sunday morning he got on the el headed north.

At Howard Street he changed to the Evanston el. He rode it to the end of the line. He saw colored getting on and off. Most of them got off at a place called Foster Street. He overheard their conversations. They lived in Evanston.

Jersey-Blue ain't never wrong, thought Wayne.

Evanston was a quiet place. From the elevated track he looked down on seemingly endless leafless tree tops. The el afforded a great view far to the east where sunlight sparkled in Lake Michigan's rippling blue pleats.

Wayne felt comfortable, relaxed. I could live here, he thought, and nobody would never know where I'd done gone. Safe.

When he went to work Monday morning he felt better than he had in a long time. He felt good enough to go back to his apartment after work. He knew he could pack up and move. He

19

had a place to go.

Wayne stared at the letter in his hand. It was all over. Since November. Since the first of November - even before the hawk came - since the first of November it had all been over. They had thought he had learned by now. The court had held a hearing on it and found no cause to charge him with anything. Self-defense. Self-defense. His people had thought he was staying in Chicago because the money was so good. His hand was shaking. He started laughing. He started laughing and could not stop. His ribs ached.

Then just as quickly as he had started laughing, he stopped.

His mind returned to that day in Bardwell.

It's like ain't nothin' happened. It's like he ain't never lived.

He did hit me in the head, but I shouldn't of killed the man.

Then something said, *if it's like nothing ever happened and they never sent nobody lookin' for me, who is the stranger?*

5

Through Remington, Wayne wrote Penny right away. Remington was the only one he knew who could read well enough to read the letter to Penny. He sent her a package filled up with the money orders he had saved for her. He wanted to come see her, he wanted to come see her without wasting a minute.

Everyday he poked and peered to see if something had come. Time after time his box was empty. Until one day a little envelope nested inside it. Wayne snatched it out. Remington's careful scrawl covered the envelope's face. Wayne tore it open and let it fall to the floor. His eyes greedily grabbed the letter, reading too fast to understand. He calmed himself, took a deep breath, then read the letter again, slowly. Penny said yes. Come home. Come home as soon as you can. Just let me know when it will be.

Wayne wrote back that night. He mailed the letter the next morning. He would come home Sunday-week on his day off. The bakery would be closed that following Monday so he could have two full days. The days and nights before his departure rose like a mountain between him and his Penny.

Wayne had not realized how small everything was, how small, and slow, and ... backwards.

He stood at the railroad station, looking at Bardwell's downtown, and shook his head. Look at these hicks, look at these hicks. And they had the nerve to call me country. He laughed.

Downtown Bardwell would not fill one block in the Loop. Especially when you think about skyscrapers, he thought. Bardwells stacked on top of Bardwells. There is fifty Bardwells on every single block of the Loop. Fifty. Fifty! Look at these hicks!

21

And they had the nerve to call me country.

He could not imagine he had once believed Bardwell was scary - so big and fancy it was scary. Man, this ain't even a good CTA bus stop.

He stepped down off the railway platform onto the street.

He felt good. I'm too big for this place.

He walked down the podunk street in his big, new Chicago suit. He had a big, new, Chicago hat on his head, and big, new, Chicago shoes on his feet.

I'm too big for this place.

Several people greeted him. He spoke back.

They even talks slow. They talks slow and they walks slow.

His pockets bulged with big Chicago money.

I'm too big for this place.

Wayne was stunned by how quickly he passed through the town and was out, trudging down the familiar country road - so much smaller than he had remembered, and devoid, absolutely devoid of traffic.

The weather was a lot warmer than it had been in Chicago. He wanted to loosen his big, new, tie, and his big, new, shirt collar. But he did not. He took out a big, new, handkerchief and wiped his big, new, Chicago face. The air smelled sweeter than it did in Chicago. It tickled his nostrils and he sneezed.

Everything was so much smaller - the fences, the houses, the ramshackle sheds and barns. Everything was much more run down than he had remembered, stained by the weather, falling apart. Mosquitoes rose off the damp ground in large, dark, buzzing masses.

Wayne did not like walking on the trail. It was hard to keep his big, new, Chicago shoes dry. Sticks hung down from trees and knocked off his big, new Chicago hat. He had to move quickly to keep the soggy ground from ruining it. After awhile he kept it off, holding it in his big hands.

Finally, he stood in front of a very small shack, a very small shack he had known as home with his mother and father, his brothers and sisters, several cousins, uncles, and aunts for all of his days. I'm too big for it, he thought. I'm so big I won't even fit through the door.

Especially with his big Chicago hat back on his head.

But Penny was even better than he had remembered - prettier and finer and softer in all the right places. Better than all those Chicago women. And she made him feel more like a man than all his big, new, Chicago clothes and all his big Chicago money. Because when they were finally together for the night he had none of that on and he felt too big for the world.

Monday morning Penny and Wayne went for a walk to enjoy each other alone in the daylight. They held hands along the woodsy trails and across boggy meadows.

"Why you goin' back to Chicago, Wayne? Why don't you stay here with me and Bobo?"

"I got my job, Penny. I cain't just leave it."

They walked on quietly holding hands.

Penny was proud of him in all his Chicago finery. Nobody around had ever seen clothes like that. They had been coming since sunrise from all over to see Wayne in his big city duds.

"My, my, my has you ever seen the likes o' that," some said.

Others reached out to feel the soft brim of his hat.

"Look like the sun comin' up over Peace Lake," said an old man talking about the shine on Wayne's shoes.

Penny let her eyes go big and smiled as she looked at Wayne. He's my man. It feel so good to be with him. She leaned her face against the expensive material of his suit. The sensation thrilled her.

23

"I been thinkin'," said Wayne. "Since I got back. We - you and me - we too big for this place. You don't know it cause you ain't never been out. But I do. We too big, Penny. I cain't come back here to live no mo.' I'm too big. And I got t'get you out. This place is too small for us. We better than this. We too good for this."

Penny did not understand what Wayne meant, but she did understand he was not talking about deserting her, he was not talking about running off with some Chicago woman. He was talking about bringing her with him.

He's my man. He gon' stay my man.

"I cain't take you back now," he said, "cause we ain't made no plans or nothin'. But I want you to start thinkin' about it. Before long I'm gon' have you up with me in the Windy City."

Windy City. That meant Chicago. He had never told her but she knew that was what it meant. He knew he would not have to tell her what it meant. He knew she would understand. That's how city folk talked about it. Big, fine city folk with big, city money. Like her Wayne. The dimples dug deeply into her cheeks. Windy City.

Wayne talked to Remington before he left. He gave him ten dollars and told him to teach Penny how to read. Sweet as she was, he could not have any ignorant woman living up in Chicago with him. He was in the big-time now. He had just realized it.

As soon as Wayne returned to Chicago he knew he could never bring Penny there to live with all those bad, crazy Chicago niggers, with all those pretty men. No. No. He could not do it. And Chicago was no place to raise Bobo.

Wayne accepted his change from Mr. Walker who owned the grocery store down the street from his building.

"Thank you," he said.

"You're welcome, Wayne," said Mr. Walker.

Wayne dropped the change in his pocket and started tearing the corner off his pack of Chesterfields. He walked back outside.

He loved Saturday afternoons.

He walked away from the store, dropping the cigarette pack into his shirt pocket and taking out a book of matches. He struck a match.

It was after he had inhaled and glanced to his left that he saw the stranger. Not ten feet away.

Wayne choked and coughed. The fit lasted a long time. While it was going on the stranger approached.

He was pretty. Long, wavy, black hair. Not conked. Not processed. Naturally wavy and pomaded to glisten. Aquiline features, complexion like darkened ivory. His lips were thin and clean. Slim, he stood slightly over six feet. He wore a wide-brimmed hat and a suit shining gold. Zoot.

"Hey, my man." He had a deep, soothing voice. "Is everything on the square?"

Wayne coughed one last time and nodded his head.

The stranger extended a long, elegant hand glistening with golden and jewel-studded rings. The cuff links emerging beyond his suit sleeve flickered ruby-fire in the sunlight.

"Claude, Claude Bonfils is my name," he said. "People calls me Light."

Wayne took his hand. It was soft, soft as a breast. Wayne dropped it.

"W-W-W-Wayne H-H-Hunter."

"Wayne Hunter," Light repeated the name.

"Where you from, my man?"

Wayne pointed. "J-J-J-Just down the street."

25

Light laughed, showing two rows of big, even, white teeth. "Naw, Jim. I mean where you *from*? Where yo people from?"

"K-K-K-Ken-Ken-tucky."

"Kentucky." Light raised his eyes to Wayne's. "I done met niggers from everywhere, but I don't believe I ever done met a nigger from Kentucky before."

He smiled again, his cheeks dimpling. "You got a job, Wayne? By the way, what do people call you?"

"Yeah. Yeah, I g-g-got a a j-job.

"Wayne. P-P-Peoples just calls me Wayne."

Light nodded. For the first time he looked away from Wayne. He watched the people on the street.

"You got a *good* job?"

"Yeah. I got a good job."

"I tell you why I'm askin," said Light. "I need a man like you."

"What ... Uh ... er ... uh ... what you mean a-a-a-a-a man l-l-li-li-li-like me?"

"A big man, a strong man."

Light turned his eyes back to Wayne's. "I got a job for you, Wayne, that you couldn't find if you went out lookin' for it, that you couldn't find in ten thousand years."

"What kind of a job?"

Light smiled.

"I couldn't tell you about it," he said. "You wouldn't believe me. And besides that, I cain't describe it. You'll have to see it.

"I tell you what. You got anything planned for tonight?"

Wayne swallowed. "No," he said.

"Good. Be downstairs in front of your place - I know where it's at - be there at ten o'clock tonight. I'll take you out with me and make you a job offer. Hey, Wayne ...."

"Uh ... er ... uh ... yes ...."

26

"Call me Light, man."

"Yessir. I mean, Light. Yessir."

"Dress to kill."

Wayne nodded.

He walked around Light. He wanted to get back to his room. He did not notice anyone he passed. He did not even notice his cigarette until it burned down so low it seared his hand. He stumbled as he walked down the street. His mind was working.

He been followin' me all this time just to offer me a job? I don't believe it. What kind of job? And why me? All the niggas it is in Chicago. Big niggas, too. Strong niggas. Why me? He don't want me for no damn job. What he gon' do with me if he get me t'go out with him tonight?

As soon as Wayne got to his building he wanted to ask Delgado about Light, ask him what he should do. But Delgado was not at home. No one was at home. For a long time Wayne sat in his room and looked at the wall.

Dress to kill. He kept hearing it and seeing Light grin.

Dress to kill. Oh, Lord, what do the nigger want to do to me?

As the day wore towards evening Wayne realized with increasing finality there was little he could do to escape. The man knew where he lived. He had followed him several times without much difficulty. If not now it would be later that the request for an evening's company would be inescapable. And if Wayne had reneged on an earlier promise to comply, the later consequences might be even more dreadful.

Now, he told himself. Now. I got to face it *now*.

When Wayne stepped out of the vestibule in the big clothes he had bought to wear back to Kentucky, they did not seem big anymore. He remembered Light's golden, shining, zoot suit. His own double-breasted suit felt shabby surrounding the contours of his huge body, too little and tight, a child's cheap suit on a man's body. The money in his pockets no longer felt big. It felt like chump change. He was sweating when the door closed behind him and the nippy spring draft tried to leap up his coat sleeves and dive down his collar.

There was no one outside the building.

Wayne looked down at his watch. Yes, it was ten o'clock.

Now how long I'm gon' have t'stand here and wait on the nigga? What if he don't even show? He felt an edge of hope.

That is when he noticed the long, white Lincoln parked at the curb.

No. His mind said, no. As his eyes lighted on the car, the back door swung open.

Weighted down, heavy with fear, he bent forward, trying to peep the interior. He could not see into the dark insides.

"Get on in, Wayne. It's me. Light."

Still trying to see, Wayne shuffled over to the car. When he got to the door he could discern a pale form against the dark on the far side. A strange fragrance greeted his nostrils.

"Get in, man."

Wayne bent over further and stepped into the car. The soft, luxurious seat seemed to rush up and enfold him. He sank back into its yielding comfort.

The sidewalk outside the door suddenly seemed as if it were part of another world. As an afterthought he reached over and pulled the door closed.

Quiet. Languorous.

Wayne felt at peace. He sank deeper and deeper into the upholstery. He did not know his eyes had closed. The mysterious scent played in his nostrils.

"Wayne, I want you to meet Nice."

Wayne's eyes did not pop open. They opened slowly as if Light had spoken to him from a dream.

He could see more clearly. The driver had turned around

and extended his hand. He, too, was pretty. He was dark, almost as dark as Wayne, but with fine features and slick, wavy hair. Wayne shook his hand. It was strong and not as soft as Light's.

"My pleasure," said Nice.

Wayne nodded. He did not know what to say.

Nice turned back around and the engine started. The car glided away from the curb.

"If you join up with me," said Light, you be working with Nice a lot. You two be a team."

Wayne looked out of the window.

He was sealed off from the outside. What people were doing out in the streets had nothing to do with him. He could ride by and watch them as a detached observer. He could not help smiling. He had not realized what being inside a Lincoln was really like.

"The war's going to make me a millionaire," said Light as they passed a crowd of sailors standing on a corner.

He leaned forward and opened a cabinet in the seat-back ahead of him.

"What's your pleasure," he said.

Wayne stared at him, uncomprehending.

"To drink," said Light. "This is a bar."

"Damn," said Wayne. He almost laughed. But he held his reaction to a wide grin.

"I likes straight whiskey," he said.

"Ice?"

"You got ice in there, too?"

Light clinked it with the tongs.

Wayne nodded vigorously. "Yeah, ice. I likes ice."

As the first ingots of bourbon poured into Wayne's stomach he relished the fiery trail they left. He held his glass out in front of him and listened to the ice tinkle in it.

He wanted to laugh. Who in Kentucky would believe this

shit? Who would believe it?

"You see, I makes my money in women," said Light, "the finest women in Chicago. You'll see. And there's always a market for fine women. But now. With all these soldiers and sailors passin' through Chicago. And with the ones they got stationed at Fort Sheridan and Great Lakes what comes here on passes - man, I makes money too fast to count. Ain't that right, Nice?"

The driver nodded. He smiled. "That's right," he said. "The eagle flies everyday."

The Eagle flies on Friday,
Saturday I go out to play.
Everyday, everyday, I have the blues ....
Pimp. Light was a pimp.

Wayne frowned to clear his head. He looked over at Light.

"I got thirty-five ladies workin' for me," Light said, "and more comin' in every week."

Wayne swallowed the rest of his whiskey in one long slide.

After the tearing in his eyes stopped, and the fire subsided in his alimentary canal, he said, "Where is we goin?"

"We gon' hit the clubs," said Light. "I want you to see my ladies in action."

Everywhere they went Light was known and a table was cleared for him. All the joints were jumping.

They hit the first club at 10:30 and they went on until five A.M. Wayne had gone to only a few clubs with his friends from the building. Though they had gone out regularly they had always gone to the same spots. Wayne had not imagined the number and variety of places available for night life.

And the women. He had seen many beautiful women in

Chicago, but he had never seen such women as he saw that night. Where do they come from, he wondered. Where do they be at the rest of the time? Why don't I see them on the street?

He drank enough so that after awhile he was not conscious of his staring, nor did he care. He could not look at them enough. He wanted to see, to see. Fine. So fine.

They stopped off for breakfast on the way home and Light let Wayne out in front of his building at seven A.M.

"I just wanted you to see what the operation was like," said Light. "I'll come by next Saturday and we'll talk."

The door closed and the beautiful car slipped away.

Wayne watched it. When it disappeared he stood for a few minutes on the empty sidewalk.

I know they wouldn't believe it in Kentucky. I don't believe it my own damn self.

7

Light had mentioned nothing about money. He had mentioned nothing about what Wayne was supposed to do. He might be out to pluck him for the country boy he was. Still Wayne could not get the sight of all those women out of his mind, or the feeling of all that luxury.

He baked bread and cakes and rolls and pies, but his mind was not on his work. He kept wondering what kind of jobs he could be doing for Claude Bonfils. Light. He wondered what kind of clothes he could wear. And he dreamed of the women. Oh, God, the women!

Being with Light had made a difference. They had not whispered behind his back and called him country. They had flirted with him. Pressed their titties against his arm. Rubbed their asses on his hand. Kissed him on his ear. O' Lord!

Wayne started drinking when he got home at night. He drank himself to sleep. He did not want to spend too much time awake. It was better being drunk. Much better.

Saturday did not want to come.

It did though.

Light sent Nice up to Wayne's room to get him and the three of them went for a long ride in the country.

Once he was inside the Lincoln, the lingering aroma clung to Wayne. He now knew it was reefer. Some time during the prior Saturday morning Light had asked him if he wanted a reefer. Shocked, Wayne had politely declined. Light and Nice and several ladies had gone ahead and lit up. Right away the smell had hit Wayne and he had recognized it from the car. Reefer.

Light poured Wayne a drink.

"I'll tell you," said Light, "why I need you. My enforcer is temporarily indisposed. I want you to be my new one."

"Enforcer?"

"Yes. The one who enforces my regulations. You see, you cain't run a business without rules and regulations. And I got mine just like everybody else. But I cain't rely on the police - the law - to enforce mine, so I got t'provide my own enforcement."

"Uh ... er ... uh ... like what?"

"Most important is this. All my ladies holds out on me at one time or another. I knows that. But I don't let them know I knows it. I makes 'em think I believes they turns in everything. So I checks 'em from time to time to keep the impression up. It's too many to check 'em all the time, so I just do like spot checks. I don't tell them when and where it's comin'. If they's messed up, they got t'face the enforcer. That's you."

"What ... uh ... what ... am I ... uh ... er ... supposed to do?"

"Nothin' - what will leave marks. Squeeze the bones in they hands together and rub 'em back and forth. Grab they biceps and cut off the circulation and rub the vein against the bone. Hold 'em down while you pushes yo knuckle into they shoulder or they arm, or they calf. Do it till they screams and cries and cain't stand it no more and they breaks. That's all I wants 'em t'do. T'break. Then it'll be a long time before they holds out on me again and when they does it won't be often or much, and they'll be very, very, careful."

Wayne didn't say anything. He tossed down the rest of his whiskey and put his glass back on the bar. Light filled it up.

"That's not something you gon' have t'do often," said Light. "Maybe I'll catch one girl a month. With you as enforcer I might not catch that many."

"What you mean? Why?"

"See, that's why I needs you, Wayne. I learned a long time ago in this business the more trouble you can avoid before it gets there, the better off you is. You can help me keep trouble away - things I won't never have t'deal with.

33

"You see, Wayne. You looks rough. You looks mean. You looks like somebody nobody would ever want t'mess with. That's what I seen the first time I looked at you. People will think twice before they gets involved in somethin' where they might have to go up against you. Just the look of you will do that. Save me a whole lot of trouble.

"Like last week when you was with us, you didn't notice no trouble, did you?"

Wayne had not collected himself enough to speak a second time. Husbanding his energy, he shook his head, no.

"That's what I mean," continued Light, "now it's some weekends when we don't run inta nothin'. But last weekend was busy. We made lots o' money - with no trouble. Didn't nobody even loud talk us. See - a ounce of prevention is worth a pound of cure."

"But ... uh ... er ... Light, seem like t'me you could get somebody with experience at it. Somebody who be knowin' what he be doin'. I don't have no experience like that, with womens."

"Oh, that's just a little part of it. It's the most important, but you don't have t'do it much. Like I said, no more than once a month. No, the most troubles I get is from cats who mess with my women - slaps 'em around, or takes they money, or won't pay 'em. We got more of that since we got all these cats from the service. At least five or six times a week. Sometimes that many in a weekend if it gets bad. You gon' have t'deal with that, too. Run them cats down and set them straight. Then there is a few tricks who got some sick ideas. They's yo job, too."

Wayne licked a chip of ice soaked in bourbon. He did not say anything. He shook his head, slowly, back and forth.

"Then," continued Light, "it's other pimps what tries to move in on my women. Now, you know, my women don't work the streets - strictly clubs and hotels. They is class chicks. Some cats tries to take some over, get them on they string. Others will

34

try to run them out of a club or a bar, fill it up with they women. All that's dead action. I cain't let it happen. Enforcer got t'take over."

"How often that happen?"

"Two or three times a year."

"Well," said Wayne, "I guess you know what you doin', but, you know, somebody with a ... a - "

"Gun," asked Light.

"Yeah. Er ... uh ... it would seem like t'me - I mean, that's rough stuff you be talkin' about."

"I'm glad you understands that," said Light. "That makes me even more convinced I done made the right choice. Yeah, you right. It's rough stuff, and anytime anything happens what requires artillery, me and Nice takes care of it. We both packs. And I carries a razor, too, though Nice don't believe in 'em. All he believe in is that little thirty-eight he keeps up under his arm, ain't that right, Nice?"

"That's right," Nice called back over his shoulder. "I want t'see what a razor gon' do t' somebody my special momma cain't stop."

"Naw, we wouldn't want you to pack no iron," said Light, "leastways not for a long, long time. See what we need you for is just three things: Number one, to walk into a room so they can just see you. Most o' the time that's all you'll need to do. Lookin' at you will take the fight out o' most people, and the word'll get around so fast, we won't have t'worry about nobody in the know messin' with our action for a long, long time. Number two, if it's necessary - to grab somebody. When you does that, you gon' pick 'em up off they feet and they gon' see how strong you is. And number three, if you absolutely has to, to knock somebody down and remove all doubts."

"Yeah," said Nice. "See, all we got t'do is walk into a place with you - and they know you our enforcer - nine times out of ten all the shit will be over. Like Light was sayin' - just by bein' with us last week, you cut out all the negative action. Peoples just figured you was Light's new enforcer. For that tenth time - when the fools ain't got no sense - Light and me packs enough lead to put down about two infantry companies. So together we keeps our shit up tight."

"Most of the time," said Light, "you won't be doin' shit. We just be ridin' around together, drinkin', goin' t'clubs, havin' a good time."

"He's right," said Nice. "That's what we be doin' ninety-nine percent of the time. Just like we doin' now. Just like we done last Saturday night. Most of the time we don't have no trouble. But in case we do, we can cut off a whole lot o' shit if we got somebody look like you along."

The whiskey was warm in Wayne's brain.

I am the enforcer, he thought. He chuckled. He smiled inwardly. He was smarter than they thought. He noticed they had told him he really wouldn't have to be doing nothing except having a good time, but they hadn't mentioned no money.

"The fringe benefits is sweet, too," grinned Light. "How did you like them ladies?"

Wayne had been trying not to think about them. He returned to the warm whiskey inside his mind.

"You could have some of 'em, Wayne," purred Light. "The finest women in Chicago - could be yours."

Oh shit. Wayne swallowed. He wanted them. He wanted them so bad.

"And they know what t'do for a man," laughed Nice, "you can take that shit to the bank!"

"I'll pay you ...." said Light.

Oh, yes, thought Wayne. Think they got me now. Talked about how easy it would be. Got whiskey in my brain. Talked about fine women till I cain't see straight. Set me up. Now they gon' come out with some chump change I cain't live on and expect me t'swallow that shit, 'spect me t'eat it right up. Ha, I'm ready fo you, Mr. Light, Claude Bonfils. You ain't gon' country-boy me.

"... one hundred dollars a week."

Wayne's eyes bolted open. He had a good job. He was the envy of everybody in the building, and he only made twenty dollars more than that in a month.

One hundred dollars a week.

Was it possible?

"To start," said Light, "then we'll see how it go.

"Of course, I'll give you a couple hundred dollars bonus for teamin' up with us. Nice can go out with you, and you can spend some of it on clothes. My enforcer, very definitely, has got to'be dressed to kill.

"I don't want you to make up your mind right away. Why don't you let us take you back home? Then you can run with us again tonight. Get a second look at what you'd be gettin' into. Then let me know a week from today."

Wayne nodded. One hundred dollars a week. A two hundred dollar bonus. Whiskey and pussy and fine clothes.

He barely heard Light tell him as he was getting out of the car to come down at ten as he had the week before.

When Wayne reached his room he took pains to become stone, cold sober. Weights had been dropped free-fall into his brain. Bonus. Money. Clothes. Fancy women. He would have to hurt them. He remembered seeing them the week before - yellows and high-yellows, deep chocolate browns, brown-skins and light brown-skins. Coal black. He remembered their laughter and the way they moved under their clothes. He remembered how their touch had felt on his skin and through his clothes. Their perfumes had wrapped his senses in a fog of desire. He would have to hurt them.

Only once a month. Mostly they would be scared of him.

37

Scared of him? How could any woman be scared of him? He was scared of them. Scared of how they made him not care about anything else.

He checked himself. He had to know he was sober. The weights his mind had to haul around did not accord him the luxury of infirmities.

He thought about how he had decided not to try to run with Delgado and his friends, just to sit back and watch. They were too fast for him. But next to Light, Delgado and his crowd were asleep. Fast? Next to Bonfils, lightning was slow.

Slow. That's me. How can I even think about running with that bunch?

Wayne remembered what it had been like going back to Kentucky as a big Chicago man. How much bigger he would be if he went back riding in a Cadillac, rings on his fingers, gold watches on his wrists, money falling out of his pockets and beautiful women like those hayseeds had never seen falling out of the back seat? They wouldn't know what to do with me. Those country hicks in Bardwell and Mayfield. Had the nerve to make fun of me. Had the nerve to call me names. Country. That's all they was. He'd show them. Smooth. Big Chicago man. Ain't never seen nothin' like it in they whole life!

Penny would be so proud of me. Except for the other women. The fast life. Penny ain't made for the fast life.

Me neither. Sweet Jesus. I wish I was. I wish I was.

A hundred dollars a week! I'll never make that kind of money. I wouldn't have t'hurt them that often. I ain't worried about the men. It wouldn't bother me to handle them. I don't want t'kill nobody else, but I would be careful. I would be real careful.

By the time Wayne went downstairs to get into the big Lincoln he had decided to stay sober and watch, to really watch the life he was thinking about joining.

8

"Reefer."

"No Thanks."

"Dance, baby?"

"I don't know how."

"I can teach you anything."

Number.

Number.

"Bee-bop-a-ree-bop!"

"Solid, Jack!"

Don't know why

"Fill it up."

Ain't no sun up in the sky

"Look at that ass!"

Stormy weather.

"I can tell you how to use cocaine so a bitch'll think yo dick's the sweetest thing since sugar. Look, I'm gon' pay you a hundred dollars a week. Would I steer you wrong? She'll kill for that dick."

Fast.

Wayne looked at the pretty women. He looked at the beautiful women. He looked at the gorgeous women. He could not hurt them. He could not hurt one of them.

Matilda joined their table. Wayne stopped thinking about anything.

He looked at Matilda's eyes. He looked at Matilda's mouth. He looked at Matilda's nose. He looked at Matilda's hair. He looked at Matilda's breasts. He looked at Matilda's arms.

He watched her tongue as it slid along her lipstick red lips. She was a yellow woman, not quite high yellow, but not too far away, either. She wore her dark hair up in a pompadour.

Her body was lush.

When she laughed he watched her teeth and the dark inside of her mouth. He leaned over so he could smell her. He breathed in deeply and kept breathing in.

She was so close. So close. He wanted to touch her. He wondered if it would be wrong to place his big, black hand on her yellow arm.

He listened to every sound her voice made and did not care what the sounds meant or signified. Each note of her voice touched him behind his stomach, against his spine where he could feel it.

When she got up to dance with Nice he watched her waist and her hips and her ass and her legs and her feet.

He stared at all of her and his eyes were feeding.

When she came back to the table and sat down she stared directly into his eyes and held his gaze, and smiled. Wayne did not know what to do. He grinned but that was involuntary. He could not speak. He did not know if he were about to laugh, or shout, or fall over dead.

Light and Nice left the table. They asked Wayne if he had cab fare to get home. He nodded yes.

Matilda's flat was two blocks away from the club, on the second floor.

They undressed in the dark. All the while he could not stop kissing her and touching her and hugging her. They lay on the bed for a long time doing just that. Her hands started moving over his skin, over his naked body.

Suddenly without warning her voice leaped out in the early morning air, shattering through the near windows, cracking - stark, above the dying streetlights, escaping the apartment into the hall and up and down the stairs.

"No!

"Oh, No!

40

"Sweet Jesus! No!"

They made love past noon because she would not stop and he would not stop and she would not let him stop until they both crashed exhausted into sleep, still joined, locked, one in the other. Neither ever wanted to leave the other's embrace. Neither wanted ever for the time together to end.

As Wayne rode the el to work on Monday his mind did not leave Matilda. Her mouth opened to swallow his. The soft wetness of her lips enveloped his. He felt her long tongue, full and thick, rolling in his mouth, and reaching down towards his throat. He wanted to swallow it. He wanted to swallow it all. He felt her body moving under him, over him, around him. He had never known what a woman could do, what a woman could be. Here he was a grown man and a father of a four-year old and he had never known. He never left her and he felt her mouth and hands all over him. He never lost his erection and never stopped coming and knew he could not, he could not - even if he tried with all his heart and all his soul and all his will - he could not stay away from her.

About Wednesday it entered Wayne's head that all the time he had been scared of Light and trying to stay away from him, the man had been trying to recruit him to help with his pimp business. All the time I was staying away from him I was staying away from Matilda.

As Wayne leaned back into the soft upholstery of Light's automobile and Nice pulled it away from the curb, Wayne blurted out, unable to keep it inside another instant, "I wants t'see Matilda."

Light chuckled in the darkness. "Funny thing," he said. "She said the same thing."

"Don't lie to'me, man. I ain't playin'."

"Lighten up, Wayne. I ain't lyin'. What did she say,

Nice?"

Nice spoke over his shoulder.

"Yeah. It surprised me. Long as I been knowin' Matilda. She told Light, 'You better bring that big, black nigger back here next weekend, and I'm not talkin' about Saturday night, either. Have his black ass over here by Friday!'"

"That's what the bitch said," confirmed Light. "I had t'school her. If she wanted to see you she had to work her ass off Friday night. Then if she did good - real good - I'd let her see you on Saturday." He laughed. "Bitch worked her ass off."

Nice laughed, too. "Shit, if she worked like that every night we could retire in a month."

Wayne felt his fingers clenching.

"Look like I don't need t'teach you about cocaine," said Light.

"Naw," said Nice, "don't teach the nigger nothin' 'bout no cocaine. He'll have every bitch in Chicago eatin' out of his drawers."

The two men laughed.

Wayne looked out the window. He wanted the car to go faster. He wanted it to fly. He had to see his Matilda.

Making sure that Wayne stayed lodged deeply inside her, Matilda nestled her head against his chest. She smiled quietly and peacefully.

"Matilda. I wants to ask you somethin'," said Wayne.

She ran her palm across his chest.

"Baby, you don't have t'ask me nothin'. Whatever you want, you got."

He held her tightly against him. It felt so good to be inside her. He did not want to move. If either of them started moving they would both go crazy again. He relaxed his hold on her, caressing her back with soothing.

"If you could still make good money and not have to work" he said, "would you - would you stay with me and not turn no tricks?"

She kissed his chest. "That would be nice, Baby, but Light would kill me."

He held her very tightly. "I mean if Light would leave you alone."

She reached her arms up over his shoulders and around his neck. She started to move on him.

"Baby, I would stop workin' tonight."

9

Wayne gave the bakery two weeks notice. He went up to Light's apartment early one afternoon when he knew Nice was out getting the car waxed.

"I wants to talk to you about the job," said Wayne after Light handed him a drink.

"It's about time. I ain't never had nobody put me off so long."

Wayne took a swallow. "I cain't bullshit you, Light."

Light nodded.

"I wants the job. But."

"Not enough money?"

"No."

"What then?"

"I - I ... shit."

Light turned his back to Wayne.

"I want the job, but ... I - I w-w-w-want Ma-Ma-Matilda, too?"

Light swung gracefully around. "My man, you have her every weekend."

"No, Light. I mean, I want her for me. Permanent —— no tr-tr-tricks."

"What!"

Wayne took another swallow.

"That's it," he said. "That's what I wants."

"Did she tell you -"

"I said. That's what I wants. Me. Wayne Hunter. I wants it."

Light poured himself a drink. He sipped it.

"You talkin' about a number one lady," he said.

Wayne did not answer.

"On a *bad* week she turn over a thousand dollars for me.

"How you go' replace a hundred thousand dollars a year?"

Wayne swallowed another drink.

"I wants the job. But I cain't take it no other way."

"Dig up," said Light. "If I say no ... if I say no, you lose Matilda *and* the gig."

Wayne walked over to the bar and poured himself a drink. "And you lose a enforcer, and maybe somebody else gets one," he said.

Light put his drink down.

He looked carefully at Wayne.

"On one condition," he said.

Wayne felt his pulse quicken.

"You make her loss good."

"What you mean, Light?"

"What I means is this. Matilda is one of my heaviest hammas. Ain't too many mommas like Matilda. If she leave my stable it's gon' take two or three GOOD WOMEN - I ain't talkin' about no ordinary, everyday ho. It's gon' take two or three good women - top-line women - to make up the money I'll lose. You bring 'em to me. Enough to replace what I'm gon' lose. That's what I mean."

"Light - how I'm s'posed t'do that? I don't know nothin' bout turnin' nobody out."

"I ain't talkin' about turnin' nobody out. I'm talkin' about replacements - workin' women - you dig?"

Wayne shook his head.

Light looked away, exasperated. "Listen up, my man, you gon' be a enforcer - dig? That means one of the things you do is make sure don't nobody intrude on my territory. Well, now, I want you to intrude on somebody else's territory and TAKE two or three of his best women."

"Light -"

"Unless you don't want Matilda."

Wayne turned up his glass and took all of the burning fluid down in two swallows.

Matilda lay next to Wayne unable to keep her hands off him.

"You gon' do it, Baby?"

Wayne pointed his toes and felt his muscles stretch as the agonizing ecstacy of her touch surged throughout his body.

"I wants you, Baby," said Wayne.

"You got me."

"No. I mean I wants you just for me. I don't want you doin' this to no other man."

She lay her weight on him and kissed him. She began grinding her pubis into him.

"Think of it as an apprenticeship," said Light. "You had to apprentice yourself to a baker when you learned how to bake, didn't you?"

Wayne nodded.

"Yeah, well, this is the same thing. Just a different kind of work. I likes the threads you and Nice picked out. Clean. But, you know. You need a little more flash - some jewelry. A couple rings. A stickpin. You got t'glitter, man. You know, when you moves, the chicks got t'see you gleam.

"But like I said, see. You takin' these women for me, that's trainin'. 'Bout time you finished, you be ready t'start workin' for me, first class."

Light blew a long, elegant stream of smoke out of his

mouth.

"Plus, it'll help make yo rep. People won't be wonderin' if you as bad as you looks. They'll know."

Wayne thought about it. Everything Light said was probably true. But that did not help Wayne. He did not know where to start.

"I don't even know why he need a enforcer," he said to Matilda in the dark. "He got a razor. He got a gun. He got Nice. What he need me for?

"To keep his face pretty," she answered. "How you think Light turn out so many fine women? They fall for his pretty face. He can't afford to get it messed up. See, Baby, once Light gets a woman's attention he can talk so much shit she won't know which way is up. Oh, yes, Claude Bonfils can talk a whole world of shit. He have bitches eatin' the shit out of his drawers. But, see, how he get their attention in the first place is by bein' so damn pretty. It don't hurt for him to be ridin' around in a long, white Continental with a chauffeur, to be wearin' silk shirts and cashmere coats. But they see all that after he's smiled at 'em, and talked a little smack to 'em. By then they's so confused they'll swear fat meat ain't greasy. They sink back in the back of that Lincoln, Light makin' eyes at 'em, mixin' 'em a drink, gittin' 'em to hit on a reefer, diamonds flashin' on his fingers, gold bracelets on his wrist, talkin' smack like a mixmaster, and those bitches never know what hit 'em. They be singin' *Summertime* in the middle of January with the hawk whistlin' all up they pussies.

"Mmmhmm, and that's before he put that cocaine covered dick up in 'em. After that he can take them straight to Kankakee. Nutty as a fruitcake. Believe that Claude Bonfils is Jesus Christ and Haile Selassie all rolled into one. King of the Jews. Lion of Judah. And Prince of Candy."

She smiled at Wayne. "See, Baby, if it's any trouble he want you to catch it on yo big, black, country face. He's savin' his. Givin' you the straight skinny, Light is one of the meanest cats around. Like you say, he carry his razor - and his gun - at all times. Know how to use 'em, too. Uh huh. He's a head hunter. Plus, he don't even need 'em. He's strong. And quick. Knows how to use his hands. Most of those pimps around here can't touch him. He'll do 'em like the Japs did Pearl Harbor. Make 'em wish they was dog doo.

"But see, all it would take would be one time - just once - when he was talkin' to one of his women who ain't come across, for her to rake her nails across his face. Claude Bonfils don't never want that to happen. He don't want the chance of that to happen."

"But Nice -"

"Nice is to protect Light. That's his job. Period. Nice cain't protect Light and enforce at the same time. Uh uh. That's two different jobs."

He reached over and touched her smoothness in the dark.

"Tomorrow I got t'go t'Willie's Club," he said.

"That's where Golden Jones keep his ho's," she said. "Baby, Light ain't playin'. Golden Jones is a murderer."

So am I, he thought.

"Baby, don't go. I can keep workin' and still make you forget all about it." She kissed him. "I'll make you think castor-oil is sweet."

"You already do, Baby. And that's why I got t'go. My woman ain't gon' be fuckin' nobody else!"

10

Wayne got to Willie's Club early. He sat in a dark corner and ordered a set up. He watched the place fill. The whores did not come until late, until the men had grown a hunger for them.

He saw Golden Jones when he came in. He was tall and solid-built. He was not pretty like Light. He was darker. His features were more colored. His thick hair was not straight or wavy. But he looked neat. Everything about him looked neat - the razor-edge around his hairline, his eyebrows, his straightline moustache. His nose was neat, his lips were neat, his ears were neat. He looked as if it would be impossible for a line to appear on his face or a wrinkle on his clothes. He even walked neatly.

A striking woman held onto each of his arms. Everybody in the bar acknowledged his entrance, raising a glass to him, nodding to him, smiling at him. Even Wayne could not help himself. He nodded. It felt like a bow. Golden noticed them all - every one - and acknowledged none. He strolled to the back of the bar where a table that commanded the whole room awaited him. He sat down, followed by his ladies, and then there was a rush as people mobbed the cocktail waitresses and the bartender to buy drinks for Golden and his women.

Wayne watched him. Golden did not miss a thing. He knew when every one of his ladies left and came back. They did not bring him the money. He sent one of the lovelies at his table to pick it up. He never moved.

The bar was very orderly. People had a good time. They laughed and drank and danced, but nobody got unruly. Everybody was aware of who sat at the table in the back of the room.

Wayne watched the whores work. They wasted little time and few words. They were efficient. Wayne studied them all night. When he left at three in the morning he knew the first woman he would claim for Light. He came back early again the next night and waited. He came early because he did not want to be at the club too late. He wanted to make his hit and be gone before Golden arrived.

Cinnamon came in and glanced around the dark room. Wayne emerged just enough from his inky corner to catch her eye.

She walked over to him.

"Can I buy you a drink," he asked.

"Maybe."

She looked him over.

"What's a big man like you lookin' for tonight," she asked.

"You."

She laughed.

"What you wanta do with me?"

He reached out and touched her thigh, letting his fingers run down the slick material clinging to her body.

"Uh-oh, watch it," she said. She took his hand and placed it on the table. "This stuff ain't free. These is expensive goods. I ain't sure you can afford it."

"Can afford it better than those dumb-ass soldiers and sailor-boys."

He showed her a wad of green currency.

"Sheeit, what we waitin' on, baby? Let's go party," she said.

Very quickly they were outside in the dark.

"I got a place across the street and up the stairs," she said.

"Not there. My place."

"It'll cost you," she said.

"Baby, for you it ain't no price tag."

"Aw, shit! Talk to me, daddy. That's what I likes to hear. Let's go!"

The cab took them to Light's territory. When they got to the Parkland Ballroom Wayne got them a table, ordered drinks, and explained to Cinnamon that she had a new employer.

She had already sized up Wayne. She knew there was no point in trying to get away. She decided she would have to play a waiting game.

"Light - huh? Well, I never said he ain't fine. I guess now I'll get some o' that sweet dick for myself."

"That's between you and Light."

"Golden ain't gon' like this," she said.

"You let me worry about Golden," said Wayne. He wondered if he sounded unworried.

She nodded and sipped her drink.

"When you get through - with yo drink - you gots t'make some money for Light."

"What?"

"He's got t'see what you can do."

"Ain't this a bitch."

"I got a room for you," he said. "And don't worry. I'll be right behind you wherever you goes. So be sure t'stay away from telephones."

She looked at him. Just wait, big nigger, she thought. Just wait till Golden gets ahold of yo ass.

The next night at the stroke of twelve Wayne ushered Cinnamon into Willie's Club.

Golden saw them before Wayne saw him. He was sitting at the same table but it took a while for Wayne to see him in the crowded, smoky room. When he found him, Golden was staring right at them. Neat. He sat neat as ever behind clouds of smoke, two different but equally ravishing women seated at his table.

Wayne picked a center table. He and Cinnamon sat down.

The woman from Golden's table reached them before the

cocktail waitress.

She did not look at Wayne or pay any attention to him.

"Golden wants to see you," she said to Cinnamon.

Cinnamon started to stand.

Wayne laid his heavy hand on her wrist.

He shook his head, no.

He could feel the blood draining from his head. His big hand was cold. Cinnamon's arm burned his fingers. He had to fight from snatching his hand away.

The other woman looked at Wayne for the first time.

She turned her gaze back to Cinnamon.

"You know I cain't go back there without you," she said. "He'll kill me."

"What's your name," asked Wayne.

"What!"

She was furious. Why was this fool butting in? Did he want to get them all killed?

"I said, what's your name?"

"Puddnin'-tane, motha-fucka. Stay the hell out of our conversation, git yo big, black paw offa Cinnamon's arm, and let us get the hell away from this goddamn table."

"What's her name," Wayne asked Cinnamon. He worked very hard not to look in Golden's direction.

Cinnamon and the other woman had no such reservations and glanced over there repeatedly.

"Peaches," said Cinnamon. "Her name is Peaches."

"Sit down, Peaches," said Wayne.

"What!" Both women reacted.

"I think you heard me. Sit down."

"Cinnamon, what's wrong with this motha-fucka? Is he crazy? Is he a dope fiend?"

Alarmed, both women looked at Wayne desperately and threw fearful glances towards Golden's table.

Cinnamon leaned forward and spoke intently to Wayne.

"I don't think you understand. Golden will kill us. All three of us."

"Golden ain't gon' kill nobody," said Wayne. He fought to keep his eyes from looking to the back of the room. "Sit down, bitch!"

He yanked Peaches into the chair beside his.

"Glad t'meet you, Peaches," he said.

Peaches dropped her forehead onto the table.

"Oh shit oh shit oh shit oh shit o shit o shit o shit," she moaned.

The cocktail waitress showed up.

"Not yet," said Wayne. He was not cool enough to handle that, to go through the pretense of ordering drinks. He could handle only so much at once. Right now it was taking everything he had to keep from looking at Golden.

"Hello, Shirley," said Cinnamon.

The other woman from Golden's table stood across the table from Wayne.

"Hello, Shirley," said Wayne.

"What the hell is wrong with you two," said Shirley.

Peaches did not raise her head from the table.

"Golden is waiting on you."

"Have a chair, Shirley," said Wayne. Under the table his foot pushed the chair that sat opposite him and easily moved it out.

Shirley flicked her eyes in Golden's direction.

"Look, Mr. Smart-ass," she said.

"Wayne."

"Wayne - Smart-ass. I don't give a shit what your name is, I don't know who you think you fuckin' with," she continued in an undertone, "but this is Golden Jones."

"Sit down, Shirley," said Wayne. He reached across the table so quickly that no one saw him move. With a twist of his wrist Shirley was in the chair facing him.

"Oh, God," she said. "Oh, no."

Cinnamon was mute. She started shaking her head back and forth. Peaches had not moved.

Golden Jones stood behind Wayne, his face a fixture of fury.

"Cinnamon, you got t'talk to me."

Wayne did not turn around, but he knew who had spoken.

"M-Mi-Mi-Mister J-J-Jo-Jo-Jones," said Wayne.

"Pardon me, my man," said Golden, "my conversation is not for you. Me and this lady got some bidness to discuss." He moved to Wayne's right and extended a hand to Cinnamon.

He even talks neat, thought Wayne.

Wayne put his massive hand over Cinnamon's, covering her forearm almost to the elbow. He looked up at Golden.

"M-Mi-Mister J-J-Jones. Cinnamon do not w-w-w-wo-work fo you no mo."

Golden gave his attention to Wayne for the first time. He doubted his ears. He stared, then shrugged him off. He spoke through his teeth at Cinnamon without moving his lips.

"Git yo ass up."

Neat, thought Wayne.

Cinnamon dropped her eyes to her hand lost under Wayne's gigantic ham.

Golden's eyes followed hers.

He turned back to Wayne.

"Look, my man, I told you the lady and I had bidness to discuss. It's plenty other hammas in here. You got two sittin' at yo table right now - special deluxe. This lady's got t'go." He reached for Cinnamon's upper arm.

Wayne's free hand blocked him.

"I tri- tri- tried t'tell you, Mr. Jones. Cin-Cin-Cinnamon do not work fo you no mo. She ain't got nothin' to discuss."

Affronted by Wayne's audacity, Golden did not hear a word he said. He stared at the offending hand, took a step back and fixed his sight on Wayne.

"Nigger - has you lost yo mind!

"Don't nobody - you hear me - don't nobody come between me and one o' my bitches."

Though the music still played from the juke box, all other sounds in the room stopped. No one moved.

"Th-that-that-that's just it. I been tryin' to t-t-t-tell y-y-you -"

"Tell me what, you no talkin', baboon-faced, black, greasy, gorilla-ass, motha-fucka!"

"She ain't yo woman no mo."

"What!"

"She ain't -"

"Shut yo country ass mouth befo I cut yo sorry head off - and git the fuck outa my face!

"Come on, Cinnamon."

"She cain't go with you -"

"Don't say shit to me, nigger. In fact, git yo ass up and git the fuck outa here. I don't like the way you looks. You too goddamn ugly and too goddamn black. I don't like the way you tries to talk. I don't like the way you smells. You fuckin' up the joint. Git outa here."

Wayne stood up, Cinnamon's hand in his.

He loomed over Golden. Broad as a wall he seemed to cut off the dim lights glowing from the ceiling.

More quickly than the eye could follow the glittering blade appeared in Golden's hand. His lips drew into a thin smile.

"Big man, you ain't takin' that bitch nowhere."

"You told me to go."

"I told YOU to go. She stay."

Golden extended a hand toward her. Light on his feet he

55

was almost crouched. The tension in him was nearly visible.

Cinnamon looked fearfully up at Wayne.

"Cinnamon work for Light now," said Wayne. "She come in here tonight to tell you goodbye."

Golden's rage exploded so suddenly it caught him by surprise. Before he knew what he was doing the deadly steel had arched through the air.

He never felt the chair.

He was on his back on top of the bar then crashing to the floor behind it. The switchblade still vibrated in the wall where it had flown when the force of the blow had dislodged it from his hand.

Only one person in the room moved. Wayne kicked a hole in the bar, walked through it, bent over and picked up Golden and sat him on the bar's remains.

Wayne spoke slowly. "Cinnamon don't work fo you no mo. She work for Light. Peaches and Shirley gon' work for Light, too. When they leaves, don't come lookin' for 'em. Just leave 'em alone. Then won't nobody mess with you. Won't nobody come lookin' fo you. Since you got mo' hammas than anybody else, we just takin' some of the load off'n you, takin' the surplus off yo hands. We doin' you a favor."

Wayne took a napkin off the bar and patted down Golden's face. He straightened Golden's shirt, tie, and lapels. He wanted him to stay neat. He bent over and picked up Golden's brim, brushed it off, and placed it neatly on his head.

"My b-b-best to y-y-you, Mr. Jones," he said. He walked away from Golden, took Cinnamon's arm and nodded to Peaches and Shirley. They followed him out of the club.

Within hours everyone in Chicago's fast-life had heard of Wayne though they did not know his name. Light's Big Nigger

56

they called him. And by the time the story got around to Light's side of town, Light's Big Nigger had whipped twenty-five niggers in a bar, busting half of them across the head with bar stools, had knocked down a whole bar and trampled it into kindling wood, and had walked out of the bar with five bitches under each arm. The only part of the story that remained in perspective was that he had departed with a gesture of respect to Golden Jones.

Ordinarily such a public humiliation would have prompted Golden to immediate retaliation. But he was so shocked he was incapable of action. He could not believe what had happened to him in front of over a hundred witnesses. He was never the same. He started shooting heroin and within months his women had deserted him and his friends had come to despise him. One day he just disappeared. His life had become a testament to the might of Light's Big Nigger, LBN, as Wayne came to be called.

From the day Wayne took on Golden Jones at Willie's Club his rep was made. All anybody had to do was take one look at him and they believed everything they had ever heard about him. That made Wayne's work very easy.

Matilda reveled in the respect accorded her man. It was different from what she had known with Light. Though everyone had respected and admired Light and though the women had been jealous of those favored to spend time with him - no matter how little - she had not been Light's only woman. She had been one of his main women and that had set her up as the *creme de la creme*, but there were at least nine other main women, and she had not been able to count the lesser ones. She was Wayne's WOMAN, his one woman. Not only that, but she did not work for him, he worked for her. Whatever respect he got, she got in triplicate. But she would have stayed with him even had that not been the case. He had her number.

Hard as cars were to come by, Wayne managed to get ahold of a Packard sedan and he took Matilda for rides in the country whenever he got a chance. He liked to look for places to fish. He kept a fishing rod in the trunk and whenever the weather was right if they found a likely place they would set up on a river bank or a pond and he would teach her the mysteries of bringing finny creatures out of the water.

One day as they leaned against the bank of the Des Plaines River, a casting rod propped on a forked stick, the multi-colored line leading taught into the murky water, Matilda took one of Wayne's big hands into hers.

"Wayne, yo hands is so heavy," she said.

"That's cause they got t'hold so much sweet meat," he said.

She kissed his hand.

"I don't think I could ever go back to bein' what I was," she said.

"I don't plan to let you."

"I mean me. I couldn't," she said. "For one thing I

couldn't leave you."

"For another," he continued.

"For another, she said, "that life don't mean nothin' t'me no more. It did then. It really did. The fast life. I mean I was big time, Claude Bonfil's woman. Diamonds and furs. And niggers after me like white on rice. Drinkin' and smokin' reefer, and a cocaine-headed dick. I loved it.

"But now I likes just bein' with you. And the country. We goes out enough. I can still strut my stuff. I knows all the mens still wants me. But they cain't have. And that's more fun. To know they wants but cain't have."

"I'll tell you one thing," said Wayne, "It's sure a hell of a lot mo fun fo' me."

They both laughed.

12

Light never told anyone or let on how much what had happened with Matilda bothered him. He never let on to anyone what went on inside him. He believed his success depended on no one's ever knowing him. Matilda's action was something he did not understand. LBN was ugly, black, and country. Yet Matilda had left Light for him. She had done it voluntarily. Light did not understand that. Slick as he was. She had gone to live with the country nigger. Light knew it was not about whoring. To cushion the shock, to come to accept it, for a few days he had let himself be fooled about that, let himself think she was doing it as a way to get out of whoring. Even that was hard for Light to take because he believed any woman should be happier to be his whore than any other man's wife. But it helped soften the blow to see it that way. Still Light made his living by noticing other people's strengths and weaknesses, and using them. He was too perceptive not to realize Matilda would have gone with LBN after that very first night even had it meant she had to keep whoring. She was his woman. That was the sole reason Light had agreed to let her out of his stable. Because he knew she was already out in spirit. And he did not understand it. Here he was the finest thing walking, talked more shit than a chimney, had diamonds on his fingers, gold watches on his wrists, a long limousine and two dozen pairs of shoes, had treated Matilda better than any woman he had ever known, and she had walked. Walked for some hick just up from the woods. He did not like it.

For a long time he did not do anything about it. He just watched them to see what would happen. Waited for her to come back. He knew she would miss his loving. They all missed it. Needed it. Nobody could love like him. Once they had it they could not do without it. He wondered how she would do it, if she would break with LBN, or if she would come sneaking back while LBN was away to get what she could of Light, to take whatever precious minutes she could have. He watched them. Nothing happened. The only times he saw Matilda were when LBN brought her into a club. She did not come slipping up to his apartment and she did not call. That is when Light began to get the idea that her break with him was more permanent than he had expected and when the enormous dimensions of his ego began to assert themselves and to insist that this could not and would not be tolerated.

Matilda should have expected Light's reaction. She knew him as well as anyone. She had survived, she had thrived, by developing the art of reading him to a science. No one was a master at deciphering Light. That is why he stayed three steps ahead of everyone. But Matilda was as close to it as anyone came; nevertheless she did not expect Light's reaction. She did not because of what Wayne had done to her. Wayne was the first man she had thrown herself over for. She gave herself to him without caring about anything. She was so caught up in her feelings for him, so overwhelmed and amazed by them that Light had dropped out of her mind. Even when she had fallen for Light she had held onto part of herself. He had eclipsed her and charmed her and seduced her and thrilled her, but all along she had intuited that there was something too brilliant, too glossy about Light and what he did to her to be quite real, so she had clung to a tiny part of herself. With Wayne, involuntarily and before she knew what was happening, she had given herself to him entirely. She had no time to be fooling around with what was going on inside Claude Bonfils' head.

13

Wayne never had to get rough with Light's women. All he ever had to do was appear as a reminder. Everyone knew some exaggerated version of what had happened to Golden Jones. And Cinnamon, Peaches, and Shirley were living testaments in Light's stable to the truth of whatever fable they had heard. As Golden had gone into decline, on the needle, and eventually evaporated, more and more of his women had come to Light. Their presence added further credibility to LBN's mythical prowess. No woman wanted any trouble out of him.

None of the other pimps tried to muscle in on him. They were all quick studies. Golden's lesson was clear enough. They would keep what they had.

Wayne's biggest troubles came from soldiers and sailors. They got crazy drunk more than anyone else and when they got crazy drunk they did not understand and were not interested in understanding ordinary rules of human behavior or communication. A lot of them were fresh out of boot camp and had to prove to everyone in the world, including themselves, how bad they were. Some had been kept in boring and uneventful duty for months or even years and had to prove they were as much men as their brothers-in-arms who had not had easy duty. And there were others who had seen and suffered such indignities and horrors either at home or abroad or both that they had absolutely nothing to prove to anyone and simply did not care what they did.

They gave the girls problems. They wanted free pussy. Or they wanted reduced rates. Or they didn't like the girls' attitudes. Or they tried to take their money. Or they wanted to beat up on them. And they didn't care what LBN looked like. The sight of him did not calm them down or scare them one bit. Sometimes one of them would come at him. Sometimes they would come at him in packs. But they never hesitated. The only way to stop them was to stop them, render them immobile. As long as they had any means of locomotion, they kept coming.

Wayne did not mind beating up on soldiers and sailors because he was jealous of them. They had been the ones to read and write before he could, the ones to tease him because he could not. They were the ones to ride the Illinois Central out of Bardwell while all he could do was stand and watch. They had branded him a country-hick. And all of them had gone places he had never gone and seen things he had never seen. He did not mind beating on them at all. He knew they would not know who a real man was unless he showed them. They thought the silly little uniforms they wore somehow made them men. He knew if he smashed enough of their faces and broke enough of their bones they would have to change their minds about him. Wayne also did not like being reminded that he was a murderer - and sometimes in the flashes of fury he felt at them he saw Joe Harrison and he remembered, which made him madder than ever. But now he knew. He knew his own lethal potential. He always held back just enough. He never killed anyone.

That's another reason he liked to take Matilda out. Anyone who saw her with him, no matter what uniform he wore or how many stripes or bars or ribbons it had on it, would know with a woman like Matilda on his arm Wayne could not be a country-hick or any less than they were. He had to be a real man.

Light appreciated Wayne. He knew he could never find an enforcer who could handle servicemen - who were at once Light's biggest source of income and his biggest problem - as effectively as Wayne. Servicemen had run many pimps out of the business. Those who stayed could make a killing, but the risks were high. LBN cut the odds considerably. Light was a good executive, he rewarded his namesake appropriately.

Wayne's eyes were happy behind his closed lids. He loved to have Matilda shave him. He never got over the luxury of it, and the wonder of it.

Light wanted Wayne to have Light's barber shave him, but Matilda did it just as well and the experience was infinitely more pleasurable. Her soft hands touched his face lightly. Her breasts lay along his chest. He tasted the scents of her breath and her body. He loved it. He even liked the feeling of the razor sliding over his throat when he knew her hands wielded it.

He smiled.

"Keep your mouth still, Wayne Hunter."

"Yes, Baby."

"That means no talkin', neither."

He opened one eye and winked at her. Then he closed it.

Matilda liked to shave Wayne. She liked being able to do whatever she could for him, to show her affection in as many ways as possible, but she also liked the daily opportunity to talk at him without his being able to talk back.

"Wayne, you gon' have t'quit working for Light pretty soon," she said. "We got enough money saved up. You could open yo own bakery. And every day you works for Light is a extra day you's in danger when you don't has t'be."

Wayne bristled. He knew one of the reasons she shaved him every day was so she could give him a piece of her mind with no interruptions. Still, he never could resist the temptation. So everyday he submitted himself to her little scoldings. Just wait. Just wait till she's finished, he thought. Then I'll tell her a thing or two.

"Plus, I don't like you bein' around all those women. You might get t'messin' around and look at somebody like Lily's big ass and not be able to help yoself. Then she'd find out what you got and I'd never be able to get you back all to myself. They'd turn

64

you into a pimp.

"No, you got t'git outa this business soon. You around too many temptations."

You my biggest temptation, he thought. I just wanta be around you all the time. I don't wanta have t'work at all. I don't never want to be away from you.

"I ain't playin'," she said. "You don't know like I do how bad this business can get."

She placed her soft lips on his. She pressed gently.

"Barber's through," she said, pulling back and wiping his face with a warm, damp wash cloth.

He opened his eyes.

She patted his face with after-shave.

He sat up. "One day," he said, "one day I'll quit. But not now. You don't know what it's like bein' where I'm from. You a Chicago girl. Been here all yo life. You don't know what it's like growin' up where you think Bardwell, Kentucky is the big town. One day, Baby, but not now. I cain't quit now."

Everybody waved at Wayne when he came into the Club Delisa.

They kept a table for him next to the dance floor. Women smiled at him from all over the room.

Wayne was happy to acknowledge the greetings with a wave and a nod as he crossed the crowded room.

Burton Humphries, the head waiter, held his chair for him.

"Will there be anything special tonight, LBN?"

"No, thanks, Burt. Just the regular."

"Yessir."

Burton was off through the swirls of people.

Wayne surveyed the room trying to get a reckoning of

65

which of Light's ladies were present.

A waiter brought Wayne a double of straight Kentucky whiskey, on the rocks.

"Thank you, Shoes," said Wayne.

"Thank you, LBN," said Shoes, quickly pocketing the tip.

Wayne took a sip. He always loved the way the first taste burned as it slid down. Burn yo guts out, too, Jersey Blue had warned him. Maybe, thought Wayne, but it ain't happened yet, and it feel so good.

Wayne felt the press of a hand on his shoulder and looked up to see Camilla standing beside him. Camilla was a free-lancer.

"Is it true what they say that you auditions all the ladies for Light," she asked, smiling at him and raising her bare shoulder, the one next to Wayne's face.

"Not all of them," he answered. "Only special ones like you."

"I didn't say I was trying out," she said.

"I'm inviting you," he replied. "Sit down."

She sat across the small table from him. She used her eyes on him.

Shoes appeared. "What can I get you, Miss Camilla?"

"Cutty-Sark," she said. "On the rocks."

He left.

"Let's talk bidness," said Wayne. "Light would love to have you in his corner."

He kept scanning the room, searching out Light's ladies.

"I don't know if I need Light," she said. "I'm not used to giving up money to a man. The way it is now I keep it all."

"Then why you talkin' t'me?"

"I don't know if I need Light. But I need protection."

Wayne was sure he had identified all of Light's ladies. He turned his full attention to Camilla.

"Protection?"

"Yeah, some army been givin' be a hard time."

Shoes returned with the drink and disappeared.

Camilla sipped it.

"Army - huh," said Wayne.

"Yeah. And I seen you handle army lots of times. You could handle them for me."

"But you don't work for Light," said Wayne.

"Listen to me, LBN. I'm talking a business proposition to you. This has nothing to do with Light. This is business between you and me."

"Light don't like competition."

"Light don't have to know nothing about this. Look. I get in trouble, you help me out. You help me out, I help you out. Just straight-up business, you and me. No third parties."

Wayne swallowed whiskey.

"I know some other ladies interested in you, too. Aint' no protection like you in this whole town."

Wayne turned so that his large head was right in Camilla's face.

"I like you, Camilla, but ain't nothin' what goes down in Chi-town what Light don't know about. If we was t'cut a deal he'd know about it. Now, I ain't worried about me, cause I can take care of myself. But, you - you know Light. He would have yo face cut up in strips, in strips. I couldn't let that happen t'you, baby."

She dropped her head.

She finished her Cutty-Sark.

"How do I get in touch with Light," she asked.

Wayne handed her a business card with a phone number on it. "You gon' like workin' with us, baby."

"Yeah." She got up and walked slowly toward the entrance.

Wayne leaned back and relaxed. He finished his drink and looked around for Shoes.

All in a night's work, he thought.

She had not mentioned it even to Wayne, but Matilda very much wanted children. She did not douche and she made sure Wayne did not wear rubbers - at any rate an act of futility - and she waited for her period not to come.

She had been thrilled by her wild life but with Wayne it was as if it had never happened. She missed none of it. All she wished for was a full family with Wayne and to get away from any connection with that past life. She wanted to feel as much a part of him as possible. That is what piqued her curiosity about Kentucky. She wanted to see where he had come from, to understand. He kept telling her she could not understand. She wanted to see. She wanted to see his people and she wanted them to see her. She wanted them to accept her. Maybe she and Wayne could stay there. Maybe he could go back to work for that Mr. Mueller or open up a shop of his own in that other little town. What was it called ... Mayfield. Yes.

Wayne said they could never live in the South, that she was ignorant about the South. That it would kill her. Maybe. But she could go there at least. She could visit at least. She could meet his people..

And we can make a baby for them.

She kept waiting for it not to, but her period kept coming.

Wayne knew he should quit. He was going to one day. But the problem was it got good. The life was good. The money was easy. He actually liked to beat up on soldiers and sailors and that was about all the work he ever did.

Oh, he watched the ladies, but that was no work. Light had nothing but foxes working for him, so all night long Wayne's job was to keep his eyes fastened on beautiful women. He laughed. Who woulda thought it? Who woulda thought it was even possible?

The rest of the time he just rode around in big cars and dropped in on clubs where everyone bought him drinks and tiptoed around him. He was big time. He loved it. And the money kept rolling in. He wore expensive clothes and bedangled his fingers with rings and his wrists with watches and golden bracelets.

He loved the way people bent over slightly when they talked to him and didn't quite dare look him in the eye and said, very respectfully,

"LBN."

Yes. He knew he should quit. Matilda wanted him to quit. To get away from those people.

But those people had been good to him, especially Light. Light had made him everything he was. He respected Light. And Light needed him.

One day. Right now he was developing a taste for expensive cigars - Havana - and Light could get them by the case. Besides, he liked being around beautiful women all the time, even if he wasn't touching them. They touched him. And there was always the possibility.

I know I cain't do this forever. One day I'm gon' quit. But not now. Not today.

Sure. We got enough money. But money ain't everything. Once I stop bein' LBN, money won't buy it back.

Just a little while. Just a little while more.

14

Matilda opened the door. Light stood smiling in her face.
"Hello, baby."

"Hello Light. Long-time-no-see. Come on in."

"Thanks."

He sauntered into the room. He put his hat on the coffee table. He opened his golden cigarette case.

Matilda closed the door and turned back into the living room.

Light surveyed her from the highest hairs on her head down to her feet and back up again. He stopped at her eyes.

He smiled. "Sure lookin' good, baby."

"Thanks. Sit down."

He lifted a cigarette from the case, returned the shiny container to his inside pocket and sat down. He lit up and inhaled.

Matilda sat across the room from him.

"So," she said, "what's happ'nin'?"

"You, baby."

Matilda watched the smoke drift out of his mouth and nostrils. Such a familiar scene, *deja vu*.

"Wayne's not here," she said.

"I didn't come here lookin' for LBN. I came lookin' for you."

"Be quiet, Light. You sound like you tryin' t'talk trash."

"Not trash. Not trash. I been thinkin' about you a lot, baby. Been wonderin' if you miss the old times. You don't get a chance t'git out much, now. You and me ... you know ... it used t'be very nice."

"It used to be very nice with you and a whole lot of ladies - I'm sure it still is."

He looked at her closely.

"All those other chics bother you, baby? You know it was never nobody like you."

"I don't think about it anymore. It's all over with."

"Yeah, that's what's been botherin' me, Matilda. It don't have t'be over. You and me ... it was too good t'be over."

She started to feel uncomfortable. She did not know where the conversation was going. The direction it seemed to be taking was not plausible.

"Light, I don't know what you came here to talk about, but I am not going back to work."

Light tilted his head back and laughed heartily.

Matilda knew she was out of practice, but she realized she had to tune into him. She had to read him.

He returned his gaze to her, a tender expression on his face. "Matilda, I surely did not come over here to try to talk you into going back t'work. I don't want you t'work. I came over here because I miss you. I came over here because I wanted to see you. I came over here because we had a beautiful thing and a lot of years going for us, and I don't want to stand by and watch it all slip away. I came over here because I needs you, baby."

Matilda was upset. A few months ago she would have been able to translate Light's little speech, to understand just what he meant, just what he was after. Now his words only confused her. She recognized - she hoped not too late - that she was too out of practice to read him. She knew she could not go one on one against him without that edge. She needed to give herself a little time, a little space.

She stood up and walked to the window, her back to him. "Need me how?"

He pushed his cigarette into the ashtray and came up behind her. He placed his hands lightly on her shoulders.

She knew she had to get away from him. He was too close. But her face was just inches away from the window. Outside, on the other side of the glass was a two-story drop to the ground. There was nowhere to go.

"Need you like I always needed you. Need you like a man needs a woman. Need my body in yours. Need you close to me." He pressed tightly into her back and cupped her shoulders. His erection throbbed between her buttocks. "I've, I've never stopped needing you." His soft lips brushed the graceful lines of her neck. His breath seemed to be scalding her skin.

Matilda felt the weakening in her knees, the swooning in her stomach. Her lips parted involuntarily.

A spark ran along the backs of her thighs.

She leaned back into him. "I belong to Wayne," she said.

"How can you belong to LBN when he belongs to me? Niggas don't even know his name. He's known by me, 'Light's Big Nigga, LBN.' *He* belongs to me. *You* belong to me." His lips along her neck were now kisses, his tongue darting out.

"No ...."

She knew she loved Wayne. She did not know how Light had made her feel crazy, but she did not even want him. She had everything she wanted in Wayne. She wanted to slap Light for turning the keys that took her body out of control. She spun around, her right hand drew back to deliver a hard, discoloring, open-handed blow to his pretty face.

He grabbed her hand and mashed his open mouth against hers. She could not help letting her tongue run down his throat.

Wayne stood in the doorway and stared at them in his bed. Matilda saw him almost instantly. With a groan she wrenched and turned and hurled Light off her. She cried out.

"Wayne! Please! I love you!"

Light landed on his back, his rigid penis spurting ridiculously into the air.

Wayne raised his arms overhead and cried out. He rushed into the room, snatched up the bed, dropping Matilda off it, and hurled it through the window. He bellowed.

Matilda leaped to her feet and threw herself onto him.

"Baby, I love you, I love you," she screamed and wept.

Wayne shook her off and yanked Light into the air.

Crawling along the floor, Matilda reached Wayne's feet and clung to them, screeching. "Yes! Kill him! Kill him!"

Wayne looked up at Light's stunned face and saw Joe Harrison and heard the pop of his neck.

Wayne slumped against the wall.

Light fell from his hands onto the floor.

Matilda climbed up Wayne's body. "Please, baby. Please, forgive me. I love you, I love you. Oh, baby. Oh, baby, oh ...."

Wayne swatted her away. He staggered through the bedroom door and down the hall. At the door to the apartment he did not stop to open it. He smashed it down and dragged himself through the splinters into the hall.

A STORY OF WIMBEY'S CORNER

Eskeridge Wimbey

Eskeridge Wimbey came to Chicago from the South while he was in his mid-teens, during the early 1870s. He didn't claim he'd been a slave. He didn't speak about the subject. He didn't act like a man who had ever been in thrall to others. He acted more like a man who had always had others in thrall to him. Following the fire of 1871 Chicago was one mad rush of hustling and rebuilding, and Eskeridge jumped right into the carriage trade, driving for a hauling firm. Something of a wizard with horses and an indefatigable worker, he soon owned his own horse and wagon, expanded that to another horse and a carriage, and just kept adding onto his business.

Eskeridge probably would have remained only conventionally wealthy had it not been for World War I. Like other rich men of his era he probably would have died leaving an estate of a few paltry million. But fate sometimes does intervene in life, and in Wimbey's case it did so in the form of some unknown Serbian nationalist and an Austrian archduke who was foolish enough to get out of his carriage to be of assistance when bullets were flying.

As soon as the European armies began to mobilize, so did Wimbey. He knew there would be business aplenty. He built warehouses all around his west side stables. He bought wagons and horses and bid on every hauling contract in Chicago and its vicinity. He hauled all over the Chicago area - anything and everything. He made so much money it was impossible to reinvest all of it in making more money. Eskeridge gave it a good try, though, and by the time the U.S. entered the war, he had to open a courier business just to haul around his own money.

Though his wartime money-making binge delighted his employees, his bankers, his stock brokers, and many formerly unemployed Negroes, it dispelled with terrible finality many of the illusions Eskeridge was wont to cherish. The facts and figures, the daily performance charts, even his own eyes told him the motor driven trucks and lorries surpassed his horse-drawn wagons by such a degree of magnitude that the jig was up.

Eskeridge learned early that the key to a business performing consistently at a high level was its personnel. Personnel were key. That was one of his guiding axioms. After he abandoned the carriage trade, he decided to replace his fancy east side carriages with a dark colony. He was determined to be as thorough in that venture as in any other, and if anything, somewhat more so.

He locked the matter up into a trust so that legally it would be impossible to get him or his Maroon Foundation out as property owner. They would own the little piece of land *in perpetuum*. But that was only the first bit of critical business and not the most important. The secret to the longevity of the festering enclave of coons in the lily-white North Shore preserve would be the personnel, the darkies themselves.

Eskeridge anchored his plan of tenant resistance on Mackenzie Sweet. The old man was the first person Eskeridge admitted into the Corner. Once settled, Mackenzie had no intention of moving. He had lived through more and seen more than all of his opponents combined. Also, he had no intention of allowing anything to happen which was going to put any stress on him. He sat on his front porch, and when the weather was cold, he sat in his bedroom, which was at the front of the house above the porch. He sat in the bedroom window and cooked up plenty of schemes to keep the wolves at bay.

A major flaw in Wimbey's plan was that no one could replace Eskeridge himself. Therefore, although Eskeridge groomed his nephew, Porter, to take over upon his death, and though his will ensured that the Scottswoman, Mary Bryce, would have a significant say in who occupied the Corner, neither Porter nor Mary Bryce had Wimbey's judgement. They couldn't read people for their strengths as Eskeridge could. Oh, they were good on people's weaknesses. Very good on that. But sometimes one had to have an eye for the odd and peculiar strength. No one had that eye like Eskeridge Q. Wimbey.

So plan as he might, Eskeridge had not accounted for every eventuality. Mackenzie Sweet played a part in that. He failed Eskeridge. His life did not evolve into a *perpetuem mobile*. He eventually gave up the ghost. Eskeridge's strategy had counted on Mackenzie's living considerably longer.

There were other glitches. A broad strategy like Eskeridge's allowed for them. Eskeridge knew that things happened which one had not foreseen. In his own life such events had momentous effects. The Chicago fire. Mary Bryce. Craziness in the Austro-Hungarian Empire. Eskeridge always tried to leave room for the unknown. But not even allowances for the unknown could accommodate what life brought to Wimbey's Corner in the person of Wayne Hunter.

1

Nasty rumors about Eskeridge Wimbey and Mary Bryce got started during the twenties and early thirties. They arose from the practice Wimbey developed of stopping by Mary Bryce's house everyday for lunch. He had provided the house for her directly adjacent - except for the narrow strip of ground which had the effrontery to call itself an alley - to Wimbey's Corner.

He came weekends as well as weekdays, holidays as well as workdays. Without exception. A man who had entered his late sixties, a bachelor without permanent feminine liaisons began to call daily on a single woman, one who in her early fifties was still of great physical attraction. This drew notice - but only from the residents of Wimbey's Corner because - with a few exceptions - they were the only ones aware of these daily appearances.

One of the exceptions was Wimbey's chauffeur and the role attached to him immensely complicated the truth or falsehood of the accusations which linked more than the names of Eskeridge Wimbey and Mary Bryce. Wimbey had refused to learn how to drive. He had been a master handler of horses, but holding and guiding a wheel attached to a monstrous internal combustion engine that somehow propelled and directed the contents of an automobile was an enterprise he could never lower himself to undertake. He hired a chauffeur who took him everywhere he needed to go. In earlier times Wimbey had employed a driver for his personal carriage, but he was quite capable of managing the carriage himself and on certain discrete occasions did precisely that. In the case of the automobile he was immobile without its driver.

In the year he began his calls on Miss Bryce his car was a brand new Pierce Arrow Imperial Limousine. Its unmistakable silhouette and shimmering surface appeared in front of Miss Bryce's house at twelve o'clock noon daily.

After Wimbey entered Miss Bryce's door, the chauffeur

drove off. In order to know when Wimbey left, one had to witness the reappearance of the vehicle and Wimbey's return to it. That was no easy matter. One would have to spend every second with eyes glued to the space in front of Mary Bryce's house. No one had the leisure to do that. As a result, it was only by chance that anyone ever saw Wimbey depart.

From this circumstance the first whispered suggestions arose. Some people said they had seen Wimbey leave promptly at one, others, late in the afternoon, and still others claimed to have seen Wimbey mount into the Pierce Arrow long after dark.

As notorious a womanizer as Eskeridge Wimbey, though now rapidly approaching seventy, spending so much unspecified time inside the home of a single woman, alone with her, was sufficient cause to set wagging the tongues of those privy to the information. These daily visits continued without interruption until Eskeridge's death in 1938.

His departure from the earthly sphere was a momentous occasion. It was as if one of the lights in the heavens had been extinguished. His housekeeper found him dead in bed, a smile on his face.

This proved the lie to all those filthy insinuations proclaimed the supporters of white female virtue and the upholders of Eskeridge's racial integrity. The man died in his own bed far away from the Bryce house yet he had been accused of every sin imaginable with the honorable woman. To others the time and place of his death proved nothing. Their suspicions focused on the mysterious smile that had graced his lips.

Eskeridge's funeral was one of a kind. Every Negro in Evanston was determined to attend. Eskeridge was such a big shot that every Negro in Chicago who had pretensions of being a bit shot was determined to attend. Because of Eskeridge's labyrinthine and extensive financial holdings, many non-Negroes felt obliged to attend, from both within and without Evanston, from within and without Illinois, from within and without the

United States.

Eskeridge's family came, dredging themselves up from deep in the South. Even Carol, his niece, was furloughed from Kankakee that she might attend her uncle's funeral ceremonies. Though the child was well into her forties, she came with all the naive hopes of her youth, exultant that her stubborn uncle had died at last, and that she had outlived him, radiating the expectation that she was about to inherit unimaginable riches.

There was some difficulty in finding an appropriate person to say words over Eskeridge's body. Not that there was any shortage of volunteers. Quite the contrary. Every one who had any smattering of a right to a clerical collar wanted to be anointed to speak to so vast and distinguished an audience. Eskeridge, however, had not been a church-going man. His peccadilloes were widely celebrated and he had never made any effort to apologize or atone for them. In addition, he had the audacity to die with a smile on his face.

The problem of who to say the words was solved when the place was chosen in which they would be said. The high school gymnasium was the only place in town big enough to accommodate the throng. Since it was his building, the high school principal was picked to say the eulogy. He had never met Eskeridge, but since even those people who worked closely with him could scarcely be called his intimates and actually knew very little about him, he did not suffer from greater distance from the man than anyone else. In addition, he added just the proper note of distinction to the proceedings, being a highly educated man, widely respected, and white.

No one remembered what the principal said. Very few heard him and even fewer listened. The noise in the room never dropped below a low roar. There was constant motion. Women screamed. Ladies fainted. Men perspired profusely.

Mary Bryce occupied a seat of honor near the family and wept continuously. There were weeping ladies throughout the hall, all the others colored and distinguished only by their rare beauty

82

despite a rather considerable range in their ages.

Members of the family did not weep. Dollar signs crashed too loudly inside their heads. Indeed, Carol laughed hysterically. It was not maniacal laughter. It was sheer joy. She could already see and feel the money. Little did she know the very car which had brought her up from Kankakee was parked nearby, its driver lounging against it, waiting for the ceremonies to end, so he could whisk her back to the asylum.

The funeral procession was a spectacle. Immediately behind the hearse and the Cadillac V-16 Madam X Limousine reserved exclusively for Eskeridge's brothers and sisters came a phalanx of Cadillac limousines bearing the rest of the family. Behind those came not only Pierce Arrows, Cadillacs, Lincolns, Lasalles, and Chryslers, but also a Rolles Royce limousine with a divider, a Bentley, two Merceded Benses, a Gazelle and a Berlina Coupe, a Citroen, a Jaguar, a Burgati, a Hispano Suiza; and a DKW F 700 Luxurious Cabriolet. People staggered at the sight. The common people were also well represented by all kinds of Fords, Plymouths, Dodges, and Chevrolets. The line of vehicles took a full hour to pass the Church Street bridge over the canal on the way to Sunset Cemetery.

The trust created by Wimbey's labrynthine will guaranteed that his colossal fortune would remain intact with various persons and lineages to benefit from it over time. Certain dispensations were granted in the document but they were all minimal in comparison with the magnitude of the Wimbey Estate, an estate whose total dimensions the trust prevented from ever being disclosed.

Porter Wimbey received outright a grant of three million dollars, but Porter was astute financially, had worked hard, and had very good connections. At the time of Wimbey's death, Porter's own estate was valued at something over five million dollars. Wimbey's bequeath did not even double his nephew's wealth. Porter was beside himself with indignation. He came as close to anyone as knowing the truly fabulous proportions of his uncle's wealth. And though Porter received certain ongoing benefits in exchange for managing elaborate facets of Eskeridge's ventures, he was livid that his outright award should be so paltry.

2

Although one would have imagined otherwise, except for genuine grief and regret, the residents of Wimbey's Corner were not thrown off their moorings by Eskeridge's death.

As Eskeridge had planned for decades, they had been the ones who preserved the Corner's well-being. They had directed its survival. Eskeridge's presence had comforted them. But it had been entirely a background presence. He had taken no part in devising or executing the schemes they had concocted to stave off the assaults of their wealthy and continually offended neighbors.

The inhabitants knew about the Trust, that it made it literally impossible for the Corner to be pried loose. They knew all they had to do was keep anyone from ousting them. They had become adept at that. Mackenzie Sweet with all his years and talents entirely devoted to survival, with his continuing arguing and experiments with different ways of thinking and approaching inscrutable questions was an incomparable strategist and tactician. He was the indispensable one. Indeed, when he died several years after Wimbey, the Corner missed his guiding hand far more than Wimbey's. Wimbey had picked the residents to be self-sustaining, which, indeed, they had been. But Mackenzie had been a crucial ingredient in their success.

3

Every time Mr. Stuart walked past the house marking the western boundary of Wimbey's Corner, he could not help thinking of Mackenzie Sweet. When Mackenzie was alive, during warm weather he was always on his front porch. He did not sleep much. Always afraid of death sneaking up on him. He took little cat naps during the night but never slept the whole night through. Said he enjoyed laughing at death too much. Caught it hiding behind the foot of his bed and sneaking around his dresser-drawers. Mackenzie said he'd sit up and holler, "I got you," and laugh as death scuttled away.

Mackenzie's life-long ambition toward which he had worked diligently was to be the oldest Negro in the world. He was not interested in being rich, famous, or erudite. He just wanted to be old - very old. The older he got, the older he wanted to be. There was no limit to his ambition.

He was aided in his quest by a remarkable constitution and matchless laziness. He was a very strong man and could work prodigious feats of energy and power when pressed. He simply strove to keep such opportunities to an absolute minimum. He had many favorite homilies, one of which was, "No strain on the brain or frame." He did not believe in undue exertion of any type if there were the slightest chance of avoiding it. That is why he married early. He put all the strain on his wives, and later, on his daughters. He outlived five wives and thirteen daughters. He outlived many sons, too, but he did not put much store in them because they died off young anyway, and besides they did not contribute much to reducing his "strain." He outlived scores of grandchildren and many great grandchildren and so on. His ultimate goal was to outlive every Negro.

Mackenzie Sweet had begun life in slavery and after that had passed through many occupations most of which he did not remember. What he did remember was how as a slave he had become an expert at avoiding work. He let that lesson guide his life. So whatever occupation he had, he spent most of his time and energy not doing it.

Sometime in his middle life he had taught himself how to read. Mostly he read obituaries because they proved how successful he was. But contrary to what one might imagine, Mackenzie was not a one-dimensional man. He loved to argue.

About anything. For any reason. He never cared about the subjects on which he disputed - unless it was somebody's age or how long so and so had lived - but he had a splendid talent for irritating and aggravating everyone about him. Their discomfort tickled him. It drove him to push his illogical, contradictory, yet irrefutable arguments to the furthest reaches of absurdity. Then at the very point when his case was about to collapse from the weight of its sheer irrationality, he became systematic, methodical, and impeccably logical, thereby dashing to bits any hope for victory on the part of his frustrated opponents. He was one of the few people who could get others literally to gnash their teeth.

Charles was one of Mackenzie's favorite people. It was partly because Charles had been a soldier. Mackenzie loved soldiers. They increased his odds. During wartime they died like flies. Even during peacetime they had a higher than average mortality rate. They got in fights. Training exercises. Ships were wrecked at sea. Men fell overboard. Trains carrying them crashed. And then after the ascendancy of the automobile they were abominable drivers. Colored soldiers cooperated more than the norm by being hanged *en masse* at Brownsville and Houston. Yes, Mr. Sweet loved soldiers, and sailors, too. He believed they had been created just for his convenience. The Civil War always reminded him of the great lengths to which soldiers would go to preoccupy death while Mackenzie used the opportunity to think up ways to outmaneuver him. He was well aware that a much higher proportion of Black soldiers had died during the Civil War than white soldiers. One-third of Black soldiers had died. For that reason, Abraham Lincoln was one of his great heroes. He shared reverence for him with most Black people, but for totally different reasons.

Mackenzie used to interrogate Charles extensively about the Negroes he had seen die during the Great War.

"How many colored you figure got killed altogether," he would inevitably ask.

Charles did not know.

"Mmmhmm. But it was plenty. Thousands. You seen plenty killed yoself, huh?"

Charles always nodded.

Mackenzie giggled. "Yessuh," he said. "Some of them boys might o' outlived me. But no chance. No chance now."

When Eskeridge Wimbey died, Mackenzie's joy was unrestrained. One of his most formidable foes had fallen. Still his exuberance did not prohibit him from exercising his critical faculties.

"Can you imagine that," he demanded. "Can you imagine that? Don't make no sense at all. I knowed somethin' was wrong with that boy, but my goodness gracious - of all things - to have a smile on his face! To be caught up with by death and be smiling about it, he was a tuity-fruity. The boy was deranged."

When death finally sneaked up on Mackenzie and caught him in a nap, even though he was asleep, Mackenzie retained enough presence of mind to die with a frightful frown on his face and clenched teeth. Try as he might the undertaker was unable to change his expression.

Mackenzie said Eskeridge's problem was he frittered away time on the insignificant.

"All the boy could think about was makin' money," he said. "Now, we all got t'make money to live, but Eskeridge was ridiculous about it. That's all energy he could of been puttin' into his life, into livin', trickin' death. He was a fool. If he had o' saved that energy for hisself, he had a good two or three hundred years left in him." When it came to life, Mackenzie did not think in diminutives. He had read the Bible and those old folks there did not spare the change. They knew how to pile on the years. Mackenzie saw no reason why the tradition should not continue.

Mackenzie had never admitted it, but he had feared Eskeridge. Wimbey was a younger man than Mackenzie and of comparable robust health. And like Mackenzie he had just kept living. Mackenzie was hurt because Eskeridge was his landlord. He believed he was contributing to Eskeridge's longevity. It galled him every time he paid rent. He thought of it as adding another year to Wimbey's life. Intolerable. Absolutely intolerable.

Mackenzie knew with Eskeridge's death he was on a long, high roll. Everything was going right. That's when he started reading the newspapers again, the foreign news, the international section. He figured there was a war on the way. Things had been going so good for him there had to be a war on the way.

He was perturbed, aggravated, and enraged because the U.S. would not go on and get into the war. "What's wrong with that Roosevelt," he asked. "That's why the Negroes love him so much. As long as he keep out of the war, them young colored mens can just keep on livin' and livin'. After Pearl Harbor, the Japanese took first place in Mackenzie's affections. He was so elated he threw a party. He danced and hopped around, encouraging everyone to drink alcohol and smoke cigarettes.

When Stephen Wenders had gone off to war it had been hard for Mackenzie to conceal the glint in his eye. A rival so close, being sent to engage in the formidable task of dodging bullets, bombs, and land mines. Mackenzie loved it. The closeness of the deceased always increased the intensity of Mackenzie'a affirmation of his own aliveness. He loved to palpitate his own living flesh.

The untimely end of Gabriel Frye, an almost matchless physical specimen, at the dewy-cheeked age of twenty-three, and the next door neighbor but one, left Mackenzie joyous for months, a condition which was lengthened indefinitely when he was afforded so much care and concern by the youth's nubile widow.

He took to hiring cabs every two or three months to drive him out west through the colored neighborhoods so he could look for service flags with gold stars in the windows, each the mark of a man lost to the war. He kept a count. He loved soldiers and sailors even more than he loved gangsters and hooligans. There were so many military men. It was just that the wars did not come often enough or last long enough. The criminal elements had to take up the slack during the off seasons.

The whole length of Charles Stuart's acquaintance with Mr. Sweet had been exhilarating for Mackenzie. It had begun with the Great War, the deaths on the battlefields. The Red Summer continued it, particularly its success in Chicago with Negroes being murdered left and right on the streets, so that when Charles had moved to Evanston, Mackenzie was in his heyday. Potential rivals were being slaughtered everywhere. On the Southside Negroes were engaging in deadly knife fights, often dispatching each other.

He had a tally, he called it the "Sweet Tally," rather elaborate, which he worked on in the wee hours when he was busy outfoxing death. Charles was one of the few persons he ever told about it. He went to the public library and checked out books on mathematics. He had learned about actuarial tables from an insurance agent and was trying to learn about statistics and probability theory. Thinking about mathematics also improved his reasoning and sharpened his arguing skills.

He was pleased to learn that the life expectancy of Negroes was much shorter than that of whites. With every year he greatly improved his odds for becoming the World's Oldest Negro. Unlike many people, Mackenzie was not at all concerned with the reasons which created such a vast discrepancy in life expectations. He was only concerned with results, the final numbers, and he was delighted that the prospects were all in his favor. He looked hopefully on scourges like small pox, malaria, syphilis, and tuberculosis. He was well aware that Negroes were much less likely to be treated for such maladies than whites and he applauded the fact. He got down on his knees and thanked God for the worldwide flu epidemic that followed the Great War. He spent a lot of time during that period visiting colored hospitals and colored wards, watching people die. It delighted him that the very young and the very elderly were most vulnerable to the frightful disease. While his central ambition centered around age, he never lumped himself into the same category with other people who were merely old. While they were simply holding on, he was *achieving* greater and greater age. He was also a big enthusiast of the high infant mortality rate for colored. It cut off the most dangerous competitors - those who had the longest period of living ahead of them. If they were stopped at the threshold, so to speak, they never got into the real competition.

Like mortuaries, cemeteries were favorite haunts of Mackenzie, especially newly filled graves. When tombstones or markers were present, he took great delight in comparing the ages of the dead with his own. Even when he was in his nineties almost none had lived as long as he had.

Charles had the uncomfortable feeling that one of the reasons Mackenzie liked him was he did not consider him a rival. He must have had very strong and definite feelings that Charles was not going to live long. Every time they were in each other's company Mackenzie slapped him on the back, looked into his eyes, and laughed.

One of the first items he showed Charles was his newspaper collection. It contained obituaries, obituaries exclusively of Negroes. But what had first struck Charles had been the amazing sample of Southern newspapers. The number was stunning. Mackenzie collected them for the obituaries and also for the records of what others were doing on his behalf.

Mackenzie was not in any recognizable sense a political man. Still he had one favorite political organization and one political organization which was to him the implacable enemy. His favorite was the Ku Klux Klan. Next to the U.S. Army the Klan was doing more to contribute to his ultimate victory than any group of people he could think of. He had a lot of clippings on the Klan. Some were quite old. One, which was perhaps Mackenzie's favorite, and which had bound him in rock-fast devotion to the Klan was printed while Mackenzie was a young man, barely in his thirties and which proved the Klan had been about his work even before he knew of his calling.

"Here, here," he had said to Charles, pointing to the yellowed passages with his gnarled finger the color of iron. "Look at this."

The article summarized the report of the Congressional Commission of 1872, appointed to investigate the activities of the Ku Klux Klan. The work was a thirteen volume study which among other things pointed to 107 lynchings in Alabama in two years, to more than 2,000 Black people killed in Louisiana within a span of weeks, details of nigger hunts and mass burials in Mississippi, 124 lynchings in the month of April alone in 1869. The Klan lynched thirty-five people in only nine South Carolina counties within a six month period. Texas had witnessed at least 1,000 lynchings of Black people between 1865 and 1868.

A kind of beatific grace emanated from Mackenzie's face. These were people who had been eliminated from the competition before he even knew he was in it. By the Klan, the Ku Klux Klan. There was thanks in Mackenzie's voice when he said the three words. He uttered them like a kind of invocation, "Ku Klux Klan." It was as if he had genies on his side.

On the other hand he hated the NAACP for it was determined to stamp out the Klan. It also had launched an all-out campaign to abolish lynching.

"Now why they want t' do me that away," Mackenzie asked Charles. "I ain't done nothin' t' them."

And, indeed, he had not. He even subscribed to the *Crisis*, the NAACP's monthly journal, because it tried to keep track of atrocities committed against Negroes. Mackenzie leafed through each edition, got the numbers, and entered them into his tables and charts.

The Southern newspapers which Mackenzie had accumulated were shocking to Charles. Not just the old ones, but the later ones, too. He read articles from the *Memphis Press* about a Negro who was burned to death by a mob and stayed alive even though the flesh had fallen away from his legs and who uttered sound only when the crowd brought his wife and tiny daughter to watch him burn.

He read of a mob in Georgia which had tied a woman by her ankles to a tree limb, soaked her clothes in oil and set her on fire. After her clothes had burned off to the accompaniment of her screeches, she had not died. A man stepped forward and ripped open her belly with a knife. A fetus fell out which was stomped to death amid much enthusiasm from the crowd.

Mackenzie noticed Charles reading the article and said. "Two. I counted two. One for the mother and one for the baby. Both gone."

When the depression came, Mackenzie was at first unimpressed by stories of millionaires leaping out of skyscrapers. They were all white and their deaths were of no consequence to him. They could jump or not jump. It did not matter. As far as he was concerned the question was how to get Negroes to jump off the high rises.

For a while Mackenzie hoped that because Eskeridge was a millionaire he might be tempted to fling himself off the top of his carriage-barn. But no such luck. Wimbey was far too rich to be threatened by the depression. Indeed, it merely increased his wealth. Mackenzie abandoned that line of wishful thinking. He soon realized, however, that the depression would bring greater and greater misery to millions of Black folk, and many of them would die.

4

Mr. Stuart was extraordinarily zealous about his appearance. He had a handicap in that regard. Of the many things one should not be, too short was one. Mr. Stuart was an even five feet tall. Even Mrs. Stuart was five feet, five inches tall, a proper height. Mr. Stuart never would have married a woman who was too short. That was something he could control. Unfortunately, he could not control the height to which his own body had decided to grow, or more aptly, stopped. It had betrayed him. Mr. Stuart had to work that much harder to maintain appearances. He wore elevated shoes. A hat with an extremely high domed crown. The hat served double duty as Mr. Stuart possessed a shining bald scalp - another no-no.

Much of his wardrobe was patterned in vertical stripes. His plain-colored clothes, except shirts, were dark colors. He always dressed nattily, a suit or sport jacket and slacks every day, white shirt and tie. His shoes gleamed with a military polish. He was smooth-faced and clean shaven. Even his fingernails were immaculate - his toenails, which no one could see. He walked with a proud, upright, military bearing and a snappy step. In his right hand he always carried a leather briefcase. When it was raining he bore an expensive, black umbrella. In the winter he donned fashionable overcoats.

The other crowning monuments to his taste were his residence in Wimbey's Corner and his wife, Rebecca. When they first met twenty years earlier, she had been the rage of the South Side - all those wild dances - the Charleston, the Black Bottom, bathtub gin. And then one night they had discovered they were both from Gary, an instant bond amid so much chaos and so many shaky linkages. An anchor. Some anchor. A shocking figure. Vital. Brilliant. Energetic. Beautiful. She drew people like some centripetal force, and then led them on dazzling forays to solve first this one's problems, then another's. Rebecca. He still thought

94

of her that way. Dancing all night. He still saw her that way.

Today's Rebecca, in her black cotton coat, rain or shine, summer or winter, would have nothing of causes. No rouged cheeks. No red lips. No shadowed eyes. Only soap and water now touched her face which even in all this time kept its baby-smooth complexion. But no heart-shuddering smile. No light dancing in her eyes. To work and home again and once a month to Gary to visit her nieces. Her hips did not shimmy and her legs did not kick. Her body plodded to and from the bus stop, and did her house work, and went no further.

In the darkness of midnight, Rebecca Stuart lay awake in bed. Her husband snored next to her. She was glad he was asleep. She was thinking of her next trip to Gary. She smiled. No one knows I'm smiling, she thought. Or why. Her smile deepened. She knew how people thought of her, drab and faded. Let them. I have more important matters to attend to than what people think about me.

Her public appearance was so different from what it had been when she and Charles first met. It was as if she were trying to erase all that, or something more, to become invisible.

She wanted no notice taken of her, not in Evanston. Gary. *Was different.* But in Evanston, her comings and goings, so regular, were like the rising and setting of the sun, forgotten, except in her case if was as if a grey sun rose in a grey sky.

She liked the middle of the nights when she could lie alone with her thoughts. She knew some people were troubled by that time, awaking in the middle of the night to have their minds ravaged by relentless and fearful thoughts. But she was not. Her thoughts were explorations and tastings. They comforted her. They excited her. She enjoyed them. After a while they brought such contentment she drifted back to sleep.

5

Wellington Cork had worked to get his wife, Genuine, with her sandy color, her long, pointed nose, her flowing, thick, jet-black hair. He had worked to get her, he had got her, and nobody else was going to touch her. Ivory had not come out just as he had wanted. As a newborn she had been perfect. Whiter than a white baby. But as she got older she had darkened, and her pretty, wavy black hair had kinked up. Now she was darker than Genuine, a café' au lait, with rounded features. Wellington knew that was his contribution, with his brown skin, wide nose, and thick lips. He had hoped somehow that Genuine would cancel him out - she was the mother - and the baby would look like her. That had not happened. Still Ivory was light, with pretty, soft features.

Unlike everybody else, Mackenzie's death hadn't surprised Wellington. He had hated him. The dried-up old fossil had always lorded it over everybody, telling them how he was going to outlive them. It would have been one thing if he really could have fought, but he was too old to fight so all he could do was talk. Argue. And he just kept running his mouth till everybody else was too tired to go on, so he always said he won.

Dirty old man. Always trying to feel on the young women. It didn't matter that he had a wife young enough to be his granddaughter. He was always trying to feel on any young woman who came within his reach. The younger the better.

Wellington had hated to go out into his own front yard when the old man was alive. In good weather Mackenzie was always sitting on his front porch - any time of day or night.

As soon as he saw Wellington he'd start cackling.

Wellington knew better. He tried. He did everything he could not to, but he never could stop himself. He always shouted in response to the old geezer's instigating.

It was always something like, "What you laughin' at, you old goat?"

Mackenzie would keep laughing. "Laughing at you." Then he'd say, depending exactly on what Wellington had said, the equivalent of, "And you right. Yessir, you right. I am old. Older than you ever gon' be. Cause you gon' die long befo' you gits t'be my age. And you know what? I'm gon be settin' right up here, still laughin' at yo dead ass."

Then he would lean back and cackle some more.

"You right about the other part, too. I'm a goat. A billy goat. You know what a billy goat do? He, he, he, he, he! Yessiree, I'm a billy goat. And I'm gon' billy goat that Indian-nigger wife o' yourn and yo daughter, too, when she get a few more years on her, and then I'm 'on sit right up here with my old - **OLD** - ass self, and laugh at yo dead ass as I billy goats yo women. You lookin' at the man what's gon' be the oldest Negro in the **WORLD!** "

Mackenzie got in every lick he could - sneaky and dirty. Like calling Genuine an Indian-nigger. While it was true Genuine had Indian blood in her, pure-blooded Cherokee, it was also true she had Irish and Scotch blood in her, too. But Mackenzie wouldn't acknowledge that. Oh, no, he called her an Indian-nigger, ignoring and canceling out her white blood, as if she had none. Wellington was glad he had died.

6

It was difficult, but sometimes Mabel Brockerton tried to think of people who might live lives like hers. When she first began such labors of the imagination, long after she had accepted the perpetuity of her personal horror, she likened her life to the lives of people who are interminably faced with some natural disaster. They live on the edge of a volcano, or in regions wracked by earthquakes, tornadoes, or floods.

But the analogy did not satisfy her. She explored it for a long time and tested it and measured it. But it would not do. The experience was not close enough to hers. It lacked certainty. Natural calamities were subject to caprice. Unlike her dreaded visitations, they were not certain.

Perhaps people who sat on death row knew a life like hers. They knew that one day the guard would come with a man of the cloth. The day could be delayed but it would come. One day he would be led down a long hall to the gallows, or to tumbling canisters of gas, or to electrodes wired to his skull and hands and feet. If a person knew that in her lifetime she would have to face scores of executions, that life might be like hers.

Her ancestors had perhaps known it. Waiting in the slave market. They had no power over it but one day a person would come to buy them and another person would sell them and off they would go, all their prayers and hopes and entreaties to the contrary signifying nothing.

She watched her husband every day when he left for work. He was a hard worker, a kind man, silent. He never showed a sign and she never knew. She watched him as if the watching would tell her something.

At first she had blamed herself, always blamed herself. She was so big and fat. The hard thing was that the bigness and fatness were nothing new. As long as she could remember she had been big and fat. As a child. Fat. Huge. That's how she'd been when he met her, fell in love with her, he said, courted her, married her. He loved her as she was he said. Still at first she had blamed herself. So big. So big. And stink. Some people said she stank. She could not smell it herself, but some people said how could she smell it, she had been living with it all her life. People get used to the oil refineries and the stock yards. Don't smell them. That's how she'd become. She did not smell herself though she smelled to high heaven. Her fault. Big. Fat. Stank.

She stopped blaming herself when she realized that he - John - made choices. He chose her. He chose to stay with her. He chose fat. He chose big. He chose stinky. She was pretty. She had always known she was pretty and everybody had said it. He chose pretty, too. He did not have to. He made other choices. He did not have to. Whatever she was, he had made choices. She was not to blame.

She watched him every day with his silent, contained, purposeful self as he washed and dressed and ate his breakfast and left for work. She watched for a sign that he would come back as a whirlwind, or a splitting of the earth, a mountain of fire. As a wall of dark and terrible water. She watched for a hint that he would come back with lightning rods on his collar and jack boots and a hand pounding on the door at midnight, or that he would return with the voice of the auctioneer and buyer to sell and buy her and hers out of their own world. But he gave no sign.

99

7

The clang of the gate behind her always made Rebecca Stuart feel good. Home. Safe in Wimbey's Corner. *Wimbey's Corner.* The barest trace of a smile slipped by her lips as she walked to the stairs leading to the top floor of the house where she and Charles lived.

Her left hand grabbed the bannister and began the effort that would help pull her up the long flight. Some of her relatives had visited her in Evanston. They had, after each visit, asked why she and Charles did not move. They assured her they could find a great place for them in Gary. A house of their own. Their own yard. No steep, interminable stairs to climb. What could she tell them? She always said, "Oh, we're fine just where we are." That was no explanation. But that's what she always said.

Her relatives said, "Rebecca, I ain't never seen such a strange bunch of little houses. And it's so few of you, all surrounded by white people. Don't you feel alone?"

She reached the top of the stairs. She opened the door to her porch, went in, and closed the door behind her. Here she was alone. She smiled broadly. She got her key out and opened the front door.

Alone?

She went in and closed the door behind her.

No, we don't feel alone. Not in Wimbey's Corner. Private maybe. To a certain extent. She laughed.

She went to the closet and hung up her coat. She looked around her apartment. Just as she left it. She walked into the kitchen, in her mind going through the steps she would take to make dinner.

What was it about Wimbey's Corner that was different?

She began, automatically, the preparations for dinner without having to think about them.

There's no crime here, she thought. Somebody is always

home in the Corner and watches out for everyone else. Sometimes two or three people are watching out. The only criminals who operate in this neighborhood burglarize the rich and wouldn't waste their time or effort on us. We leave our windows open and our doors unlocked all summer when we're home. There has never been a reported crime in Wimbey's Corner.

It's peaceful. It's quiet. The birds wake us up in the mornings, and in the evenings when the wind is right we can hear the lake two blocks away. We're surrounded by trees and shade. We know everybody and everybody knows us. There are no strangers. It's comfortable to be where everyone is a known quantity and where the population is stable. Over the years the same people are always here. They don't leave - unless it is the way Mr. Sweet did. We always know what we're coming home to.

She thought about how Tary Street was always cleaned because it was a street rich people lived on. She thought about how Wimbey's Corner garbage was always picked up on time because it was right on the route for rich, white people.

She thought about how the trees were trimmed of dead wood and how the police patrolled the streets - quietly, courteously, but efficiently. The street drains never got stopped up. Sirens never wailed in the middle of the night. She could not think of another colored neighborhood with such a benevolent environment.

She walked out onto the back porch and looked down, out through the screen door past Wimbey's Corner and the alley, into Miss Bryce's back yard. Tall, leafy trees. Rich, green grass. A flamingo fountain spouting water into a little pond teeming with sparkling gold fish. Grape vines. A tiny green-house resplendent with flowers. Sweeter than the gardens of Babylon, she thought.

8

When Wanda was a baby, Mabel could read her mind. There was so little to read. She laughed. When she liked the food she was eating she opened her mouth wide and waited for her mother to spoon it in. She mouthed and swallowed it greedily, sometimes still chewing after she had swallowed most of it, as if to get every bit of taste. She smacked her lips. How easy that was to read - or when she crinkled her face and kicked her legs when it wasn't coming fast enough. When she did not want it she turned her head aside from the spoon. All that without a spoken word.

When she got older, crawling, and she wanted something, she fixed her eyes on it and made straight for it, hands and knees covering the floor at a rapid pace, one-track, unswervable. After she learned, haltingly, to walk, if she did not want to come, she ran, tottering, in the opposite direction, often falling in her pell-mell flight. Direct communication.

I used to be able to read her mind. What she thought, she did. What she did, she thought. Clear. Simple. No concealing. The brain expressed what was going through it by what the body did. O yes! I used to be a mind-reader.

Mabel believed that sometimes she could still read Wanda's mind. Wanda felt a deep ambivalence toward her. She loved her mother and felt closer to her than to anyone. At the same time she hated her and was ashamed of her. Mabel knew - probably with greater articulation
than Wanda - the reason for those paradoxical feelings. It lay in what they shared. In what they alone as members of the human family had as a mutual bond. There was first of all their immense weight. Wanda loved her mother because she too bore that burden. She too was uncommonly huge and like an odd pair of twins, one tall and one short, they possessed the same physical identity, the same painful physical identity and Wanda was ever grateful for her mother for being a partner in bearing such a cross. Her mother

suffered with her, her mother was shunned with her, her mother was humiliated with her. They were sisters in sorrow. But that bond was also something for which Wanda despised her mother. If Mabel had been svelte, with the slim, clean lines of a dancer, maybe Wanda would have been, too. When Wanda looked at her mother and saw herself she was mortified and outraged. Why did anyone have to be so monstrously large with unending folds, and creases, and mounds of flesh? She found the sight of her mother disgusting and repulsive. To know that in seeing her mother she saw herself was unforgivable.

The other thing they shared, that brought Wanda closer to her mother, locked to her, but at the same time alienated daughter from mother because mother had chosen it, had accepted it, and had mired her daughter inextricably in it, was life with John Brockerton. Mabel, too, made choices.

Baby, sometimes I can still read your mind. O Lord, I wish I could read his.

Busying herself with preparing a nice dinner took Mabel's mind off what she faced every evening. Waiting. She hated it. The very instant she awoke in the morning her terror began. It was acute at first, then gradually subsided. It built up again as he prepared for work and was almost tactile, slicing, ubiquitous, infusing itself into every breath, the very color of the day by the time he left. Her hands literally shook with fear as she cleared the breakfast dishes. When he walked down the stairs, through the yard, out of the gate, and out of sight, the terror lifted. For the rest of the day it appeared only fitfully - in flashes - until mid afternoon, when her mind began to orient itself toward leaving work, toward coming home. Then it began to grow again, slowly but without surcease, until by the time she reached home it was heavy, like another woman her own size settling down on her shoulders.

103

If she could just get through cooking dinner she knew, she knew she would be alright. If she could just get through cooking dinner she would be alright because by then he would be home.

If he were coming.

Mabel began to set the places on the kitchen table.

Where was he? He was usually home by now. Maybe he missed his bus. If he did, he would have to wait another fifteen minutes. Fifteen minutes!

No. Maybe ... I just cooked one vegetable. Only warmed up those mashed potatoes. Maybe it's not as late as I thought. I'm probably setting the table earlier than usual. Yes. She felt relief rush through her as she sighed.

Still she took her time setting the table and tried to keep from looking out of the window as she worked. Was he coming?

I'll go into the bedroom and look at the clock after I finish the table, assure myself that I'm just early. I'll give myself that time. I'll wait till then to assure myself.

She avoided Wanda's eyes which she knew were following her around the room. She knew her father was normally home by the time the table was set. She knew.

Mabel kept her back or her profile to Wanda and did not look at her and told herself that in a few minutes she would look at the clock to prove she was early.

She heard the click of the gate and looked up through the window.

He was there! Oh, thank God he was there! She felt so happy she wanted to sing. John was home. She looked at Wanda and smiled.

9

From their living room Rebecca and Charles Stuart could look through the window into the leaves and branches of an ancient elm. They sat enjoying a late, Sunday afternoon.

They savored the quiet.

They indulged themselves in the stillness.

Charles held back. He wanted to speak, but he held back. He was enjoying his wife's company and he didn't want to intrude on her mood.

Finally, she looked at him and smiled. She reached over and patted his hand.

He reached over and patted her hand on his.

"I'm glad this wasn't your weekend to go to Gary," he said. "It's good having you here all day."

She smiled.

"I've enjoyed it," she said.

He withdrew his hands and eased back into his chair. He watched the leaves.

"You know, I've been thinking a lot about Mackenzie since he died," he said.

"I know."

"The strange thing is, when you think about Mackenzie, and when he was here, you have to see him as sharp, abusive, cantankerous - divisive."

She chuckled. "I'd say that's a fair summary of his nicer qualities," she said.

"I know, I know," he said. "Always out to look for the weakness, and probe it, and widen it, and pour salt into it. Hateful. Mean. Attacking people. Driving them apart."

"He didn't have much appreciation for human life," said Rebecca.

"Oh, yes, he did," said Charles. "For one."

"Such a nice man," sighed Rebecca.

105

"No, he wasn't nice," said Charles, "but the one thing that surprises me is that I've realized in thinking about him, he was the glue."

"The glue?"

"Yes. It was him that held us together. He knew ... he knew what was important about each person - and how to use it."

Rebecca's face lit up. She turned to her husband, inspiration radiating in her face.

"Because ... because," she said, "our performing at a high level insured his well-being. He kept us together - so we could protect him, take care of him!"

"He was the glue," said Charles.

She leaned back.

"What do we do now that the glue has gone?"

"You know what kids do?"

"No, I don't," she said.

"They mix up some flour and water and make paste. It's not as good as the real thing - but it works."

"Tell me one thing."

"Yes, Ma'am."

"How are y'all going to turn John Brockerton into paste?"

They both laughed.

They held hands and watched the wind playing in the leaves.

106

WAYNE'S STORY IN EVANSTON

1

He came into her bed so quietly and so gently, yet so customarily, that his arms were around her and he was holding himself against her back before she became awake enough to recognize that anything was different. At first she only smiled with her eyes closed and snuggled back against him because her awareness was still more dreaming than consciousness.

She awakened because she had never heard him cry. The joy of her discovery made her want to sing yet she could not because of whatever great misery was afflicting him. She turned around and brought him into her arms. Whatever had hurt him - she could not help herself - she was happy, so happy. She comforted him and kissed him and rubbed her little hands on his vast back.

"I'm sorry, so sorry, Penny."

She did not know what he was sorry about. He was back, that's all she knew. He was back as she had always known he would be. She did not know how long it had been since he had written or sent money. She had known he would be back and here he was. She was very happy and she had no idea what he was sorry about but she was glad he was sorry about it in her arms.

For a long time Wayne was just thankful he had some place to come. He did not go to Bardwell. He stayed in the country. Mostly he kept close to Penny and helped her with her reading and writing and played with Bobo. Sometimes he took them fishing. While he was awake he did not let either of them out of his sight for more than five minutes. He slept much less than they did and when they were asleep he liked to have some light in the room, even if it were only moonlight, so he could keep looking at them.

Matilda was an extremely beautiful woman and she had opened his heart in ways he had not known it could be opened.

109

Wayne felt as if he were being cleaned, the way you clean a fish, or a chicken, or a hog, whenever he thought about her. Somebody was just cutting him open and pulling all his insides out. Only if I would bleed, he thought, only if I would bleed. But he did not.

After a few months, though, Wayne knew what he had learned before. He was too big for his natal place. He did not bother to go into Bardwell because he was too big for it, too. I couldn't even fit into a town that little, he thought. I'm a big city man, a Chicago man.

That is why Wayne knew he could not stay. He was bursting out, bursting out of the Western Kentucky backwater. He had not only seen what lay beyond, he had lived it. He could not be shrunk back down to country size.

He worried, though, about Penny and Bobo. He was not ever going to leave them again, but Chicago would gobble them up. If he had been worried about Joe Harrison - Lord, he had been a babe in the woods. Chicago would eat up Penny and Bobo for breakfast, smack its lips and ask when the real meal was going to start. He could not stay, but he could not leave them and he could not take them, until one day he remembered Evanston.

2

The first place Wayne and his family lived in Evanston was a room in Mrs. McCracken's house. The room was in the back on the second floor. Mrs. McCracken, a lady in her mid-seventies, had paid for the house by taking in roomers. Rumor had it that the house had originally been built by Albert Moore's grandfather. Albert Moore was the undertaker. He followed in the profession of his father and his grandfather before him. In his grandfather's day the house and the address were said to have been very prestigious, but the Moores had moved further west with the fashion and eventually the mortgage had become Mrs. McCracken's possession. After the mortgage had been paid off, and that happened years before Wayne and his family took up residence, Mrs. McCracken had found the roomers such a convenient source of income she kept them. Indeed, she became preoccupied with trying to devise ways to squeeze more in. She became ingenious at it, and her inventions only drove her to greater heights of ingenuity. None of the city officials or building inspectors were worried by the number of people Mrs. McCracken squeezed and packed and jimmied and mashed into her house. Rather, the more she could fit into it, the greater the capacity of the west side to absorb Negroes, and the less danger they would spill into other parts of the city. By the time Wayne and Penny and Bobo came along even Mrs. McCracken had forgotten how many people lived in her house.

Bobo, at five, was quite gregarious, and quickly met and befriended other children both within and outside the McCracken labyrinth. Penny and Wayne met many of the children's parents and before long they had a sizeable number of acquaintances. They discovered that unlike the denizens of the rooming house, many of whom did not even know one another, the Negro residents of Evanston at large often exhibited a great deal of mutual friendliness. Many had come from the same sections of the South, even the same towns and knew each others' family histories for generations. It was not unusual to hear someone quote a neighbor's genealogy back four generations and out to cousins ten and twelve times removed.

Penny liked the town right off and in no time felt superior because she, too, did not live in Chicago, though the only time she had ever been there was coming from the Twelfth Street Station to Evanston. That tickled Wayne because he liked Chicago even though for reasons known only to himself he had to stay away from it. He nevertheless gradually became infected by the notion that a higher class of Negroes lived in Evanston - he and his Penny and Bobo among them.

Wayne's most pressing concern was finding work. Unlike many people he knew, he hoped the war was in no hurry to end. He knew when the white boys came back they would be claiming jobs that had snatched up colored boys during the war. He had a much better chance of getting and keeping a baking job while most of the white bakers were making their pastries for battleship and aircraft carrier crews, for messes all across Italy and England and the Pacific. He would not care if the war went on forever except he was tired of seeing soldiers and sailors and the way everybody loved them.

In Evanston all somebody had to do was show up in a uniform and everybody was oohing and aahing all over him. With Great Lakes and Fort Sheridan so near, servicemen were always looking for Evanston girls. Wayne tried very hard to keep Penny out of their sight. They had no respect for wedding bands or engagement rings or anything else. Any woman was fair game as far as they were concerned and since he and Penny were not even married, she would be open season to any of them.

He remembered how he used to beat them up in the night clubs and sometimes he wanted to do it again, just bust them up into bloody messes right out in the middle of the street. He never did it, though sometimes it was very hard not to, especially when there were bunches of them

112

together acting arrogant and as if they owned the world and because there was a group of them how tough they were. Wayne wanted to show them but he did not. What made it worse was that Bobo loved uniforms. His eyes lit up and his face danced whenever he saw one. The stores sold little ones for kids and Bobo wanted one. He wanted to know why his daddy did not have a suit like the "soldier-mans." Penny did not say anything about uniforms. Wayne did not know whether she liked them or not. She kept as far away from the subject as possible.

Three weeks after arriving in Evanston, Wayne got a job at Elmer's bakery on Custer Avenue. The hours were long but the money was good and there were plenty of extras for Penny and Bobo.

3

Penny did not know how to bring up about the marriage license. Wayne was happy with things as they were and she did not want to do anything to upset him. She did not think he had anything against marrying her formal-like. She did not know - but she did not think he did. Everything was fine as it was. Except Penny wanted to feel like a real Evanston woman. She knew a real Evanston woman would not be a common-law wife.

She did not like it when the women talked about their weddings. They talked about them a lot. Justice of the Peace. Church. In my father's house. Short sheets and rice in the beds. It embarrassed her. She never said anything about herself. She smiled and laughed at their stories and felt self-conscious.

She did not even have a wedding ring but she had remedied that very soon after her arrival in Evanston at the five and ten cents store. She wore a very pretty silver-looking ring. She had not thought about a wedding ring until one day someone had asked where hers was. After much embarrassed flustering and blushing she had said her finger had grown too fat for it. They told her it was easy for jewelers to enlarge it and not long after that she made her trip to the five and dime.

Wayne had never noticed. He did not know she wore the ring, though she never took it off.

Sometimes she watched him as he slept and thought that as wonderful as their life was how much better it would be if he were her legal husband.

In Evanston, Wayne never felt intimidated as he had at first in Chicago. He felt free. He liked to wander around

114

and see the town. He got off work early in the afternoon and he liked to take Penny and Bobo for walks along the city's elm-draped streets. Most Evanstonians were proud of their trees and Wayne and Penny started being proud of them, too. Penny and Bobo, even when Wayne carried Bobo, could never walk as long as Wayne wanted. So since Wayne woke up early every morning whether he worked or not, he started going for long Sunday morning walks by himself.

One Sunday morning as he was walking east on Davis Street he inhaled air saturated with the smell of water. He ran the two blocks to the lake front. He stopped, transfixed by the vast inland sea, a shining, smooth sheen stretching in every direction to the farthest horizons, the sun tinting it gold, the crystaline water drinking color from the sky.

The song came off the water in such a distant and uneven way that when Wayne first heard it he did not think of it as a song at all, but as a trick of the wind or the echo of distant bells or an illusion in his mind. But he kept hearing it - hollow - in catches and vanishing strains.

He climbed over the great hunks of broken pavement and massive blocks of stone tumbled against the shoreline as a barrier to the water, protecting the park made on landfill. The park also buffered the mansions across the lakefront drive from the beaches where the common people cavorted. Wayne used both hands and moved his feet slowly as he clambered over the jumbled rock to stand at the water's edge.

Ripples lapped gently and inaudibly against the shore.

Wayne heard the song.
0-0-0^0 ... 0-0-0^0
Got to
Got t'get some ....

115

HAA ... A ... ALL ... HAA ... A ... ALL ....

Some distance to Wayne's left a long, concrete pier plunged into the lake. A lone figure sat at its far end. Fishing.

Carefully, Wayne made his way over the heaps of masonry to the pier. He climbed onto its flat surface and rested. He had never seen the lake when he lived in Chicago except in snatches between buildings or from the el windows. Now, elevated on top of the pier and a few feet from the shoreline, he had a chance to take a long, deep look.

He felt as if he stood on the edge of eternity.

One of the Great Lakes.

He saw a flash of yellow as a cane pole arched in the morning sun, a fish deep under the water drawing the line taught and bowing the tip of the pole toward the surface.

It's a long way out there, he thought, watching the man lean back and pull up on the pole.

Only then did he notice that the song had stopped.

He walked cautiously out on the pier, his fear moderated by his eagerness to see what the man was catching.

The man had just strung the fish on a long stringer that dropped five feet from the pier to disappear in the smooth water. Below the surface Wayne could see a mess of fish shapes tugging and pulling on the stringer.

"What you catchin'?"

The man, busy hooking a minnow under its dorsal fin, looked up. He wore a broad brimmed hat with a pointy crown. The hat kept his eyes in shadow, but he had a long, hooked nose and a wide mouth. He had a tanned complexion and Wayne could not tell by looking at him what race he was.

"You must be new around here," the man said. "Waterton's my name."

116

"Yes. I am new. How'd you know? My name's Wayne."

"Glad to meet you, Wayne. How'd I know you was new? Number one, I ain't seen you around here before and I know damn near every nigger in Evanston, and number two, ain't but one thing to be catchin' off these piers - leastways this time o' year, and with a southwest wind like this. Take a look." He pointed to the stringer.

Wayne reached over and pulled up on it. Heavy. When the first fish broke free from the water, flipping and thrashing, Wayne saw right away they were yellow perch. But they were not like any yellow perch he had ever seen. He studied them. They were deeper bodied and broader across the top than any perch he knew of, and the fronts of their heads were shaped differently, not as elongated. Their color was all wrong. They were not yellow or yellowish-green. They were almost colorless, almost silver, except for the broad, vertical stripes along their sides, stripes which were wider and darker - almost navy - than on any perch in his experience. They were big, too, very big for perch. He could not remember ever having seen any that big. He let them back into the water.

"Perch," he said.

The way he said it made Mr. Waterton laugh.

"Ain't never seen none like them, is you," he said.

"No," replied Wayne.

"Them's lake perch," said Mr. Waterton. "The lake changes 'em. I suppose if they was raised up anywhere's else they'd be plain, old yellow perch. But not here. These here is lake perch."

The tip of one of the man's poles started twitching. Suddenly it took a deep dip.

"Hot damn," the man said. He snatched it up.

After a brief, sweeping run, and a short, tugging struggle, two fat, long perch came sailing up out of the

117

water.

Wayne grinned. "They really bitin' today," he said.

"You damn right," said Mr. Waterton. "Anytime you get a southwest wind like this, make the top o' the lake like glass - the perch comes in."

"Comes in?"

Mr. Waterton laughed.

"Yeah," he said. "Look at this lake. You see how big it is?" He was busy taking the fish off his hooks and putting them on his stringer.

Wayne nodded his head.

"Well, big as it look," Mr. Waterton continued, "you cain't see hardly none of it from here. It go all the way cross to Michigan. It go all the way south to Indiana, and all the way north past Wisconsin and up to northern Michigan. Why it's ships what sail this lake big enough to sail the ocean. You think these perch set up under this pier all the time. No siree. You get a strong east wind and the waves'll be comin' in here five feet over the top o' this pier. A fish would be a fool to be settin' up in here then. You get a north wind and it'll be cold, and there'll be whitecaps and the waves just beatin' at the north side of this pier. But goddman! Don't let the southwest wind blow. The minnows comes in. It's all peaceful here and the minnows just set up here under the piers without fightin' no waves and the perch comes in and eats 'em up.

"Come here, let me show you somethin'." He motioned for Wayne to sit down beside him.

Wayne was afraid, but he did it. His fishing instinct overcame his fear.

"Look yonder," Mr. Waterton pointed out fifteen feet from the pier.

Wayne's eyes adjusted quickly to looking under the water. He saw what at first seemed to be a dark mass lying just under the surface, maybe six inches down. Then he recognized it was not solid. Its separate parts were moving. It was a stream of minnows - continual, unbroken. It appeared to be at least twelve feet wide, and he could not tell, maybe three of four feet thick, and packed so closely together Wayne was sure they formed a solid mass. He could walk on them. They just kept coming and coming.

When Wayne recaptured his voice, he said, "How long they been there?"

"I don't know. I don't know when this southwest wind started. But they was here when I got here about 4:30 this morning and they gon' be here all day, or as long as this wind last."

"How long will that be?"

"I don't know. It could change in two or three hours. I know it ain't gon' change no sooner than that because the minnows starts breaking up about an hour or so before it really change. So it could be gone this afternoon. Or it could last all day. Longest I ever seen it last was three or four days. By the last day my hands and arms and back was just wore out from catchin' fish."

"You mean the minnows kept runnin' - like this - for three or four days?"

"Uh huh. They'll keep comin' - just like this - long as that southwest wind last. And right up under them is them lake perch, stuffin' they guts. You cut open one o' they stomachs, it's just full o' minnows."

Wayne was flabbergasted. "Then why, why you the only one fishin'?" He could not imagine he had come to a place - with so much water, with such incredible fishing - where no one fished.

"Because nobody know when the southwest wind gon' blow. I comes down here every morning. If the waves ain't too bad I comes out here and fishes. If they is too bad I goes on back home. I ain't got nothin' else to do. I'm retired.

119

"There'll be some others later on. But I'm always the first one here. Saturday there'd be somebody else here by now, but Sunday morning they likes to get they sleep. See, yesterday it was a southeast wind. That ain't too bad a fishin' wind if it ain't too strong, and it wasn't. But didn't nobody expect no southwest wind today - includin' me. So they'll get here late. Shit, I'll be ready t'go home. I catch too many more as it is now, I won't be able to peddle 'em home on my bicycle."

Wayne looked at the endless river of minnows. A cane pole dipped. He knew where he would be spending a lot of Sundays.

4

Penny and Bobo knew nothing of Matilda or that part of Wayne's life in Chicago. He did not want them to. He had told them only about his job in the bakery near the loop and made it seem that he had done no other work. There was only one external vestige from that period in his life. Under Light's tutelage Wayne had developed a taste for fine clothes. It was one in which with Penny and Bobo at his side he did not much indulge himself, but every now and then he made a purchase which was altogether out of keeping with his station in life. Such extravagances puzzled Penny because Wayne had never had much of an interest in clothes, but she remembered the figure he had cut when he had returned to Kentucky and she deduced that the fashions in Chicago had overwhelmed his earlier disregard for apparel.

Wayne always got restless when he put on his fancy clothes and it was then he was most likely to think of Matilda. The problem was that in Evanston there was no place to go all dressed up. It was a dry town so there were no night clubs. Wayne was not about to go to Chicago where he might run into his old life and even commit murder again. Church was a place where people wore their best, but Wayne had never been a church-goer and was not interested in becoming one. Besides, there was something in Wayne's flashy clothes which marked them as not precisely suitable for a house of worship. So when Wayne donned his finest garb he usually strolled around on Mrs. McCracken's front porch for upwards of an hour before he retired upstairs and changed back to his everyday clothes. Going through the whole experience with its attendant memories was not pleasant for him. Nevertheless, he found himself periodically, irresistibly, repeating it.

121

One way Wayne sought to avoid throwing himself into a state of distress was by spending time - not only on Sundays, but afternoons as well - at the lakefront with Mr. Waterton learning how to catch lake perch. As often as they were up to the walk, he took Penny and Bobo with him.

Being the trained fisherman he was, and as often and as long as he fished off the pier, it only took Wayne a few weeks to master many of the tricks for catching lake perch. On a good day anyone could haul them in by the bushel, but on a bad day tricks were required to catch any fish at all. Even on a good day only master fishermen constantly caught big ones. The run-of-the-mill fishermen spent too much time throwing away little ones and stringing up those just in the "keeper" range. But the master fishermen left with strings full of the long, fat, deep, "jumbos."

Wayne loved it when his pole dipped and he felt the surge of a heavy perch against his line. He leaned back and loosed the almost obligatory cry, "Jumbo!" It let everyone within hearing know that big fish were hitting. The frequency of its repetition marked the level of excitement for the day. Very few fishermen - even on the best of days - launched into the self congratulatory shout almost every time their poles bowed. Within a short time Wayne was one of them.

On good days Wayne caught far too many fish for his family, so he gave them away to other fishermen on the pier, to Mrs. McCracken, and to several roomers in the house who confessed to their unabashed passions for fresh fish.

Mr. Waterton seemed too young to be retired so after a couple of months Wayne broached the subject. Mr. Waterton confessed that yes he was only in his forties, but that he had already been retired for over twenty years.

"Retired right after the war," he said.

"Oh ... uh ... you ... er ... was in the G-G-Great War,"

asked Wayne.

"Uh huh. Though as much as I done thought about it, I cain't think of a goddamn thing about it what was great."

"Uh ... er ... uh ... w-w-wa-wa-was you wounded?"

"Why'n the hell you think I'm retired? Damn tootin' I was wounded. My body was wounded. My mind was wounded. My soul was wounded.

"I was so goddamned wounded I cain't work no more. Just cain't do it. Cain't work."

Mr. Waterton did not mind talking about the war. "Them Frenchies was alright," he often said.

"Yessir, we served right with a French division. We was the 371st Infantry Regiment. Served with the Fifteenth French Division. Red Hand they called it. Had a little red hand .. uh ... insignia, yeah, insignia. We got one for our uniforms, too. Yeah, them Frenchies was alright.

"We made a good team - colored and Frenchies. Whipped the shit out o' the Kaiser's boys. You should o' seen the way we fought up that Observatory Ridge. Kickin' ass left and right. Course, we ... we lost a lot o' men, too. But I'm gon' tell you one thing. Them Frenchies was alright."

But no matter how Mr. Waterton started out, if it were praising the courage and skill of the men of the 371st, the brotherly affection of the French Red Hand, or cussing the prejudiced white bastards of the American Army, he always ended on the same note. "I cain't work."

Whatever his wounds , they did not keep him from making babies. He had a wagonload of children, some now grown. His wife worked as a domestic, the money was slim, but well-managed, and whatever fish he could bring home always helped. Though that is not why he fished. He even fished days when he did not catch a fish and when he had known before he left his house he would not catch any.

On those days he just sat out on the end of the pier by himself and sang his song. It was the song Wayne had half-heard that first morning over the water.

"O-O-O-O^O, O-O-O-O^O.

"O-O-O-O^O, yeah. O-O-O-O^O, yeah.

"Got to, Got t'get me some, Got t'get me some

"Ha-a-dachol! Ha-a-dachol!

"Oh, it's good for the body and it's good for the
soul,

"Ha-adachol! Ha-adachol!

"Put some in ya, and you'll do the jelly-roll -

"Ha-a-a-da-chol!"

In midsummer when even the nights were not cool, sometimes Wayne fished until the predawn hours when he had to go to work. Usually there were about a half-dozen men staying on those hot nights, chiming in and out of the richly textured polyrythmic conversations orchestrated by Mr. Waterton. Lanterns hung over the water.

There were days, though, when by the wind Wayne knew it would be pointless to go to the lake with the intention of catching fish. Those days he resumed his walks around town, sometimes with his family, sometimes without them.

Being a fisherman, there was one place in all Wayne's tramps that fascinated him. The western boundary of Evanston was marked by what everyone called the canal. It was a pea-green, viscous body of water which moved sludge-like, almost imperceptibly, to its merger with Lake Michigan at Wilmette Harbor. Its steep banks were covered with thick bushy undergrowth and a few stubby trees. The gluey channel was bridged by the major east-west streets. Under the bridges and in assorted places along the banks derelicts and hobos had made both individual and group shelters which they camouflaged.

Wayne liked to stand on one of the bridges,

124

particularly the Church Street Bridge, and watch the opaque murk slide by. Sometimes he walked along the top of the pitched bank staring into the heavy fluid. He was looking for fish signs. It appeared to him that occasionally he saw some, which was puzzling. Because he never saw anyone fishing in the canal - not even little kids, who fished anywhere - puddles just formed from rainstorms, and sewers, and gutters. Not even the derelict men who lived along the canal fished it. Yet they were often desperate for food.

He became increasingly tempted to try it. But in such a long stretch of water - it ran for several miles - with no one even trying to tease a fish onto a hook, he could not understand how there could be any fish in it. He did not want to appear a complete fool - fishing where absolutely everyone knew there were no fish. Just to make sure no one fished there, he began checking the canal at different times of the day, and at night, throughout the day and night. He began to survey various sections of the canal.

He never saw anyone fishing. He remembered the day he'd seen Mr. Waterton fishing all alone at the lake with a stringer full of jumbos. Nobody was there because they didn't know the fish were biting. Maybe here - at the canal - nobody knew the fish were even there. The more time he spent near the water the more his highly trained eyes saw fish signs. Maybe they don't know, he thought. Maybe the people here been away from the country so long they cain't tell where there's fish at.

He decided that one evening, just at dusk, when no one could see him, he would go to a place he had picked out - a place out of sight from any of the hobo camps, out of sight from the road, but one which was also a natural fish place. He would go there to try his luck and skill, to see if he could coax a living fish out of the canal. But he would have to wait until the time was right.

Wayne spent most of his free time fishing at the lake. It felt fresh and exhilarating just to be there. The endless sweep of water was resplendent with changes. He never knew what to expect - great, smooth, blue-green swells, raging grey waves showing white caps, choppy, blue tent-tops; or the marvelous glide-clarity of the southwest wind. Besides, there was company, the robust, warm, and spicy company.

Sometimes when Wayne lay on his bed at night with Penny beside him, as he tried not to think about Matilda, he passed beyond a state of yearning for her, missing her, and felt seeping through his body and his feelings a deep peace and contentment, a gratitude for the tranquility of his days. He thought about the first time he had stepped off the el onto the platform at Foster Street and had seen Northwestern's serenity. He treasured that feeling because it represented what Evanston was to him. When he walked home from fishing through the east side, he took his time, soaking in the stillness of the elegant homes.

Sometimes when he lay awake at night he grieved, too, for though he tried to keep it out of his mind, he had killed a man. The court had said he had not murdered. He knew that, but he had felt his hands on Joe Harrison's body and heard the terrible crack that had ended his life and he knew what no court could ever know. He knew what it was to steal the sun at midday. He tried never to think about it, but sometimes he failed. Sorry, he knew, wouldn't bring him back.

And Matilda. He had been away from her long enough to know how much he needed her and missed her. He wanted to see her again. He had to see her again. He did not know what had gone on between her and Light, why they had lain in his bed fucking like dogs. But as time passed he had let himself visualize the scene again.

126

Gradually, he had let tiny portions of it out of his memory and into his mind. Bit by bit. He knew as soon as he let some remembrances into his consciousness he had to block them out forever. There were others he could stand. After a while, he knew, he truly knew that for whatever reason she had fucked Light, she had regretted it.

She really did love me, he thought. She was sorry for what she done. She wished she wouldn't of done it. She was sorry. She really did love me and she wanted me to kill him.

He heard her words.

He saw her horrified, desperate face looking up at him.

"Baby, I love you. I love you," she had said. He saw the tears running all down her beautiful face and she did not care how she looked.

All she could do was reach for me, he thought. He remembered how the tears merged with the perspiration on her body and how her breasts looked. Her nipples were swollen.

Suddenly he wanted her in the same, terrible way he had always wanted her.

She hated Light.

He heard the venom in her voice demanding, *"Yes. Kill him! Kill him!"*

She hated Light.

Then why was she in bed with him?

He remembered the way her body had felt against his arm as he had brushed her away.

"Please forgive me."

She loved me. She still loved me. No matter what she done, she still loved me.

Wayne let himself know that and he knew he had to see her again.

Wayne was excited as he walked down the darkening streets toward the canal. He had a sectioned cane pole broken down in his hands so no one could spot right off what he was carrying. He had a stringer in one pocket and a tied-up handkerchief filled with moist earth and night crawlers in the other. No one would know what he was up to. He giggled. Even Penny and Bobo did not know where he was going. He had stashed his fishing gear under the back steps and told them he was going for a walk.

We'll see, he told himself. We'll see if there's any fish in that canal. He looked around him before he stepped off the sidewalk into the thickets. No one was looking. He bent over and moved quickly. Soon he could not be seen from the street. When he reached the top of the bank he stopped. He listened.

He could hear an occasional car passing on the street. Far away he heard a dog barking. A screen door slammed. Around him there was nothing. Every now and then leaves moved in a light breeze. Nothing. Nothing else. The sound of himself standing on twigs and dead leaves.

He strained his eyes into the gloom. He could see the lighter shape of the water between the two dark banks, the silhouettes of a few scruffy trees. Nothing was moving. He could barely make out the place close to the water he had chosen. He waited a minute longer, alert. Then he began a careful descent down the steep, overgrown incline. The water's unpleasant, not quite stagnant smell rose into his nostrils.

Wayne had decided the best bet was to fish on the bottom. If the canal had any fish in it, they would be bottom feeders. He let the tip of the pole down slowly, easing the heavy weight into the water. The fluid was so thick the line, sinker, and bait took a long time descending. At last he felt the weight settling into a mushy bottom.

He exhaled.

He felt he could hear his heart through his shirt.

Almost instantly his hand trembled in disbelief.

A nibble. It felt like a nibble.

Not the current.

Not a snag.

A nibble.

His hands tightened around the pole.

Yes.

He ain't took it yet, but, yeah, it's a nibble, a nibble!

I just got here!

I just got here and I got a nibble!

The fish started to move away. Either the hook was inside its mouth by now or not, but the fish had the worm and was moving on.

Now is the time.

Wayne knew when he flipped his wrists he would either set the hook or bring the sinker and stripped hook flying out of the water. One or the other.

Now is the time.

He flicked his wrists.

The tip of the pole jerked down.

The heft of the fish bore down on the line.

Wayne grinned.

The hook had sunk home.

Wayne stopped fishing after forty-five minutes, but only because he had run out of worms.

He sat on the sticks, and dead leaves, and weeds, leaned against the embankment and collected himself. His whole body was charged with excitement.

He had fifteen fish on his stringer, the smallest would go at least two and one-half to three pounds. He had bullheads, catfish, suckers, carp, and two red horse that had to be twenty-five pounds apiece. He shook his head. He had thrown back as many as he had kept, fish of around a pound or less. He blew out a long breath.

He was not yet ready to stand. He leaned his head back and closed his eyes.

Nobody fished here! They must be crazy. They must all be crazy. I couldn't be the only one who knows ... but maybe I am.

Wayne kept two medium-sized catfish for his family. He gave the two big red horse to Mrs. McCracken. The others he gave to men at the bakery and families in Mrs. McCracken's house. Like all good fishermen he told no one where he caught them. He was keeping this place as his personal secret. The fish were especially tasty. Even Bobo smacked his lips over them and everyone Wayne had given some made a special effort to tell him how good they were.

Wayne still did almost all his fishing at the lake. The setting was more pleasant and plenty of times he could take Penny and Bobo. He also had to be very careful when he went to the canal, sneaking so no one would discover his secret place. But every now and then when the wind was out of the east or the north, he slipped down to the viscous, green water and caught fish such as no one in Evanston had ever seen or tasted.

Penny was very pleased with the way they were living. Wayne had a good job. He made more money than anyone they knew. Bobo had made lots of friends and was growing up strong and smart. They were able to save. Penny did not have to worry about the war taking Wayne away. All around her women were seeing their boyfriends and husbands and sons go off to war, or they had already gone. She had only two worries. Small worries and only two.

She wanted Wayne to marry her. She had made up her mind that she wanted a legal marriage. How could she be better than the country and Chicago niggers as all the other Evanston women were if she did not have a legal marriage license? But she did not know how to bring it up. She had to think of some way because it tortured her too much.

The other thing was she had noticed right around the time Wayne caught that first mess of big, fat fish he had started acting distracted every now and then. It wasn't often, nor was it anything to put a finger on. Most of the time he was his usual jovial self, full of love, full of kindness. But then sometimes ... he wasn't there. He just wasn't there. He was sitting beside her but he was gone. It didn't last long and she did not know how she knew it when it happened because sometimes he even kept talking, but he was not there. She did not know what it meant, but like the marriage license, it troubled her.

6

Wayne was trying to figure out how he was going to find Matilda and then get to see her. He was convinced that whatever she was doing she still loved him and would come back to him. Imploring images of the last time he had seen her inundated his mind. If he asked her she would come back.

He did not know what that would mean about Penny. He loved Penny as he always had, and she was the mother of his son. Penny was his "heart." He did not know what it would mean and he did not want to think about it as every time a picture of Matilda came into his brain he felt the same need, the same craving for her he had never been able to slake. He had to find her and he knew if he asked she would come back to him.

He figured she had gone back to working for Light. That would make it very hard to reach her. Light kept close tabs on his women. He would have a new enforcer. Light would also kill Wayne if he found out where he was. Having been in mortal jeopardy at Wayne's hands was a thing Light's vanity, his pride, and his profession would not countenance. If Wayne ever appeared on the Chicago scene again he would have to die - even though only three people knew what had happened between them. He would have to find Matilda without alerting Light. That would be very, very hard.

Wayne's mind kept returning to his problem. Until he remembered Jersey-Blue.

Wayne had been going over characteristics of each of Light's women to determine if there were one or two whom he could trust, whom he could absolutely trust, whom if he asked it of them would not reveal him to Light.

He came up with three names: Camilla, Lily, and

Cinnamon.

Wayne got in touch with Jersey and asked him to try to locate one of the three, and when he did, to get Wayne her phone number. As always, Jersey came through.

Camilla answered the phone on the fourth ring.

"Hey, LBN," she said. "Tell me what happened. I want to be the first one to know the true story."

"It's a long story, Camilla. I don't want to tell you over the phone."

"Well, where you at, baby? I'll come to you. This story is worth a little movement."

"Not now. Later. We'll get together some place and I'll tell you."

"Soon?"

"Yeah. Soon. Soon."

"Okay, baby, what you want?"

"Camilla, where's Matilda?"

It was as if they'd been disconnected.

"Camilla?

"Camilla?"

"LBN?"

"Yeah, what happened? We get cut off? Where'd you go?"

"You ain't playin'? You don't know about Matilda?"

"Know. Know what?"

"Wayne. Light. Light killed her. Killed her over a year ago. Right after you left."

Wayne dropped to his knees. The receiver dangled against the wall.

When he stood up he leaned against the wall and placed the receiver to his ear.

"He in jail," he asked very softly.

133

"No, baby. They said it was self-defense."

Wayne dropped the receiver again. He slumped back to his knees, his back against the wall.

Self-defense. Self defense. He knew about self-defense. As if she never lived. As if she had no right to live.

When he picked up the phone he said, "Meet me at the State Street Theater. I want you to tell me everything."

Camilla told him everything.

Wayne told her what had happened that night in the apartment.

They sat on opposite sides of the booth at Walgreen's and stared at each other.

"You know," Wayne said, "Light cain't get away with this. I loved her."

"She loved you, too," said Camilla. "That night, before it happened, she had a long talk with me. She was crazy - I mean she was crazy - but what she said made sense. She said she loved you. She said she couldn't live without you. She said she hated Claude because of what he done to her - she didn't say what it was. She just said he was cockroach shit. The lowest thing on earth. He was cockroach shit. She screamed it and she hated him and she couldn't live without you. She broke down crying."

"I wonder how he got her t'do that," puzzled Wayne. "I mean, like sh-sh-she l-l-loved me and everything. H-H-How, how d-d-di-did he get her t'd-d-do it?"

"Oh, honey you don't know Claude. I mean you might know him in one way. But you don't know him like we do. He could talk the bark off a tree. Believe me. He could get you to believe, for a little while anyway, that a pot of chittlins was a mink coat and git you t'try t'wear that sucker." Wayne shook his great head. "I shoulda killed the nigger then. Just like she told me. Him and his skinny, little dick shootin' cum in the air.

"She'd still be alive today."

Wayne cried out.

People all over the drugstore looked at him.

Camilla lit up a cigarette. She ignored the staring people. She watched Wayne.

She clicked her fingernails against each other.

She exhaled.

"Claude got the biggest dick I ever seen," she said, "and I'm a ho."

Wayne looked up at her. He grunted. "That little ol' punky thing. I shoulda broke it."

Camilla stared at Wayne, a new intensity dominating her.

"Matilda said one other thing. I didn't pay it no attention because she was talkin' so crazy and because she was wild in love with you. She ... she said, she ... never wanted nobody to know," Camilla inhaled from the cigarette. She exhaled and tapped her fingernails on the tabletop. She stared at Wayne.

He looked back.

"She said she was afraid what would happen if other women found out, but now that she'd lost you she didn't care and she wanted the whole world to know, especially she wanted all Claude's women to know."

She inhaled again.

"Know what?"

She exhaled.

She looked steadily into his eyes.

"That you got the biggest dick in the world."

Wayne broke out laughing. He laughed so hard his whole upper body fell across the tabletop. People turned their heads to stare at him again.

"What's so damn funny, Wayne? I know you don't

135

have no little dick. I seen the bulge, and then when you said that about Claude - who got a giant, horse-ass dick - I remembered what Matilda said. So what's so damn funny?"

"I ain't never heard nothin' so crazy in my life.

"Matilda must have ... Light did that. He made her ready for the looney-bin. And then the dog killed her." Wayne gritted his teeth and clenched his fists.

"Let me see it."

"What?"

All of her attention was focused on what she was saying.

"Let ... me ... see ... your peter."

Wayne thought he was going crazy. What was wrong with Camilla?

"Oh, I'm just gon' pull it out, right here in Walgreen's?"

"I don't care. I want to see it."

"Camilla I'll get arrested. Everybody's already lookin' at me."

"Let's go outside. We'll get in a cab. You can show me there."

Camilla screamed.

The cab driver looked into the rear-view mirror but he could not see what she was screaming at. He did not dare turn around because he saw Wayne's eyes staring back at him in the mirror. Wayne was a very, very big man.

"Let me touch it! Oh, God! I've got to touch it!"

She reached out both hands and grabbed it.

Wayne felt her body trembling. He saw the goose bumps on her arms.

"Oh, God, and it's not even hard."

She mashed ten dollars into the cabby's shoulder and told him to take a walk around the block. As he closed the

136

door he saw her hiking up her skirts, a wild, frightening expression on her face.

The cabby was ten feet away when he heard her shriek. He kept walking.

On the el Wayne tried to pull his thoughts together.

He could not think about any one thing. He had learned so much so quickly. It all kept going through his head.

Matilda dead.

Light had killed her.

The nigger got t'die.

The biggest dick in the world.

Matilda crazy.

Camilla grabbing him and crying as she humped up and down on his dick.

Camilla mashing another ten dollars in the cabby's hand when he opened the door.

"Walk! Walk, fool," she had said.

Matilda.

Shot her down.

Like a dog.

What lies had the nigger told her?

Why did I go?

Why did I go?

Why didn't I kill him?

Why didn't I get out of the life before like she told me? We had enough. We had everything we needed. Uh uh. It was too good. I thought it was too good to get out. In a little while, I kept saying. In a little while.

Baby, be my pimp. Baby, be my pimp. I'll work for you - just keep bringing me back this sweet peter - ooh, ooh, baby! Ooooh!

Up and down she humped. Fast, fast. Then slow.

Then stopping. Then - again and again.

I can't stop. LBN. I can't stop.

Wayne had tried to fit everything together but the pieces kept flying at him. He gave up trying to make sense out of it. But he could not keep the pictures out of his head. They kept flying at him faster and faster.

He put his massive hand to his head.

The el rocked as it hurtled along Chicago's North Side.

Penny did not know what took Wayne on his trip to Chicago but she knew when he got back whatever had sent him there in the first place was worse than it had been before he left.

He was not only "gone" most of the time, he also stopped eating and stopped talking. He would not mention his trouble.

"Somethin' botherin' you, baby?"

Most of the time he did not hear her.

When he did, he said, "No ... no ...." and then returned to wherever he had been.

He went to work.

But he did not go fishing.

He did not go for walks.

Winter was coming.

It took Mrs. McCracken to pull him out of it.

She stopped him one day after work when he was walking up the stairs to the front porch.

"Now, Wayne," she said, "you know I don't be the one t'go around askin' people for no favors."

"Yes, Ma'am," said Wayne, a big smile on his face. "What we talkin' about?"

"We talkin' about the glory of God."

Wayne looked up at his landlady's face. He wanted

to see what kind of expression she could possibly have on it. What in the world was going through her mind?

"Ma'am?"

"Son, I need you to do me a big favor. But it's not exactly for me. It's for my church."

"Rock of Ages?"

"That's right. Now, what will it be?"

"Well, uh ... Mrs. McCracken, I'd be glad t'do whatever I can, but ... uh ... er ... uh ... I don't know. I mean, seein' how as I'm probably the biggest sinner you got livin' here -"

"Wayne, you ain't the biggest. I don't believe you even middle-size, far as sinnin' go. But never mind that. You can help me even if you is the biggest. Yes, you surely can. Maybe make up for some o' them sins what you talkin' about."

"Yes, 'M."

"We havin' a big fish fry Friday night. And what with the price of fish bein' the way it is, I wonder if you could catch me a big mess o' fish for the church. It's almost time for winter t'break and it won't be no more fishin' for a long time."

Wayne smiled.

It was as if she had opened a door for him.

Where has I been, he thought. Where the hell has I been? This is my life - a fishin' pole in my hand, my Penny and Bobo. He looked happily at Mrs. McCracken.

"Well," he said. "I cain't tell for sure if they gon' be bitin' at the lake."

"Now, Wayne," she said, "I would like some o' them sweet perches if you can get 'em, but I'd like you to get me some cats, too, and some red-horse, you know, some big fish like you done sometimes and won't tell nobody where you been catchin' 'em - if you can do that?"

"Yeah, Mrs. McCracken. I think I can manage that.

I think I can manage that just fine."

Wayne caught perch on Monday and Wednesday. Mrs. McCracken cleaned them and put them on ice. Tuesday he could not catch a thing. He waited until Thursday evening to go to the canal because he could catch them there whenever he went and he wanted them to be as fresh as possible.

And did he pull them in - the longest, biggest, heaviest fish he had ever caught there, and so many of them. They were feeding heavily, putting on their last fat for the long winter.

He fished with two hooks and it seemed that every time he rebaited them and threw them out, fish just jumped out of the water to grab them. He had a great time. If he had not been so strong it would have been impossible for him to carry the staggering load of fish back to Mrs. McCracken.

"Wayne, you done yoself proud," she said when she saw the fish. "Thank you Jesus.

"I ain't never seen a mess o' fish like this, and I'm a old woman." She patted their sleek sides. "You cain't find no fish like this in the market. Look like they been raised up on butter." She licked her lips. "I tell you what," she told Wayne, "you done such a good job I'm gon' invite you to the fish-fry, free o' charge."

"Thank you, Ma'am." Wayne smiled. He felt honored. Mrs. McCracken and those church ladies could cook some fish. He knew. He had tasted them before.

That night as he held Penny in his arms he told her, "I had some trouble in Chicago, some trouble from when I was here before. It's been on my mind. I'm sorry, baby. I didn't mean it to hurt you. But sometime ... sometime it just gits on my mind." Gently he pressed his lips to her forehead.

She snuggled against him. "Oh, Wayne," she said,

140

"don't you know I love you?" For her that said everything. In the darkness she was smiling deeply.

Wayne's head cleared after that. When Penny talked to him he was there. He laughed and teased her. He played with Bobo. He took them fishing again. He sang Mr. Waterton's song along with him and went walking with his woman and son in the last afternoons of Indian Summer.

Wayne was getting everything straight. His mind was fine and clean and methodical. He did not have to think about his work at the bakery. Everything he did there had become automatic, a reflex action. He could use his time there to think about other things, which is what he did. When he left work his mind was free. He could give it to Penny, and Bobo, and good times.

While he was at the bakery his brain worked very hard, very systematically, very efficiently. Wayne faced the one terrible thing he knew about himself. He was a murderer. He had taken human life. That could not be changed. He was capable of killing. He was not only capable, he had done it. What he had done once he could do again. What he had done to the undeserving he could do to the deserving. Claude Bonfils, the women's pet, Light, the ladies' delight.

When I done this, Wayne told himself, that whole part of my life, that Chicago part, will be over with. I want to cut it out of me. Finished. The only part of it what was any good - Matilda - is dead. Murdered. Ain't nothin' left. Nothin'. I don't want none of it. When this is done I'm gon' start all over again. No Chicago. Like it never happened. Me and Penny and Bobo. New beginning.

We gon' have t'move. Not out of Evanston. I got a good job. But away from Mrs. McCracken's. New beginning. We gon' get married, too. We gon' get a marriage license and she gon' be my legal, wedded wife. New start. New day. Begin again.

He started talking to Penny about how maybe they needed more space than they had at Mrs. McCracken's and maybe they should think about looking for a new place. They didn't have much privacy, either, and it would be good if Bobo had a little yard he could play in without going all the way from the second floor and past all those people's rooms. It would be nice not to have to share a bathroom and maybe get a telephone of their own. They could afford it.

Penny was very happy at Mrs. McCracken's but everything Wayne said about why they should at least think about a bigger and better place made sense so she agreed they should think about it though she had not the slightest idea where they might go or how they might find a place. But it did not trouble her because though she agreed it was a good idea she was perfectly content where she was.

One day while Wayne was at work it occurred to him that the kind of break he was thinking about might be more complete if they moved away from the west side altogether, moved to a new part of town. Where that could be, he did not know, as the only place he knew where colored lived was the west side. But he did know Mr. Waterton did not live on the west side. Wayne did not know where he lived, but he knew it wasn't on the west side. He decided to bring it up the next time he went fishing. There would not be many days left.

When Wayne got to the pier Mr. Waterton and Hadlon Fields were holding each other back from falling into the lake. They were laughing so hard they both were in danger of tumbling in.

Wayne sat down beside them. He did not say

anything. He unwound the line from his cane pole, baited up, and tossed his line out. The familiar sensation of release washed over him.

"Young Blood," said Mr. Waterton.

"Old Blood," replied Wayne.

"I may be old, but I'll tell you one thing," said Mr. Waterton, "I's clean." He started laughing again.

So did Hadlon.

"I know one thing," said Wayne. "You two 'bout ready for Kankakee."

They laughed louder.

"He think we the ones ready for Kankakee."

"It's somebody more ready than we is," said Hadlon.

"Might of just escaped," said Mr. Waterton.

Both of the older men laughed, pointing at each other and shaking their heads.

Wayne shook his.

"You think we crazy," said Mr. Waterton, wiping the tears from his eyes, "but you know what ol' Hadlon told me?"

The two older men shook back and forth again, holding each other from falling in as mirth convulsed them.

Wayne kept shaking his head.

"Wayne, Wayne. Listen, listen," said Mr. Waterton, "Hadlon said he walked across the canal last Thursday night to get hisself a half-pint. And he swear that when he was comin' back home over the Church Street Bridge he seen by the moonlight - it was a full moon - somebody *fishin'* in the canal!"

The two hooted again.

Wayne felt the heat around his ears and moving into his head.

His hands shook on his fishing pole.

"Wh-wh-wh-wh-who-who-who w-w-w-was it," asked Wayne.

"I don't know," said Hadlon, taking out his big, white, dirty handkerchief and blowing his nose. "It were too far away and even with the moonlight it were still dark. But can you imagine some fool *fishin'* in the canal?" He stuffed his handkerchief back into his pocket.

"N–n-n-n- no," said Wayne. "I-I-I-I ain't –n-n-n-n-ne–ne-ne-ne-nev-v-v-ver s-s-s-s-see-see-seen n-n-n-n-n–no b-b-b-body f-f-f-f-f-fi–fi-fishin' in th-th-th-there."

"Who have,"said Mr. Waterton. "Oh, it's plenty of fish in there alright, but even in '32 people wouldn't fish for 'em. Nobody. Who in his right mind would even wet his line in that mess?"

Wayne stared at the place where his leader dipped into the lake. He felt he must have visible flames on his ears. He wanted to talk, at least to ask questions. But there was no point. He knew the words would not come out. He was just glad Hadlon had not recognized him. What in the world was wrong with fishin' in the canal?

"Yessir," said Mr. Waterton, "I want t'know who the nigga was, so I can stay away from his ass."

"You and me both," said Hadlon.

"Can you imagine?"

Wayne could not look either of them in the face. He studied his line.

Mr. Waterton sat back. "That's why I don't even fish Wilmette Harbor no more," he said.

"Biggest perch in the world in Wilmette Harbor," said Hadlon.

"Mmmhmm. Biggest red-horse, too."

"No, now, now I wouldn't keep no red-horse out'n the harbor," said Hadlon, "cause likely as not they done come out'n the canal. But perch - they don't go up in the canal. It kills 'em."

"You could be right about that," said Mr. Waterton, "but how come the perch gets so big in the harbor? How

144

come they don't get that big nowhere else?

"I'm gon' tell you, ever since my uncle caught this big red-horse in the harbor in '34 I ain't never fished there since."

"Why's that," asked Hadlon.

"Never will forget," said Mr. Waterton. "He was such a big one, must o' gone eighty pounds. My uncle caught him on fish bait. We wanted to see what he'd really been feedin' on, so we could use some o' that as bait the next time we went to the harbor, maybe catch us some more like him. So after we cleaned him - we done filleted him and everything. Had enough steaks to feed a regiment. We had his guts in a pile. We took out the stomach and cut it open - goddamn. The first thing what come out was a great, big, ol', thick wad of used toilet paper."

"What!"

"Sure as I'm settin' here right now. A wad of toilet paper twice as big around as my fist, and whoever used it must o' had the runs."

"Oh, shit."

"That's right. That's what it was. Pure shit. And that was one, big, fat fish."

"What else was in his stomach?"

"We didn't git no further. We all got sick. Throwed up right there. All over the grass. Throwed them fillets in the garbage. I tell you one thing - the flies loved 'em.

"See, they supposed to have some kind o' screen or somethin' what keeps that shit from gettin' into the harbor. But if they do, how can them big red horse move back and forth from the canal into the harbor? If it's a screen, it got some huge holes in it. I'm gon' tell you one thing - that wad o' shit paper couldn't o' passed through no screen."

Wayne's stomach started churning.

"Every sewer line from every house in Evanston empty directly into that canal," said Mr. Waterton.

145

"I know myself," said Mr. Waterton, "I pisses about a gallon of piss every day - and makes five pounds of shit."

"Ha, ha, ha, ha, and them fish just eatin' it up," said Hadlon.

"Gobblin' it up. And some fool gon' be out there tryin' t'catch 'em."

Mrs. McCracken's church, the Rock of Ages Missionary Baptist Church, had hosted a very successful fish fry the preceding weekend largely on the strength of Wayne's catch. Everybody had raved over the fish. Wayne, Penny, and Bobo had gone, guests of the church. Each had eaten plates full of the delicious deep-fried fish. Fat as butter everyone had said.

Wayne felt his tongue and the insides of his mouth swelling up. His throat was thickening. He believed he could feel his stomach twisting slowly and turning.

He was off the pier and onto the park's lawn when the first warm puke gushed over his lips and onto the ground. He dropped to his knees. He stayed there for a long time as his convulsing body pushed the contents of his stomach up past his esophagus and out onto the freshly mowed turf.

It took him two days but he had to get himself together quickly. Snow was already threatening. He had to find out where Mr. Waterton lived before the winter drove him away from the lake. Wayne's face was still slack and a deep, grey purple color when he returned. But he could stay away no longer. Time was relentless.

"So, you thinkin' about movin, boy," said Mr. Waterton. "What you gon' do - make another baby?" He laughed. " Yessuh. Have some Hadachol. Put lead in yo pencil - that's right - lead in yo pencil!" He laughed again.

"Bout time you made anothuh baby with that cute,

young thing you got. Uh huh. You need t'be fillin' her up with babies, one after the other. I'm gon' tell you somethin', son; that is a tasty piece o' blackberry pie you got theah. Yessuh. The blacker the berry the sweeter the juice! And she is put together like a woman should - hot dog - git me some Hadachol!"

The two of them were alone on the pier. The fishing season had ended for almost everyone else. The cold wind was light from the southeast. They each had several healthy keepers on their stringers.

"Well, I'll tell you," said Mr. Waterton, who loved to hold both sides of a conversation, "ain't too many places for colored t'go out of the west side. Now, if you was domestics you could live on the place. But you ain't domestics. You a cook, though, boy. Why don't you git a job cookin' for some rich, white family? Then you could move right in with them."

"No, sir. My job's too good. And I ain't a cook. I's a baker. Plus, that's what we want t'do - git away from livin' in somebody else's house."

"Uh huh. Well one thing's fo sure. You cain't bake babies. No suh. You got t'make them with the original recipe. Yessuh. Love that home cookin'.

"Well, Wayne, if you don't want t'get a job where you can live on the place, you ain't got too much choice in the matter about movin."

"But, Mr. Waterton, where does you live at? It ain't on the west side, is it?"

"No, no, it's not. But you ain't in my situation."

"What you mean?"

"I'm a settled man. All my children is either teenagers or grown. Yessuh, I done made some babies in my time. I'm gon' tell you, Wayne, that Hadachol is good t'you. I'd make some more, too, if I didn't have t'raise 'em up. Yessuh. Mmm, mm, mmm. I loves t'make babies - hot

147

dog! But I ain't made none in a long time. If you let me close t'that little Penny, though, that's another story. I always did like 'em young and sweet. My boys has t'keep they girls away from me. They picks some pretty ones, too. Oh, Lord, did I tell you about them French womens? I betcha I left plenty little brown babies over there in France. Yessuh. Nevuh seen none of 'em. But I betcha it's a lot of young frenchmens walkin' around over there what looks jest like me. Love that Hadachol!

"But, uh - you - you ain't in my condition. You got yo baby makin' days ahead of you. Mines is behind me. Lord, I wishes they wasn't - but you never can tell what's left in the old water pipe - hot dog! Anyways, Wayne, where I lives at it's about nine colored families in a block and a half. The rest is whites. But, you see, all nine Colored owns they own house. Now, you ain't in no position to buy."

"You right about that."

"I know I am. See, that's the only way t'get into our neighborhood because the ordinance won't allow nobody t'rent out rooms lessen it's t'familiy.

"It ain't hard t'buy in there because the whites what lives there will sell to get away from the colored. But buyin' is the only way t'get in and it ain't too many colored what's in a position to buy."

"Yeah, I see what you means," said Wayne, "and I ain't one what is."

"There you go, boy. You know what I'm talkin' about."

"But it must be some other places."

"Well, it is. A flat here and a flat there what rents t'colored. But the ones what's in 'em ain't movin' out, and ain't tellin' where they's at. You got t'hunt 'em out, and then most likely you ain't gon' find 'em. It ain't no place out o' the west side where you can find colored rentin' t'see

- except for that pinch there at Wimbey's Corner and it take beatin' the devil t'git in that place. They some dicey niggas ovuh theah. Yessuh, my sons was runnin' afta them Wenders girls and they think they too high and mighty t'fool with nobody. 'Cept Electa. And she was too good for anybody 'ceptin Gabriel Frye, Mr. High and Mighty hisself, and she ain't nothin' but a teenaged girl, married, got a baby by him, and she ain't even finished high school. I'm gon' tell you, boy, them sisters is somethin' else."

"M-M-M-Mi-Mi-Mi-Mister Waterton ... uh, uh, uh wh-wh-wh-where i-i-is W-W-Wi-Wimbey's C-C-Co-Corner?"

"Don't worry about it none, boy. You cain't git in there. All them places is taken and ain't nobody movin' out. Not out of Wimbey's Corner, uh, uh.

"Eskeridge laughed hisself silly every time he talked about it. All his doin', he said. He put eight nigger families - as many as thirty individual niggers - livin' in weird buildings in the middle of Evanston's high society, with pickaninnies and everything goin' t'school with they children - and that's only countin' what folks *calls* Wimbey's Corner, the north side of Tary Street, not even talkin' about that big house - used t'be a barn, next to the alley on the south side of Tary."

It took Wayne one half hour longer to get Mr. Waterton to tell him where Wimbey's Corner was. He was shocked to learn it was just six blocks from where they sat. On the way home he detoured down Tary Street just to make sure.

When Wayne stood in front of the group of strange, little houses, he could not believe his eyes. The houses were weird enough in themselves, but he could see colored faces peeking through the windows - on the Eastside, in the heart of Evanston's fabled wealth - colored!

Through one window he got a glimpse, just a

149

glimpse , of a woman's face so exquisite it frightened him. It was true. *Negroes who lived here could not be ordinary.* The face, the face underlined that. It was like none he'd ever seen. Here. Here. In Wimbey's Corner. He saw the flashing limbs of colored children playing in the back. Colored could live here. Colored *did* live here. It was possible. As with his first sighting of Mr. Big he experienced the startling revelation that the unbelievable could be real. He shook his head. He blinked and opened his eyes again.

Still there.

From that moment on, Wayne knew he had to live in Wimbey's Corner.

7

"Baby, baby, I been waitin' on you. Where you been? I been goin' crazy. I got t'have it!"

"Camilla, I got a lot of things t'take care of," said Wayne.

"Take care of 'em! Take care of 'em! I don't care. But you got t'take care of me, too, sweet daddy. Nobody else makes it anymore after you, baby. Not after Mr. Big."

Wayne grinned. Mr. Big, he thought.

"I just cain't go nowhere right now," he said.

"You don't have t'go nowhere. Just tell me where you's at. I'll come to you."

"Not now."

"Wayne. I'm tryin' t'tell you. I got t'have it."

"Camilla -"

"Wayne. You want me to help you out?"

"You know -"

"Then you got t'help *me* out, baby. I done told you. You done ruint me for other men. Cain't no other man do nothin' for me but tell me where to find you. Wayne, I told you. I'll ho for you. I'll do anything for you. But you got t'take care o' me, baby. If you don't, if you don't, I'm sorry, but ain't no way I can help you. Baby, I don't want t'be no bitch about this, but this is push comin' t'shove. Please, baby, just help me out. That's all I'm askin'. That's all. I'll do anything you want me to. Just please. Just please be good to me."

"Alright, Camilla. Alright. I'll c-c-come d-d-down this, this weekend."

"Oh, baby, you won't be sorry. You won't be sorry. I'll be so good to you."

When Wayne hung up he dropped his head. He knew what he had to do but he hated to have to act so

151

doggish to do it. Doggish. Doggish. Just like that damn
Light.

8

After Eskeridge Wimbey's death the mantle of responsibility for the old man's vast holdings had fallen on the broad shoulders of his nephew, Porter. Porter inherited the responsibility for Eskeridge's staggering wealth but he did not inherit the wealth itself. The will reduced him to the caretaker of an estate of such magnitude that his failure to possess it kept him in a perpetual state of indigestion.

Wayne could not have known Porter had a standing policy that no one in his office was ever to issue applications for Wimbey's Corner. As a result, Wayne was not deterred when he was fed a whole line of Porter's obstacles and showed up every single working afternoon for a month asking for an application. He became so persistent and his large, forbidding appearance so regular a feature at Wimbey's offices that even Porter Wimbey himself was moved to push a chair next to his office door, stand on it, and peek through the transom at the upstart. Porter learned through that act that this determined fellow was indeed a very, very big man. He stopped peeking but each day grew more uncomfortable at the knowledge that the massive presence had returned.

At the end of Wayne's second month of attendance Porter asked that Wayne be shown into his office.

"THIS ... is Mr. Hunter," said Porter's secretary, pointedly, as she ushered Wayne into his office.

Shocked by the size of the man, up close even greater than he appeared through the transom, Porter rose quickly and scurried around his desk to extend a hand to Wayne.

"Pleased. Pleased, I'm sure. Very pleased to meet you, Mr. Hunter. Please. Please. Have a chair."

"Th-Th-Tha-Tha-Thank y-y-y-you, M-M-Mist-t-ter

153

W-W-Wi-Wim-Wimbey."

Wayne sat down.

Porter was as surprised by Wayne's stutter as by his size. But the stutter put him more at ease. A sure sign of weakness

"I understand," Porter said, sure that the man's huge frame was a mere facade, "that you have an interest in occupying one of our houses on Tary Street."

Wayne nodded as he spoke as if to emphasize his spoken words. "Yessir. That's right, sir."

"Well - first of all - let me make it very clear to you: that is impossible. There are no vacancies on Tary Street. There have been no vacancies on Tary Street for ten years, and we do not anticipate any. I wish I had better news for you, Mr. Hunter, but unfortunately you have put your hopes upon the most distinguished residence for Negroes on the whole Northside. That says nothing at all against you, we simply have nothing there to let. Why if Joe Louis himself wanted to live in Wimbey's Corner, there would be no room for him."

Porter leaned back in his chair and leveled his self-satisfied gaze at Wayne.

Wayne looked up briefly then lowered his eyes.

"We have other properties," said Porter, "I'm sure we can find you something very suitable in one of them."

"No," said Wayne. His voice resonated in the depths of his cavernous chest. "We only interested in Tary Street."

Jolted, Porter sat straight up.

Wayne was very, very big.

"Well," said Porter. He cleared his throat.

Wayne's hands tightened on his cap. His eyes remained clamped onto Porter's.

"Yes," said Porter. "Well. An application. Nothing lost filling out an application." He bent over, unlocking a drawer in his desk. He rummaged in it then brought out a

154

legal size, thick sheaf of papers.

He rose and walked them around to Wayne.

"Yes, Mr. Hunter. If you have any trouble filling these out, I'm sure Miss Mason in our front office can help you. Now. Now. Thank you for coming in. *Tempus fugit, tempus fugit.*"

After he completed his application and turned it in, Wayne walked by Wimbey's Corner everyday to see if anyone had moved. Wimbey's Corner Negroes were not like any Negroes he had ever seen. He never dared approach one of them, but whenever he saw one of them walking along Tary street, he nodded and said, "Good-day," even to the children, even to the little boy who could not have been more than three years old. They were always very polite and nodded and spoke in turn, but with such absolute dignity that Wayne could not help admiring them slavishly. *I want to be one of those Negroes.*

Wayne thrilled at the way they pronounced their words. They were so proper-sounding. "Hello." It was as if he could hear each "l". "How are you?" Clear as a bell. "Fine, thank you; how are you?" They had to be the most proper Negroes in the world. Wayne loved it. He started talking like that, too. It was very much the way he had talked when he had tried to talk like newspapers when Mr. Mueller had helped him improve his reading. The sounds felt good in his mouth, on his tongue, on his lips - felt good to his ears. In the evenings and weekends when he listened to the radio, he practiced saying words and sentences as the announcers did. Wimbey's Corner Negroes spoke even more high-fallutin than that, but talking like a radio announcer was a first step.

Wimbey's Corner Negroes even began to influence the way Wayne dressed. Though Light's taste for flashy

155

clothes had made an indelible impression on him, Wayne began to pattern his day-by-day dress after some of the Wimbey's Corner men. He also began buying clothes for Penny which mimicked the fashions of the Corner's women. Bobo found himself dressed in new styles. He did not know they were dictated by a three year old boy who lived with his mother on the first floor of the house on the southeast edge of Wimbey's Corner.

Bobo and Penny, in fact, did not know Wimbey's Corner existed. Wayne was keeping it as a surprise from them until that fateful day when they would be lucky enough to move in. But when that happened he wanted them to be ready. He wanted them to be, like him, Wimbey's Corner quality.

They had to walk and carry themselves in a certain way, a way which Wayne began to perfect. They had to have all the social graces and Wayne began to read books about them and insist that Penny read them, too. Every day they practiced diction and worked on improving their grammar and expanding their speaking vocabularies.

Wayne went to the library and checked out literary books. Both he and Penny read them. Wayne acquired a list of children's classics from the librarian for Bobo.

For their part, Wimbey's Corner residents became accustomed to seeing Wayne pacing slowly in front of their homes, leaning against one of the great elms in the parkway, gazing at their houses and yards.

Wayne knew he could not move on Light until he got into Wimbey's Corner. He could strike at Light only simultaneously with starting his new life. That new life could only be in Wimbey's Corner.

He had to keep seeing Camilla who became increasingly jealous, increasingly possessive. She wanted to know where he lived. Just a passing glance or a friendly nod from another woman was enough to send her flying off in a fit of invective at the woman, only Wayne's strong hands restraining her from physical assault.

9

Mackenzie Sweet brought on the crisis.

He died.

In many ways the act was one of betrayal. Most betrayed was Mackenzie Sweet himself who was only 102 at the time of his premature demise.

He betrayed, too, all the people who were plotting to get even with him. All the people who had worked up the perfect argument on some obscure subject and were just waiting to spring it on him. They came to his funeral in droves and wept copiously - not at his parting - but at their lost opportunities.

Mackenzie never got sick and was not sick when he died. In fact, the sole cause of his eclipse was that death caught him by surprise. Had that not been the case he would most likely still be alive today as he was an expert at what he did.

One afternoon Mackenzie took his nap and slept too long. While he was asleep death caught him. If he had awakened at his usual time Mackenzie would still be laughing about how he tricked death. But as it was he slept too long and death grabbed him before he could wake up.

Mackenzie's widow asked to be put away. She said she would be no more good without her Mr. Sweet.

Mackenzie's death was also a betrayal of Evanston's funeral directors. He had made it a habit to cultivate funeral directors as acquaintances. He liked to visit them late at night when they were working on their clients because the sight of the grisly business made him all the more convinced he had chosen the correct profession. It sharpened his already acute sense of self-preservation. He teased his funeral director associates, telling them he would see them in their coffins long before they could get their hands on him. The teasing had not bothered them much until he got into his late sixties, that is when he began to outlive them. By the time he was in his late eighties he had begun to outlive the sons of the first funeral directors he had outlived. He had cultivated the sons just as assiduously as he had the fathers. Funeral directors could not escape his familiarity. He had a horrible fascination for them. They were irresistibly drawn to him, the way a spider's victim is mesmerized, or the way a bird or a mouse can be entranced by a cat and sit quite still, almost invitingly, while its nemesis advances to devour it. They were powerfully attracted to him, yet they knew - he never concealed it - he gleefully awaited their dooms.

When they learned of his death they were beside themselves with joy. They vied with each other to see who would get the body. But Mackenzie betrayed them. As many times as he had promised each of them he deserved the right to drain, stuff, and plug him, if he should ever be so stupid as not to outlive him, and that he could have his body should so unlikely an event take place, he had held no intention of ever being humiliated by the descendants of any of the many funeral directors over whose burials he had chortled. He had seen to it that should any unforseen circumstance such as his death occur, the arrangements were to be handled by a Chicago funeral home.

Finally, Mackenzie betrayed Porter Wimbey, because by dying and leaving his wife in no condition to live an unsupervised life, he left the house vacant and open for occupancy. Although Mrs. Wenders wanted the house and had first call on it because of the length of her residency in Wimbey's Corner, her move would leave her place unoccupied and available for the only party who had an application on file for Wimbey's Corner, Wayne Hunter.

As soon as Wayne learned of the vacancy, he rushed to the Wimbey offices, made sure his application had been accepted, put down a deposit, got a receipt certifying that he could move in when the place was ready, and called Camilla.

"Get ready, baby," he said. "The chickens are coming home to roost."

10

Claude Bonfils leaned back in the comfort of his limousine's rear compartment. He swirled a glass of sherry under his nose. The alcoholic aromas dilated his nostrils and the blood vessels inside them. He liked to inhale sherry or brandy fumes before sniffing cocaine. It greatly enhanced the effect. After he had taken the cocaine he would sip the glowing liquid.

There's no doubt about it, he thought, I knows how to live.

He could not imagine what was so urgent that Camilla wanted him to come to the St. Laurent. What a scumbag of a hotel. He did not like his ladies to work places like that. Gave them and him a bad name. Light liked class, only class. Camilla had said the trick had insisted on it, a favorite place of his. Then he had got her in some kind of trouble, she did not want to go into it on the phone. So she had called Light, to help her out.

And here I comes to the rescue. I sure am good to my women.

Light took in the cocaine one nostril at a time.

Aaaaah. Yes! Baby, I does know how to live.

He did not know what was wrong with Camilla. She had been acting strange for a long time - months. It was nothing to put your finger on. She seemed to be acting as she always had, but Light was very sensitive to his women. He had to be. And something was different about her. Had been. For too long.

He sipped sherry.

The money was still good. She made top dollar. But ... something ....

Maybe she's coming around now. Maybe after I get over here to this fleabag hotel and saves her ass she'll straighten out. Know how much she needs her Daddy-Light. Come home to Papa.

The wine felt fiery coasting down his throat. With the coke working on him he could feel it burning in his veins.

Yeah, Daddy'll straighten everything out.

It was a certain coldness. Yeah, that's what it was about her. A certain coldness. He had not experienced that in one of his women since ... yes ... since the first night Matilda spent with that countrified nigger, LBN. The recollection drew a red screen of rage across Light's eyes.

I'd like to kill the nigger.

It's a good thing for him he run out of town.

He remembered the humiliation of being held above the giant's head, come still dripping out of his dick.

In one gulp he swallowed the rest of the sherry.

I hate his ass!

Ruint my best bitch!

It was my fault. It was my fault, though, for turnin' her onto the nigger. I wonder what he done. I wonder what he done to make her so crazy for him.

After me, too - after she done had Claude Bonfils!

Claude was incensed.

He poured himself another glass of sherry.

Camilla better not have no dude.

I'll kill the bitch!

Yes, I will.

Oh, no. She better not.

He sipped sherry.

Light's gon' take everything in hand tonight, once and for all.

Wayne watched from the fifth floor window as the big limousine pulled up to the hotel.

162

It felt good to be dressed in city-slicker clothes again. Wayne felt clean, felt like he belonged in the night, in the city, felt like a man in charge.

He reached up and pulled down on the front brim of his hat. The finely woven shirt felt good across his chest. He imagined he could see the jeweled cuff links fastened at his wrists and the gleaming shine on his shoes.

Yeah. Feels good.

Nice came around and opened the door for Light.

Light got out. The two of them stood beside the car talking.

"He's down there," said Wayne.

Camilla flew to the window.

She reached one arm up Wayne's back, hooking her hand over his shoulder. She looked down into the street. She slipped the other hand under Wayne's waistband reaching urgently for Mr. Big.

"Good," she said feverishly, "soon all this gon' be over and you gon' be mine, all mine."

Light walked into the hotel.

Nice leaned back against the Lincoln.

Wayne kept watching Nice. He wanted to know if he were going to have to deal with one of them or two.

Nice did not move. He took out a cigarette and lit it up.

"Baby, we got work t'do," Wayne said to Camilla.

He removed her hands and guided her to the door.

"When he comes in, you goes out," he reminded her.

"Yes, daddy, whatever you say." She rose on her toes, threw her arms around his neck and hurled her open lips at his, slinging her tongue at the roof of his mouth.

They separated when they heard the elevator door open.

Light's footfalls were inaudible.

One knock on the door.

163

"Camilla," very softly.

"Yes, Light. Yes, Daddy."

The door opened.

Light saw Camilla standing in front of him and stepped in.

Iron bands sprang around his neck and clamped his arms to his sides.

He heard the door slam.

The room was pitch-black.

Instinctively, Light knew.

LBN! Wayne Hunter!

Before Light could react, Wayne had him stomach down on the floor, his arms pinned behind his back. Wayne went through his clothes, taking out his blade, his heat, and his razor.

"Say, Wayne."

"So you know it's me, huh?"

"Yeah, my man -"

"Don't 'my man' me. You killed Matilda."

"Hey - Wayne, listen. I didn't - look. It was self-defense. I didn't want to. The razor - man - the razor was in the air. It was almost at my throat before I fired."

Light felt Wayne kneeling on him, the big man's entire weight in the small of his back.

"Uh-huh. I understands that," said Wayne. "But you had no business goin' t'see her at my place from jump street."

"You right, Wayne. It was a mistake. I apologize, man. I'm sorry. I never should of done it. I made a mistake."

"Uh huh. A big one."

"Look ... Wayne, I'm sorry. I didn't know what was gon' happen. I didn't know what it would lead to. I made a mistake. You right. But everybody makes mistakes now and then. Wasn't no way I could know how bad a mistake

164

it was. Man, I ... I know I cain't bring Matilda back. I know it's no way to undo the wrong. But I want you to believe me, I didn't want to kill her. I waited till the last second - the blade was in the air - I didn't want to shoot. Man, I cared about Matilda."

"Yeah. Well, so did I."

Light was thinking that maybe any minute Nice would be coming up. They had a standard arrangement that if Light went in alone and didn't signal within five minutes, Nice would come up. LBN knew about that, but Light was hoping he'd forgotten.

Oh, just get me out from under this big nigger, he thought.

Wayne pushed the side of Light's head relentlessly into the floor.

"She hurt a lot before she died," Wayne said.

"Oh, no. It was quick."

"I mean she hurt inside. Because of what you done to her."

"I'm sorry, man. What can I say? I'm sorry. Look, Wayne, I know you don't want t'have nothin' t'do with me right now, and I appreciates that, I respects it, but I just want you t'know, whenever you ready, I can turn you onto some action - set you up with bread, rides, a crib. I know I was in the wrong. I'll be straight about it. Ain't no rush. Ain't no hurry, but whenever you ready, I'll try to make it up to you in some way."

"Don't you worry, Claude Bonfils. You gonna make it up to me alright."

"What you mean, Wayne?"

"Light. ... did you know I killed a man?"

Where's Nice?

"That's why I come to Chicago."

I know five minutes is up. Where's Nice?

"Killed him over a woman, too."

165

"Wayne! Please! I got over a thousand dollars on me right now! It's yours. Anything you want is yours! Please!"

Light also had $5,000 more in the car he could offer immediately, but he didn't want to draw Wayne's attention to thoughts of the car and Nice.

"I can get you more - big money - within an hour! Just let me get to a phone. Listen, Wayne - please! I didn't want to do it. Give me a chance."

"I am Light. I am gon' give you a chance. Just like you give her a chance."

"I did - God! I waited till the last second!"

Where the hell is Nice?

"I killed that man with my bare hands. And he was a bigger man than you, Light."

They heard the elevator door at the same time.

Wayne's big fist came down on the base of Light's skull.

All the tension left the pimp's body. He lay inert, but breathing, on the floor.

Wayne peeked through the keyhole.

Nice was moving toward the door, no more than a foot away from it, a .38 held in front of him.

Nice was tense. His finger was ready to squeeze the trigger at the slightest stimulus.

He knocked lightly on the door and took one step back. He kept the .38 trained on the door, gut-high.

The door opened on a darkened room, but Light stood in the aperture. His brim shaded his eyes; he stood strangely.

"Hey, Light," Nice stepped forward, drawing the gun barrel down to his side.

Nice could not register that Light was actually flying through the air toward him until he felt his boss' dead weight against his body. He crashed to the floor, Light's

166

motionless form on top of him.

He felt the gun ripped out of his hand, then Light was off of him and he was staring up from the floor at LBN.

Nice was speechless.

"I ain't gon' hurt you, Nice," said Wayne. "My business is with Claude Bonfils."

A few minutes later Nice was bound and gagged inside the hotel room's closet.

He heard the door close as LBN took Light out of the room.

A NEW STORY IN WIMBEY'S CORNER

1

Wayne and Penny went to the Justice of the Peace in Chicago. Otherwise, the notice would have appeared in the *Evanston Review*. Everyone would know their little secret. Penny often wondered if anyone had a right to be as happy as she was. Life was supposed to be full of suffering, but hers was not. Hers was always good and getting better every day. They were married and Wayne had even found a new place for them, one that was their own, where they would not have to share the stairs, or the hall, or the bathroom. It was almost like having their own house. But more wonderful than anything it was on the east side. She could not get over that. She had not even known colored lived on the east side. Few did. And now she would be one of them. Special. With her Wayne and Bobo.

When she first saw the little collection of houses she had been surprised because they were like nothing she had ever seen, yet they seemed surprisingly familiar. It took her days to realize what it was. The books. The children's classical tales and nursery rhymes Wayne had been bringing home for Bobo. The houses could have stepped off the pages of *Mother Goose*, drawings of tall, narrow houses, twisting and leaning. Houses with doors and windows in unconventional places and missing where they should be. Odd porches and crazy roofs. Stairs that seemed to lead nowhere, running up the sides of buildings as if tacked on by someone who did not know the purpose of stairs. Wimbey's Corner looked like a child's imagining of a medieval town.

She realized why they had been practicing proper-talking. The folks in Wimbey's Corner did nothing but proper-talking. That's why all the books. Wayne said they had fancy manners and everything; it was as if they were hardly colored. Wayne told her she was going to love them; she knew she would. How could she not? And now she was going to be one of them. Already she could act like them, talk like them, and dress like them. Wayne had seen to that.

Just one block away from Wimbey's Corner was a school where almost nothing except white children went. It would be Bobo's school. Two little girls who lived in Wimbey's Corner attended it. They and Bobo would be the only colored children in the school. Penny could not imagine it. On the west side all the colored children went to the same school and they were the only ones in it. Foster School. But now - she could not believe it - next year her Bobo would be starting in an all-white school. She giggled uncontrollably. Two years ago she could not read. And now she was a cultured, east side Evanston woman married to her Wayne. The world was her oyster. She laughed out loud, filled with ecstacy.

2

As soon as the Hunters moved into Wimbey's Corner the first thing on Bobo's mind was how to get the girl who lived upstairs, directly over them, to do it. He had seen the big kids over on Emerson Street doing it all the time. They had let him watch. Sometimes they had even done it just so he could watch. Now he wanted to do it.

The girl who lived upstairs was very pretty. She had the cutest, prettiest, little face. Bobo wanted to do it to her until he fell off her onto the ground as he had seen some of the big boys do. They had told him later that only happened when it was very, very good. Oh I busted a nut on her they said. Bobo wanted to bust a nut on the pretty little girl who lived upstairs.

She was fat. She was the fattest little girl Bobo had ever seen. She was the same shape as her mother who was huge. Bobo often watched them go up the stairs. There were so many stairs they did not rise straight up. There were two apartments above just as there were two below. One upstairs apartment sat over each downstairs apartment. Each downstairs apartment had its own set of stairs which led to its front porch and its only door. The stairs which went upstairs started in the middle of the building.

He liked to watch them climb the stairs. He did not understand how they ever made it. He did not see how the steps could hold them. The fat lady always stopped three times on the stairs. She stopped in the middle of the first set of steps, holding onto the bannister, leaning forward and breathing heavily. She stopped again on the landing, posturing herself in exactly the same way, and once more in the middle of the flight which led to her own porch. She stopped again when she got onto the porch.

Bobo was always afraid the stairs were going to break. He wondered what would happen if they did. Would the fat woman crash through and fall all the way to the ground? Would she get stuck half-way and hang there with her great, balloon legs dropping and swinging in the air while her stomach lay lodged in the wooden staircase, her huge, rounded titties, spilling out all around her? Would she scream? Would she cry? Bobo knew he would run under her, to look up, to see what he could see. What would she look like up there? He wanted to know.

Their porch worried Bobo the most. Everytime the fat lady reached her porch and stopped to rest, the floor sagged. One day, Bobo knew, it would break. Would she crash down on their porch and then down through it and keep on going? Or would she just hang there up above his head where he could look up between her fat legs?

Unlike her mother, the girl could go right up all the steps without stopping. The mother made the trip twice a day - once down, and once up. Once she got there she did not come down again until the next day. The little girl on the other hand was up and down all day - quick - like a huge, round, ball that could bounce up the stairs or down.

Bobo wondered how he was going to get the little girl to do it. He waved at her everytime he saw her and he had spoken to her several times. Her name was Wanda.

174

3

Wanda stood on her porch and watched the little pee-behind boy from out west playing below her on the square of pavement in front of his apartment. She knew he was a bad boy because he was from the west side. Her mama had told her plenty of times about those bad west side boys. He smiled and waved and spoke to her, but he could not fool her. He was bad. He would try to do things to her.

He was cute, though.

When he looked up and caught her watching him she moved away from the railing. She knelt down on her porch and started playing jacks. She wondered why Miss Bryce had let those west side people move in. No telling what they would do. The man was the biggest man Wanda had ever seen. He could not hide that he was from out west. Nothing that black and ugly would ever come from the east side of town. Wanda could not imagine why Miss Bryce would let such an obvious devil of a man into their nice little neighborhood. The woman was cute. Little and sweet, leaning to plump - not fat like Mama and me, she thought - but just about right. Like her man she was dark. All three of them dark as soot. The little boy got his cuteness from his mother. Lucky for him he didn't get his father's looks.

Why they want t'move here anyway? Should have stayed out west where they belong, where there's people like them. They don't belong here.

She peeked through the railings. The little boy was doing tricks, turning cartwheels and standing on his hands.

I don't care, she thought. He's not going to fool me with his bad, west side self. He's not going to do things to me. Though he was not watching her, she stuck her tongue out at him, then went back to playing jacks.

4

Wellington Cork pictured himself as the rock, the cornerstone of Wimbey's Corner. He often thought of himself with respect to a song he'd learned during his youth in the South. *"I shall not, I shall not be moved. Just like a tree that's standing by the water, I shall not be moved."* He was the physical Peter of Wimbey's Corner. "On this rock I will build my church." He had a commanding presence. He saw himself as magisterial, even as he sat at his dining room table.

His wife daintily slid peas onto her fork. She shot a glance from the corners of her eyes to make sure her daughter was following proper decorum. Satisfied at her daughter's deportment, she returned her attention to her meal.

Between bites, Wellington said, "What you learn 'bout that new family?"

Genuine's back stiffened. "Black as coal," she said. "There's nothing else to learn about them except what's obvious. They came from out west."

"Now, I wouldn't be minding about their color," he said, though he did not mean it. He mentioned color because he wanted to take a dig at the Wenders. "All those Wenders men is black as night. Look at Fends. Look at Stephen."

Genuine took a sip of water. When she put the glass down, she said, "The Wenders are not your run-of-the-mill, west side Negroes. In them it is permissible to reveal the taint of the tarbrush. Besides, that man looks ... he looks as if he just stepped out of the jungles of Africa."

Ivory glanced at her parents. She had seen the little boy. He was younger than she was and for a few minutes she had fantasized that although he was a boy she might be allowed to play with him because of his age. The drift of the conversation, however, made it plain that she would no more be allowed to play with him than she was with Wanda.

"I don't see why that kind of Negro just doesn't stay out west where they're fitted," said Mrs. Cork. "They have no business coming over here trying to mix with their betters. First thing you know they'll try to get that little, black, knotty-headed boy to play with our Ivory!"

She extended a hand protectively on Ivory's shoulder.

5

The wind was light out of the southeast. A few keepers were hitting and every now and then a herring. The slight, rolling waves were tinted a transparent greenish-blue. Only Wayne and Mr. Waterton sat on the pier, as far out as they could go.

"Mmhmm," said Mr. Waterton, "day like this, if I work at it, I can get a red-horse or two. Might do it, too, just t'do somethin' different."

Wayne watched his bobber. He was using two poles, one with a bobber and one without. He was experimenting with the best way to fish under the conditions.

"Yessir," continued Mr. Waterton, "See, when the wind gets like this, those red-horse takes t'cruisin' 'round the shore. They comes in schools of about three or four, sometimes more. Sometimes two or three schools 'll go by in a hour. Then it might be another couple hours before another one. But they's cruisin' alright. Yeah, I think I'm gon' git me one or two."

He pulled in one of his poles and started rigging it for red-horse. He glanced at Wayne.

"You know, Wayne, I never did figure you for Wimbey's Corner."

Wayne smiled. "I don't know why. I told you it was the place for me."

"Oh, I don't mean that. I knowed you wanted t'git in. Most niggas wants t'git in. What I'm surprised about is that you did get in.

"You know, I knowed ol' man Wimbey 'bout as good as anybody 'round here knowed him. 'Cept for his wimmins." Mr. Waterton chuckled. "Most people was afraid of him. Not me. I didn't see nothin' t'be 'fraid of. He was just a man like everybody else. Only thing, he had more money. Hell - I wasn't worried about no money. Don't work no way. Do what I want all day long. I figured my life was as good as his. So I wasn't scared of no Eskeridge Wimbey. Lots of folks was, though.

"Anyway, ol' Wimbey used t'talk t'me about his tenants. What kind of folks he wanted in there. He was kind of like braggin' 'cause he always got 'em. And, Wayne, you don't fit the bill."

"Maybe I didn't once, but I do now."

"I guess so," said Mr. Waterton. "You in there." He finished setting up his pole for red-horse and tossed the line back out. "Course Wimbey's dead and gone. But like he told me, his will made it so Porter and Miss Bryce was s'posed t'follow the same guidelines as him."

Wayne was getting a nibble on the pole he was holding.

"Course I guess you got the main qualification. You wanted in there bad, and you wants t'stay there. But, see, Wimbey had certain classes of people he thought would want to live in the Corner bad enough t'be the kind of tenants he wanted."

"What do you mean by classes of people?"

"Well ... like, uh. I mean some kinds of people would fight t'stay more than others. Like, they, had, uh, good reasons t'want t'be there. I mean, it was good reasons for them. Wimbey thought some of 'em was silly, but he knew it was somethin' those people believed in."

"Like what do you mean?"

A fish took the bait on the pole Wayne was holding. At the same time the bobber on the other pole dove under. He snatched up the pole he was holding with his left hand and reached for the other with his right.

Mr. Waterton laughed at his predicament.

"Look out there, boy. You don't want t'fall in."

He reached over and took the pole out of Wayne's left hand while Wayne pulled in the other one. There was a keeper perch on each line. Wayne strung them both up.

"Boy, didn't you look the fool," said Mr. Wateron.

They both laughed.

"Thanks," said Wayne.

" They'd almost got you *in* Lake Michigan before you got them out," said Waterton.

They both laughed again.

Wayne started rebaiting his hooks.

"But, uh," said Wayne, "what did you mean about people believin' in things?"

"Well," said Mr. Waterton, settling back, "like one class of people was those what believed in good education for they kids. They'd do anything to keep they kids in Carter. Ain't but one place colored could live in this whole city and have they kids go to Carter."

"Wimbey's Corner."

"That's right. And Eskeridge knowed when he had some Negroes crazy about the education of they young kids that he had found hisself some tenants he could count on."

"Well, I qualify on that point," said Wayne. "Me and Penny got Bobo."

"Shit, lot o' niggas got kids. That don't mean nothin'. Did you know about Carter School before you moved in?"

"I knew it was a school just down the street."

"Did you know about *Carter* school? Did you know anything about it?"

"Well ..."

"Don't 'well' me, boy. You don't qualify. You don't qualify on that score. Wimbey was talkin' about people what was crazy to get they kids into *Carter*. They knowed all about it. See, you don't fit."

181

Wayne dropped his rebaited lines back in the water.

"What were some of the other classes of people he wanted?"

"Alright, alright, it was another class of people who had to live where it was quiet. No loud parties. No fights. Niggas shoutin' up and down the street. Dignity peoples. You lived at Mrs. McCraken's, so I know that ain't you. That's strike two for you, Wayne."

"Yeah, your're right. I don't fit on that one. But come on. It's got t'be some other types he had in mind."

"Yes, there was. People who hated white folks. Who would do anything to get under their skin and stay there."

"I ain't crazy about white folks."

"What Negro is?

"No, what Wimbey meant was people who had a long, deep hate for the fays. Who would soon as slit they throats as look at 'em. People who thought they should be wiped off the face of the earth and wanted to contribute to doin' just that."

"No, I ain't like that."

"I didn't think you was. See what I'm talkin' about?"

"What else?"

"People who couldn't stand bein' around niggas."

"What?"

"People who couldn't stand bein' around niggas."

"Mr. Waterton, what sense do that make? Everybody in Wimbey's Corner is colored."

"Yeah, but look at it this way. "How many Negroes do you have t'live around in Wimbey's Corner compared to the westside?"

"You got a point."

"No - Eskeridge had a point. The smallest collection of Negroes in Evanston - probably the whole North Shore -

182

except for those what lives on the place - is at Wimbey's Corner. It is perfect for niggas what can't stand niggas."

"I don't meet that qualification either."

"Now. Do you see what I'm talkin' about?"

Wayne looked over at Mr. Waterton without saying anything.

"You don't fit none o' them classes," said Mr. Waterton, "but the thing what really convince me you don't fit is that Eskeridge wouldn't take somebody if they only fit one of those classes. They had to fit at least two. The more the better. The best was somebody who fit all of them. You don't fit none! Not one! Wasn't no way in the world you would qualify."

Wayne looked at Mr. Waterton and started laughing.

"What you laughin' at, boy?"

"You must think I'm a fool," said Wayne. "You took all that time just to tell me a fairy-tale. Either that - or Mr. Wimbey never got anybody who met every one of his qualifications."

"You're wrong," said Mr. Waterton. "He had plenty."

Wayne started laughing again. "Uh huh. And fat meat ain't greasy. Tell me - tell *me* - how somebody gon' hate fays so bad they want t'kill 'em, and at the same time cain't stand bein' around niggas. It's either one or the other."

Mr. Waterton shook his head. "Wayne, I don't believe I'm settin' here list'nin' to you, a grown man, with some sense in his head, settin' here sayin' this. Do you mean to tell me, that you has never met Negroes who hated white folks *and* Negroes. Who was filled with hatred for white folks and at the same time couldn't stand for a Negro to get near them? You ain't never seen a Negro who would turn his head with shame every time he saw another colored

183

man, but who every word out of his mouth about a white man was devil and skunk and no-good and mean and evil?"

Wayne knew plenty of people like that. He nodded.

"You're right," he said.

"I know I am. And like I said. Wimbey had plenty of tenants who met every one of his qualifications. You ain't one of 'em."

6

Bobo hid under the stairs as the fat girl came down. His eyes darted with excitement but he held himself absolutely still.

Wanda was glad the bad boy was not around. She felt safe coming downstairs to play. She was thinking about drawing a hopscotch pattern when she skipped off the bottom step onto the ground.

"Betcha don't know what I got!"

The boy was in her face, eyes bright and shining, teeth gleaming white in a pink mouth working up and down.

Wanda shrieked. She stumbled backwards.

Bobo laughed, bending over with glee.

"Scared you, didn't I?"

"No," she shouted, suddenly more embarrassed than frightened. "How's something as little as you going to scare me?"

He stood still, staring at her. His eyes were big and round. A smile stretched across his face.

I want t'do it t'you, he was thinking.

"What you lookin' at, black boy?"

"You."

He grinned.

She turned her back to him and started walking away.

"Why you lookin' at me?"

"Cause you a pretty, little ol' fat girl."

She flushed and started to skip. "Didn't your Mama tell you it's not nice to call people fat."

"But you are! You're fat. You're fat, but you're a pretty little fat girl."

He caught up with her.

"Betcha don't know what I got in my pocket."

She stopped and leaned against the tall elm tree which dominated the little scrap of yard beside their building.

She raised her eyes to his.

"Don't know and don't care."

He is a cute, little black boy, she thought.

He stuck his hand in his pocket and seemed to be fingering something.

"I'll let you see," he said.

"See what?"

"What I got."

"What is it?"

"First you got to promise."

"Promise what?"

"You won't tell."

She looked into his eyes again. He was cute enough to kiss right on the cheek.

"I promise."

Suddenly Bobo felt warm. He felt good and hot and warm all at once.

"You have to come over here ... closer. I don't want anybody else to see," he said.

She took two steps toward him.

"Okay. Show me."

"A little closer."

I could hug and kiss this little, ol' girl, he thought. But there's no place to do it. We can't do it right out here in the yard.

She took one step closer.

He could reach out and touch her. If he bent over very far he could kiss her on the cheek.

He was already imagining doing it.

But not here.

"Okay," she said.

186

"Okay?" Bobo's mind hadn't left the thought of kissing the girl, so, naturally, he thought she was talking about that. Had she agreed already? Did she want to do it here in plain sight, right out in the yard?

"Yeah. Show me."

Oh. She was only talking about his secret.

He started to pull his hand out of his pocket. Then he thought about the stairs. It was dark under the stairs. He grinned. He ran under the stairs.

"Come over here," he called. "I don't want anybody else to see."

Standing in the bright sun Wanda could not see under the shadowed stairs.

Quickly she put her hand over her mouth.

What was he trying to do? What was he trying to do? He had almost fooled her. Bad boy. Bad boy with his westside tricks. Trying to do things to her.

"I have to go upstairs," she said running for the steps.

"Wanda - wait," he called, stepping out into the sunshine.

But she was already half way up the landing.

Mama told me about those bad boys from out west.

"They smells, Mama."

"Who smells, Bobo?"

"Those Brockertons, those big, fat, Brockertons."

"Bobo Hunter. You know it's not nice to talk about people that way. The Brockertons are very fine and proper people."

"I know, Mama, but you ain't never been close to 'em."

"Bobo. Talk the right way."

"Okay. Mama. What I mean is ... well, I don't want to talk about the Brockertons. I know that's not nice. But, Mama, what should I say? I mean, they *are* fat. What should I say about that?"

"You don't have to say anything about it. If you don't have something nice to say about someone, don't say anything at all."

Bobo nodded.

He sat watching his mother for a few minutes.

"Mama, is it wrong to be fat?"

"No, Bobo. It's not wrong. Some people are just fat and some are not. Just like some people are short and others are tall. Your Daddy's tall and I'm short. Neither of us is wrong. We're just different. That's all. Just like some people are colored and some are white. Nobody's wrong. We're just different."

"Like Gabriels's skinny," said Bobo. "It's not wrong to be skinny."

"That's right."

Bobo ran his finger around the chipped enameled edge of the kitchen table.

"Then if the Brockerton's are fat, why is it wrong to say they're fat? If it's not wrong for somebody to *be* fat,

188

why is it wrong to say they're fat?"

"I don't know, Bobo. It's not wrong. You just don't need to mention it, that's all. We all know who the Brockertons are. We know what they look like. You don't have to say anything about it. Sometimes ... sometimes it hurts people's feelings."

"But they aren't here."

"I know, but you shouldn't say something that would hurt people's feelings if they were here. You shouldn't say anything about someone you wouldn't say in front of that person. And you should never say anything that would hurt someone's feelings."

Bobo drummed his fingers on the table top.

"Like they smell."

"Yes. Exactly. Like they smell. Wouldn't it hurt your feelings if somebody told you that you smell?"

"But I don't."

"But what if somebody said you did?"

"It's different if I don't smell. Then they would be lying on me. I'm not lying on the Brockertons. See, Mama you're never around them. You run and hide whenever Mrs. Brockerton comes down her steps or into the yard. You've never even seen them up close. But I have. I come right up to them all the time. Close. And they smell. It must be the fat that makes them smell that way."

"Bobo what if someone said you were small for your age? Would it make you angry?"

Bobo looked down at the table. He nodded.

"Would it be true?"

He waited a long time. Then he nodded.

"See, somebody can say something that's true, and it still hurts. There are some things you don't have to say. So why say them?"

Bobo looked up. "I used to think it was because they didn't take baths," he said. "But now I know they take baths. I can smell the soap. But I smell the fat smell up under the soap. Baths don't take it away."

"That's enough of that, Bobo Hunter."

"Okay, Mama."

He would not. He would not talk about it anymore. But that did not mean they didn't stink.

Penny was the first to hear Gabriel's screams. She ran out on her front porch, stood there trying to locate the sound, then rushed down the steps, stopping on the ground, still not knowing where the noise originated.

Standing on the sidewalk she heard Gabriel's little fists pounding on the cellar doors, saw the doors, ran around and flung one open.

His voice tore a swath of goose bumps down her flesh as he sprang out of the dank basement. The sound was so loud Penny couldn't connect it with the tiny body which emitted it. Both the sound and the contortions on his wee face conveyed abject terror.

Yet in a bizarre fashion he appeared almost comic as he vaulted through the air, nude from the waist down except for his shoes and socks.

With the adeptness of one used to small children, Penny caught him as soon as he landed on the ground and swept him up into her arms. She held him there against her chest and patted his back.

"There, there," she said, "it'll be alright." She was already walking toward his house.

His sounds stopped as he drew a deep breath, filling his lungs past their normal capacity.

In the sudden silence, holding and patting him as she walked, Penny asked, "What's wrong, little fellow?"

The answer was in the first part of the screech that damaged Penny's right ear almost permanently.

"MYYYYYY   Teeeeeeee-Teeeeeeee! AIEEEEEEEE!"

By the time Penny reached Gabriel's front door, Electa Frye stood there, her face blanched, her arms thrust forward to receive her son.

The two women learned, with Electa's persistence and under Penny's calming presence, that Wanda had done something to his teetee, put something in it, through the hole, put something inside his teetee. Finally, in a hysterical gasp they learned it was a pin.

Somehow Electa summoned up a car. Penny hurled Bobo into the back seat and jumped in after him, while Electa, holding the now almost petrified Gabriel, sat in the front seat with the driver as they rushed to the doctor's office.

X-rays confirmed the presence of the pin lodged in the boy's urethral canal. All five people stood looking at each other. Then the doctor turned back to study the x-rays, scratching his head.

Electa reacted to the shriek first. She sprinted across the examination room to the open door. Gabriel stood on the shining tiles in front of the toilet.

"I see it! I see it," he screamed.

The index finger of his right hand pointed into the toilet bowl, the water tinted by his urine. A straight pin lay on the bottom of the bowl.

The x-rays confirmed that he had indeed pee'd the pin out.

From that time on Penny and Electa became close friends.

As for Wanda, her mother administered the first beating. The sounds of the child's howls were heard for three blocks around. Unfortunately her father returned home while the backs of her legs and buttocks were still frighteningly tender. The man was slight of build yet possessed an uncommon strength. For a mile in every direction the girl's pleas and protestations filled the air. Three times the police arrived at Wimbey's Corner each time to be told simply that a father was administering justice. Wanda was not seen for a month. When at last she

192

returned down the stairs she had not the slightest inclination to peer at what boys had in place of her pussy-willow.

Besides, by then she knew.

Bobo, in the meanwhile, had despaired of ever seeing her again and had turned his attention to other fields. He had learned that some little white girls lived in the Thames Hotel. Why not do it to them, he thought. They had pussies, too.

Mabel's grief, her humiliation, her rage, were almost too much to bear. Her Wanda. Her perfect Wanda. How could she do such a thing?

As Mabel had beaten Wanda she had asked, screamed at her, tried to rip and beat out of her where such a devilish idea had come from.

"Did it come from that black boy! Did it come from that westside devil! Tell me the truth!"

She did not hear her baby's cries as she beat her, though neighbors were closing windows at the sound and more distant neighbors were calling the police. Mabel beat on, hearing only the insistent sound of her own voice.

"Tell me! Tell me! Tell me the truth!"

When at last Wanda began to answer her mother in words, she said she did not know where the idea came from. "No, Mama, No, Mama. No, Mama!" She insisted it had not come from the boy downstairs. She had kept away from him. He had not whispered devilment in her ear. She did not know, she screeched, she did not know where it had come from but she promised never never never never never to do it again.

"I know you won't! I know you won't! I'll kill you first! Do you know that! Do you know that! I'll kill you first!"

The effort of beating her child almost killed Mabel. But she could not stop. It was the first time she had ever

193

laid a strap to her, the first time she had ever had the need, and she could not stop.

Oh, help me Jesus, she said inside her head even while her mouth spewed venom and her arms rose and fell with terrible persistence.

Deep, deep down inside, the center of Mabel's world had slipped off its moorings. Wanda had been her celebration, her joy in the morning. Wanda had been her trumpet call to all those who cast aspersions on her and pitied her. Because of John. Because of her husband. Wanda was the answer.

Now her statement, her testament to the world, was sullied. Mabel felt a hole emerging and widening in her innermost self and there was no bottom to it. How could such a thing be? Was there no justice in life? When John came home from work. She could not do otherwise. She had to tell him.

He said nothing. He just looked at his wife, walked into their bedroom, took off his hat, his coat, and removed his belt. Belt in hand, he climbed the small flight of stairs which led to the upstairs room, Wanda's room.

Wanda screamed though there was a long time before the first sound of leather striking flesh. It was a loud sound, a painful sound, and it went on, relentlessly. The shrieks bore no relationship to it. They went on during, between, and through the horrible lashes. Lashes which continued during and after the police visits, monotonous, terrifying.

At last he came downstairs, his yellowed white shirt open at the collar, stuck by sweat to his lithe, muscular frame. He had not as yet said a word. He dropped the belt over the back of the kitchen chair, sat down, and waited for dinner.

Mabel did not know how she was going to leave the house in the morning, descend that interminable flight of stairs. She would have to walk all the way from the back of the Corner, in front of the new people's place, then between Electa's below and the Stuarts' above on one side, and the Corks' on the other, past both houses to the front, then through the gate and down the street past the Corks' and Mrs. Wenders'. How could she do it? The humiliation.

She had apologized abjectly to Electa. Had she been physically able she would have crawled on her knees before her. Her shining star, the light of her life, her Wanda, had reduced her to that - groveling on the pavement before her neighbor, still a girl herself.

Oh help me Jesus.

Upstairs she did not know if her Wanda were broken. In the dark upstairs all the crying wrenched from her body. Mabel hoped she were not broken but she did not know ... if all the light had gone out of her eyes. She had to be stopped. She had to be punished. She had to know what could never, never, never be done. If she were strong the lesson would not break her. But being broken would not mean she was weak. Only a strong person, a very strong person would not be broken. Mabel did not know if alone in the gloom upstairs her body rent with wounds, her insides an agony, her daughter lay as if her spine had been snapped - limp - never to stand on her own again, or if somewhere within her she clung to the dignity and wholeness of her own spirit, indomitable within a humbled body. She did not know.

There was something Ivory's parents were trying to keep from her. Everybody in the Corner was excited about something and Ivory did not know what it was. She had to try to figure it out. She had to try to figure out almost everything because her parents told her so little. She was the oldest kid in the Corner and everybody was told more than she was, even little Gabriel. The boy from out west had to know more than she did because of where he came from, and he was younger, too. She envied him. And Wanda. She knew a lot. Everything Ivory knew she had to find out on her own. Hiding. Her parents were always hiding things from her.

Like Mr. Sweet. They had not wanted to let her know he had died. She had known, though. She had known right away. Mr. Sweet was always in the same places at the same times everyday. It helped his routine, he said. He did not like to break his routine. He had liked Ivory.

Always smiling at me and saying nasty things, she thought. Daddy hated him.

But Ivory enjoyed the dirty old man and the first morning she got up and he was not in his bathroom window trying to peek into her bathroom while she was in it, she knew something was wrong. At breakfast Mama and Daddy had acted strange, pretending they were acting normal, being very careful to act normal. She had known right then he was dead.

They probably never would have told her except that Mrs. Wenders and her daughter, Virginia, had moved into his house. They couldn't tell her he had moved away, because Mr. Sweet always swore he would never move again.

That's the way they were, though, always trying to keep things from her.

Ivory patted her feet. She would figure it out. She already knew it had something to do with Wanda. Her parents had tried to make a lot of noise when Wanda had been screaming the night before, but they could not drown out her yells, then they had taken Ivory out for ice cream to get her away, but she could hear Wanda way down the street.

She did not know what it was, but she would figure

196

it out. Just as she had figured out what they did not want her to know about Mr. Brockerton. Sometimes she got so angry at them she could not stand it. They did not want her to know anything.

Amazed. Wayne was amazed at the Wimbey's Corner's people's reactions to Wanda's perfidy. He expected them to be streaming up the stairs, pounding on her door, to visit vengeance upon her, and have her thrown out - out! That's where *he* wanted her - out!

But they did not. They did nothing.

He watched. He waited. The expected reaction never came.

He kept it in himself until he could contain it no longer. He spoke to Penny.

"The mother," he said, "just take for instance the mother. Doesn't she want something done to the girl? Doesn't she want her son to feel safe?"

I would do something, he thought. I would avenge her if she asked me.

Penny dried the dishes. She was wondering where the car had come from so fast, how Electa got somebody driving a car almost like magic. But she answered her husband.

"Electa says Gabriel's alright. He wasn't hurt. He pee'd the pin out. It didn't do any damage - no bleeding or anything."

Wayne slammed the side of his fist down on the kitchen table. "The boy's got to live with that girl around everyday!"

"Electa says Gabriel's not afraid of Wanda. He knows she got punished. Everybody knows she got punished. Nobody expects her to do it again. See - Baby, they been friends a long time. This is just something that happened. One thing. It won't end the friendship."

"Penny - Penny - we're not talking about something that happened out west - this is Wi -"

"I know. I know. And that's why .... Well. She did wrong. Everybody knows she did wrong. That had to be corrected. Hard. It was. You know it was. You heard that child -"

"Should of broke her neck."

"From the sound of it, that was about the only thing he didn't break. But, Wayne, see - everybody knows she was punished. Punished bad. That's what they expect. That's all they expect. She knows and now everybody goes on about their business. She's been a good girl all her life. They expect her to keep on being a good girl. They're going to help her do that the best way they can. That's why they're not mean to her. That's why they smile at her and speak nice to her and hug her. That's over and life's got to go on.

"You keep talking about how could she do that in Wimbey's Corner. But don't you see, that's just it. She did it *in* Wimbey's Corner. Nobody outside knows she did it. Nobody outside will ever know. And for them it's been taken care of. The boy's all right. Punishment. See ... Baby ... *she's one of their own.*"

Things might have turned out differently if Wayne had understood what Penny meant. They might have turned out differently if he had confronted his own incipient emotions. But he did not.

198

9

Electa Frye frightened Wayne. She drew men like bad meat draws flies. Soldiers and sailors. Wayne hated seeing them come around. The fancy boys. The uniforms. Drew them like clover draws bees. She was proper enough. She went out on dates with one soldier or sailor , or another, sometimes a civilian, usually once a week. She never stayed out all night. They always brought her home early. Her mother stayed with the little boy while she was out. She was proper enough. But they kept coming around. Buzzing. Buzzing.

Wayne was troubled the times when he came into his house and saw Electa there. Both Matilda and Camilla had been voluptuous, feasts for the eyes and hands. She was not like that. Beautiful. You had to catch your breath. Sometimes you had to sit down. Beautiful. Sometimes it hurt to look at her. Slender. Subtle curves. Elegant. Sometimes you did not know whether to talk to her or put a frame around her and just look at her.

Wayne did not think she should be like that in his house - laughing and smiling and sometimes being serious with her great, dark eyes and her light-complected, smooth skin. He thought she should not be sitting in his kitchen chair with her delicate wrist bent as she held a cup, her trim ankle showing where her legs crossed.

He feared the way she moved as if the world belonged to her and moving that way in his house, befriending his little, simple wife, his Penny. Moving right into their lives as if she had a place there and he was afraid and he did not know what he was going to do about it because it was important for Penny to make the right friends and if Electa Frye weren't right, nobody was. But still he had to keep seeing her and hearing her and knowing she was there.

And then the soldiers and sailors kept buzzing and buzzing and buzzing.

10

At first it had not bothered Wayne that people in Wimbey's Corner did not cotton to him. He understood that Mr. Sweet had just passed away, somebody who had lived in the Corner ever since there had been a Corner. He understood how people would take some time to adjust to a new person. Even though he had an excellent job. Even though he spoke the King's own English. Even though he had a wife and son who were as proper-talking and as proper-acting as anyone could hope. He understood it would take some time to be accepted. So it was quite a while before it bothered him.

Wayne had not expected to be welcomed with open arms, and when he saw the insular character of the place he understood he'd have to wait even longer than he'd guessed. He was patient. In his life he'd proved that over and over again.

What really started to bother Wayne was when he noticed that there were some strangers who came into the Corner and how they were received. They were servicemen. They all came to take Electa Frye out. Wayne noticed that they got a smile right off from Mr. Stuart, and a nod and a wave from Mr. Cork. Of course Electa just lit right up for them.

So these ... foreigners, these ... no accounts, got more recognition in the Corner than Wayne, *who lived there*. And Wayne was somebody. He lived in the Corner. He was a family man. Respectable. Responsible. And here were these tin horns getting more respect and acceptance than he was.

If these Wimbey's Corner Negroes are going to take their time about me they better damn-sure take their own, sweet time about everybody else - especially about some jokers they don't even know walking around in uniforms.

Bobo and Gabriel sat on Bobo's steps drawing. Bobo, at least, was drawing. His hands could magically reproduce what his eyes had seen. He drew some dolphins he had once seen in a *National Geographic* magazine. Gabriel made scribbles and lines on the cardboard. Penny had given them sheets of white cardboard from the shirts Wayne brought back from the Chinese laundry; she had also given them colored pencils. She was excited by Bobo's artistic ability and encouraged it in every way she could.

"You ain't never had none is you," said Bobo.

Gabriel kept scribbling.

Bobo stopped working on his dolphins and looked up at what Gabriel was doing. He shook his head. He watched Gabriel for a while.

"I asked you a question," he said.

"What?" Gabriel looked up.

Bobo looked back at the door to see if his mother were there, then he returned to his work on the dolphins.

"I'll ask you again," he said. "This time I'll ask you in proper-talk. Maybe then you'll understand."

He paused.

"You have never had any, have you?"

"Any what?"

Bobo glanced at the door.

"Any pussy, that's what."

"Pussy -"

"Shhh. You don't have to talk so loud."

"Okay." Gabriel lowered his voice, coming as close to whispering as he could. "Pussy. What's that? I don't know what pussy is. All I know is pussy-cat."

"I thought so," said Bobo. "You're just a baby. I'm not talking about any pussy-cat. I'm talking about *pussy*.

203

I'll be your teacher. Teach you the facts of life.

"I can make a baby."

Gabriel stopped scratching the cardboard with a pencil and looked up.

"How?"

Bobo grinned.

"It takes me and a girl and I can make a baby. I coulda made you."

"How? Mamas makes babies."

"No. Mamas don't make babies. Daddies make babies. Mamas just has 'em. I told you I'm gon' teach you. You're just a little kid."

Gabriel stared at Bobo.

"You're not a daddy."

"No, but I could be. I know how. Pretty as your Mama is I would love to make a baby with her."

Gabriel's scream was intuitive and inarticulate. He flew off the step onto Bobo, the fingers of his left hand grabbing for Bobo's face, his right hand stabbing the pencil like a dagger.

Shocked by the surprise of the attack and overwhelmed by its ferocity, Bobo fell over backwards, bashing the back of his head against the boards of a step.

He lay stunned for seconds while Gabriel unleashed his bawling fury. Outraged at his own violation, Bobo retaliated. He kicked and punched, using his size, motor skills, and experience of twice Gabriel's age to his advantage.

Gabriel found himself tumbling down the steps to the concrete patio. He immediately rushed back up the stairs, silent now, but as mindless as before, only to be pummeled back down again.

He rose and rushed the stairs again.

The scene repeated itself nine times.

Finally, Bobo caught Gabriel as he charged, wrapped

his arms around him, and pinned his arms. Gabriel butted frantically with his head.

Bobo felt he was in a nightmare, that it was never going to end unless he killed the little boy.

"What's wrong," he asked. "Why are you doing this?"

"Take-take-take it back," wailed Gabriel.

"What? What? Take what back?"

"My M —a-m—a! What you said about my M—a-m—a!"

"Okay. Okay. I take it back. I'm sorry."

"Say you didn't mean it."

"Yeah, yeah. I'm sorry. I didn't mean it. I apologize."

Bobo felt Gabriel relax.

He let him go.

Gabriel started wiping his face. He kept staring at Bobo. "Don't ever talk about my Mama again."

"I won't. I won't. Sit down."

Gabriel sat down.

The pieces of cardboard were bent and torn. The pencils were scattered. Bobo started picking them up.

Gabriel did too.

"I'm sorry for what I said about your mom," said Bobo.

"Nobody talks about my Mama," said Gabriel.

"Mmhmm. I see why. But you will never be able to play the dozens."

"What's that?"

"Never mind. Living down here, you'll probably never get a chance to anyway.

"Besides. Those two white girls who live in the hotel?"

Gabriel looked up at Bobo.

"I can make a baby with them. You can watch. I'll

show you how to do it."

"Then I can make a baby?"

"I don't know. You might be too little. You might have to wait until you grow and get big like me."

Bobo was pleased with himself. Now he had to do it to those two girls. He had to prove to Gabriel that he meant what he said - that he could do what he said he could do. The first problem, he thought, will be to get them down out of that hotel and into our yard. He glanced up at their window. He was sure he saw one of their faces disappear.

12

It was going to be so easy, like picking berries off a vine. Bobo could not get over it. He was really going to be able to do it to those two white girls. They went along with everything he said. He could lead them by their noses. He had already kissed each of them, felt in their panties. He could not get over it! It was so easy. He said. They did. All he had to do was find a place.

Perched on his steps he watched Gabriel playing on the cement below him with a toy car.

"Hey Gabriel!"

The smaller boy stopped and looked up.

"Your house has a basement, doesn't it?"

Gabriel nodded.

"What's in it?"

"Pipes, wheels, some funny machines, dirt, spiders, and camel crickets."

"What's a camel cricket?"

"They're poison."

Bobo lapsed into silence.

After a while he said, "Do they bite?"

This time Gabriel kept playing with his car. "Do what bite," he asked.

"The camel crickets."

Exasperated that the older boy should be so ignorant, Gabriel, on his knees, took his hand off his car and leaned back in a sitting position, his butt on his heels, and faced Bobo.

"No," he said. "They don't bite. They got sharp little spikes on them that are poisonous."

He canted his head slightly to the side, then turned it back facing Bobo again. "They don't look like other crickets, either. They're bigger. And they're white with

207

brown stripes."

Bobo started laughing.

"You're making up stories," he said. "There ain't no such thing as a camel cricket."

"Wanna bet?"

"Then how come I ain't never seen one?"

"They only live in the basement."

"Liar!"

"I am not!" Gabriel picked up his car and stood up, defiantly posturing himself before the older boy.

Bobo eyed him for several seconds. "Aw, go on," he said at last.

"Bet you a dollar," said Gabriel.

"You don't have a dollar."

"Bet you anyway."

Bobo turned his head away. "What else is down there?"

"Where?"

"In the basement, dummy. What else do you think we're talking about?"

"I told you - those pipes and things, secret things. We're not supposed to talk about them, and there's some junk, junk they use to hide the secret things."

"What kind of junk?"

"Oh, I don't know. Old things. Junk."

"Let's go see."

"Why?"

"Bobo lowered his voice. "It's a secret. I'll tell you after we take a look."

Gabriel awakened to adventure. He tingled. His eyes turned up, shining.

"Okay. Come on. You have to be careful of the camel crickets, though."

Just a bit timorous, not knowing whether to believe in camel crickets or not, but exuding self-confidence, Bobo followed the little boy.

The heavy, wooden hurricane doors were too heavy for Gabriel, so Bobo opened them.

The cement walls and steps leading down to the basement were damp. Bobo studied the descending vestibule carefully. He saw spider webs and beetles, but nothing unusual. Feeling a bit less wary, he said, "Okay, go on."

"I'm scared of the camel crickets," said Gabriel.

"Do you see any camel crickets?"

"No. But what if they jump down on us?"

Bobo started laughing. "Go on. Nothing's going to jump down on you."

"You go first."

"I would, but it's your house."

"I give you permission," said Gabriel.

Well, that was that. He had permission. Bobo started edging down the steps. "Scaredy-cat," he spat back over his shoulder.

"I'm only four years old."

There was a door at the bottom of the steps.

"How am I supposed to open it," called up Bobo.

"It's not locked. Just open it."

Bobo turned the handle.

The door swung inward at a touch.

There were shafts of light, but Bobo could not see anything except the few, narrow rectangles from which daylight slanted into the gloom. He did not move.

"See. The door's open. Come on down."

"I'll wait."

"If you don't come down, I won't tell you the secret."

Timidly, Gabriel began to inch down the steps. He sat on a step, eased his feet to the lower step, braced his hands on the step where he sat, then slid his rear end off that

209

step as his feet descended to the lower one. He repeated the process over and over again, very slowly.

"Where's the light," asked Bobo, trying to make out shapes in the dark, dank interior.

"There isn't one," said Gabriel, at last joining Bobo on the threshold.

"This is where you really have to be careful about camel crickets," said the smaller boy.

"Oh, shut up about those stupid camel crickets!"

Bobo was now able to see in the room's dim interior. Immediately before him was an expanse of dirt floor. Eight to ten feet across the dirt was a huge pile of stuff, junk, as Gabriel had called it, concealing some kind of secret. *I'll bet*, thought Bobo.

Bobo studied the pile. For a while he was not willing to credit his eyes, but - yes - it was undeniable. As an answer to his wildest dreams - there - lodged in the pile, was the edge of a mattress.

He stepped eagerly onto the dirt floor.

He tugged and pulled at the mattress. Eventually, he got Gabriel to come help. Finally they got the thing out of the pile and on the floor. They collapsed onto it, exhausted. Bobo was very, very happy. He could picture the future. Those two little girls were going to be lying on this mattress as he did it to them.

He was getting ready to share the secret with Gabriel when something happened which nearly caused him to pee his pants. There were white flecks on the basement's filthy brick walls. Bobo, over-ripe with the thrill of his secret, ready to burst it out into the waiting ears of his little friend, was gazing absent mindedly at the wall, when one of the speckles moved.

Both boys sprang to their feet and hurtled themselves screaming through the open door and up the stairs.

210

13

The black, 1937 Buick Special gleamed. Within seconds it was surrounded by wondering admirers. A cigar in his mouth, Wayne leaned back behind the steering wheel into the plush upholstery. When Penny and Bobo appeared, almost crazy with excitement and pride, he reached over, opened up the front passenger door, and let them in. Bobo sat between his parents. Penny closed her door. For a few minutes all three of them, looped in drifting swirls of cigar smoke, sat and grinned.

Wayne had paid cash for the car. It was all his - top to bottom - front to back. He patted the steering wheel. The choice had been difficult. He had been particularly attracted to a 1940 Cadillac. What could compare with the opulence of a Cadillac? He thought back on it ... the extra wide grill, the long strip of chrome running from the grill to the trunk. Magnificent. He had been sorely tempted. He had the cash. He could have driven it off the lot as much his as the Buick now was. Still. It had been a bit too much. People were always talking about niggers' irresistible love of Cadillacs. He had just proved it was resistible. He did not need to be seen in a Cadillac. And his Buick was the next step down the line, second to the top, truly a luxury automobile - but not a Cadillac - not too showy. Just right. That's what his car was - big and powerful, stylish and comfortable - but not overdone. Just right. He laughed again. The Fords and Chevies and Plymouths had not even tempted him. He could have brought home a lot of those. He had the money. He turned up his nose at all of them. There had been one Pontiac, though - a '37 with a sun visor - which had allured him. It had looked very, very good. But the Buick had won the day. It should have. It was a better car. A bigger car. A more prestigious car. And here he sat, Wayne Hunter,

211

behind the wheel, his wife and son beside him. The smile bunched up his cheeks and showed his big, white teeth. A line from the Bible sang in his ears, "Where is he that was crowned king of the Jews?"

14

A big, black, Buick car. A big, black, Buick car. It was just like a nigger.

Charles stood in his back porch and looked through the window down to the alley. He could see the bumper and grill of the out-sized monstrosity, the flashy hood ornament a half-naked woman. He was beside himself with frenzy. The garish vehicle had no place in Wimbey's Corner. No place!

He knew what he could do. He could drop a lighted rag down the gasoline tank and that would be the end of the fancy car. He chuckled. He knew what to do alright. He could show that bum a thing or two.

Nobody else in Wimbey's Corner even had a car. There were some things which were unnecessary, supercilious. An automobile was one of them. Of course, Fends had one before he got sick, but Fends was a settled man, not a boy wet behind the ears. How much must a thing like that cost? Where in the world could he get the money to afford it?

Miss Bryce had said he made an exorbitant amount of money. How could he? How in the world could he? A mere juvenile. He had not even served his country, had not even served in the war. And here he was leaning back in the lap of luxury.

Charles hated him.

He didn't have to blow up the car. He could break the windows. Slash the tires. That would set him back a peg or two. Charles laughed. Old Mackenzie would have enjoyed some action like that. Put some dents in those shiny fenders. There he was lording it over everybody. It was time he learned some humility.

213

15

Bobo thought at first he would be able to use the car as his place of assignation with the two little white girls. To get inside that dream of steel and glass and soft cushions they would have permitted him anything, would even have given him money on top of anything else he wanted. He knew that. Therefore his mind had raved wildly with glorious delight as he sat in the front seat with his mother and father, the people clambering around outside. He had pictured himself not long hence, one little girl naked on the front seat, the other on the back, while he hopped gleefully from one to the other, little Gabriel perched on the hood and peering through the window. "This is how you do it, Gabriel. This is how you make babies." Bobo's father, however, remained much more inflexible about the car than Bobo would have imagined. It stayed locked at all times. His father had the only keys and unlocked it only when he was going to enter it. The sole times Bobo could get in was when he was going somewhere with his mother and father. The rest of the time he had to stand around and look at it from the outside just like everybody else. There would be no "doing it" in the Buick.

That turned him back on his only remaining resources. The basement. Somehow he and Gabriel were going to have to master the camel crickets. Otherwise, there would be no baby-making, no naked little white girls. No fatherhood. No showing a four year old what a big boy could really do.

Thus began a long, fear-inducing process of the two boys' trying to coax each other past the hurricane doors, down the cellar steps, and into the darkened room that was the camel crickets' domain.

Gabriel tried to convince Bobo that making a baby

was not that important, that if he had to go down into the basement with camel crickets in order for a baby to be made that it just wasn't worth it. He was happy being a little boy playing with toy cars and balls who would never know how a baby was made.

Often the argument sounded convincing to Bobo and he would put off descending the damp, cobweb flanked stairs. Other days he thought about seeing the two little girls without any clothes on and him with his thing, his peter, his dick out and sticking it into them and he knew that no little white bug with brown stripes on it was going to keep him from doing it. On those days it was only when his foot had left the bottom step and he stood in front of the cellar door that he remembered the little white bugs were poisonous.

Sometimes at night Bobo could hear his mother and father "doing it." That gave him greater incentive to master his fear and claim the basement for his own. Yet he recognized that his fear was based on prudence. He was afraid because he did not want to be killed. He had to find some way to use the basement without being killed. He realized what he needed was an ally, someone who would have more insights on such problems than the little boy and him. That is when his mind returned to Wanda. She had never given him a chance to get close to her before, and ever since her episode with Gabriel she had been very scarce, but now Bobo had a weapon to use in recruiting her he had not had before - the 1937 Buick Special. She would not know he could no more get into it than she could, and he could use it as his bargaining chip. That pretty, little, fat girl probably knew all about camel crickets.

215

16

Freedom. That is what the car gave Wayne that he had not thought about. He had pictured it as transportation, a way to get to fishing places. It became as well a bearer of freedom. He saved half an hour every day driving to work and home. Shopping was easy and could be done less frequently since they could pile as many groceries as they wanted into the car. Even going fishing to the lake was quicker and easier. Freedom.

Wayne had not realized how much he would love his car. It got him, as he had intended, to those distant places to fish. He took Penny and Bobo to the Pond and to Skokie Lagoon and to the Des Plaines River. He took them to Fox Lake and the Fox River. He took them north as far as Wisconsin, and south to the Kankakee River. He drove them around the foot of the lake to Southern Michigan. They always came home with a tub full of fish.

Fishing the way he knew how to, in all the varieties he knew, worked its old magic on Wayne. He was once more a child of the waters. He was once more in pursuit of Mr. Big. He rejoiced in the exultation of his rediscovery.

Electa was one of the principal and most grateful recipients of their largesse. She loved fish, especially fresh caught fish, and she also deeply appreciated any gift which supplemented her budget and freed a few more dollars for her son.

Penny had told her that she and Wayne were going to want to take Gabriel fishing with them and Bobo sometime. Electa had heard but forgotten, so when the invitation came, it caught her by surprise.

Bobo had caught on quickly to the different kinds of fishing - pond fishing and lake fishing and river fishing. He picked up trolling and drifting and bank fishing and night fishing. He was very good. But Wayne saw that his son's heart was not in it and he remembered that he and Penny had agreed to take Gabriel sometime and he thought with someone closer to Bobo's age along, the spark might be struck in his boy. Since Bobo was a good fisherman, if nothing else he could show off to Gabriel. That should excite him. That boy loved to show off.

After the first time, the Hunters frequently took Gabriel fishing. Wayne had seen, that very first day, when the little boy walked to the edge of the water, the excitement, the ineffable joy which coursed through his tiny body. It put music in him.

Wayne saw Gabriel anew. He wasn't just a skinny four-year old hanging onto his mother's skirts. He was a lonely little kid, barely out of babyhood, who did not have a father, and whose horizons had been limited almost entirely to the walls of his house and the small yard on Tary Street.

There was a terrible vulnerability about him, yet around the water he assumed a powerful vitality. Wayne had to laugh when he looked at him. He could see Electa shining through.

Wayne's favorite place to take Gabriel was the Pond because it was just the boy's size. Shallow. It covered about two acres, mostly three to four feet deep except for several holes eight to ten feet. It was framed by water reeds with a few pockets of lily pads. It teemed with bluegill, sunfish, crappie, real yellow perch - not lake perch - and bullheads. There was also a sizable population of largemouth black bass. The boy could always be assured of catching something, and he could learn. Wayne thought it was just the size of a place where Gabriel could handle the

217

Mr. Big who lived there. We'll teach him to fish this, he decided. We'll get him ready for Mr. Big.

Wayne liked to go fishing early in the morning. He would ask Electa the night before if he could take Gabriel the next day. When he had her consent he would tell Gabriel. Wayne would be up before grey-light, while it was still dark. He loaded all his gear and his wife and son into the car in the dark. Then he walked to the Frye's. As he passed the bedroom window a small face pressed against the glass and the eyes stuck right to him.

They got to the water before the sun was up when there was a lightening around the edges of the eastern sky. That's the way Wayne liked best. It was the way Gabriel came to savor, too.

Wayne taught Gabriel how to bait a hook, whether it was worm, or minnow, or cricket or crayfish. He taught him to put on the different kinds of worms - nightcrawler, and red wiggler, and pale babies, and to make combinations of them. He showed him how to vary hook placement with the size and kind of minnow and how to pick the size of the hook to fit the bait and the fish he was after. He showed him the knots that would unite catgut with fishing line, and how to attach the hooks to the leader. He explained how to put on weights and the different kinds of weights for varieties of fishing.

He introduced him to fishing with a bobber, and straight-line, and jig fishing, and to the wonders of a casting rod. In all this the little boy's eyes stayed big and round and his tongue ran out of his lips with the taste of it.

Gabriel learned patience, to untangle the mess of a backlash, to sit still as a log while he watched a bobber ride the ripples, to follow each nod made by the tip of a casting rod, the taught line running out from it, knowing the difference between the motion imparted by a light breeze or the movement of water, the peck-pecks of little fish nibbling, or the slower, more subtle motion of a bigger fish testing the bait.

Wayne observed him. He saw his excitement when he caught a fish, the happiness, the peace that enveloped him when he was on the water. He grew close to the boy.

17

Fishing brought Bobo and Gabriel back together. The camel crickets were what had driven them apart in the first place and Bobo proceeded to remedy that breach by putting his plan for dealing with the camel crickets in motion.

Every day he lounged around the bottom of the steps, waiting for Wanda Brockerton to come down. Every day when she finally did, he marveled at two things - how she kept getting both prettier and fatter at the same time. He could not get over it. It did not make sense, but it was clearly true. The girl was both a raving beauty and as fat as a walrus.

For several days Bobo did not say anything when Wanda came down. He just kept his distance and watched her play.

By the fourth day she could not stand it any more.

"What are you looking at, west side boy?"

"The prettiest fat girl I ever saw in my life. The prettiest girl I ever saw in my life. The fattest girl I ever saw in my life."

"Well, I'm looking at the blackest, knottiest headed boy I ever saw in my life."

"Maybe so," he answered.

"No maybe about it."

Bobo smiled. "You seen our new car?"

"What of it?"

"Oh, nothing .... I was ... just ... wondering."

"Wondering what?"

"Oh, never mind." Bobo turned, bounded up his steps, and went inside.

He stayed away from Wanda for four days.

On the fifth day he was hanging around the steps

again when she came down.

"I see you got back," she said. "Where'd you go, on some monkey business?"

"If you were my friend, I could tell you," said Bobo.

"I don't want to know that bad," she said.

"Well, if you were my friend, I'd tell you anyway," he said. "Gabriel's my friend."

"I know. You have to have babies for friends since you can't make any your own age."

"I would like you to be my friend," said Bobo.

Wanda laughed and started skipping around in circles. "Join the crowd," she said.

"Because Gabriel's my friend he gets to ride in our big Buick all the time."

They were both quiet for a spell.

Wanda squatted down and started playing jacks.

Bobo could not get over how pretty she was. All over again he wanted to kiss her.

"If you were my friend, do you think your mama would let you ride in our big car?"

She caught her ball and looked up at him.

"I don't know."

"I was just wondering," he said as he turned on his heels and sprang up the steps into his house.

He did not come out again any time Wanda was in the yard for two more days. He watched her from his windows. He saw her first staring at the car, standing inside the back yard and staring at it. He saw her when she went out in the alley to be a little closer to it, to walk around it and see it from every angle. He could not repress the smile that slipped onto his lips. The second day she touched it. She put her hand on the chrome strip and walked all the way around the car, trailing her hand behind her, her fingertips

221

soothing the shining finish. She held onto the door handles and stepped onto the running board. She pressed her face against the glass and contorted and twisted her position to look inside, to look at everything she could see.

On the third day Bobo danced in the stairs' shadow when Wanda came down.

"Hey, good lookin,'" he said.

She jumped.

He laughed.

He sauntered into the sunlight, hands in his pockets. "When are you going to let me kiss you?"

She cast her eyes down and walked away from him, swinging the lower half of her body.

"We're not even friends yet," she said very softly.

"Do you wanta be my friend," he said running up behind her.

When he got close to her he smelled her fat smell. But he did not mind. He was too excited.

She turned around lightly on her toes. "Maybe," she said, facing him. "What about you? You were the one asking. Do you still want me to be your friend?"

"Do flies like dead meat?"

Wanda grimaced. "What are you talking about?"

"I mean, yes. Of course. I want you to be my friend. I want to be your friend. I want to kiss you, too."

She turned her back to him again and started walking away, sashaying. "Maybe ... we can be friends," she said, pointedly omitting anything about kissing.

She walked to the back fence where she could see the Buick parked under the windows of the Hunters' flat.

Bobo focused every scintilla of his consciousness on her.

He saw her flick her eyes in the Buick's direction without wanting to let him know what she was doing.

Bobo walked over to the fence, leaned on it, and

222

stared at the car.

That gave her the excuse to look at it, too.

"When we're friends," he said, "we can sit in my car together, maybe even go for rides in it."

He sighed. "I sure would like to be friends with you," he said.

"If we make friends," she said, "we don't have to kiss.."

"No, we don't HAVE to," he answered, "but I sure want to. You're the prettiest, fattest little girl, and I just want to get my mouth and my hands on you." He did not care about the smell any more. In fact, he liked it. He liked it because it came from her.

Wanda ran away from the fence. "Oooh," she said, in the softest voice she could manage. She did not want any adult overhearing her. "You shouldn't say things like that. That's bad!"

Bobo ran after her. He chuckled. "Are we friends?"

She turned around quickly. He almost ran into her, but he stopped just short of collision. She laughed at him.

"Okay. Friends," she said. She extended her hand.

"Friends," he said, wrapping both of his around her right one. My, what a soft, fat, little hand, he thought. He didn't want to let it go.

As his initial lever in sustaining the friendship Bobo could offer no more than promises of ensconcing Wanda in the plush upholstery of the magnificent vehicle. But since it was no secret that the extravagant automobile was the Hunter family car, and since Bobo was very good at making promises, they sufficed.

Wanda was more than happy to tell Bobo about the camel crickets. Just as he had expected, she was an expert on them.

But the more they talked, the more convinced Bobo was that he had to do it with Wanda before he did it to either of the little white girls. Wanda, after all, had been his first choice. He had only gone to the white girls when she was taken out of the field of play. Now she was back in it. She was so pretty. Prettier every day. And her voice had a nice sound to it. He *wanted* to do it to her. He wanted it very badly. With the white girls it was just to show Gabriel he knew how to make a baby. That was the other thing. He knew how to do it. He had watched it done dozens of times. But he had never done it himself. Before he put on a show for anybody he had better have some experience. He could get that experience with Wanda. Many times. Many times before he put on the exhibition with the white girls.

Wanda assured him the camel crickets were not a problem. You could do whatever you wanted in the basement as long as you knew where they were and stayed away from them. They tended to favor certain places. Damp places. The darkest places. They were ugly, little, pus-looking creatures, but they would not bother you if you stayed away from them and the long spikes on their hind legs.

Wanda took Bobo down into their own basement to show him. They had to be careful about that because Wanda had not only been forbidden to play with Gabriel after their unfortunate episode, she had also been forbidden to go into the basement. But like most children Wanda and Bobo were good at sneaking and stealthily made their way into the basement their two apartments shared.

There, after Bobo finally got over his terror, after Wanda had shown him pockets where the loathsome little beasts hid. After he had restrained himself from shrieking, and fleeing, and got used to it, and got comfortable, he kissed Wanda for the first time. The sweetest kiss he ever had. So sweet it turned into ten kisses. In the dark. In the

224

basement. With the camel crickets in the shadows.

The friendship was transformed after that. Bobo did not even have to make any more promises about the car. In fact, one day Bobo and Wanda were playing outside when Wayne left to go to the store. Wayne had never forgiven Wanda for what she had done. But it seemed to have been taken care of quietly. No one outside knew it had happened. The serenity of the Corner had been preserved. And it was good for Bobo to make as many Corner playmates as possible. Making such friends was impossible to overdo. He took them for a ride together in the back seat. But from the time of the kisses on, the car had become of secondary importance. Bobo and Wanda were locked together in mutual infatuation and events pressed inexorably to the moment when the last restraints would be hurled aside and they would finally "do it."

18

As she spread the plates out on the kitchen table Mabel glanced out the window.

No one.

She knew she was not early. She had taken a long time on this dinner. It was one of John's favorites. She had expected him to come home in time to smell it while it was still cooking, to sit at the table talking to her, or at any rate listening to her, in eager anticipation of the feast she was readying. He would not mind eating a little bit later than usual when it would be so good. She knew she was not early.

She did not look at Wanda. She did not want to see her. If she saw the terror in Wanda's eyes it would only confirm the conviction that was clutching at her insides.

Please, John. Please.

Mabel straightened the napkins and peeked out the window.

Nothing.

She would wait for a while before she started ladling out the meal. It would cool faster once it was on the plates. John liked his food hot.

She kept her back to Wanda.

What else could she do to keep busy? She could fill up the salt and pepper shakers. Yes. Mabel walked awkwardly to the cabinet making sure never to face her daughter, never to give her a chance for eye contact. She knew if Wanda made eye contact she would speak. Then she would be forced to look at her, and not only to see the panic in her eyes, but also to hear the hysteria welling up in her voice. Well, thank goodness she hasn't said anything yet.

The gate clicked.

Mabel lurched for a point in the room where she could see out the window.

Aaahhh. Mr. Stuart. It was only Mr. Stuart.

Mabel leaned back against the wall. She closed her eyes. If she had opened them she would have seen Wanda.

He's coming, she said to herself. He's coming. Steering away from the wall she opened her eyes and returned to the salt and pepper shakers. What am I going to do when I get through doing this? I have to keep busy. Busy, busy. Until he gets here. Until my John comes home. Please. John. Come home. Please.

Wanda watched her mother. She did not see her but she watched her. She did not see her because she was using all her energy to focus on not talking. She knew if she opened her mouth to speak she would not speak. She would scream. She knew exactly what she would scream. "Mama, where's Daddy!" She did not want to scream and she did not want to hear her mother's answer so she used every bit of her strength not to talk. She watched her mother with huge eyes which moved back and forth as her mother moved but did not see her. The faculties she would have used for seeing were concentrated on holding her mouth closed. It was clenched in a tight line across her face.

Wanda knew how her mother would answer the question.

"Oh, he's coming home. He's just a little late. Maybe he missed his bus, or maybe he had to work overtime. He'll be here soon."

Wanda did not want to hear the lie.

She also did not want to face the truth so she kept her mouth in a tight line and watched her mother without seeing her.

Well, I'm going to have to feed Wanda. It's going to get cold so I 'll have to feed Wanda.

John will get upset if his food's not hot. He loves

hot food. I ... I can warm it up when he gets home. It won't be as good. Warmed over food. Bad as left overs. But that way he can at least still have it hot. He's late and Wanda has to eat. I have to feed her now, still he can have hot food - even if not as good - if I warm it up when he gets home. Home. Hot food. For you, John. I can warm it up for you.

The gate made its noise.

Mabel held her breath. She did not like the shaking in her knees. Her knees were too big to shake.

I'm not going to make a fool of myself jumping for the window this time. All I have to do is wait. If it's John I'll hear his shoes on the stairs. All I have to do is wait.

She smiled as she ladled out Wanda's food.

Just in time, she thought. Just in time. It's still hot. She giggled.

Downstairs the door slammed.

No. Oh No.

Mabel listened.

Nothing.

She listened.

No creaking stairs.

No feel of his pulling on the bannister as he carefully trod one step at a time.

Nothing.

No.

Oh, no.

Wanda was able to get through her meal without speaking. Mabel never had to hear the question shrieking from her lips. Never had to tell the lie.

Wanda washed the dishes and went right to bed. She could not stay up. She could not stand it. She ate, washed the dishes, and went to bed without saying a word. But she could not stop what was going on inside her head. She could not silence the awful words.

Where's Daddy?

228

That's all she wanted to know.

Where's Daddy?

She did not want to know at all, but she wanted not to have to ask the question, the unanswerable, not-want-to-be-answered question.

Where's Daddy?

19

Mabel was thankful for her daughter. Thankful for her silence. Thankful for her early departure to bed. To leave her alone in the night. Staring out the window. She could see the whole cement walkway. It was lighted from the gate to the downstairs apartment by the streetlight. From the downstairs apartment to the front of her stairs, the light from windows kept it illuminated.

She watched. She did not eat. Lord knows she could skip a meal.

She waited. She did not acknowledge until the lights had gone out in all the other windows, till she could see only that part of the walk illuminated by the streetlight, that he was not coming.

So. Here it is.

Here it is.

Oh God.

Please.

Oh.

Where is he?

When will he come home?

Oh.

My God.

Please.

She left her vigil only to go to the bathroom.

Once.

In all the night.

She could not think. All she could do, all she could do, was wait.

When Wanda came down for breakfast her eyes asked the question though her voice did not.

She was so good to me last night, thought Mabel. I can't keep the child under a strain like this.

"Your Daddy didn't come home last night," she said. "I haven't heard anything from him, but I think he's alright. I'm sure he'll be home in a day or two."

That's what I'm scared of, thought Wanda. Lord, Jesus, that's what I'm scared of now.

Mabel managed to get Wanda off to school and herself off to work without thinking.

The whole day only one time - and then for but an instant - did her mind betray her.

I hope he's there when I get home.

But he was not.

Wanda was listless, sleepwalking through every movement.

Mabel faced another day without eating and another night without sleep except that about four AM her head crashed to the table and remained there until six AM when she awoke.

She got through the day without knowing how and returned home to let her eyes ask Wanda the question her mouth was afraid to utter.

"Daddy's not home yet," said Wanda.

"Well ... soon," said Mabel and hugged her daughter and patted her.

The next day was Friday.

He did not come then or Friday night either.

Early Saturday afternoon Mabel sat staring out the window when the familiar hat atop the familiar head appeared over the front gate.

She stood up and walked to the window. She pressed her fingertips against the glass. Her eyes adjusted to the distance and locked him in perfect focus.

He was having some trouble opening the gate. From where she stood Mabel could not hear what he was saying, but his lips were moving and his face was making exaggerated expressions. There was no doubt he was talking. But to whom? Since no person was in sight he had to be talking to the gate.

At last it swung open and John stumbled through it. Several steps into the yard he turned and looked at the gate as if recognizing he was supposed to close it. He quickly abandoned the idea, waved at the gate with a downward thrust of his free hand - his other clutched a brown, paper bag - turned away from the fence and staggered forward.

He tripped, ran, stumbled down the sidewalk, then off the sidewalk across the patch of dirt, and up into the wall of the Cork's house. He leaned against the wall, supporting himself by the point of one shoulder.

Now that he was closer Mabel could see him more clearly. The lower part of his face was covered by a thick, beard stubble. His clothes were crumpled and stained. Mabel could almost hear him belching as the Cork's outer wall supported him by the point of his shoulder. His lips and face worked in oversize expressions. Mabel leaned forward and tried to hear and read his lips at the same time, by the combination grasping what he was saying.

"Shit.

"Shi-it.

"Damn right.

"Shi-i-it."

He shook his head and laughed. He kept shaking his head.

"Oo-ooowhee, I gotta pee, Oo-ooowhee, I gotta pee."

Clumsily he stuck the bag into one of his coat pockets.

With both hands free he began to reach for his pants fly.

No, said Mabel silently. Please don't John. Please

232

no.

It took him many seconds but finally he got two buttons open.

He reached into the opening with his right hand.

Please John don't. No. Please John.

He pulled out his long, limp penis. He held it with his fist.

With his left hand he pushed himself off the wall and stood swaying in independent suspension for at least a minute. When he had gained a modicum of stability he pointed his penis at the wall.

The yellow liquid spurted against the wall. John started laughing.

"Oo-oowhee, lookit me pee. Oo-oowhee, lookit me pee."

The urine made a splattering noise as it splashed against the wall and onto John Brockerton's clothes.

"Pee the shit outa this mothafucka. Pee the SHIT OUT OF IT!"

He began moving his penis right to left and back again, urine flying and splashing.

"I'm gon' saw this mothafuckin' house down. Saw the motha-fucka down."

He laughed loudly.

"Shit.

"Shi-it!"

When he finished he pushed his penis back into his pants but did not attempt to fasten the buttons.

He pulled the paper bag out of his pocket and brought it to his lips. He turned it up and sucked greedily.

He burped as he took the bag away from his mouth. He started to return it to his pocket, thought better of it and once more lifted it to his open mouth. After a long, slurping gulp during which miraculously not a drop of liquid spilled, he managed, finally, with much misdirection to stuff the bag back into his pocket.

He turned, putting his shoulders at right angles to the wall of the Cork's house. Standing, facing his porch with the Hunter's porch below it, he kept his feet planted while his body wove.

He belched.

"Aah," he said.

His neck unsteadily raised his head and tilted it up toward his porch.

Like a sailor shipboard on a heavy sea he stood swaying, his head tottering on top of his neck as he tried to focus on his porch twenty feet above the ground.

"Where's the bitch at," he said.

Mabel felt all the strength and will sapped from her body.

"Where's the fuckin', fat bitch at?"

He reached into his fly, pulled out his penis, and brandished it in the air.

"You gon' git yours, you fat, fuckin', sloppy bitch - you gon' git it all," he bellowed.

He dropped his penis which hung outside his pants as he pitched forward, somehow with an extended foot preventing his body from collapsing to the ground. He managed to career ahead, talking as he went.

"You know what I'm 'on do to the motha-fuckas - you hear that? To the MO-THA FUCK-AS! MOTHA FUCKAS! Goddamn right!

"You know what I'm 'on do? I'm gon kick they mothafuckin' asses. That's right - kick they motha-fuckin' asses! You hear me? You hear me - you mothafuckin' dogs!"

He had a hard time turning to head for the stairs, but he kept his feet and eventually reached the railing, holding onto it with both hands.

"Aha, I gotcha now," he said, slobbering over his

234

chin and onto the front of his shirt, thick stringy saliva. "I gotcha now you motha-fucka.

"Bitch!

"Bitch, I'm comin' up these goddamn stairs!

"You fat 'ho! You mothafuckin' fat 'ho, I'm gon' come up these sonofabitchin', mothafuckin' stairs and beat the cock-suckin' shit out of yo fat, jelly-roll ass!"

He laughed, he laughed for a long time as he clung to the bannister.

Then he put one foot on the first step. "Ready or not," he said, "here I comes! Mama and daughter, butter ball one and butter ball two, big Miss Pumpkin, and little Miss Pumpkin," he surged up the steps, slowly, but with much awkward deliberation, one step at a time. "Ready or not, here I comes. To whip yo' asses. To teach you who's the boss. To beat the motha-fuckin' shit out o' you. Here I comes. Ready or not."

When at last he reached his door he beat on it.

"Open this motha-fucka up," he shouted. "I'm here to beat yo' fat asses. Open up the goddamn do'. You know what you got comin' to you."

Mabel heard Wanda sobbing behind her. But she could not help herself. She bowed to the inevitable. She opened the door.

20

Wynfried Wenders sat at her kitchen table staring at Charles Stuart, who sat across from her. She shook her head.

"Mrs. Brockerton and the girl," she said.

"Wanda," said Charles.

"Yes, Wanda," said Wynfried. "They are not the question. Wanda had the one problem. Nothing before. Nothing since."

Charles nodded.

"And they help," continued Wynfried. "Wanda brings us more information about the neighborhood than you can imagine - and Mrs. Brockerton. Well, we just couldn't schedule our *wimmin's work* without her."

Charles nodded and chuckled at her allusion to the invaluable work of the Corner's women.

"But, John," she went on. She shook her head. "This can't go on. This is the Corner, Mr. Stuart."

"Well, you know John," began Mr. Stuart. "He ... has his periods."

"His ... periods ... as you call them, are intolerable. This is the Corner."

"Yes, Ma'am," said Charles. "I understand. I think Wellington and I can do something about it -"

"Think?"

"Yes, Ma'am, I know. I know. Thinking is not enough. I agree. But let me tell you this. For our security. We need him. He's invaluable.

"When he's drunk as a skunk?"

"No, but -"

"Mr. Stuart, I'm just going to tell you this. The ladies have come to a conclusion on this. And Mr. Brockerton's past behavior shall no longer be tolerated. I

236

hope you and Mr. Cork will take that message to heart. This last episode was ...."

"One too many," he said.

"Right."

He nodded.

"We won't let the ladies down," he said.

21

One of the things Charles had learned from Mackenzie Sweet was the importance of being careful. Mackenzie had always stressed that it was never possible to be too careful. That is why he had lived so long.

Especially, he watched people. He said a person had to be more careful in Wimbey's Corner than elsewhere because everyone had secrets. Sometimes people were not careful enough and if they lived in the Corner Mackenzie found out those secrets.

He winked at Charles and laughed. He knew everybody's secrets he said. He knew secrets people didn't even know they had.

Charles had blushed. He had not said a word. Being careful meant just that. His face flushed and swelled but his lips did not open.

Mackenzie had watched him. Grinning, the old man had popped a lime-drop in his mouth and said, "I'll give you a for instance."

Charles had braced himself and waited.

"Look at old Fends Wenders up there. I calls him old, but he ain't nothin' but a boy next t'me. A pipsqueak. But look at him. His wife, Wynfried, says he got took ill all of a sudden. Had t'take him away to the hospital.

"Mmmhmm. He been in the hospital two years. Two years, you hear me? Now what's gon' keep you in the hospital two years? After two years you either supposed to be well or dead. But Fends Wenders is still settin' up there in the hospital. You ask Miz Wenders how he's doin', she'll say, 'Oh, he's about the same.' About the same after two years. He, he. Now you know somethin's supposed t'happen in all that time.

"You know how much that woman love Fends. The

238

sun rise and set where he walk. The man can do no wrong. But she don't go to visit him but once a week. Somethin' strike you about that? I'm talkin' secrets now, secrets and how t'keep 'em. You got t'be careful. Look'a here. You know of a hospital what's got only one visitin' day and that is the same day every week? Say he's out of town because of specialists and cain't nobody visit but family. You ever hear her say what town? Listen to me, Charles, now listen to me. I'm talkin' about what folks don't know.

"The Wenders about the most respectable folk in Evanston. They don't do nothin' what ain't proper. Electa almost spoiled that when she popped up pregnant, but that didn't last. She got married and to the most somebody, colored young man in Evanston. No sir, you don't expect nothin' but righteousness out o' them Wenders.

"Do you remember what old man Wimbey used t'say was visitin' day for his niece at Kankakee?"

"Sunday," said Charles.

"Sunday, echoed Mackenzie. "What day is it Miz Wenders go t'visit Fends?"

"Sunday?"

"'Sunday.' Ain't no question mark. Sunday. She been doin' it every week for two years. You know she go on the train cause she got that coal dust smell on her when she come back - and when do that last Illinois Central get in Sunday night?"

"Eight," said Charles, stunned. "Eight."

Mackenzie cackled. "I told you, boy. I'm talkin' about secrets. You got t'be careful.

"Kankakee ain't the all of it. Did you notice Fends actin' strange in the head before he went off to the hospital?"

"No."

"Me neither. Funny thing, though. They was makin' preparations weeks in advance. Like somebody

239

knowed he was gon' lose his jelly beans though he was actin' just as proper as me and you. Now how much sense do that make?"

"None."

"You right. None. Unless."

The old man had chuckled and rocked back in his chair. A generous smile had spread across his features. He had closed his eyes.

"Unless what," demanded Charles.

The centenarian had rocked forward.

"Unless ... it was predictable."

He had spoken in subdued tones.

"Predictable?" Charles had not understood.

Mackenzie had maintained his modulated volume. "It's some diseases what has predictable stages."

Charles had stared at Mr. Sweet.

The old man had winked.

"Oh no."

"Secrets," had said Mackenzie. "You got t'be careful. Look at stupid-ass Wellington. The boy think I don't like him. I ain't got nothin' against Wellington except he too damn dumb. Now, there's a man with secrets what needs protectin'. He think he protectin' 'em by keepin' 'em locked up in the house all day."

"You mean Genuine and Ivory?"

"He got somebody else locked up in there?"

Charles had lowered his eyes.

Mackenzie had laughed. "Sometimes you act simple, too," he had said. "He think if he keep 'em locked up won't nobody know what's goin' on.

"You know why he don't let that little girl play with nobody?"

Charles had shaken his head.

"Cause kids don't only play. They talks. And little Ivory, there, would ask somebody's daughter, 'Do yo Daddy

240

do this to you?'"

Charles' lower jaw dropped open.

"That's right. That's why they don't even let that child walk home from school alone. Walks up every day t'meet her and carry her on home.

Mackenzie had slid his eyes over at Charles. "You got secrets, too," he had said.

He never mentioned another word about it.

But Charles was very, very careful. Appearances were of first importance.

His shirt, his underwear, his socks, clean every day. His clothes neatly pressed and his tie unrumpled. A spit shine on his shoes. He knew how a dignified businessman should dress. High-crowned hat. He knew.

On weekends he oiled and rubbed his briefcase to a high gloss. When he closed his door on Monday mornings and started down the long run of stairs he was a man to handle the world. Once he turned onto Tary and started the walk to the El station he was the mark of efficiency. Crisp. Clean. Competent. By Princeton Avenue, one block from the El Station, he had joined the swarms of executives headed for Chicago. Except for color he was indistinguishable from them.

He picked up a *Tribune* at the downstairs stand next to the ticket booth, marched up the stairs and stood on the platform with his peers waiting for the 7:28 train.

On the train and seated he devoted himself to the newspaper, scanning the news stories first, then turning to the financial pages and giving them his full attention until it was time to get off at Madison.

Off the train he joined the streams of busy people flowing across the concrete plain between windowed massifs blotting out the sky.

He walked, briskly, all the way to Michigan Avenue where the air fresh from the lake always delivered its greeting. The foot traffic was much sparser there and his immaculate reflection bounced back at him from gleaming marble cornerstones and the fresh-washed windows of the city's most elegant shops.

He nodded to the doorman at the Hilton, turned under the awning and entered the Hotel's elegant foyer. He strode across the lobby and disdaining the elevator took the stairs to the mezzanine. He made his way to the men's room where he placed his briefcase on a sink, took off his hat and observed himself in the mirror. Large eyes. Spotlessly clean face. Smooth shaven. He ran the fingers of his right hand over his cheeks and chin, under his jaw line. No resistance. Not one trace of stubble. He washed and dried his hands.

He opened his briefcase and took out a freshly pressed, neatly folded grey smock. He closed the briefcase. He took off his suit coat and laid it over the briefcase. He put on the smock and tied the cloth belt securely, but not pinching, around the waist. He observed the perfect hang of the smock in the mirror. He picked up his suit coat and hat in one hand and briefcase in the other. He walked to the restroom vestibule where he hung his suit coat on a hanger and placed his hat on a hook, and the briefcase on its stand. He reached into his briefcase and pulled out a clothes brush and a clean, white towel. He put the clothes brush into his smock pocket and draped the towel over his left forearm which he held across his midriff. He fastened his briefcase and made a final trip before the mirrors. In work as in all things appearances were important.

TOMMY'S STORY

1

Every sailor who could find a reason to get on deck lined the ship's railing and leaned into the ocean spray, straining for a glimpse of the fabled city. So accustomed were the blue jackets to the short, choppy wash of the waves they did not feel the ship's rolling. They concentrated their attentions on the horizon ahead of them, oblivious of their hands wet from the ocean splash, tight on the railings.

The tanker rode evenly through the grayish-blue sea. Even though she had long ago discharged her burden of oil, the running flanks of whitecaps did not trouble her measured passage. Gulls wheeled, and rose, and dropped, and hung in the air, as landward, heaps of green hills, surf breaking at their feet, continued to shield the long-awaited view from the eyes of the eager young men.

Though the air was cool and the ocean water cold, and though Tommy Brown and Billy Jones wore only sleeveless white undershirts above their work trousers, neither was uncomfortable. Tommy stood six feet tall. His naturally peanut-butter brown skin, burned a deep, copper-red by the sun, covered a solid muscular build. His kinky hair, parted at the side, was a light-brown, sandy color. A pencil thin moustache, shaped like a reclining "L" on each side of his nostrils, adorned his upper lip. He squinted as he peered at the coast line.

Beside him, Billy was taller, six feet, three inches, skinny, though the wiry muscles on his long bones were strong. Billy's complexion was a dark, dark brown. He brushed his black hair straight back.

Their young muscles tightened and flexed with the rising and falling of the ship. All their senses focused toward the east, toward the jumble of hills and crashing waves they fast approached.

245

"Yo-ho!" The joyful shout erupted from the lookout high on the bridge.

"There it is." Tommy let go of the railing, clamping down on Billy's shoulder with his right hand, pointing with his left.

An orange shaft leaped into an opening between two hills, waves slamming into its base, its top piercing the sky.

"That's it, that's it, huh," said Billy.

The voice of one of their crewmen sang. "Hot damn, the Golden Gate Bridge!"

The space between the two hills slowly but steadily widened. Greater and greater portions of the bridge spanned the growing gulf. Every man knew it from pictures and postcards. Even though it was newly built, its familiarity was startling, its simple clarity, striking. All across the deck sailors stared, transfixed.

The spell lasted only a minute. Jubilation erupted as the battle-painted tanker rode the flow of water rushing toward the landmark.

Tommy and Billy looked briefly at each other, then turned their attention to the harbor they were entering.

"Alcatraz is somewheres up there, ain't it," said Tommy.

"Yeah, yeah, it's supposed to be," said Billy. "The rock. They call it the rock."

"Yeah, it 'posed to be a island. Ain't nobody never 'scaped off'n it, neither," said Tommy. "Hey, ain't that it over there?"

"I don't know. Maybe. Hey - hey, Tommy. Look."

On the starboard side of the ship, the city rose from the sea. White. Pastels. Houses, shops, buildings, one after another, white and pastel rising in hills from the sea.

"It's a fairy-city," said Billy, "from a fairy-tale."

"San-Fran-Frisco," said Tommy.

The U.S. Ship Monongahela slipped easily through

246

the waters of the Bay bringing her crew home from war. The date was February 16, 1942. Twenty-one days would pass before the Monongahela would sail again.

2

Tommy, Billy, and the other colored sailors were busy packing. Some sang. Many laughed and joked. A few talked non-stop. Energy and excitement electrified the tight space.

Tommy whistled. "Hey, Billy," he said, "you sure you won't spend just one night with me in Frisco? Man, we could have a time."

Billy stopped his quiet, methodical packing.

"No, thanks, man." He looked at Tommy, " I can't lose one minute, one second, getting back to my little Marva. We got twenty days. And I wanta spend fifteen, sixteen with my Marva."

"Okay," said Tommy. "I was in love once, too. Got over that, though. I'm free. Free like them seagulls. Like them - you 'member them flyin' fish - like that. Free like that. I'm a free man and I'm gon' be out on the town TONIGHT. Get ready womens, your lover-man is on the way! "I was married once. I was in love. No days, jack. No mo' days like that! Why should I make one woman miserable when I can make so many happy? "

Billy finished packing. He began putting on his navy blues. " You gon' spend your whole furlough in Frisco?"

Tommy laughed. "Me? I'm just gon' go where the wind blow. I told you - I'm free!"

"Ain't no nigga in the world free," said Red Mule.

Red Mule got part of his nickname from his literally red, almost orange, dense hair. The rest of it came from the broad shoulders and powerful build carried by his five-foot, ten-inch frame. A few freckles adorned his light-brown skin.

He butted into Tommy and Billy's conversation.

248

"But a nigga can sho' have a good time on leave in San Francisco - hot dog!"

He broke into a song. "The buzzard took the monkey for a ride in the air."

Tommy and Billy joined in finger popping on the next line.

"The monkey thought that everything was on the square.

"The buzzard tried to drop the monkey off his back,
"The monkey grabbed him by the neck and said,
"Now listen, jack!
"Straighten up and fly right!
"Straighten up and fly right!"

The three young men burst into laughter, clapping each other on their shoulders and backs, too carried away to finish the song.

Mule, tears of laughter in his eyes, looked at Billy. "Hey, man, you sure you won't come with us? Even for just one night? We gon' have a real good time. "

"I know," said Billy. " I just got t'get back t'my baby."

"Alright, fool," said Tommy, "me and the Mule won't miss yo' behin'

"As long as plenty womens, we can find."

He and Mule laughed together, winking conspiratorially.

Completely dressed, Billy fastened his ditty-bag, put his cap on his head, and picked up his pea-coat. He tucked the pea-coat under his left arm, and lifted his ditty bag with his right hand.

"I'll see y'all in about twenty days," he said. " I don't wanta come back and find y'all in the brig."

Red Mule and Tommy laughed.

"If we ain't, it won't be cause we ain't tried," said Tommy.

"Be careful down there in blip."

Billy turned quickly and made his way through the den of festive sailors.

Tommy and Red Mule strolled along Market Street, their gear safely locked in the bus depot.

"Oh, will you look at the wimmins," said Mule.

Tommy did not say anything. He grinned. He could not think of a thing to say as his eyes popped out of his head, as his neck swivelled his head around, first to the left, then to the right. He could not think of a thing to say. Every now and then he managed to suppress his grin long enough to let out a long wolf whistle.

The two made a neat pair, long and lean in navy blues, bell-bottom trousers, white caps cocked on their heads. Mule's broad shoulders accented Tommy's tighter physique.

"Hey, Mule," said Tommy. "It's time t'pick us up some chicks. Where we gon' do that?"

"I don't know," said Mule. "Ray said somethin' about Filmore. Filmore's the place to go."

"Where's that at?"

"Tommy Brown, how I'm 'on know that?"

They continued their stroll down Market, double-taking everything in skirts, laughing, occasionally breaking into a shuffling dance for two or three steps.

The soldier who approached them wore his olive-drab uniform with pride. He strutted as he walked, his face stiff and unmoving. He was young, his face so smooth after shaving its dark brown sheen almost matched the spit-shine on his shoes.

Tommy spread both his arms in an expansive gesture of greeting. "Hey, Army," he said, "we just off the ship and wants t'have us a good time. You know where Filmore

Street is at?"

The soldier stopped and broke into a wide grin. "Private, first-class, Theadoshius Williams, Houston Texas, at yo' service, Navy. I'm on mah way t'Filmore maself."

Tommy and Red Mule quickly extended their hands for a shake.

"Tommy Brown, Petty Officer, second class, Tuscompany, Alabama."

"George Johnson, Petty Officer, first class, Little Rock, Arkansas - just call me Mule."

They shook hands.

They stood in a triangle.

"Well, you say you goin' there," said Tommy. "You know where it's at?"

Theadoshius laughed. "Was there last night and the night before." He winked. "The finest young things this side of the Mississippi - and loves a uniform!"

All three laughed uproariously, bending over and clutching themselves with glee.

"Hey, uh sailors, y'all wouldn't have a cigarette, would you?"

Tommy produced a pack from his breast pocket and flipped one to Theadoshius.

"Thanks." Theadoshius looked at the cigarette appreciatively, smoothing it between the thumb and forefinger of his left hand as he held it with his right.

"Ca-all for Phillip Mo-oriss," he said, mimicking the famous commercial. "Good cigarette. I likes 'em."

He put the cigarette in his mouth. Tommy gave him a light.

Theadoshius took a deep drag and exhaled. "Aah," he said, "that feels better."

"Yeah, we just goes down t'this corner here, and we can catch the trolley there and ride it all the way to Filmore. Stick with me y'all. I knows the places to hit."

251

Tommy and Mule gave each other a quick look, overjoyed with their good luck.

The three servicemen walked off, the soldier blowing large, sophisticated smoke rings which floated slowly over their heads.

Outside the door of the Club Louise the soldier and the two sailors huddled briefly.

"Now, the thing t'do when we gits in there," said Theadoshius, "is to order a set-up. The chicks really likes it when they sees a bottle and the mixes settin' on a table. Then, they knows you ain't cheap, you know. So we'll order a set-up, and I'll scout around for the most terrifyin' chicks in the place."

Agreed, the three entered into the bopping, smoky darkness.

Theadoshius ordered a set-up of Gilbert's gin with gingerale and got up to cruise the club to see if there were any game young women he remembered from his earlier nights in attendance.

Mule and Tommy went halfs on the set-up when it came. They were keeping their eyes peeled for Theadoshius to see if he had come up with anything, but he had disappeared.

Suddenly, he materialized out of a thick cloud of smoke. He sat down and poured himself a drink, heavy on the gin.

"All new talent tonight," he said, "but the joint is jumpin'."

He took a deep drink. "Hot damn," he said. "Gilbert's 'll curl the hair on yo chest." He popped his fingers to the music.

Tommy scanned the room, his bright eyes still

252

unable to focus clearly in the dim lounge.

Mule leaned back, letting the liquor penetrate his bones.

The way the fog sometimes parts at sea, the dense smoke separated slightly, and in the V of unpolluted air Tommy saw across the room, a soft, heart-shaped face, the color of ripe peaches, eyes large and liquid black.

Her eyes caught his through the break in the haze, and as his teeth broke out in a spontaneous grin, her lips formed a quiet smile.

A crush of bodies and a surge of smoke obscured her from his view. He stood.

Mule looked up. "Hey, spook, where you goin'," he asked.

"I just saw me somethin' fine on the other side of this room," he said. "I'm goin' over there."

"Okay," said Theadoshius, "but these Frisco chics is hep. It don't hurt t'play it cool, 'less they thank you just got off the farm. Cause they don't do nothin' but play with country boys."

Tommy heard the street wisdom in the voice. Reluctantly, he sat down. "You 'bought right, The'doshus, man," he said. He took a drink of Gilbert's. "You 'bout right. I'm 'on take my time with that little filly. But she's gon' be mine tonight!"

All three men hooted together and turned up their glasses.

The long, chocolate woman who appeared beside their table was beautiful.

"Y'all got room for some company," she said.

"Is fat meat greasy," said Theadoshius. "Sit yo' fine self down."

"Pardon his manners," said Tommy. "But my name is Tommy Brown. And I don't never fail t'introduce myself to a lady. And if you ain't a lady, the Pope ain't Catholic."

253

She sat down and reached across the table for her drink, letting her hand touch Tommy's as he handed it to her.

"Barbara," she said, "Barbara Walker."

"Well, I know we gon' boogey tonight," said Tommy. "By the way, this here's The'doshus, and Red Mule."

"Pleased ... I'm sure," said Barbara.

Tommy looked, for an instant, away into the gloom, but he could not see across the crowded floor. He could not see the face.

Theadoshius had moved his chair up to Barbara's. He sat hunched over, his elbow propping him on the table in front of her.

"Look here, Darlin'," he said, 'you here all alone - somebody as red-hot as you?"

Mule poured himself another glass of gin. He figured he was out of the running.

Tommy sipped his gin. He was torn. The face across the room had enchanted him. He wanted that girl. He wanted to meet her. At the same time, Barbara was fine, and he had received very clear indications she was interested in him. The other girl was still an unknown. There was no guarantee - if he could ever get over there and still maintain the appearance of being cool - she would take notice of him. He did not know if she were there with someone. Still ... her face ... parting the smoke.

He glanced at Barbara. Theadoshius was leaned all up into her. She flicked her eyes over at Tommy, smiling slyly. Yeah, he thought, she was his if he wanted her. And no doubt about it, she was fine. He sipped his gin.

"What you say, Mule," he said, "we let these two alone for awhile. Cause when we gets back, we gon' break this lovey-dovey up."

Mule bolted down the last of the gin in his glass.

"Sound good t'me."

Barbara looked over at Tommy. "Don't y'all stay gone all night, now," she said.

"Yeah, hurry back," said Theadoshius, not taking his eyes off the woman.

"Don't worry 'bout that," said Tommy. "We ain't crazy." He smiled at Barbara.

She smiled back.

Red Mule pulled on Tommy's sleeve as they pushed their way through the crowd.

"Hey, why you open the door like that fo' that nigger? You done gone blind? All that time at sea done lost you all yo' stuff? Couldn't you see she got eyes for you?"

"Hey, Mule, she be there when we get back. This ain't gon' do nothing but help me out. All the while we gone, she gon' be wonderin' what I'm doin'. Meanwhile, I know what she doin'. She ain't doin nothin' but messin' up that soldier's min'. Makin' his peter hard. Sides, Mule, didn't I tell you I spotted me a fine young filly I wanted to see?"

"I ain't gon' try t'outguess you, Tommy. I done seen you operate befo'. Still, it do seem crazy t'me just t'walk away an' leave a woman with a fool talkin' his smack ninety miles a minute."

"Well," said Tommy, pulling a cigarette out of his breast pocket, "long as he keep talkin', he cain't do nothin' else."

He stopped to light his cigarette, shook out the match, and dropped it on the floor.

People were up jitterbugging. The two men had to stay close to the wall as they circled the lounge.

She was sitting at a table with four other people. There were three women altogether. The two men were civilians. He stopped where he could watch her. He had to try to figure out if she were with a man. He hunched Mule

255

in the shoulder, and nodded at her. "That's her," he said.

Mule swallowed heavily. "I see what you means." He paused, feeling the evening slipping out of his grasp. "Look, I got t'look out for myself." Mule moved off into the swarming people.

The girl was not looking in Tommy's direction. Most of the time she kept her eyes on the other people in her group. Just every now and then she looked out over the dance floor. Tommy could not figure out who was with whom at her table. None of them moved, and the two men sat in the middle, one woman to their left, two to their right. She sat on the outside. He became convinced she would never see him where he stood. He had to catch her eye again.

The band was getting ready to play a new tune. A tall, leggy woman stood patting her foot next to Tommy. He touched her arm.

"I just got off my ship today," he said, "I been looking' all night and I ain't seen nobody as pretty as you, so I's 'shamed t'ax. But could you spare a poor sailor a dance?"

She laughed. "I'm glad t'do my part for the war effort. Specially with a handsome devil like you."

They twirled out onto the polished wooden floor.

The woman loved to dance. It showed in her every movement. The music penetrated her body and set it to flowing. Her feet twinkled over the floor, skipping and tapping. Her hips swayed sensually. Her face lit up with the joy of movement. Her dress flew out from her in a graceful arch.

Tommy led her into rhythmic steps with consummate ease. His eyes sparkled at his partner's ability. He rose up on his toes, clicked his heels, and set his feet to dancing. He leaned into her, and held her out, and whirled her through spinning turns. He picked her up, catching her first on one hip, then the other. He tossed her into the air, caught her, and flung her out again through dazzling, arrogant whirls. Their broad grins flashed in the darkness and sweat shone on their foreheads.

On a floor full of fine dancers, a space cleared around them, and heads turned to the music taking flight in them.

When the band stopped, applause followed the pair as they walked of the floor, hand in hand.

"Sailor, if you ever wants a dancin' partner, you don't have t'look no farther than me," she said. "My name's Finnie-Marie Atwater, and you'll find me here every night the joint's open. I've danced with the best, and I ain't found none come close t'you."

Tommy was open and expansive. "Well, thank you, Finnie-Marie. But dancin' with somebody who can dance like you ain't somethin' a man gits t'do everyday. And when he gits the chance, he's got t'live up to it. Tommy, Tommy Brown is the name. And I hopes you saves a dance for me everynight. And if I ain't here to have it, then you just saves 'em all up for me, and maybe one night we'll dance the night away."

"I can't wait, Tommy Brown. I can't wait."

"Thank you for the dance, Finnie-Marie. Thank you very much."

"Don't you worry, Tommy. It's a lot more where that one came from. And I'll be waiting."

Tommy smiled at her then stepped away. He looked up for the girl and found her eyes waiting for his.

He started moving purposefully through the throngs of people. Many wanted to stop him and shake his hand, or plant a kiss on his cheek, to tell him what a wonderful dancer he was and how long it had been since they had seen anything like that. He smiled broadly at them, and laughed with them, and shook hands and hugged women. But all the while he was fixed on the little woman sitting at the table with her four friends.

When he caught her eye, she smiled openly at him, and feigning shyness, looked away. But she returned her glance quickly, smiling with the promise that there was a secret between them.

Tommy was no more than three good steps from the table when the band started up again. One of the men at the table asked her to dance. It was obvious she agreed only with great reluctance. The people at her table would not have understood had she refused. She waved at Tommy as she made her way out onto the dance floor. He waved back. He was willing to wait through one more song.

The music was slow and romantic, just right for holding close, for swinging and swaying. Tommy felt a loss as the crowds of dancers shielded her from his view.

He was surprised to see Barbara standing straight in front of him.

"I thought you was comin' right back," she said.

"I am. I am. Just givin' soldier-man time to hand out his line and git it over with."

"Sure of yourself, ain't you?"

"No. No, I just thought, let him shoot his best shot. After all, if he's the one you wanted, wasn't nothin' I could do about it."

"Well, he's not the one I wanted. And the only way I could get over here to you was t'ask him t'dance with me, and then t'send him back after a drink."

"You done good. You done real good."

"Don't you like me?"

Tommy looked at Barbara. She was slim and curvy. Beautiful. Just beautiful. She licked her lips and Tommy knew she wanted to be kissed. Her perfume smelled good, and she was so close he could feel the heat of her body. He had been at sea a long time. He could do nothing to still the erection that pumped up between his legs.

"Hold me, Baby," she said. "And let's dance slow."

She was softly into his arms, and cheek to cheek, tightly entwined, they moved smoothly out onto the dance floor.

Tommy's eyes searched for the girl, but his body enclosed in Barbara's silken softness, responding to her grinding hips, was not concerned about the girl, wanted only more of the warmth it felt, wanted only to press more and more into Barbara.

"You know I'm all yours, don't you," she said.

Tommy felt hot. " I don't know if I can handle as much woman as you," he said.

She rolled her pelvis onto, up, over, and around his penis. "Don't tell me that," she said. "Don't tell me that."

Promise of relief from months at sea surged through Tommy's body. He held tightly to Barbara.

I want to find that girl, he thought. I want to talk to her. I want to meet her.

Barbara's fingers were on the back of his neck.

But that girl ain't here in my arms. That girl ain't the one who's bein' so good to me. There was no doubt in his mind. Barbara could be his that night. He wanted her badly. Her lips brushed his cheek.

The girl is so pretty. Her face was etched into his mind.

She is pretty, but I'll just get to meet her tonight. I'll spend the night here with her and her friends. If I'm lucky, I'll get a goodnight kiss. If I'm lucky. The rest will have to wait for later. But I can have this woman I've got here, right now. Tonight. She's beautiful. And she's all mine. I can get that pussy tonight. I know I can. I been at sea a long time, and it's so good, so good.

He pulled back and looked at Barbara. She had a beautiful face. Her lips were wet and full. As he leaned back to look at her, she leaned back, too, letting her pelvis rock forward to meet his. He pulled her shoulders into him then, his face sweaty against hers.

I can always come back. I can always find that girl another night.

"I ain't got no place t'stay tonight," he said, huskily.

"I now a nice hotel. Close."

When the band stopped, he said, "Let's go."

He took her by the hand and led her through the milling people. As he was about to go through the door, he looked back over his shoulder. The girl's eyes locked on him. The smile had left her face. He grinned at her. She saw it, but did not respond. He waved at her. She did not wave back.

3

Tommy did not sleep much that night. Things had not turned out as he'd expected. "Barbara" had turned out not to be Barbara at all. After an explosion of violence and a bout of nausea, Tommy had fled into the night and spent the early morning hours walking the streets filled with self-loathing and disgust.

At noon the next day he went to the bus depot. He and Mule had agreed to meet there.

He found Mule at the lunch counter with a hot-dog and a coke.

He sat down beside him.

Mule looked over at him, bent over, and broke out laughing. His mouth was full of food, and he had to fight to keep it in. When he had almost finished chewing and swallowing, he banged his fist down on the counter. "Look like you done had one hell of a night! Look like that big Barbara 'bout wore yo ass out!"

He chuckled and took a drink of coke.

"Tell me 'bout it, Big Time," he said.

"Mule. I don't want to hear about it. I don't want to talk about it. Cool?"

Mule looked over at Tommy. His quick inspection told him Tommy was serious.

"Well, said Mule. "I know I had a good time last night. No place in the world like Frisco." He took a bite of hot-dog. "Mmhmm."

"You said it there," said Tommy. "No place in the world."

"Well," said Mule, his mouth full again. "What we gon' do tonight?"

"I don't know what *we* gon' do tonight," said Tommy, "but I ain't gon' stay in no Frisco."

"You ain't go stay in no Frisco? Well, what you gon' do, Big Time?"

"I don't know. Go t'Oakland. I heard they be boppin' in Oakland."

Mule laughed. "Well. You bop on over to Oakland. I know where it's at, Daddy. It's right here - in good, old San-Fan-Frisco. I know where it's at, cause I had it last night." He laughed again.

"Yeah? What happened after I seen you?"

"Hot-dog, Tommy. Let me tell you about it."

Red Mule told his tale of wild good luck and loving, of waking up in the morning with a beautiful, honey-colored sweetie lying beside him.

Tommy ate two hot-dogs, a swedish roll, and drank a root beer as he listened.

"Yeah, Big Time," said Mule, " she got up this moanin' and made me a breakfas - eggs, bacon, grits, coffee, toast, orange juice - Hot Dog! And when that was over - when that was over - don't y'know we got right back in the rack! Oh, what sweet lovin'. Darla. Darla-Anne. Hot Damn!" Mule could not stop grinning.

"I'm glad," said Tommy. He patted Mule on the back. "What you say we walk around town today, see the sights? Befo' I head over to Oakland. Befo' you gits back to yo little Darla-Anne." He smiled.

Mule laughed. "Sho. Sho 'nuff, Big Time."

They rode the cable car to Chinatown, walked around for an hour, rode the cable car down to Fisherman's Wharf where they ended up buying beers and watching the fishing boats. They got a cab to take them up to Coit Tower. They climbed it and looked out over the bay and the city.

"This sure is a beautiful place, ain't it," said Tommy.

"Yeah. It is. Look. Look over there. You can see the fog comin' in."

262

It was true. The fog was moving in from the ocean - up the seaward hills, cloaking them and lifting high above them. It was covering the great, red-orange bridge.

Tommy watched it for awhile, then turned around to look at the hills on the bay-side still bathed in sunlight. "Damn pretty," he said. " What did Billy say - like a fairy city. Like a fairy city.

"It is, too. In mo' ways than one."

Tommy had a good time in Oakland. He stayed three days. When he came back to San Francisco he went to Darla's. Mule had given him the address.

He walked up to the second floor apartment and knocked on the grey door marked "5."

Mule opened the door.

"Big Time," Mule beamed. "Darla, come here, I want you t'meet the man I been talkin' about so much."

"Wait," said Tommy. "Here." He thrust a brown paper bag into Mule's hands.

Mule looked down into the bag. "Champaign - zoot, zoot!"

Tommy broke into a big smile. "Genuine California," he said. "Nothin' but the best for the Reddest Mule in the Navy."

"Come on in here, Tommy," said Mule.

Tommy walked in. Mule closed the door.

Standing in front of Tommy was a little, yellow-colored woman, not more than five feet, one inch tall, with wavy black hair and a shy, small smile. She had a wispy figure with a big, heavy bathrobe draped over her tiny, soft curves.

"Oh, Mule," said Tommy. " What'd you tell me? You knew where it was at? Well, my man, you was right. Cause here it is. Right here."

He walked up to Darla, hugged her, and pecked her on her cheek.

"Man, uncork that champagne, and let's get t'gettin' it." He winked at Darla, "And, Mule - when you gets ready to let her go - let me be the first one to know."

"See what I mean," said Mule. "He just takes over."

Tommy walked into the kitchen and sat down at the table.

"Y'all got a victrola," he asked.

"Sho' do," said Darla. "Got a victrola and somethin' to go on it, too. Got some records by Duke Ellington, and Count Basie, and Ella Fitzgerald, got -"

"Hoy! Hoy!," said Tommy.

"Zoot! Zoot!," said Red Mule, taking the champagne bottle over to the sink.

"Let's hear somethin', then, you pretty, little gal," said Tommy.

Darla pulled some records out of a record holder. She took off the brown, paper covers.

Pop!

The cork exploding from the bottle startled Tommy and Darla. All three laughed.

Red Mule expertly caught the bubbling liquid in a glass. Quickly he filled three. He handed a glass each to Tommy and Darla. He raised his glass in a toast.

"To eighteen more days of freedom. Hep them be as sweet as these is."

"I say A-men to that," said Darla, and she gave Mule a look that surrendered her soul.

"Goodness gracious," said Tommy looking from one to the other. "Y'all gon' mess around here and fall in love." He drank to the toast.

"That's good stuff," he said.

"It sho' is," said Mule. "Thank you, Big Time."

"Yes, thank you, Tommy," said Darla.

"Anytime, anytime. Let's hear some o' that music."

Soon *A-Train* sparkled through the small flat.

Tommy had dinner with Darla and Red Mule. He thanked them, then left to ride the cable cars and walk around the city. In the darkness he stood on the towered hills looking at sprinkled lights and black waters. About midnight he went down to the bus depot, retrieved his belongings, and got on the bus for L.A.

He stayed a week in L.A., went to Las Vegas, to Nogales, Mexico; stopped off again in L.A., and got on a bus back north that stopped in San Francisco at eight PM on the last night of his leave.

There was one thing on his mind. An image. A heart-shaped face the color of ripe peaches, eyes large and liquid black.

He put his gear in a bus station locker and went into the station restroom where he spent thirty minutes getting his appearance as close to perfect as he could. When he was satisfied, he popped on his sailor cap and strode out the door.

He went to the Club Louise. It would be his last chance before they sailed. He had grinned and waved at her as he left. But she had not waved back. Her mouth had become a grim line. But, oh, before ... how she had smiled and laughed and called him with her eyes.

He got on the trolley. He sat down and looked out the window. He remembered Theadoshius. The army boy, The'doshus Williams from Houston, Texas. He should o' let The'doshus keep Barbara. Wouldn't that o' been the trick! As it was, Tommy thought, I was the one what got tricked.

He could not see much out of the window in the dark. Yep, he thought, I was the one what got tricked.

When Tommy got to the Louise he handed the man at the door a dollar. The man looked strangely at Tommy.

"What's that for," the man asked.

"Cover. Cover-charge," answered Tommy.

"Ain't no cover charge here," said the man. "Not for no servicemens. Never was."

"Well, I'll be damned," said Tommy outloud. He and Red Mule had each given Theadoshius a dollar so he could hit the man with their cover charge on the way in. "I'll be damned."

Inside the club was as loud, and as crowded and as smoky as he remembered. He could not see well in the gloom. It was a long time before he could distinguish faces. But he made the rounds. He walked over the whole club.

After a while he began to recognize a few faces, a few figures he had seen almost three weeks earlier. But there were only a few. He had no recollection of most of the people.

Every now and then the way a woman turned her head or the hue of a woman's complexion fluttered his heart. Yet rapidly and continually his hopes dissipated. He could not find the girl who had shared a secret with him in her smile.

Finally, he sat at a table by himself and tried to get down to the corner of a bottle of Gilbert's.

"Tommy Brown!"

He looked across his table, up the pair of long, swaying legs, up the rhythmically rocking torso, and into the vibrant, shining face of Finnie-Marie Atwater.

"Dancin' Lady," he said.

"Dancin' Man," she echoed.

"Zoot! Zoot!"

"Hoy! Hoy!"

"Did you save 'em up for me?"

"One for every night," she said.

He sprang up. "Feets don't fail me now."

She laughed. They made their way out onto the

gleaming boards and turned the place out. They danced until the band started packing up. They went home to her place, where they shared coffee, and kisses, their bodies easy and complete, and a deep, short, sleep. Tommy had to leave at six in the morning to get to the depot for his belongings. But he had her address, and she his. He kissed her lying in bed as he left. He told her how important it was to get mail at sea, and said he would write when he could.

He ran into Red Mule at the bus station, and they both ran into Billy on the way back to the ship. They were all glad to see each other, but each drawn into himself, too. They were on their way to board their ship. But their minds were not there. Their hearts were not there. Their hearts and minds were back where they had left them, in warm arms, touching sleepy lips. Their hearts and minds had not accepted the reality their bodies obeyed. Shore leave was over.

4

"AAOOHA! AAOOHA!" The loud, harsh horn belted out its alarm. The bosun's whistle sounded. The ship's talker enunciated loudly and clearly.

"General Quarters! General Quarters!"

The words were superfluous. All over the Monongahela sailors jumped hell-bent to their battle stations.

A lookout on one of the outriding destroyers had spotted the periscope. The word had gone to the whole fleet. The ships responded with a beautiful movement zigzagging in unison away from the menace while five destroyers zagged directly after it.

Tommy sat beside his gun. He was a pointer. He turned his head to watch the destroyers' pursuit.

"Watcha thank about that, boy, said the gunner's mate, who as the sighter, sat directly on the other side of the gun. He was a warrant officer named Pearson.

"Think about what?"

"Watcha thank about them tin cans gittin' right after that dirty, yellow, jap sub?"

"I think," said Tommy, "I hopes they gits him."

"I used to be on a tin-can," said the gunner's mate. "Don't know why'n hell I got orders to sail on this hunk o' junk."

He looked over at Tommy. "I guess they need some real seamen where they got stewards workin' guns. Hell, they don't want us to blow our own damn self outa the water. Somebody got t'be in charge." He wanted to talk. He did not want to watch the tin-cans. They reminded him of his lost chance for glory. He had been serving on a destroyer just ten months earlier.

Tommy tried very hard not to listen to Pearson. He

268

remembered his ear plugs. Gratefully, he put them on under his steel helmet. Then he glanced at the warrant officer just to watch his lips moving with no sound coming out. Tommy chuckled.

He shifted his attention to the destroyers. He was amazed at how rapidly they reached top speed.

Suddenly, all the destroyers began turning, cutting back across each other's wakes. Depth charges flew through the air.

There was a long pause. Then in rapid succession the force from the repeated blows drove him back against his seat and held him. The sound reached him dully through his protected ears. He opened his mouth to relieve the pressure.

As Tommy watched the charges going off behind the destroyers, he could make no connection between the plumes of white water and the shocks which buffeted him. They seemed totally distinct, two different and unrelated phenomena.

He looked at the gunner's mate. Pearson had stopped talking. He, too, was braced against the blasts.

Tommy knew when a pack of destroyers was out after a sub sometimes the safest thing for the sub to do was go right in among the convoy. There it was extremely difficult to detect with sonar and to fire upon, with so many friendly ships in such proximity. At the same time the sub was free to pick out the choicest targets and fire at will with plenty of escape routes from the tell-tale paths of its torpedoes.

The fleet had opened a considerable distance between itself and the working destroyers. Tommy wished he had field glasses. It was getting difficult to tell what the destroyers were doing. It was obvious enough when they dropped depth charges, but they had stopped doing that.

Tommy hoped they had not lost contact with the sub.

If they had, his fears might be realized. The sub might be among their own ships. He wished he had field glasses.

He watched the lookouts. Each was busy covering his own sector of the sea. No hints from them whether anything unusual were afoot. He looked around at the racing waves. No way I'm 'on spot a periscope from here, he thought.

The ship moved on, everyone still at general quarters.

We got a whole fleet at general quarters, thought Tommy, and nobody knows where that damn sub is at. We should have some subs of our own with us. Hell, at least they could find out if he was up in here, with us.

Tommy saw that the gunner's mate was talking again. Tommy had to fight to keep from busting up laughing. Fool thinks somebody's listen'in' to him. Big, red, Adam's apple goin' up and down. Boy, he got some bad teeth. Tommy held himself, keeping his expression down to a wide grin and turned to peer after the distant destroyers.

There had not been any depth charges for a long while. For the first time Tommy noticed an acrid sweat running down his sides. He realized then there was something wrong - odd - about the destroyer formation. They had spread wide apart again, but the trouble was, the trouble was, they were racing back toward the battle group.

Tommy checked the lookouts. Nothing. They were not speaking. They had not signaled. No sign of a hit. They searched the sea methodically.

Hell, I got t'fix dinner, he thought. When this foolishness gon' be over? His right foot shook almost imperceptibly.

He did not want to look at the warrant officer. His yammering mouth with its bad teeth would no longer amuse him. Anybody that stupid, he thought, to run his mouth on and on t'somebody what's not listen'in', needed to have a fist rammed in his face. Tommy knew if he looked at the dumb gunner's mate, he would have to jump up and hit him, but he did not want to look at the destroyers either, because the closer they got, the less distance he knew there was between him and the sub.

When he had been in the Atlantic in '40, before the U.S. was even in the war, Tommy had seen a lot of ships sunk by subs. Sometimes they went down very fast. There was no time for anyone to get off. Sometimes when they went down, even those men who had abandoned ship were sucked down with the undertow. Usually the ocean was on fire and many of those rescued were badly burned.

If this ship was t'be hit, he thought, it wouldn't be nothin' but a wall o' fire. A wall o' fire. Couldn't nobody get off this sun of a gun. And then if they could, the ocean would burn 'em up. The ocean wouldn't be nothin' but rollin' fire. He could not stop shaking his foot.

He hated submarines, especially enemy ones. There was something about the whole idea that was so sneaky he could not stand it. You never know where they's at, and then them torpedoes is comin' straight at you. What can you do? I like a ship you can see to fight. Even a airplane you can see though they does come awful fast.

He looked up at the sky. Nothing there. Nothing there he could see. They likes to come out of the sun, though, he thought. That way you cain't see 'em. Caint' see 'em t'shoot at 'em. But there ain't no planes up in this sky. It's down below we got t'worry about.

The destroyers closed fast.

The whomp of the blast from the depth charge caught Tommy by surprise. He jerked his head up.

Yes. Great eruptions of spray towered behind each destroyer. Again, they cut back over each others' wakes.

They must o' found him, thought Tommy. Sonar.

271

They must o' found him. Tommy strained his eyes to see. He looked and looked, as hard as he could. Every wallop from a depth charge felt like a burst of sunlight.

"Drop them ash-cans, drop them ash-cans, " he whispered. He looked up to see one lookout point. He was focusing in the destroyers' direction. The other lookout turned his glasses to the area, too.

Tommy lowered his ear plugs. Sound assailed him. "Oil slick!"

The lookout's shout was clear.

Tommy peeled his eyes in the destroyer's direction. He could not see any oil - just the circles and spouts of white water, the broad wakes, and the battle-painted tin cans.

He continued staring. Finally, he could make out a change in the texture of the water. It seemed to smooth out, to have a flatter, heavier surface.

Oil, he thought.

He kept looking. The smooth area spread, and spread. He stood up and cheered. He waved his hands in the air. All across the task force men were cheering and dancing. Many could not hear because their ears were still protected. They did not care. They shouted and celebrated.

Forty-five men were dead and dying beneath the sea.

5

The waves were mild when the ships began to come alongside for fueling. By then the whole armada had assembled. There were two aircraft carriers, seven heavy cruisers, two light cruisers, and thirteen destroyers. There were five tankers; there were destroyer tenders, submarine tenders, ammunition ships, a repair ship, and a storeship.

Tommy and Billy stood on the rail and watched as the fueling operation proceeded. Alongside them a heavy cruiser drank oil.

"Yessir," said Tommy, "they be makin' heap bad medicine for somebody."

Billy nodded. He watched the lines stretching taught between the two ships. "Well, where'll we go now," he asked, "while they're doing whatever they do?"

"I don't know. We'll probably meet 'em someplace after the action - fill up some o' them destroyers what's been chasin' around like crazy."

The ships drifted closer together. Billy looked squarely at a seaman who stood on the cruiser's rail, staring blankly ahead of him.

"I wonder what he's thinkin' about," said Billy.

"What was you thinkin' about when they spotted that sub?"

Two days after the battle of the Coral Sea, the carrier Yorktown emerged from the vastness of the Pacific. The Monongahela maneuvered close up to refuel her.

The reports were that the Yorktown had escaped the battle virtually unscathed. Gaping holes ran along her hull the whole length of the water line. Her flight deck held a chasm - blackened, twisted steel and charred wood adorning

273

its edges. Many of the planes parked on the flight deck appeared incapable of flying again. The sailors on the tanker who were not working on the refueling stood and stared. Many of them wondered how the planes had ever landed.

The crew learned the Monongahela and her little group were to accompany the Yorktown back to Pearl. The men rejoiced. They dreamed sweet dreams of liberty.

Their reveries were shattered by general quarters.

Someone had sighted a sub.

Each ship in the formation, now eight ships, broke directly into evasive maneuvers.

The three destroyers seemed to leap forward as they accelerated to search out the submarine.

"Boy, I wish I was on one o' them tin-cans," said Warrant Officer Pearson as he and Tommy settled in beside their gun. "I'd git me a pig-boat today!"

Tommy watched the angling, swift pursuit of the little vessels. They did bring a kind of music to his heart. He was so glad they were there. They were as quick as greyhounds after their prey. He waited for the first ash cans to fly.

"Fish! Fish!" The lookout's cries conveyed more terror than information.

As the ships had zigged and zagged, the Monongahela had swept broadside into the angle once occupied by the Yorktown a mile to port.

The submarine had launched a spread of torpedoes at the Yorktown's former position. They came in two pairs spaced along the flank of the Monongohela. The first pair ran directly toward the forward part of the ship. The second pair, forty seconds behind, raced toward the stern.

The commander, alerted by the lookout, picked out

the unmistakable trail of the torpedoes with his field glasses. His reaction was immediate. He ordered a left full rudder. The bow of the ship began to swing to the right.

From their high perch beside the big gun Tommy and Pearson saw the torpedo tracks clearly. They also felt the ship beginning her turn. Every expression except terror fled Pearson's face.

"You people's religious, ain't you," said the mate.

Tommy stared at Pearson.

"I mean, y'all knows how t'pray, don't you? Prayin' and hollerin' all the time! Put that shit t'good use - pray, boy! Pray!"

Pearson's lips quivered. Tears ran down his face.

Tommy looked back for the torpedoes. They were much closer.

Pearson closed his eyes and started mumbling about Jesus. He wrapped his arms tightly around himself, and rocked himself back and forth, his lips moving and making low sounds all the while.

Relieved by the loss of hundreds of tons of oil, the ship turned quickly. The two torpedoes headed for the bow missed.

From the bridge it was evident the very tail edge of the stern would not move fast enough to miss the first pair. That fact increasingly imposed itself on Tommy's consciousness as he watched the relentless progress of the torpedo wakes. He crouched down and braced himself.

The ship was strangely silent. It creaked and groaned. But there was no human sound.

Tommy felt he had never taken so long to breathe.

He touched his pulse just above his collar bone. His life.

"Crossed under! Crossed under!" A great shout erupted from the ship. The torpedoes had been set to hit a big ship far below the water line. The tanker, emptied of

275

oil, rose thirty feet higher in the water than when fully loaded. The twin fish had run under her. They joined their sister warheads running endlessly out into the Pacific.

Tommy dropped his head. He could not say anything. He sat, drained. Unable to move. His shirt was soaked with sweat.

Pearson forgot almost immediately about Jesus. He remembered the nigger, though. The nigger had seen him almost lose it. Not good for a nigger to see a white man in such a state.

6

When the Monongahela arrived at Pearl Harbor, orders awaited Tommy and Red Mule. They were assigned shore duty. They were not to return to the Monongahela. They were to wait instead for the fast tranport, McNamara, which would take them stateside.

They went to their quarters to pack. Ten minutes later Billy trailed in after them. He leaned against his bunk as he watched them sorting and arranging.

For two or three minutes the only sounds in the tight space were the rustles of skin moving against fabric and the soft plops of folded garments deposited in ditty bags.

"Hey, uh," I've sailed with you two ever since I got my first stripe. I don't know what I'm gon' do."

Tommy stopped packing to look up at Billy. "Everything's gon' be alright," he said. "They gon' send me and Mule away for a few months, but we gon' be back. Everything's gon' be alright. These ain't no permanent orders. We gon' be back."

He resumed packing.

"You don't think it's permanent, huh," asked Billy.

"No. These ain't no permanent orders," said Tommy. "We gon' be back on this fat, ol' tub."

Billy smiled. "I hope so."

"We will," said Tommy. "I'm gon' miss yo skinny ass - even if you is got yo nose open a mile wide. I'm even 'on miss hearin' bout yo sweet Marva."

Mule laughed. "Me, too, Billy. I'm 'on miss you. But like Tommy said, we gon' be back t'this floatin' oil can 'fo 'you can turn around."

Mule secured his ditty-bag and sat down on his bunk. "They got some special duty for us," he said. "We'll be back. Like he said, these ain't no permanent orders."

277

Billy felt alone. He was going to be on his own for sure. The Pacific was a lonely place, and the Monongahela would sail without the two men he now knew best in the world. He touched his friends on their shoulders. He shook their hands. He left the room. None of them was any good at saying goodbyes.

The fast transport McNamara was a converted destroyer with a destroyer's speed. She stopped at Pearl for refueling and picked up a number of sailors who had eastbound orders. Among them were Tommy and Mule. After lifting anchor the McNamara sped ESE for San Diego. She arrived after seventy-two hours at sea.

San Diego was Tommy's and Mule's duty port. Scores of ships were being built. Hundreds of thousands of sailors were being trained. Somebody had to cook for those sailors, and the cooks had to be trained, too. Tommy Brown, and George Johnson, alias Red Mule, had come to San Diego to train stewards.

They were happy to be out of the combat zone. They slept well, ate well, gained weight, and waxed content. They were not too hard on their charges. They knew what lay ahead of them, and did not wish to add unnecessary burdens to their lives. Their primary emphasis was on teaching, on making them good at what they were to do.

Mule used his rather generous allocation of passes to travel north and spend all his free time with Darla-Anne. Tommy made the first trip with him. He went to the Club Louise to look for the girl with the heart-shaped face the color of peaches. He did not see her. He got into a fight and was arrested by the shore patrol before he had a chance to talk to Finnie-Marie. He did not accompany Mule to San Francisco again.

He used his passes just to leave base and stay in San

Diego where the young girls flocked to sailors like ants to sweets, or he traveled to Tiajuana where he paid a considerable sum of money to spend his whole liberty in the company of a beautiful woman.

Tommy and Mule did not talk much directly about their good luck at being assigned to a training mission. They marveled at it - laughing, or grunting, or shaking their heads over it - like a sunset or a whirlwind or the first snowfall. It was a wonder, so they marveled at it with gestures and exclamations, but they did not talk about it except to agree, "That's somethin', ain't it?"

They did ponder, though, how it was their luck as single men to be safely at home, while Billy Jones, with a wife he loved with all his heart, rode a steel and oil sandwich far out on the ocean as war raged all around him.

New orders came. Tommy and Mule had short duty left at San Diego. Their next duty station was Norfolk, Virginia. Neither of them liked that.

"They mostly use Norfolk as a dispatch point," said Mule the first night after they received their new orders.

"Don't I know it," said Tommy, "many times I've sailed convoys out of Norfolk cross the Atlantic."

"Nope," said Mule. "Don't look like no trainin' station."

"I'd ruther take a whuppin' than go out amongst them U-boats again," said Tommy.

"Eight or nine whuppins," said Mule.

"Why you figure they wanta pull us outa here," asked Tommy.

"Don't know. Maybe. Maybe they figure we's trained enough stewards."

"Damn," said Tommy, "there ain't a thing I likes about Norfolk. And it's in blip, too."

279

"Jim-Crow," said Red Mule.

"That's right.   And I'll end up killin' some peckerwood if he tries t'nigger and boy me."

"Just stay on the base."

"I'm gon' have to. It's Jim-Crow, too. But they ain't so crazy."

"That's one thing about Norfolk," said Mule. "You won't have to stay on base too long. They'll be sendin' you out'n there befo' you can get ants in yo pants."

They did not mention that the assignment meant they were not going back to the Monongahela. Neither of them asked the other whether that meant that the Monongahela no longer floated. Neither of them said a word about Billy Jones.

After their initial conversation about their new orders, they became very quiet. They avoided the subject. They did not sleep either. Insecurity crept back into their worlds. For the first time in a long while they could not relax. They could not greet the night as a friend promising rest. It reasserted itself as an abode of dread, filled with nightmares and forebodings, filled with horrors.

7

The ocean was rough. Tommy was scared. The little landing craft jerked up and down. Whomp! Whomp! The cold spray flew in, drenching the soldiers who stood huddled in the well of the vessel, each man locked inside himself. Many had already been sick, and many more would be sick before they reached the beach.

Tommy dreaded thinking about the beach. It was pitch black. He could not see a thing ahead of him except the phosphorescence of wave tops. He worked carefully to keep the compass heading he had been assigned. Otherwise, he would not know where he was going. But he dreaded thinking about the beach. He did not know what waited for him there - heavy guns, machine guns, mines, underwater obstacles. He did not know and the dark gave him no clues. Heavy seas had been known to break up landing craft even in practice missions.

He regretted the decision, whosoever it was, not to shell the beach beforehand, not to tear up whatever resistance they might meet. He knew he would feel a lot better if shells from the battleship, the cruiser, and the destroyers behind them were screaming over their heads into the beaches, destroying whoever and whatever was there. They had been told there would be no "softening up" because it was a surprise attack and they wanted to have captured the beaches before the French even knew they were there. He did not believe a word of it. He wanted to see the beaches on fire.

"What's your heading, coxswain," asked the lieutenant, (j.g.) Who was commanding the craft.

"One-forty-five," answered Tommy.

"What's our assigned heading?"

"One-forty-five," Tommy repeated.

281

He could hear the engines of the other landing craft around him. One of them was Mule's. He remembered the number, PX-35. He wondered how Mule was doing. He wondered if Mule was as scared as he was.

The heavy waves kept throwing the craft off course and Tommy had to adjust continually to keep it on the proper heading. The changes in throttling from the other tubs told him they were having much the same trouble.

Sometimes when the landing craft was broadsided by a wave and turned sideways, a whole sea would wash into it, completely soaking the already cowed soldiers. After one particularly monstrous wave, when the soldiers were struggling to their feet, coughing and spitting water, the lieutenant turned to Tommy and shouted.

"Sailor, are you a pilot or a truck driver!"

Tommy, who was more exasperated with the conditions than anyone on board but could not take his eyes off his work, replied, "I'm doin' the best I can, sir. But if the captain is unhappy with my work, he can take control."

"Just keep it level, keep it level," said the lieutenant.

"Womp! Whomp!"

When the first hints of grey crept into the sky, Tommy flashed his eyes where he knew the horizon had to be, trying to will some of the landmarks from his maps and briefings into visibility.

The light came up quickly and very soon he could at least see the horizon and the beach where a heavy surf crashed, though no landmarks were as yet discernible.

Must be about a mile and a half to shore, he thought. At least they ain't seen us yet. Ain't opened up on us.

As they got closer to shore, into shallower depths, the waters became even more turbulent. Tommy tried not to wrestle with the craft. He had a natural touch, but even so the journey began increasingly to resemble some demonic amusement park ride.

Looking around him, Tommy saw other craft in even worse shape. Many seemed almost swamped. Sometimes as they bottomed out in the troughs, they spewed out great gouts of water. Many wallowed, seeming ready to tip over onto their sides.

Tommy scanned the other boats, checking their i.d. numbers. He smiled as he recognized PX-35, slightly behind him to his right. *Good Ol' Mule.* Mule's LCV(P) rolled and smashed into the waves. It was making headway, doing better than most. Looking at all his companion landing craft, Tommy was sure it was nip and tuck whether any of them would make the beach.

"What's your heading, coxswain," shouted the lieutenant.

"One forty-six, sir."

"Damn it, it's supposed to be one forty-five!"

"Aye, aye, sir. I'm correctin' -"

"Well, keep it corrected, sailor!"

"Aye, aye, sir."

Tommy wanted to punch the lieutenant in the mouth, but he could not let his temper get out of hand.

"Sailor, you got a reading on any of those landmarks up on the beach?"

Tommy checked his heading to make sure he was steady on one forty-five. Then he glanced at the shoreline spotting for landmarks he had memorized.

"Sir, the ridge on the left is where it's s'posed t'be far as Grey Wolf Able, Sector five maps is concerned. That's the only landmark what I sees."

The lieutenant put his glasses on the beach and began observing it as closely as the violent pitching and smashing of the vessel would allow.

Tommy glanced back at Mule. He's alright. The Red Mule is doin' fine.

The roar of the surf had risen to drown out the loud

283

growl of the diesel engines. Tommy felt like turning the landing craft around. We could break up in that surf, he thought. We could break up.

Every time he got a chance he scanned the beach. There was no sign of movement. No sign of gunfire. No sign of enemy. Just the awful surf. From what Tommy could see, Grey Wolf Able, Sector Five, looked like the bottom of Niagra Falls, like a landing craft smasher. The landmarks were there. His heading was correct. What would he do if he were wrecked on the beach? He did not even have a gun. How could he get back to the ship? He would have to stay with the soldiers - with no gun, no unit.

"Shit," he said softly to himself.

"Uh, coxswain," the lieutenant had taken his glasses down.

"Uh, you see over there to the left. That stretch of beach in front of that landmark wall section?"

"Aye, aye, sir."

"Uh ... well, uh, would that be - according to your recollection - in Sector Five?"

"No, sir," he said. "That's Sector Four. It's off our heading."

"It's next to our sector, though, isn't it," persisted the lieutenant, "next to the edge?"

"Aye, aye, sir."

"Well, I'm gonna tell you somethin', pilot. Our job is t'get these soldiers on the beach - so they can do some fightin'. Not t'drown 'em. If we take this LC into Sector Five, the thing will break up, and with them all weighted down with that gear, most of 'em will drown. You and me'll probably live, but we'll be stuck on the beach.

"So ... take it onto that corner of Section Four. Hell, if I can't make a command decision, what good am I?"

"Aye, aye, sir."

A heavy fear lifted off Tommy. He smiled as he

284

adjusted his heading and rode with the craft into a big wash.

That damn j.g.'s good for somethin', after all, he thought.

Many soldiers fell getting to shore in the rough surf, but heavily laden as they were, they got to their feet again and made the beach. They were relieved just to be off the landing craft. They grouped on the beach. There was still no hostile fire. They fanned out, moving rapidly.

All along the front landing craft had made it to the shore and were discharging their complements of soldiers. Tommy could not make out PX-35, but he was sure it was there. Somehow, all the LC's seemed to have made it into shore without swamping.

"Ready to get on out, pilot," asked the lieutenant.

"Aye, aye, sir."

"Then let's get the hell off this beach."

As they turned around Tommy took a last glimpse of the soldiers deployed all along the beach. They were moving fast.

Lot o' men in there, he thought. Lot o' men.

Tommy had thought it had been hard coming in, but going out was worse. If the vessel had been loaded, it would have been impossible. He had to steer diagonally across the waves. If he tried to go into them head-on, he made no progress and faced the distinct possibility of being flipped over backwards. If he ran broadside to them he could not escape being swamped.

Even with an empty craft running out diagonally was a perilous undertaking. Once he had made 200 yards from the beach, Tommy could see the second wave of landing craft coming in. They appeared to be having even more difficulty than his group.

Tommy had been looking around for PX-35 and at last saw him breaking through a wave on his port side, some distance back. He turned all the way around, peering to see if there were a chance Mule could see and acknowledge a wave if he made one. He guessed not. He would wait until they got further out to throttle down some and get within hailing distance of the Red Mule. He turned his attention back to piloting his own boat.

Soon he was among the LC's coming in. He gave them a wide berth. He waved at them when they were close enough to matter. They waved back but were not diverted from their nearly impossible navigational tasks for more than an instant.

The high, screaming whistling sound seemed to come to Tommy from another world. He could not place it. He knew what it was, he just could not make the mental connection with it. He was too immersed in trying to get his LC through the steadily roughening water.

"Jesus Christ!"

The j.g's exclamation and brightness on Tommy's visual periphery locked the linkages in his mind. Tommy snapped his head to his left to see a geyser of water outlined by the rushing, dark waves and the grey sky.

BOOM! BOOM! The sound arrived.

He looked back to the hills above the beach where he saw repeated bright flashes.

"They finally opened up their guns," said the lieutenant.

Great spouts of water were knocked into the air throughout the array of landing craft.

The sounds became continual, like overhead thunder directed by a timpani drummer.

BOOM! BOOM!
BOOM! BOOM!
BOOM! BOOM!

"Damn it," said the j.g., "Why we got all those ships settin' out there? Just t'let those shore gunners take pot shots at us? They haven't hit anything yet, but if they keep

286

on shooting, out of pure, blind, luck, they'll get some of us."

As if in answer to his complaint, bright flashes appeared ahead of them, rapid and unceasing. In seconds, high, tearing sounds rent the air above their heads. Concussions slammed into the little landing craft almost as hard as the breaking waves. The fleet's guns were speaking.

"It's about time," said the j.g.

Tommy looked behind him to his left. PX-35 broke free from a wave. Tommy smiled.

He watched PX-35 slide down a wave trough and explode.

One instant it was sliding down the side of a wave. The next it was disintegrated in an eruption of flame and spray. The wave rolled on.

Tommy doubled over. He lost control of his craft. The j.g. saw the motion and jumped to his side. He grabbed the steering mechanism just after a giant wave had broadsided the LC, pouring a couple of tons of water into it.

"Mule! Mule," shouted Tommy.

"What's wrong, sailor? What's wrong," cried the lieutenant. He had not seen the direct hit. He was afraid the colored boy had gone crazy.

"Oh, Mule! Mule!"

"Would you get ahold of yourself. What's wrong? You're gonna drown us."

Tommy looked back. The towering waves rushed on, toying with landing craft, sprinkled with columns of white, up lifted waters. Screaming missiles tore overhead. Shock waves slammed through the air to the accompaniment of incessant booming.

Tommy looked back and tried to picture where PX-35 had been. The whole vision went through his mind. Mule's boat had ridden cleanly down the wave. The incredible explosion had taken its place, and then nothing was there. Nothing was there.

The lieutenant was wrestling with the controls and failing. He was keeping them from being swamped, but not for long.

Tommy moved the lieutenant out of the way. The bulky craft responded to him.

When Tommy got back on board the transport, he could not force himself to return to the quarters he had shared with Red Mule. He stayed on deck and could not drive from his mind the recurrence of one, irretractible instant.

8

Tommy had new orders when he got back to Norfolk. He was to report to base command in San Diego. He had a week to get across the country.

As Tommy read his orders he felt an irrepressible rage. Mule wanted to go back to San Diego, he thought. I ain't the one. I ain't the one.

He did not know what he had done to be alive while Red Mule was dead. He wanted to tell Mule he didn't know. *I'm sorry.*

Tommy sat down on a park bench after he left the base. He knew what he had to do. He did not feel up to it, but he knew he had to. There would be no record of her. She was not next of kin. They wasn't, he thought, they wasn't even engaged. The navy would never notify Darla-Anne. That would be up to him. He would have to tell her.

Red Mule had talked about Darla so much Tommy knew just what her schedule was. He knew at the time the ferry from Oakland was due to arrive in San Francisco, she should be in, and would probably be in for the rest of the evening. He thought about calling her from the station to be sure she was in, and to let her know he was coming. But he did not. He did not know what to say over the phone.

As he stared out the trolley window he thought about how much Mule had loved the city. What had Billy called it, "a fairy city." With its white buildings set on hills, all sparkling in the sun.

Mule loved this town. Met Darla his first night here. Damn, I was with Mule three weeks ago. With him on the other side of the world. Now I'm here without him. Alone. In his city. It don't seem real.

He pulled his eyes back into the trolley. He lowered his head.

In front of the door with the "5" on it, he stood still. He inhaled deeply.

He exhaled.

He knocked.

A cheery voice called out, "Just a minute."

Darla opened the door wide. It took her just an instant's pause to recognize Tommy. A series of expressions passed over her face in rapid succession - surprise, bafflement, joy. She turned around, leading the way into the room.

"Tommy Brown. Come in, come in. You look good."

She moved behind Tommy to close the door. He faced into the apartment, his white cap between his hands in front of him.

Behind him, turning away from the door now, she chattered on. "I thought you and Red were way out t'sea somewhere. Where is that ol' Red, anyway? When's he comin' back to his little Darla-Ann? Let me take your hat. Can I get you something? Sit down, sit down."

She took his hat and placed it on top of a knee-high rack beside the door. A couple pair of her shoes occupied the bottom of the rack. She turned back to him.

He still faced the interior of the apartment. He would not sit down. What he had to do required standing. He also could not force himself to look at her. She would have to look at him. His eyes picked out articles in the room - a knick-knack shelf on the wall, the polished wood of a high-backed chair.

She stood slightly behind his left shoulder, looking at his back, puzzled. She wondered why he did not turn around. "Am I imagining things," she asked, "or haven't you answered a thing I've asked you, Tommy Brown? Where is that Red man-of-mine?"

Tommy turned to her. He kept his eyes down.

She saw his face.

"Tommy - is something wrong? Tommy, what's wrong? Where's Red? Why isn't Red with you? What's wrong with Red?"

"I ...." He looked at her. He moved a step closer in anticipation of her reaction. "Darla. Red. Red ... is dead."

She looked at him. Her mouth opened.

"Oh, no! She raised her arms in front of her face. "Oh! No!"

She fled out of the room into the bedroom.

She ran back into the room waving a piece of paper.

"He can't be! I just got his letter this morning. I just finished reading it. He can't be! He can't be! I just read his letter!"

She pushed the letter into Tommy's face.

Tommy took her hand and lowered it. He shook his head. His chin dropped onto his chest.

Her eyes begged his face.

It returned unceasingly, the same heartless message.

She closed her eyes.

She collapsed.

Tommy caught her in his arms. He shifted her weight around, repositioned his arms, picked her up and carried her to the couch. He laid her out on the couch and sat down with the back of her head on his lap. He stroked her forehead.

Her eyes opened slowly. She held them wide open for a slow second. She bolted up into a sitting position and whirled to face Tommy. She stared into his face for confirmation yet again.

"Darla ...."

She dropped her head, shaking it, and held tightly to Tommy's shoulders, one hand on each shoulder. Her diaphragm began to contract and expand violently. Tommy placed an arm around her shoulders and drew her against his chest. Her face, pressed into his jumper, soaked it immediately. He looked out over her head into the room, shocked and angry at the erection that had accompanied her warmth and closeness.

He held her that way for a long, long time.

At last she drew back a little and looked up at him.

"When ... when did it happen?"

"November eighth."

"Oh!" She stood up. She bent over, holding tightly onto her own arms. "So long." Her voice stressed each word. "So. Long."

Tommy stood up. "I know."

Her voice was rising, slightly out of control. "He's been dead so long. My Red. My Red. I didn't know. I didn't even know. He's been dead all this time. All this time!"

She stumbled.

He brought her back down to the couch. She cried. He held her. She cried. She could not seem to stop. He held her.

Her voice was broken, and sobbing, and wet. "Why didn't I know? Why didn't I know?"

"It's. I ... Darla ... Casablanca is a long ways away. I ... I come straight here."

"Oh, I know. I'm sorry. I'm sorry. But it's been so long. He's been ... gone ... so .... long. And I didn't even know. I didn't even know." She shook heavily as she wept.

She pulled away. She sat back against the couch. She put her hands to her face. Her head inclined slightly forward.

Her voice came muffled through her hands. "Do you know ... what happened?"

He said what he'd already said in his mind a thousand times. "His landing craft got a direct hit.

292

Everybody in it was kilt."

"Did he ...."

"I seen it. Red didn't suffer none. It was instant. He never knowed."

"You saw it! You saw it!"

She stared at him in horror.

"Oh, God!"

She turned her face up. Her eyes wandered crazily as if searching the ceiling.

She dropped her face back into her hands. Her fingers moved down over her forehead, down her tightly shut eyelids, down her cheeks.

She pushed her forehead into Tommy's shoulder.

She whispered. "you saw it."

She was quiet.

"What about the burial?"

Tommy swallowed. He had rehearsed this, too. "He were buried at sea."

"Oh."

They sat.

Darla turned to look at the sailor who sat beside her. His face mirrored the pain she felt throughout her body.

"Tommy. Thank you for comin'. I know it was hard on you. You and Red was such good friends. I ...." She caught herself for a moment. She pressed one hand to her face, the other to her chest. "I know it was hard. But there wasn't no other way I could have found out. I wouldn't of known. I would of just kept writing him letters ...." She sobbed. "Thank you, thank you, thank you ...."

He put his arm around her and patted her on the back. He let his hand rest there. "Darla-Anne, you don't have t'say nothin'. Mule loved you. He wanted t'marry you. In a way you is his next of kin. I know the Navy ain't knowed that. But I does. I had t'tell you. 'Sides. I had t'be with somebody who cared about Mu- Red, too."

293

"He wanted to marry me?" She looked up at Tommy.

"Said. Said it was the first thing he was gon' ask you when he got back."

She stood up and turned away from him. "Tommy, I thank you for everything and I don't want to seem ungrateful, but I need to be alone now."

"Sure, Darla." He stood.

He patted her on the shoulder as he walked beside her.

He turned the door handle.

"Tommy - I'll write you."

"Thank you, Darla-Anne. I'd appreciate that."

"Thank you for everything, Tommy."

She handed him his cap.

He closed the door behind him.

9

Tommy arrived in San Diego to learn he had new orders. The Monongahela. The ship was in port. When he checked in with the duty officer he discovered that most of the crew was on leave. Only a work crew remained to get the tanker back in ship-shape. Tommy immediately became a member of that crew. The work was hard, but it kept his mind occupied and exhausted his body, which enabled him to sleep at night.

No one returned early from leave voluntarily, though the Shore Patrol brought a few burned-out sailors back to the ship before they were due. Tommy kept a watch on the dock, hoping to see a friendly face arriving. He had not been personally acquainted with anyone on the work crew from his earlier tour on the Monongahela. He recognized some of them, but they were all white, and he had not been on a first-name basis with any of them.

The ship was in total readiness for getting underway when the sailors started lining the gangplank, back from liberty. Tommy stared at each face as it came within visual range. He knew many of them. He smiled as he saw many of the colored men he had shared room and board with. It warmed him to see them. Their presence made him feel more at home. It warmed his heart to see them all, but he waited for one face.

He burst out with a "Yahoo!" when he saw Billy Jones' lean, dark face appear in the line. Billy's expression was glum. He did not seem happy to be back.

Tommy took off his hat and waived it wildly in the air. "Jones! Jones," he shouted. "Jones - you old Marva-lovin' fool!"

The sound of Marva's name caught Billy's ear. She had been on his mind and he had closed his consciousness to all the sounds surrounding the ship. The shouting, the waving, the greetings had all passed by him. He had been sunk deep in his own reveries. But the name rang out like a crystal bell.

Marva.

He jerked his head up, casting his eyes around. There were sailors all along the rail. Many were shouting down to friends. A few were waving. But there was one wild man, one wild, Black man. He was shouting. He was jumping up and down. He was flinging his arm back and forth.

Billy's breath caught.

Tommy! Tommy Brown!

Billy's face erupted into a smile. He snatched his own cap off his head and waived it. He did not bother to shout. He was sure Tommy would not be able to hear him in the general din. For the first time ... he was eager to get on board.

Warrant Officer Pearson stood a little behind Billy. Tommy did not see him, but he saw Tommy. Saw him and cursed.

When Billy broke past the watch officer, Tommy rushed up to him.

"Hey, you little, skinny, Jones-boy, you looks good. You looks good, and congratulations!"

"Hey - Tommy - how'd you know?"

"Billy, Billy - long's I been in the navy, I knows two stripes when I sees 'em, Petty Officer, second class, Jones."

Billy bent over laughing. He straightened up. "Oh, that's what you're talking about. Thanks. But I thought you were talking about something else, and I wondered how you knew - I'm a Daddy!"

"A - a - a Daddy! Well, I'll be ... hey, man - that's somethin'." Tommy gave Billy a big hug. Well, what d'you know? Boy or girl?"

"Little ol' girl. We named her Yvonne."

"That's a pretty name, a real pretty name."

"Yeah, we like it. I'm glad you do, too. Uh, we - uh, Marva and me, we uh, we'd like you to be her Godfather. Don't - you don't have t'tell me anything now. Think about it. It would make us very happy.

"You know what, though? You know how most people say how cute their babies are, even when they're as ugly as sin? Man, I know cause I've looked at plenty of those ugly babies. Well, I'm not like that. When a baby is ugly, I say it's ugly - even if it's my own. And I got to tell you the truth, Yvonne, my baby, Yvonne, is the prettiest baby I ever saw. I ain't lyin'. I admit - most babies are ugly, but this baby is beautiful!"

It was Tommy's turn to dissolve into laughter.

"Hey, Tommy, Tommy, I'm not lying. She's beautiful.

"Say, where's Mule?"

The Monongahela steamed back to the Southwest Pacific where she gave support to many warships which were active in the Solomon Islands.

The Monongohela stayed out of the battle zones, but she was occasionally spotted and attacked by wide-ranging aircraft and submarines. By deft zig-zagging, the use of her anti-aircraft guns, and the support of escort destroyers, she managed to avoid direct hits, though her crew suffered several casualties from near misses.

With the great increase in the number of sailors since the beginning of the war, petty officers had been spread more evenly throughout the navy, and under the Chief, Tommy and Billy were the only petty officers in the mess on the Monongohela. They worked very closely.

As they worked, Billy often steered the conversation

around to trying out to puzzle out the vagaries of assignments in the Navy. He was perplexed because throughout the war his sole assignment had been the Monongohela, while many men had been transferred all around.

"You know, Tommy, I wonder. Why me? Why do I get to stay on this ship when you, for instance, get moved around. I just don't understand the Navy. They are always yankin' you off to pilot a landing craft. Why don't they just assign you to a troop transport?"

"I don't know. 'Cept they makes up them transports at the last minute. The way they uses me, they keeps me in action all the time. If this ship's in a theater where they's got a invasion, they kills two birds with one stone.

"I tell you what, though. I wishes they would let me be. I don't want t'go on no more o' them invasions. I figure my luck cain't do nothin' but run down. The more I goes in, the worser my chances gits."

Tommy, however, did not get his wish. His services were appropriated for the invasions at Rendova and Vella Lavella. Everyone who worked with him knew right away he had a touch with the boats. There was no question about that. People remembered his name and ship, and sought him out.

That fired Warrant Officer Pearson's hatred. He not only had his personal reasons for retribution, it was also clear to him that petty officer first class, Tommy Owens, was developing an exaggerated impression of his own importance. That was an abomination to Pearson.

Somewhere near the eastern edge of the Central Pacific Basin on the way back to Hawaii, with a sea running hard, the wave tops blown off white by the strong, steady wind, under a sky so clear the blue seemed almost to chime,

298

Tommy Brown received a battlefield promotion to Chief Petty Officer.

That was the straw that broke the camel's back as far as Warrant Officer Pearson was concerned. To see the self-assured, cocky, Black sailor striding about the ship, a grin flashing on his face, covered with all the awe attendant upon a participant in the Tarawa landing, and wearing the eagle-mounted chevrons of a Chief Petty Officer, to boot, was more than Pearson could stand. He felt he could not let the coon clown go one step further. He watched Tommy. It did not take long for Pearson to find him alone.

Tommy was swabbing the floor of the Warrant Officers' mess when Pearson stepped in. It was all Pearson could do to hold himself back from rushing the Black man.

"Feel like a cup of coffee," said Pearson, almost inaudibly.

Tommy did not hear him. When he looked up from his mopping he saw the warrant officer take a chair. "Uh ... something' I can do fo' you, sir?"

"Didn't you hear me, boy," Pearson let the irritation show in his voice. "I said I feel like a cup of coffee."

Tommy resumed his mopping.

"Is you deaf?"

Tommy stopped, and looked up. "You talkin' to me, sir? I didn't figure you was talkin' t'nobody in here, as I don't see no boys."

"Oh," said Pearson, "I see you is one o' them kind."

"One o' what kind, sir," Tommy resumed his mopping.

"Never you mind that. Is you gonna get me that coffee or not?"

"Oh. Did you want some coffee? I'd be pleased t'git it for you, sir."

Tommy put down his mop and went into the galley. He kept a pot of coffee perking for the stewards and for occasions just such as this, when a sailor stopped by for a cup.

He spit into the cup. He poured the hot, black liquid over the thick mucous. When he had filled the steaming cup, he stirred the mixture with his spoon. He brought the coffee back to Pearson.

Pearson smiled as he saw Tommy coming back with the cup.

"Special just for you," said Tommy.

Tommy put the cup down and prepared to go back to his work. Pearson did not thank him. He said, "That's better, boy."

He picked up the cup and took a sip. "Good. You make good coffee, boy."

Tommy had resumed mopping. He smiled. You don't know how good, you red-neck dog.

Pearson looked over at Tommy. Nigger's still on his high-horse, he thought. Thinks he's somethin'. Everybody come askin' for him to pilot their landing craft. Look at him. Still grinnin'. Grinnin' coon.. Damn, they're ugly. That's alright. Keep grinnin', coon. I'll fix you.

"Yessir," said Pearson. "That's one thing you people can do. Fix a good cup o' coffee." He laughed. "That's about all. Sure can't make sailors out of your asses."

Pearson knocked over his coffee cup, spilling its contents on the floor. He stood up, farting loudly.

"Pick it up, boy," he said. He walked toward the door.

Tommy stood watching him, incredulous.

Pearson turned just before he reached the door.

Tommy looked from the coffee to Pearson and back to the coffee. He shook his head.

"Boy! When I tell you t'do somethin' - you do it - quick!"

300

Tommy felt heat inside. He tried to hold it back.

Pearson walked up to Tommy and leaned into his face. He jabbed his index finger at Tommy's nose - they were about equal in height, though Pearson was heavier.

"You got to learn your place, boy!

"When a white man talks to a nigger, the nigger jumps! And - boy - you is a ni -"

It was a left-right combination.

Pearson hit the dining room door on his way down.

Tommy did not move in on him. He just held his ground.

Pearson tried to leap to his feet, but he was too dazed. He fell back down. He struggled to stand, his face contorted by rage, hate, and fear. Finally, when he stood again, he turned his venom- filled gaze at Tommy. He shook his index finger at him.

"I'm gonna kill you, nigger," he shouted. "I'm gonna kill you!"

He pushed quickly through the dining room door and was gone.

Right after the noon meal Tommy received a message to report to the ship's captain.

When he reached the captain's door, he knocked immediately.

A distinct pause elapsed before a clear voice sounded from within.

"Come in."

Tommy went in and closed the door behind him. He stood at attention, bringing his right hand up to a crisp salute.

Lieutenant Commander Weatherby, pale, dark-hair, long and lean, sat behind his sea-desk looking at Tommy. He let Tommy hold the salute for a long time. At last, he

301

returned it.

Tommy brought his hand down sharply.

"Chief Petty Officer Brown," said Weatherby. "This is the second tour of duty you've served on this ship, am I not right?"

"Aye, aye, sir."

Weatherby turned away from Tommy. He stared at some charts on his wall.

"Brown, you've put some time in this navy, you've put some service in the navy. You're a good cook."

Weatherby turned back to face Tommy, looking into his eyes.

"Yes, Brown. I hear good reports about your work during the landings. Milne Bay. Rendova. Vella Levella. Tarawa."

Weatherby spun his chair away from Tommy.

"Damnit, Brown! Don't you know that striking a superior officer is a court martial offense!"

"Aye, aye, sir."

"You're not stupid, Brown. Why did you do it? Why?"

"If I could have the captain's permission to speak?"

"Go ahead. Go ahead. Why the hell you think I asked the question?"

"Sir. I hit the warrant officer because he called me out of my name."

Weatherby's face flushed red. He slammed the side of his fist down on his desk. He snapped to his feet.

"He what?"

"Sir. He called me out of my name, sir."

Weatherby let his body crash back into his chair. He kicked his desk, then spun around, his back to Tommy.

He said very softly. "So he called you out of your name. My. My. My." He began turning back toward Tommy. "You say he did not threaten you. He did not pull

302

a weapon on you. He did not strike you. No. He called you out of your name."

The lieutenant commander again faced Tommy. "And for this you struck - struck - a warrant officer! I don't believe it." Weatherby slammed his fist on his desk again.

"And just exactly what did Warrant Officer Pearson call you?"

"Sir. He called me a nigger, sir."

Weatherby did not say anything. He looked down at his desk. He began drumming his fingers on it. He did that for a long time. Finally, he looked back at Tommy.

"He did, huh?"

"Aye, aye, sir."

Weatherby stood to his full height. He was six feet, three inches tall. He leaned over his desk and looked into Tommy's eyes.

"Well, if you aren't a nigger, what are you?"

Tommy felt as if someone had slammed him across the face with a two-by-four. He did not reply at once. He had to fight to keep his closed fists at his sides.

"Sir. I am a *Negro*, sir."

Weatherby plumped himself back down into his chair and spun away from Tommy.

"So you grow your niggers, do you?"

Tommy felt the red reeling inside his brain. He fought against it.

"Sentry!" Weatherby no longer spoke to Tommy.

The door opened. Two big sailors wearing pistols and billy clubs stepped into the room.

"Take this nigger to the brig."

The two sailors did not take Tommy to the brig. Eventually, six other guards ended up taking Tommy and the two sentries to the ship's infirmary. Lieutenant Commander Weatherby had escaped. For even though Tommy had ignored the sentries and gone straight for him, one of the sentries had knocked Tommy to the floor with a glancing blow from his billy-club. In the melee that followed, Weatherby had dashed out of his office unscathed. The sentries were not as fortunate. One suffered multiple broken ribs and a compound fracture of the collar-bone. The other received a ruptured spleen and a dislocated elbow. They both had a number of cuts and abrasions, particularly about their faces and hands.

For their part, they had not left Tommy unharmed. They gave him two hair-line skull fractures, a hairline fracture of the left shoulder blade, two black eyes, innumerable cuts and bruises, and a compound fracture of the left tibia.

Pearson was pleased. He was not satisfied, but he was pleased.

Lieutenant Commander Weatherby decided not to pursue the court martial. He believed Tommy's injuries constituted suitable punishment for his effrontery, and Lieutenant Commander Weatherby prided himself on not being vindictive. Moreover, there was the slight consideration that a court martial would pry into every aspect of the incident, trying to figure out what had caused such a violent eruption. It might prove a little messy. Therefore, Weatherby ordered an official report stating that all three sailors had been injured by near-misses from dive-bomber attacks. They were scheduled for immediate medical evacuation.

That was the combat injury that earned Tommy Brown a purple heart and put him in the U.S. Naval Hospital at Great Lakes, Illinois, a week before Christmas of 1943.

A TALE OF THREE STORIES:
ELECTA'S, WAYNE'S, AND TOMMY'S

1

Electa would have had no reason to believe in love-at-first sight except that it happened to her the instant she saw Tommy Brown.

When Electa thought about it afterward, she told herself it had to be his smile.

She had gone over to the rooming house where Betty stayed. They sat on the steps and waited for Betty's boyfriend, Kenneth, and his older brother. He was a war hero, wounded in the war, somewhere out in the Pacific.

Betty remembered him from when she had been a girl in Tuscompany. He had been the big hero there, starred in all kinds of sports. She didn't remember that. She'd been too young to know about such things, but she knew the stories everybody told. Years later people still told them. So she guessed he had been the best. Kenny could never stop talking about his big brother. Betty remembered him from a later time, when he was a grown man, right before he went off to join the Navy. She'd remembered him as a great, big, beautiful man. But she hadn't seen him since, and that had been five or six years ago. She'd grown up a lot since then. She hadn't seen him until he arrived at Great Lakes. Kenny had gone up to see him and had taken her.

As they sat on the steps, Betty said, "Girl ... he is so fine."

Electa looked nervously down the street. She didn't feel comfortable doing this.

"I thought you said nobody could ever be as fine as Kenneth," said Electa.

Betty giggled. "I didn't say he was fine as Kenneth. But ... girl ... he is so fine." She grinned from ear to ear. "Wait 'till you see him. I didn't believe it. I'll tell you this, if I didn't already have Kenneth, you wouldn't be the one

307

sittin' on these steps to see him."

Her enthusiasm swept over her in a rush. "Girl ... we gon' have such a good time together - the four of us."

It was then that in her fidgetiness Electa saw the two men coming down the street. They were both dressed in navy blues. Kenneth was wearing his white, sailor's cap. He walked beside a slightly taller, slightly slimmer man on crutches, one leg in a cast. The man on crutches wore what looked like an officer's cap, with a shiny, black bib.

Electa noticed that he swung along on his crutches at an easy pace. She could at last hear their voices, though she couldn't distinguish the words. She couldn't tell what they were saying.

Betty grabbed Electa's forearm and squeezed it.

"Girl ...." she said.

She was more excited than Electa.

By then they were very close.

The man on crutches had been looking at the ground in front of him. He stopped and raised his face.

He saw Electa.

He smiled.

That was it.

It was everything Electa could do to keep herself from falling down the steps.

She didn't even hear what Betty was saying. Her ears were ringing.

She knew one thing. She couldn't stand up. Her knees would not hold her.

So she kept her seat on the step and kept staring at the man with the beautiful smile and did not know if she were grinning back or what.

The first thing she remembered hearing Betty say was, "The girl ain't got no manners. Just look at her sittin' there on her rumpty-dumpty."

And then he laughed.

2

Wayne hated Tommy Brown on sight. He was on crutches wearing a cast. He had ribbons on his chest and stripes and anchors on his sleeve and he was grinning. He had a wide smile, pretty, white, even teeth, and a thin line of a moustache like Errol Flynn's. He was tall, broad in the shoulders, the color of highly polished blonde furniture, and handsome. He stood in front of Electa's door talking and grinning at her.

Tommy had never met anyone like Electa Frye. She reminded him of the woman he had seen at the club in San Francisco through the haze of smoke in the dim light. Heart-shaped face and almond eyes. A smile to part the darkness. He had let her get away. He had not even met her. But he had met Electa Frye. Made you scared to look at her and sometimes you couldn't take your eyes off her no matter how hard you tried. Delicate. Seemed like she'd be delicate and fragile and need protection. But there was a wire inside her. Quiet, with a son. She loved her son and protected him with the wire inside her and nobody could touch him. Intelligent. Tommy had never known anyone so smart. Not just because she talked proper, and he did love listening to her. But smart way past that. She saw things. And understood things. And could figure out things. All in that body with the steel wire inside and the outside so startling and woman-looking he had to convince himself she was real.

The phone rang infrequently and when it rang Electa was always a little nervous.

309

"Hello," she said.

"Hello. Miz Frye?"

"Yes, this is she."

Electa could tell from the sound of the phone that the party-line had picked up the phone and was listening.

"Hi, this is Tommy Brown. You remember me?"

"Tommy," she said. "Kenneth's brother. Of course, I remember you."

"Good -"

Electa remembered the party-line listener.

"I think you should know we have some company on this phone-line."

He paused just an instant.

"I hopes we does," he said, "cause the reason I'm callin' is that the Navy is puttin' on a drive axin' peoples t'donate ration cards to the war effort. We wants as many peoples as possible t'hear about it, and we's axin' that most specially ration cards for milk, meat, gasoline -"

They heard the click as the snooper hung up.

They both laughed.

"You sure think fast on your feet," she said.

"Well, more like on my butt," he replied. "I cain't hardly hold a telephone and stand on my crutches at the same time, so I'm settin' down with my cast propped up. But, no, uh, nobody never accused me of bein' slow at thinkin'. Course, I know I might not sound like it - the way I talks. I ain't never got the education what I wanted. I'm shamed o' that. And ... I guess part of talkin' this away jest come from livin' in blip."

"Blip?"

"Yeah, that's what we calls the South - Kenny and me. That's where I'm from and gon' stay from cause I ain't never goin' back. Blip. Cross the Mason-Dixon line."

"I'm from the South, you know."

"Uh-huh. And water ain't wet, neither."

310

"No, Tommy. I'm telling you the truth."

"Now, now, Miz Frye -"

"Electa. Electa, please."

"Thank you, Ma'am. Okay. Electa. Now, I done been around the world. I done spoke with peoples from everywheres. I knows sailors from everywheres. When somebody's from the south, I knows it. I can hear it. I might not can tell you exactly where they's from - but mostly I will get pretty close. And you ain't from nowheres near the South."

"I was born in Waycross, Georgia. All my mother's and father's people are from Jacksonville, Florida - well, not exactly Jacksonville, outside Jacksonville, a little place called Mandarin."

"You wasn't raised up in no Waycross, though, was you?"

"No."

"See - see - I told you. I knowed you wasn't from the South, I mean raised up in the South. That's what I'm talkin' about. I done been around. I done seen too much."

"I was raised ... in Brunswick, Georgia."

"Please Miz - uh, uh, Electa. Please, Electa, don't be playin' with me. You wasn't raised in no Georgia."

"By my grandmother, my father's mother, till I was ten years old."

"Well, I'll be ... I would of swore ... I would of bet cash money."

"And lost," she laughed.

He laughed, too. "Well, looka here," he said. "How come you don't talk like you's from blip?"

Hearing "blip" again made her laugh.

"I don't know for sure," she said. "The Wenders, my father's people, those are some high-fallutin' Negroes. Think they're better than everyone else. And when Mama married one of them she just fell right into that. So, you

311

know, they always told us we had to act like Wenders - which to them meant better than everybody else. That included the way we talked. I didn't really fit into their plan too well."

"How you mean?"

"Well ... like, I mean, I was a tomboy. Rough. Always wanted to fight somebody. Wouldn't do what I was told. Tore my clothes running through bushes and climbing trees. Wenders girls were not supposed to behave that way. My sisters didn't."

"Somehow I jest cain't picture you -"

"I know. I know. That's what everybody says. But I was a tough little heifer. Mama didn't know what to do with me when I finally came up here to live with her when I was ten. She put me in a convent school - till they threw me out after about a year."

"Was yo Mama and yo Daddy both up here?"

"No, no, just Mama. She came up here to work, to make money. She sent money back down there to take care of us, and then, one by one, she brought us up here as she could afford it."

"How many of you is it?"

"Four - three girls. I'm the youngest of all four of us, and I'm the only one who married. My brother's the oldest. He's in the army. In Italy."

"There's nine of us. Seven boys and two girls. I'm third from the oldest. I ... uh ... I been married, too."

"Well, aren't you full of surprises, Mr. Brown. You aren't still married, are you?"

"I wouldn't be callin' you if I was."

"Oh, I don't know. You know what they say about sailors - a girl in every port."

"I knows what they says - but - I'm serious about this. You - you is special. And, besides, I - I ain't speakin' for nobody else. But *I* - *I* wouldn't be callin' you if I was

312

married. I don't believe in it. I'm divorced."

"Oh."

They both thought for a while, neither one saying anything.

"I likes your little boy," he said at last. "I'm crazy about kids."

She did not want to open that up. She knew how Gabriel was with men.

"He's kind of shy," she said.

"Takes after his Mama, huh?"

"Yes - I guess you could say I'm shy."

"Tomboy and all?"

"Yeah, being a tomboy doesn't stop you from being shy. I don't know. Raised in the country and all, I never was used to being around a lot of people. Coming up here was a big change for me."

"Mmhmm. I guess it was pretty hard for your Mama, too. Four kids. By herself?"

"Yep. By herself."

"Does you ever - I mean, does you ever hear from yo Daddy."

"No. They. In 'blip'. As you say. They killed him."

"Oh. I'm. I'm sorry."

"So am I."

He didn't know what to say.

"You know," she said, "normally I don't talk much. I am - as you guessed - shy."

"Don't make it seem like I guessed it. Kenny done told me. He said you was shy. 'Beautiful, prettiest thing you'll ever see,' he said, 'but I don't know if you'll get two words out of her.'

"Well, he was right on the first part, so I figured he was right on the second, too."

Electa had become accustomed to men telling her

she was beautiful, but as she did not ever know how to take it, she ignored it.

"Well, I am shy," she said. "And most people *wouldn't* have gotten two words out of me. But, I don't know. I like talking to you. I - I don't know why."

3

Electa had to be careful. Not just for herself. Gabriel. Because he was only three and she a single mother, people assumed she had developed an especially protective attitude about him. There was a touch of truth to that but not in the way most people imagined. She had to protect people from Gabriel, especially men. She had dated but the only man she really cared about since her husband died was her brother, Stephen. The men she went out with were usually fun. No more than that. She didn't get close to them. One of the reasons was her son.

He had assumed responsibility for protecting her. His mother. He had to defend her from the ravages of the world. Even the pin. Once he had lived past the panic of the terrifying metal intrusion into his body, he had simply gone on and pee'd it out so he could get on with the business of taking care of his mother.

She remembered the auto accident. She had trouble accepting what had happened, that it had not been a dream. It had seemed too unreal, too ... unnatural that her little son should behave the way he did. They had been coming home from a picnic, riding with friends. The darkness was refreshing. Everyone had been wonderfully relaxed. She sat in the front seat with Phil who was driving, and Gabriel was in the back with the other children and Rhonda and Betty.

A car ran into them from behind. The driver was drunk, so drunk he felt no pain from his broken collar bone and the rent in his head that first showed bare bone then rapidly filled with blood. He had staggered out of his car, taken out his wallet and incongruously begun giving big wads of cash to everyone, explaining incoherently in nonsequitors why they must accept his money.

315

Gabriel had been knocked from the back seat into the windshield. The glass had not broken, but his forehead had immediately swelled to the size of the rest of his head. The whites of his eyes had hemorrhaged, blackened swirls surrounded them.

The crash had bumped Electa's lips against the dashboard. A trickle of blood ran out of her mouth. She had cracked a tooth.

"Mama!" Gabriel cried.

Before she could reach out or speak to comfort him, he had sprung into the seat by her side. "You're hurt," he moaned. Tenderly he placed a hand against the side of her face. He turned fiercely and stared at the people outside the car milling around in confusion. "Don't worry, Mama," he said, "I won't let anything else happen to you. I'll take care of you."

She tried to cradle him. "Gabriel, oh, Gabriel," she sobbed.

"Don't worry, Mama, I'm alright." He patted her. "I'm alright." Then he had jumped out of the car and grabbed Phil who had been trying to make sense out of the drunken driver.

He pulled Phil away from the sot. "My Mama's hurt," he had told him.

When he had seen Phil break away from the drunk and go off to find a telephone, he had climbed back into the car to comfort her.

"It's going to be alright, Mama. I love you, Mama."

The world had to be protected from him. Especially men.

No further proof was needed than Toby Hammond.

Once Electa had started going out after her husband died, Toby was one of the first men she had seen. Little Gabriel had not liked him. He had not wanted his mother to go out with him.

He made that clear.

He told Electa and he told Toby.

He did not like him.

Still, Toby was comfortable and fun to be around, and he was not trying to get her in bed, so Electa felt at ease with him.

One evening he sat in the living room waiting for Electa to get ready. He was nicely dressed in suit and tie. Toby was 4-F.

Gabriel sat on the couch beside him. "I don't like the way you look at my Mama," said Gabriel.

Toby laughed. "Boy, your Mama's pretty, that's all. Any man's going to look at her that way. Go on. I'm not going to hurt her. I like her."

"I don't like you."

"Maybe not now, but you'll like me after a while. I like little boys. I like you, Gabriel, even if you don't like me."

He reached out a hand to pat Gabriel.

"Don't touch me.

"Why don't you go home. I don't want you to take my Mama out."

"Don't worry, Gabriel. I'm going to take your Mama out so she can have a good time. Don't you want her to have a good time? I won't even keep her out very long. Soon I'll bring her back to you."

Gabriel jumped down from the couch and walked back through the house to the kitchen. He opened one of the kitchen drawers and pulled out the big hammer. He closed the drawer. He walked back into the living room. Toby was thinking about Electa and did not pay any attention to Gabriel when he climbed back on the couch. He did not see him raise the hammer with the full extension of both arms and bring it down on Toby's head with all the strength of his three-year-old body.

Any man she cared about would have to be protected from Gabriel. She could not let herself show how she felt about Tommy Brown. Her son might kill him.

4

The Chicago police investigated Light's murder for two weeks, then they dropped it. Except for the police he had paid off, they were happy he was dead anyway. The ones he had paid off soon hunted down new pimps or numbers kings to pay them off so they did not grieve long. Murder. For reasons unknown. By persons unknown. Case closed. That is the way the police wanted it. Who could be punished for killing somebody like Claude Bonfils? Send them a plaque.

Not everyone agreed with the police. Some people missed Light. He had maintained a very large payroll. No one else was capable of holding together all the ladies necessary to sustain it. Many, many people found themselves out of work and out of money, people who had been used to very long money. They did not like that. And they knew who had killed Light. Because Nice had seen him. LBN. They were looking for him.

Camilla was looking for him, too. He had betrayed her. He had used her to get Light then he had disappeared. He had gone and taken Mr. Big with him and she could get no satisfaction anywhere. She was going crazy. She roamed the streets of the Southside and the Westside looking for him. Periodically, she took on dozens of men consecutively in marathon attempts to achieve sexual gratification. Failing, she became even more desperate and obsessed with the need to find LBN.

When I find him, she thought, I will fuck him. Then I will kill him. I will fuck him to death then I will kill him and I will kill myself. What he done to me, what he done to me, I will kill the nigger and die. Die! But I must have him before I die, fuck, fuck, with that big thing so huge in me then I will die and so will he.

319

She began to think, trying to remember anything and everything he had said and done for a clue about where he was. And she began to cooperate with the others who were looking for him. She gave up her bouts with long lines of men and channeled all of her swelling and burgeoning energies and looming madness into single-minded pursuit.

5

Tommy Brown tried to figure out what it was. He liked having a lot of women. Suddenly he did not want them. He liked seeing a different piece of chocolate every time he went out. Suddenly, he wanted to see only one woman.

It was a mystery to him. He knew no women who looked like Electa, or who were like Electa. Still ... why not Electa AND the other women? That was the part he could not understand. He could see being crazy about a woman, but why JUST her? It did not make sense to him. But he could not get around it. He did not want the others.

For days Electa had been feeling on top of the world. Sometimes riding the El home from work, or playing with Gabriel, or "heaven forbid," even washing dishes she felt as if she and the world were alive - radiant - filled with sunshine.

Sometimes the recognition of how good she felt and had been feeling hit her - especially when she was doing something like scrubbing the floor or hammering rivets home into a DC-3. She wondered why. She knew there was a reason for her outrageous *joi de vivre*. She just could not place it.

Then every now and then she remembered.
Tommy Brown.
Oh, God. How good I feel to know that man.

6

The music was not exciting. Camilla was not paying any attention to it. She was also not paying any attention to the big, greasy man who sat across the table from her trying under the table to run the mammoth palms of his hands across her stockings above the knees.

She was paying attention to Wayne Hunter. She had not realized when they had been setting up Light how careful he had been not to disclose where he was living or working. She had by now, she was sure, triple-checked the furthest reaches of her memory, recalled every syllable of each conversation they had shared. He had not once let a single hint slip. At the time she had not thought about it. But going back over it as she now did several times every day it was clear he had never intended to let her be able to find him. He used me. He used me. All along I thought I was going to have him after he killed Light, and he never intended to see me again. He did the whole thing from hiding and never let me know his hiding place or anything about it.

She would have to rely on other things she knew about him, things Matilda had told her, and things she knew from his life in the street. To begin with, she knew he was in Chicago. He had not gone back to Kentucky as everyone believed. He was in Chicago because he had been able to meet her at various rendezvous as quickly as he had. As long as he was in Chicago she could find him. She knew too many people not to be able to find him, and there were only so many neighborhoods where colored could live.

She took her cigarette case out of her purse and extracted a cigarette. The pig across the table fumbled all over himself lighting it for her. She exhaled in his face.

He loves it, she thought. The idiot.

Wayne was not in the life anymore. That was clear. Had he been, she or one of the others would have located him long ago. No, he was in Chicago but he was not in the life. Matilda ... Matilda had told her what he had done before Light had hired him. But she could not remember. She hadn't cared then, and she hadn't been paying attention. If she could only remember the work he did, she would have two places to find him - where he lived and where he worked.

When I find him, she thought, I'm not going to tell them right away. He's going to satisfy me first. Again and again and again. He's going to give me everything I've been agonizing for all these months. Again and again and again. He's going to fuck my brains out and then when I'm quite sure I can't take another inch for another second, I'm going to turn him over to them, and when they get through with him, I'm going to cut it off for a trophy. Personally, I'm going to hold it with one hand, and reach down with the other, and cut it off. I'm going to get it stuffed - in full erection - and hang it on my living room wall. No one will believe it's real.

She looked across the table at the sweating face, dilated nostrils and distended eyeballs.

She knew there was not enough liquor in the world to get her through the night.

7

"Are you sure you want to go for - well, you can't exactly call it a walk. You can't actually walk with a crutch under each arm and a cast on your leg." Electa laughed. "Are you sure you want to accompany me while I walk," she asked.

Tommy Brown enjoyed simply looking at her. Listening to her voice made him feel good all over and the prospect of sharing her company while she went for a walk was at that moment everything he wanted in life.

"Sure. Sure. Absolutely, positively sure," he said.

"Okay, let's go."

She took the two steps down to stand by his side.

"I would love to take your arm," she smiled, "but that is out of the question."

He followed her to the gate. She opened it for him. After she closed it, they proceeded east on Tary, toward the lake.

"Sure is pretty around here," he said.

"Everybody around here is a millionaire. That's why it's so beautiful."

"You ain't a millionaire, is you, Electa?"

She laughed. "Well, Wimbey's Corner is a little different."

"Yeah," he said, rising to the subject. "You got t'admit it's a strange little place where you lives at."

"You said it. I don't know of - **ANYPLACE** - like Wimbey's Corner."

He swung along easily beside her, adjusting his pace to her stride. She moved with a fluid, athletic grace.

"You get along pretty good for a crippled man," she observed.

"Better than most men without crutches and a cast," he shot back.

"Listen to you. You must be the very devil when you've got your legs under you."

"I am. I am. I always been good at sports. That's one reason the professor, he were my teacher at school, that's one reason he wanted me to stay in school - for the sports. He done told me I could do anything I wanted in sports. I guess he were right. I was the best at everything what I tried. Tuscompany - that's where I'm from, Florence, too. The twin cities. Everybody knowed me. 'That there's Tommy Brown,' they'd say. I was the best. Even in the eighth grade I was better than the high school boys. But. It wasn't meant t'be. We had all them kids at home.

"My mother raised us up by herself. Jest like yourn. 'Cept my Daddy wasn't dead. He were right there in the same town, with another woman here and another woman there. He had the idea he was somethin' special with the womens. He were half-white. Even looked like a sorry-ass white man. I hated the way he looked. I never claimed him. But he claimed us. Yeah. He claimed every kid what he ever made. Proud o' that. Makin' us. Makin' kids. But he didn't do nothin' about raisin' us up. Hell - scuse my language, but when I thinks about my Daddy I cain't help gettin' mad. That's another thing. I gots a bad temper. But around you it's like it go away. My temper is somethin' what I gots t'work on. It git me in a whole lot of trouble. But like I were sayin' - even a goat can make kids. So I don't see nothin' special about that. It's raisin' 'em up what makes a man. And my Daddy didn't do none o' that with his half-white self. Had kids all over Tuscompany and Florence and didn't raise up none of 'em. Always tryin' t'take credit for 'em, though. Like he had somethin' t'do with 'em.

"And Mama, I don't know. Mama jest loved him. He was the only man what she ever knowed. Of all his womens, she was the only one what he ever married and she thought that meant somethin'. I don't know what as he dogged all his womens the same.

"But since Mama was tryin' t'raise all of us up by herself, I had to leave school and work. Do what I could t'help the family. I were a good worker, too. Kenny. Kenny went through high school. I'm proud o' that."

They reached Tary Park on the lake.

The water smelled of life.

She slipped one arm around his.

"Look," she said, pointing to the left as they faced the lake.

A small, stony beach backed onto the drive that ran along the lake. The waters lapped languidly against the shore. In the light, the slightly winking surface seemed grey. The ripples sighed against the pebbles.

"That's free beach," she said. "That's where colored can swim.

"I'm a good swimmer - what about you? I mean, when you can?"

"Well, when I gits out o' this cast," he answered, "we'll have t'see jest how good a swimmer you is." He radiated confidence. "Cause, far as I'm concerned, you lookin' at the best."

She squeezed his arm. "We'll see," she said.

Fire burned in her eyes.

In the darkness of her living room Electa leaned back into her couch. As she thought about their goodbye, she could feel his arms coming around her, she could reach up and extend her arms over his shoulders. She could feel

326

the closeness of their bodies.

Get a hold of yourself, girl. You have to know what he's up to. After his leg heals, after he's out of Great Lakes with new orders he may simply be on to the next filly, your broken heart left in his wake.

She breathed deeply, slowly, for a long time.

That's better. Better.

Don't let yourself go crazy.

You know what's happening with Kenneth and Betty. They seem serious. You know for you with Tommy it will have to be serious, too.

From the first time I saw him.

8

Late afternoon, almost dusk, Tommy and Electa sat on her back steps watching Gabriel and Bobo playing catch in the little, communal back yard. It was supposed to be catch, but more accurately, it was Bobo throwing the ball and Gabriel waiting until it hit the ground and rolled slowly enough to pick it up, then Gabriel threw the ball and if it went anywhere near Bobo and remained in the air long enough, Bobo caught it.

"I loves kids," said Tommy. "I always wanted to have a kid of my own - boy or girl - it don't make me no difference. I love 'em all."

"You ... and ... your wife. You didn't have any," ventured Electa.

"No. I ... I don't like to think of that woman as my wife. I guess I really did love her - up to the last. But I don't now. She kilt that. She ain't my wife no more. We's divorced. Through. Quit. And I don't like to think of her as my wife. She ain't my wife. Not no more. I ain't got no wife. And no kids. That woman didn't have no kids by me."

Electa put her hand on his shoulder. She massaged it. It was hard to think of Tommy as a gentle man - with his temper and all - she had seen flashes of it. But he was. Gentle. And even *he* said it was due to her influence. She didn't know about that part, but he repeatedly asserted that his temper was coming more and more under control. She turned to look at his profile and smiled. Handsome. Handsome, gentle Tommy.

"I ... I don't like to think about that woman," he said. "Her name is Jessica. But seem like to me I wants to talk to you about everything. Would you mind?"

"No."

She moved her free hand to his right hand and squeezed it.

"I was crazy about that woman," he said. It was hard for him to tell a woman he loved and wanted to love him how strong his feelings had been for Jessica, but the story would not be true unless he did, so he made himself.

"She was the prettiest girl in the twin cities, wild and crazy. I knowed she had told some girls, 'That sandy-headed nigga's gon' be mines.' They done told me she said it, and done said it like she was braggin'. They done told me so's I wouldn't pay her no mind, so I would take it on myself to prove her wrong. Cause they was sweet on me theyself. But it didn't work like they wanted it to. What they done said jest made me pay her mo' attention, cause then I knowed I had a chance. So I got bold. I axed her out. We went out a few times. It jest made her want me mo'. I knowed her reputation - how fast she were and everything, and I wanted her bad, I don't mean jest to go to bed with, I means I wanted her like she done tol' them girls she wanted me. I wanted her to be mines.

"So, you know, I wouldn't sleep with her. That upset her somethin' turrible. Liked t'drive her crazy. She ain't never run into that befo'. She didn't have no idea of what t'do. So ... uh ... we got into all kinds of situations but we always got out of 'em without doin' nothin' cause I done told her how special she were to me and I couldn't be doin' nothin' to her less'n we was married, I didn't care what she done with nobody else.

"She thought she was losin' her mind the way she felt. She had t'have me. So when I finally axed her would she marry me, she couldn't git the yes out fast enough, and she done made me the happiest man in the world. Once we was married she right away stopped workin'. I done everything for her. I worked two jobs, brought home all my pay and give it to her, except the little bit I kept t'give my

329

Mama. That woman didn't even have to cook. I cooked. And when I didn't, I'd take her out somewheres - it was a couple chicken places in town and churches was always sellin' dinners, or we'd go to a boardin' house. I cleaned the floors, washed the dishes, the windows. Everything. That woman didn't have to lift her little finger. I was a fool in love.

"Then one day the man on my second job done told me he didn't need me that day. I was jest as happy as I could be - t'get home early to my baby.

"She was laid up in my bed with another man. I walked away from blip that day and ain't been back since. We done the divorce through the mail. I turned around and walked out of that room and out of that house and out of that town and out of the South. Because if I wouldn't of turned around that second and got t'steppin' it, I would of kilt them both.

"So, I. No, I ain't got no wife. Never had one neither. But I didn't know that then."

"So, I guess you're very careful about women now ... since that happened." She squeezed his hand.

"To tell you the truth, no. Because it were like my heart turned to stone. I ain't had no reason to be careful. I ain't never been in no danger, till now."

9

"Where's the kid?"

"He's at Mama's."

Tommy looked along his left arm which lay draped on top of the couch. Six inches away from his left hand, which draped over the edge of a cushion, was her lovely face.

"You sent him over there cause I was comin'."

She smiled, looking straight ahead. "Not exactly." She dropped her head and glanced at him briefly, then looked away again. "His grandmother likes to take care of him. And besides ... I thought we should have this time to ourselves."

"Well, yeah," he said, "but I never do get t'see him."

"I know. But you will."

"When?"

"After the war."

"That could be a long time from now."

"Maybe. Maybe you won't have to go back."

"I don't believe in no fairytales," he said.

"What do you mean?"

"I mean my leg is gettin' better, and when it gits all the way better, they gon' send me back, and the fightin' gon' be a long way from over."

"Let's not talk about that," she said.

They sat quietly for a few minutes.

She was wondering if he were planning not to come back after the war and that's what he meant when he said it was a long time. He didn't believe in fairytales. Was he trying to tell her something? No happy endings?

She threw a desperate glance in his direction. Oh, god. What am I going to do if he leaves me?

He looked at her delicate hands cradling each other

in her lap.

"Wanna play some gin?" he asked.

She smiled.

"Sure."

He grinned. "Wanna drink some, too?"

She laughed. She stood up and walked toward the kitchen. "You get the cards," she said. "I'll get the refreshments."

10

Wayne watched the sailor close the gate, wave, and disappear up Tary Street. Electa stood on her porch, the wind blowing her dress against the curves of her figure, one hand raised in farewell.

Wayne turned away from the screen door.

"I don't think anything's wrong with that sailor," he said.

"You mean Tommy Brown," Penny asked. She smiled, her dimples showing.

"I don't know the nigga's name. The one comes around here carrying that cane."

"Tommy Brown," said Penny. "Electa's sweet on him."

"Not a damn thing wrong with the nigger," said Wayne. "The way he uses that cane I don't ever see him limp. He uses it like it's somethin' t'be proud of. They need to ship him back out in that war somewhere."

"Don't say that, Wayne. That's horrible to wish on anybody. Besides, they say he's very nice."

"Who does? Who says he's so nice?"

"Oh ... well ... Electa ... and Virginia, and Mrs. Wenders, and Betty Cutter."

"Betty Cutter! You listen to her? That woman's a fool. She's a simpleton. She say's he's nice - why he must be a goddamned pervert!"

"Wayne! What's wrong with you? You don't talk like that. Betty might not be too smart, but she's very nice. She has ... woman's intuition. And, besides, she isn't the only one. You just hate sailors."

"Soldiers, too," said Wayne. "And I'll tell you one thing. There's nothing wrong with that one. He's no cripple. But he ought to be."

"Wayne Hunter!"

Wayne hated that grinning, yellow nigger in his uniform. He would like to get the chance to take him apart. To take him apart right in front of little Miss Electa. Then she would see who the real man was.

11

One morning early Wayne took Gabriel alone, to the Pond.

It was dark when they arrived on the water. Every sound seemed to violate the night-tinted air. The car doors creaked open and slammed shut. The tackle boxes rattled and clattered. Wayne's and Gabriel's shoes scraped and scuffed over stones.

Like shouts their whispered voices stabbed into the quiet.

Overhead a black sky held scattered points of white fire from a hundred stars. The moon - half a brilliant disc - cast a pale glow in the sable heavens.

Wayne and Gabriel stood beside each other a moment. Silent.

They could smell the water.

A frog chugged.

The air felt cool and sweet to the lungs.

A bird cried.

They heard fish rising.

A stretch of dark water reflected the moon and stars. Silhouettes of water reeds and cattails framed the Pond's surface.

After a while Wayne chuckled, a full, deep sound. He patted Gabriel on the shoulder.

"There's nothin' like it, boy," he said.

Gabriel smiled unseen.

They walked quietly, respectfully, toward the water's edge.

"Did I ever tell you about Mr. Big," asked Wayne.

"No."

"Well, it's best to talk about him now, before the sun comes up. He's too busy eating now to pay much

335

attention to us. But later on he'll hear everything we say."

"Who is he?"

"A fish. He lives right here in the Pond. He's the biggest fish you'll ever see."

"How big is he?"

"Bigger than you, Gabriel."

Gabriel's eyes widened.

"Yes, Mr. Big is the great, great, great, great grandaddy of all fish. The biggest, smartest, oldest fish in the world."

"Why does he eat in the dark?"

"Because he's smarter than other fish, that's why. When do all the fishermen come out?"

"In the daytime."

"That's right. And Mr. Big just sleeps the day away so he won't have to be bothered with us."

"Where does he sleep?"

"Under a ledge, behind a log, in the deepest part of the Pond. He keeps turtles, and snakes, and tadpoles, and other fish all around him to warn him if any trouble comes his way. Besides, if he gets hungry during the day, he can just reach out and gobble one up without worrying about somebody trying to catch him."

"How can he hear us if he's asleep?"

"Well, he doesn't go to sleep right away. First he listens to see if there's anybody up here he has to worry about."

" Like a Master fisherman?"

"That's right. If not, he just goes to sleep. If there is, he posts a special guard before he settles down. Has one of his smartest lieutenants keep an eye on us."

"Can he really understand us."

"Sure. He's not like other fish. That's how he got to be so big. Special. Special brains."

"And he eats at night?"

336

"Yep. He comes up when the last fisherman leaves. Swims around the Pond and checks who was caught during the day. What damage we fishermen did. What we threw in the water. What piece of bank we crumbled. What water plants we broke. What we pulled out of the water. What lines we snagged. When he's inventoried everything and made sure nobody's around, he starts eating."

"Have you ever seen him?"

"I've seen him, and I'm going to show him to you before he goes to bed this morning."

The man and the boy set out their lines - Gabriel first, Wayne helping him, and showing him, teaching him. Then Wayne set out his own.

They waited.

They caught fish, Gabriel laughing in his excitement, forgetting all about Mr. Big.

In the dark they had to go by tactile sensations - the quivering, twitching, tugging tremors transmitted from the hook, to the line, to the pole handle where the hands, alive with expectation, waited.

"I got him," Gabriel would cry out.

Or, "Oh - I missed him."

He was just as excited after a miss as after catching a fish. The excitement when he missed was wrought out of loss, fired by a determination that it would not happen the next time. *Only let him come back. Only let him come back.*

Wayne put his big hand on Gabriel's tiny shoulder. He pointed with the giant index finger of his other hand. A red line seeped up along the edges of the horizon, above it a slight glow lightened the sky.

They could see, clearly now, the mists rising off the surface of the water dimpled by feeding fish.

Having Gabriel's full attention fixed to his pointing finger, Wayne swung it to a patch of smooth water standing

337

off a clump of water weeds. The mist lifted for an instant off that span of the pond, clean, smooth. Like glass, like sliding glass. Then water rose up and swelled, the surface split open, something dark, long, huge, and rounded like a log, emerged and rolled over, submerged, sucking water down in its descending wake. The flat plane of a giant tail fin sliced up through the troubled topwater and was gone.

Gabriel. Four years old. Never. In his whole life forgot the sight.

12

Electa and Tommy, Betty and Kenneth double-dated a lot . They thought of themselves as a foursome. Each couple thought of itself as just like the other. The men, after all, were brothers. And the women were best friends.

More than that, Tommy and Kenneth were both sailors, and Electa and Betty both worked at the Douglass plant. They had so much in common. They had the future in common.

They laughed, rode the el, and took taxi-cabs together. They picknicked and sat in clubs and listened to music and loved it all.

They did not talk about the war. The newspapers were full of it. The radio was full of it. The newsreels were full of it. They did not have to talk about it.

They were not always together. Sometimes Electa and Betty had an evening or a weekend morning or afternoon in each other's company. Sometimes each couple had time alone.

But more often than not the four were together.

"The Four Musketeers" Electa dubbed them.

The uncertainty of when the Brothers would have to go back to the war required them to fill every minute of their lives. There was a tremendous energy, a zest in everything they did.

They never asked what was going to happen in the future. It dominated their thoughts - but none of them ever mentioned it.

Kenneth, however, could not live with that uncertainty. Betty was too important to him. He had to know what the future held for the two of them.

That is why he asked her to marry him. He was

unable not to ask her.

That is what separated the two couples. Until then they had been the same.

They never were again.

In the darkness Electa could not stop the sobs from shaking her shoulders. She stifled the sounds, though. She could not let Gabriel hear her.

She could not help hating herself. She was a bad woman. A good woman would be happy. A good woman would be overjoyed. A good woman would be ready to celebrate.

And here she was ready to die.

Oh, I can't help it. It hurts so much.

She was bad. She was bad. She hated herself.

The happiest day in Betty Cutter's life. Kenneth Brown had asked her to marry him.

She had said yes.

She had wanted to make him wait a few days but she had not been able. She had said yes right away. Almost as soon as the words were out of his mouth.

Electa could not stop her shoulders from shaking.

She hated Betty but she really hated herself. She hated Kenneth but she really hated Tommy.

Why not me? Why couldn't Tommy ask me?

I love him.

I love him.

I love him.

She wanted to kill him she hated him so much. She never wanted to see him again in her life. She wanted to hurt him. She wanted to hurt him as badly as she could.

Like some giant from a mythological age. That is how Wayne looked to Electa as he stood with his back to her, looking over the alley fence toward Miss Bryce's yard.

She did not intentionally flirt. She wanted to stab Tommy Brown. She wanted him to know he was not the only man in the world. She wanted to feel human contact with another man. She did not intentionally flirt. Wayne Hunter stood alone, his massive back to her, he who had been so good to her son. She felt close to him. She walked up and put her delicate hand on a vast muscle spanning his back.

He turned his head around, looked down and saw gazing up at him a face of such angelic beauty he wanted to cry out. The hand on his back which had merely been a pleasant and unknown touch began to sear his flesh.

"Thanks, Wayne," she said.

She patted him.

Each repetition was like a jab from a branding iron.

"I don't know that I've ever seen Gabriel as happy as he was when he came home yesterday."

She stood beside him, her hand still on his back.

They both looked across the alley at the long, white wall that was Miss Bryce's fence.

Wayne did not try to speak. He knew that all that would come out would be a stuttering rush of sound. Or a howl. A howl of pain at the hole her hand was burning in his back.

341

13

The lights rocked by the el window. Many flats had their shades up. Tommy could look right into the kitchen windows. People were doing everything. Eating. Playing cards. Lots of times men were in their undershirts. The women were usually dressed, but here and there one wore only a slip. Tommy looked greedily forward to each window, wondering what he would see next.

There were arguments. They were easy to tell by the poses people struck, sometimes by the violence of their gestures.

People's business all out in the street, thought Tommy. He did not like that. He liked to keep his business to himself, though he did not mind looking in on somebody else's.

He kept watching the windows and looking forward to the next scene. He did not want to think about his own business. He could take a hint.

Electa was through with him.

We should be celebrating tonight.

Kenny and Betty were going to get married and we should all be celebrating together.

I'm gon' celebrate anyway, thought Tommy. He pressed his face against the glass.

She ain't home. The kid said she wasn't there. Tommy hadn't believed him. He had called two more times. He bet the party line loved that. The kid had always answered. She ain't here. He didn't talk like that. He talked proper. But that's what he meant.

Tommy finally had gone by there. Nobody had answered the door. But he knew she was there. Gon' just shine him on. Tommy Brown could take a hint. He didn't have to put up with no shit like that and wasn't about to.

342

Who did she think she was? Who in the hell did she think she was?

That's alright. I'm goin' to Chicago tonight. By myself. Gon' have me a good time! Shoulda done it a long time ago. But never mind. I ain't gon' waste no more days. You can believe you me. Uh-uh. No more. That shit is over.

Goin' to Chicago. Sorry but I cain't take you.

The woman he met in the club and spent the weekend with wanted to know how to get in touch with him. That is when she learned he lived in Evanston. Her name was Camilla.

The news was too good to be true. Wayne pulled out a kitchen chair and settled down onto it. His tongue toured the inside of his mouth.

"Uh, well, uh, what you say happened to our little neighbor?"

Penny was almost crying. "You heard me, Wayne. She and Tommy broke up."

"Mm, mm, mm. Ain't that a pity."

"I know you can't stand him. But you should think about her. It's breaking her heart."

The corners of Wayne's lips slowly turned up. I am thinking about her, he thought. I am thinking about her. "So the crippled-ass sailor put her down," he asked.

"No. No. The way she told me, she decided she wasn't going to see him anymore."

"Oh. She put him down and you're up here telling me she's got a broken heart. That doesn't make too much sense."

Maybe it had something to do with me, he thought.

"I don't know why she decided she wouldn't see him anymore. Maybe it was Gabriel," said Penny. "I don't

343

know."

Some things are meant to be, thought Wayne. I fought this as hard as I could. Now this happens. I tried. God knows I tried. Now I've got no choice. And the way she touched me the other day. She must want me. Maybe I'm the cause of her break-up.

He felt the imprint of her small hand on his back. It will never go away. Now. Now there's no need for it ever to go away.

He cleared his throat. "Uh, well, uh, maybe it would help out her and Gabriel if we asked them over for dinner."

Penny lit up into a smile, walked over to Wayne and held his head to her bosom. "Thank you," she said. "You're so good. I never can get over how lucky I am to have you."

Wayne closed his eyes. He had betrayed Penny once. She was such a perfectly good soul. He clutched her. He had to try, he had to try not to yield to the demon within him. He rubbed his face against her breasts. He did not want her to feel the tears. I can be a little stronger, he thought. Just a little stronger.

14

Camilla got into Nice's cadillac and shut the door behind her.

After Wayne had murdered Light, Nice had left Light's line of work and gone into the numbers. He had done very well.

He accelerated away from the curb into the flow of traffic.

"So what's on yo mind, Mama?"

"What do you know about Evanston?"

"It's on the other side of Howard Street," he said, returning his attention to the cars around them.

"I thought it was a rich, white folks town," she said. "Do any niggas live there?"

"Who you think takes care o' them rich, white folks? Yeah, niggas lives there."

She placed her hand on his shoulder. "Look there," she said.

He turned his head sharply to look at her then back to the street.

"What?"

"Look there. For LBN. We know Chicago. We done looked every place in Chicago. He ain't here. Look there. In Evanston."

"Baby, you said when you was seein' him he was in Chicago -"

"I didn't know where he was at. I just knew he wasn't in no Kentucky. He was up here someplace. I didn't know nothin' about no Evanston."

"Yeah, yeah, I see what you mean. But what I'm sayin' is this - when you was seein' him he was up here someplace. Did you ever think that after he dusted Light he split? I mean, like he was here and now he's gone?"

345

She looked straight ahead out of the front window.

"He's here," she said. "He's still here.   Look in Evanston."

Nice smiled. "Alright, Mama. I'll do it. Who knows? I might can set me up a lightweight operation out there."

Camilla took a deep breath.

15

It always took a while for Betty Cutter to realize why she was not absolutely floating on cloud nine. Eventually, she remembered. But it took some time. Because she was the happiest woman in the world. She and Kenneth were going to spend their lives together. Navy didn't matter. War didn't matter. They were pledged to each other for life.

Why, then, did she have this undercurrent of sadness?

Sometimes she didn't remember until she saw Electa.

Sometimes the recognition hit her when she realized the Four Musketeers no longer existed.

She asked Electa one day, "Wasn't the name of that story, 'The Three Musketeers,' anyway?"

Electa laughed.

"Yes," she said. "But there was a fourth one. His name was D'Artagnan. So why not call them what they really were? Anyway, what sense does a third musketeer make without a fourth?" Then she was crying.

Betty didn't know what had happened. Whatever it was, she knew there was no good reason for it.   S h e did know there was no longer a foursome. There was a couple, she and Kenneth. That was all she had ever wanted in the world which was why sometimes it took her a while to realize why such a deep sadness underlay her joy.

This is the couch where Toby got his head busted open, thought Kenny. He smiled. Good. It served him right.

Kenny was uncomfortable, but Tommy was his

brother and there were some things a brother had to do.

Electa appeared in the doorway. She put a hand on the door frame. She watched Kenneth.

"You appear uneasy on my couch. Don't worry. Gabriel's not here. Your head is safe for the time being."

They both chuckled.

"I'm here about Tommy," he said.

She nodded.

"He's goin' crazy."

"Is that why you came? Because HE is going crazy?"

"No, Electa, he is. He won't move offen his bed."

"That doesn't sound crazy to me. More like lazy."

"Electa. Look. I know from Betty you still cares about him. Ain't no reason ... the boy just wanta know what he done wrong. How he can make it up to you."

Electa walked across the room and looked out one of the windows.

"Nothing. There's nothing he can do. He has his life to live and I have mine."

"But, Electa. What did he do? I mean everything was goin' fine. As far as anybody knew wasn't nothin' wrong. Then bam! You cuts him loose. Why? What did he do? You could tell me that. I mean don't you think he should get some kind of explanation, and since you won't see him or talk to him, tell me."

Electa put her back to the window and faced Kenny.

"Let me just say that I made the recognition that it wasn't going to work out between Tommy and me."

"Why?"

She lowered her head, then raised it.

"We're too different, that's all."

"That's what make the world go 'round," said Kenny.

"Kenneth. I appreciate your concern. I respect your interest in your brother's life. But you asked me and I told you. That's that."

Kenny stood up.

"Alright. There's just one more thing I think you should know."

She waited.

"He got his orders."

"What?"

"He's got to be on board a ship in San Diego in two weeks. "They's shippin' him out."

The movement of her hand to her throat was involuntary.

"Betty said she'll call you tomorrow. I guess I'll see you in a little while. Tell Gabriel 'Hi' for me."

Kenny turned away as he went out the door.

Electa stood in the living room, her back to the window, her hand on her throat. She felt as if she were drowning, as if she could not cry for help.

16

"Well ... uh, er ... uh ... I ... uh, I ... uh, heard y-y-you b-b-broke up w-w-wi-wi-with y-y-y-your b-b-b-boy friend."

Electa looked out of the passenger window. Wayne's big Buick was very comfortable.

"Yes, I did," she said. "It was awfully nice of you to give me a ride."

He beamed. "I'm g-g-gl-glad to."

"Lucky for me that Penny didn't mind watching Gabriel while he plays with Bobo. Sometimes that boy's a little more than I can handle. Both of you are so good to him."

"I-I-I ... l-l-l-like him. He's a n–n–n–nice k-k-kid."

She turned her eyes to him. The warmth showed. "I know you do," she said. "He likes you, too. You may be one of a kind. He really doesn't like men. But you - have been very good for him. The things you've done with him. I ... I'll never be able to thank you enough."

Wayne laughed.

"Well ... well ... uh, uh, just a r-r-ridin' to the store with me. That's - that's - that's thanks enough."

She smiled. "You act like I'm the one doing you a favor."

"You are."

That's sweet, she thought. That's a sweet, gentlemanly thing to say, much sweeter and more gentlemanly than Tommy Brown.

He wanted to turn his head to look at her so she could see what was on his mind, but they were coming to a busy intersection. He had to keep his eyes on the traffic.

He swallowed. His brain was a blur. He felt his palms sweaty on the steering wheel.

He was realizing this was first time he had ever been alone with her.

The beginning, he thought.   This is just the beginning.

17

"How are you this afternoon, Mrs. Wenders?"

"Oh, just fine, Miss Hepple. Won't you come in?"

Ruth Wenders opened the screen door of her back porch and welcomed Miss Hepple in. They walked through the porch, the kitchen, the dining room, and into the living room.

"Please, sit down," said Mrs. Wenders.

"I'm worried," said Miss Hepple.

"What's got you worried?"

"That new boy."

"Wayne?"

"The very one. You know, you know he was never properly approved, don't you?"

"Yes, I do. Mr. Stuart explained that to us. He had a talk with Miss Bryce."

"Yes. And I think, I think if he had gone through the proper procedures he never would have been approved."

Mrs. Wenders raised her eyebrows.

"I see him," said Miss Hepple. "I look out my kitchen window or my living room window and I see him. And that's why I wanted to talk to you, Mrs. Wenders. I don't like the way he looks at Electa."

"Looks at Electa? What do you -"

"A man. You know the way a man looks at a woman when he wants her - when he wants her and is bound and determined to get her."

"He -"

"He thinks nobody is seeing him. But I do, I look out one of my windows and there it is. I see it in his eyes, in the tilt of his head, in the lean of his body - the way he shoots out that pink tongue to wipe along those big lips. I don't like it, Mrs. Wenders. It's not right, and I think you should know about it."

Mrs. Wenders leaned back against the couch. "We've never had anything like that in the Corner," she said. "Everything from outside, but nothing in the Corner before."

"I know," said Miss Hepple. "That's one thing that worries me so about it. I don't know what this world is coming to - in the Corner!"

The two women looked into each other's eyes, shaking their heads in dismay.

18

Evanston was a funny town.

It did not take Nice long to find out where the niggers stayed. On the west side. He spent a long time cruising around, getting a feeling for the place, watching the people.

Something was missing but he had not been able to figure out what it was. He parked the car and walked. There were corners where men congregated; some corners were controlled by boys. That was normal. But something ... he could not put his finger on it ... was missing.

As he approached a group of men clustered on a corner next to a drugstore, and as he framed the question he was going to ask them, about where he could get a drink, it hit him. That was it. He hadn't seen any bars. Come to think of it, he hadn't seen any liquor stores. He reworked the question in his mind.

"Say, what's happ'nin'," he said to the little group of men.

"You got it, Big Daddy," said one.

"Naw, you got it, Home," said Nice. "Say, look, my man." Nice spoke to the man who held the paper-wrapped treasure, "I don't want to cut in on your action, but I'd like to know where I can get a hit for myself, you dig?"

The man with the bottle turned it up to his lips.

Someone else spoke. "Across the canal, Big Shot."

The drinker passed the bottle to the speaker.

"Canal, what's that," asked Nice.

"The canal, the canal, the Evanston sanitary canal," said the man Nice had spoken to at first. "You got to go across the canal to get some liquor. Into Skokie, my man. Evanston is dry."

354

"What?"

"Gotdamnit! Don't this nigga know how t' say nothin' but 'what?'"

"Pardon me," said Nice, "but I didn't know it was no dry towns left - outside the South."

"The South, my ass," said one of the men. "This where the whole thing started. Evanston, Illinois, the Women's Christian Temperance Movement. This here town is what brought prohibition."

"Well I'll be godamned," said Nice.

"Uh huh, you will be, too, says them nice Christian ladies, if you goes across the canal and buys a bottle of that demon rum."

The men laughed.

"Yeah, that rot-gut."

"Uh-huh, that sin-juice."

They laughed uproariously.

"So it ain't no bars in Evanston, huh?"

"Can you catch the clap in heaven?"

They started laughing again.

"Now that's a good question," said one of the men, "now I never thought about that. I mean, what happen to yo dick in heaven? What if you gits a hard on?"

"Shit - nigga - it ain't no bodies in heaven. Just souls."

"Well what do a soul look like? How can you tell a female soul from a male soul? Don't tell me a dick ain't involved in some kind o' way."

"You done had too much to drink. That's what's wrong with y'all niggas. You done had too much to drink."

"Well, lookahere,," said Nice. "If it ain't no bars, where do people hang, you dig?"

"We hangin'."

"Yeah, we hangin' right here on the corner."

"You mean it ain't no place for people to hang but on the corners? I'm sure the bitches ain't hangin' on no corners."

"You right about that."

"Sure ain't. You don't see none, do you?"

"So, I mean, what if I wanted to scout me out some bitches?"

"You'd be shit out of luck."

Nice started to say, "What," but caught himself. Instead he said, softly, "Damn."

They laughed at him.

A man took the bottle down and said, "You see, my man, it's this way. If the bitches wants t'have a good time - you know - go out on the town, then that's what they do. They goes down to Chicago. The South Side. Cabaret. Partay. You dig?"

"Uh huh," said another, "unless they goes to a house party here in town. But that would only be on the weekends. Most likely Saturday night."

"Except since the war, some of them be goin' up to North Chicago or Waukegan."

"Yeah, they can party with the soldiers and sailors up there - Great Lakes and Fort Sheridan."

"So it ain't no place in town where people can get together?"

"You got it, Slick."

"Hey, man, this bottle is dead."

"Looka here, Money," said one of the men, addressing Nice, "you give one of us a ride across the canal so we can get a bottle and we can turn you on t'some fine brown frames."

Nice agreed. He could see that without bars or clubs it was going to be hard gathering information in Evanston and he was going to need every connection he could get.

356

19

The faces on the screen were huge, maybe two stories high. Wayne could not pay them any attention. He had not the slightest idea what the movie was about. The voices and music coming into the car through the speaker attached to the window were just so much noise to him. He was using all his energies to concentrate on Electa, to watch her surreptitiously, to figure out how to get close to her or even touch her without being detected by Penny.

Penny and the boys were in the back seat. Electa, as the guest, occupied the seat of honor beside him in front. Wayne was pleased with himself for manipulating that little stratagem. But he had not counted on the heat. He had not thought how hot it might be with the five of them sitting up inside the car. In a way it helped. It made Electa want to be more loose. Keeping her legs open, spreading her arms away from her sides, loosening her blouse, raising her skirt a little. She did not think it would make any difference in the dark. She wore a perfume but the heat made it fuse with the musky smell of her body.

Her hot smell filled Wayne's nose.

Mr. Waterton said she was a hot number. Wayne could smell her woman.

In another way, though, the heat hindered him. It was not natural, simmering that way, to get close to someone. It was natural to stay as far apart as possible, to avoid the humid touch of another's skin.

Her scent intoxicated him, lured him to her, yet the heat told him, acted as a sign, to keep his distance. The temperature declared that everyone must have space. Unbuttoned blouses, parted legs, the smell of woman notwithstanding.

The boys, Penny, even Electa, all commented on

357

the movie. Wayne could not. He was sliding his eyes over Electa's face, down her blouse and along her legs. He was inhaling the vapors rising off her body. He was trying to figure out how to draw her attention to the giant mound growing on top of his thigh, molding the silken fabric around it.

He got out of the car twice to buy popcorn and sodas. Each time he was careful to ask if anyone needed to go to the ladies' room. He would be happy to be an escort, he said. He knew Penny wouldn't go. She did not like to use public restrooms. Unfortunately, Electa didn't want to go either. The most Wayne could hope for was that he cut a sharp figure passing under the lights in his stylish silk suit and his wide brimmed, brushed, felt hat.

When he got back into the car, each time he managed to brush against Electa's leg, and to brush her arm when he passed out the popcorn and sodas.

Her skin was soft, soft and smooth and damp from the heat.

It would be so easy to stick to her, he thought, stick like glue.

He watched her hand reach into the box of popcorn.

He wondered what that little hand would feel like touching his body. He knew that little hand could not fully encircle the thickness of his huge male member.

What would it be like for that hand to pull back on the foreskin?

She never seemed to look at him. But maybe that was alright. Maybe it was enough for her to get used to being close to him, to having his body close to hers, to get comfortable being next to him. One step at a time. Maybe this was enough for now.

20

Had she been more herself, Electa would have been conscious of Wayne's advances. She did know he was paying her more attention and attention in different ways than he ever had. But she thought of it as innocent and friendly, as innocent and friendly as her one and only flirtation, her non-intentional flirtation with him had been. She was not herself, though. She was scarcely conscious of anyone outside herself. Only Gabriel. And she was often distracted and inattentive even around him.

All she could really focus on was that it was less than a week before Kenneth had said Tommy would have to leave for San Diego. He was actually going. He would be leaving her life for good. The fact assumed such an enormity that it obliterated everything else.

He had not called or come by.

They said he was still in his room. Kenneth and Betty said it. Still in his room, pining away.

Should she believe them? And even if she did, why didn't he come to her? If it were killing him so much to be away from her, why didn't he come? She could not go to him. She could not call him. That was not a woman's place. That was for a man. That was his job. If he really wanted her.

Electa was glad to be invited over to the Hunters' for dinners and out to drive-in-movies. Going distracted her. It made her have to think about something else for a little while. She was glad whenever Wayne offered to give her rides to places because she increasingly felt she did not have the strength to continue on her own.

It was all she could do, all she could do, to get Gabriel to nursery school each morning, continue on to work, survive the day, return home, pick up Gabriel, and get him back to the house. After that she was finished. A hollow body living off its own pain.

She did not notice Wayne's change in wardrobe or how much more than usual he stuttered when he was talking to her. She was not even aware that his giant body kept creeping closer and closer to hers. She never glimpsed the perpetual protrusion in the front of his pants.

Much closer to being comatose than fully alert she often awoke in the mornings with no recollection of the entire past day.

It was probably for that reason she only nodded affirmatively when Wayne asked her one afternoon if he could come over to see her after Gabriel had fallen asleep that night.

Penny did not know what had gotten into Wayne. She did not know when she had seen him so demonstratively happy. He was always good natured, that is one reason he was fun to be around. But this was different. Singing. And laughing. And cracking jokes. He couldn't stop laughing or giggling. Whatever it was, Penny was thankful for it. Her man deserved to be happy. She loved him so.

He cooked dinner and made her and Bobo stuff themselves. He baked a delicious apple-crisp desert. They could barely get up from the table. He washed all the dishes and cleaned the kitchen. Laughing and joking all the while. Teasing them. Playing tricks on them. Then they went for a long ride in the country. Wayne was singing the whole time.

When they got home, he made their bed and Bobo's bed with newly washed sheets. He tucked them each in. Penny's head barely hit the pillow and she was asleep.

Wayne ran his bath water. He ran it very hot.

Because of his size he had to double up to sit in the tub, but he scaled and scrubbed himself and hummed one tune after another. He was doing everything he could to kill time. Still it moved slowly. He didn't care, though. He knew eventually the time would arrive. Penny and Bobo were already asleep. Deep in sleep. Not to be awakened.

Wayne would walk the few paces to Electa's door and she would let him in.

Then what? Then what.

He would hold her in his arms for the first time.

He would press her body against his for the first time.

He would kiss her lips for the first time.

He would slip his tongue down her throat for the first time.

He would hold her titties for the first time.

He would squeeze her ass for the first time.

He would see her naked for the first time.

Wayne closed his eyes in anticipation of delight. His giant sex rose out of the hot water, its monstrous head wagging in the air, cooling as the water evaporated off its enormous dimensions.

What would it be like getting in her?

It will take a long time. He knew that. It was always very hard to get in the first time, even though they were wet with wanting him, even though they were soaking with wanting him. It was very, very hard to get in. Even with Matilda and Camilla who were used to taking all kinds of men.

His thick tongue slid out around his big lips. Uh huh. It would be hard getting into Electa at first. He would have to keep grinding and pushing. Gentle pressure. Constant gentle pressure. In a few minutes he would actually be doing it. In a few minutes.

He leaned his head back.

361

His dick throbbed wildly.

When he first got the head in she would scream. With delight.

What had Camilla said? At first she was afraid he would split her open, then she said - she screamed, yes she screamed it - she could fuck anything now - horses, bulls, elephants, giraffes! Then she had laughed hysterically, screamed and cried and fastened herself onto him. "Anything! Anything!"

When he finally got it into Electa it would happen to her. She would go crazy. She would be his forever. No one else could satisfy her.

Tonight. Tonight.

In a state of near ecstacy he grabbed his big meat.

Oh, hold on. Hold on just a little while longer.

Clear, high, and fragile. Gabriel's voice seemed a presence, an actual physical existence in the blackness of the room.

Electa listened to it. Like a bell, she thought. Like a bell.

She had not heard what he had said, only that vibrant sound.

He spoke again.

"Where Mama?"

"Where, what, Gabriel?"

"What I'm talking to you about. Where's Tommy?"

"Tommy. What Tommy? You don't mean sailor Tommy?"

"Yes, I do. That's who I mean. Sailor Tommy. His last name is a color. Tommy ...."

She held her breath. In the deep quiet of the night she was sure that the soundless holding of her breath was audible.

"... Brown. Yeah, that's the color. Brown. Tommy Brown. Where is he?"

"What made you think about him, Gabriel?"

"He used to come by to see us all the time. Now he doesn't come any more. Did he go back to the war? Where is he?"

"No. He hasn't gone back to the war yet. But he will soon. He's still here. In Evanston."

"Why doesn't he come by to see us anymore? Doesn't he still like us?"

"Oh, I guess he just got busy, Gabriel. People can't spend all their time coming to see us."

"Oh."

"Gabriel?"

"Yes, Mama."

Do ... you ... like him?"

"Yes, Mama. I miss him."

"I - Gabriel, I thought you didn't like men."

"I don't like some men. I don't like Toby." Gabriel knew he should not have hit Toby in the head with a hammer. He could not help it. He hated him. He wanted to apologize for hitting Toby in the head with a hammer except he hade done it for her and if Toby showed up he would do it again. "I'm sorry for hitting him in the head," he said very quickly. "I don't like Maurice, either."

"They are both civilians," said Electa. "Are civilians the only ones you dislike?"

"No," he said, and rattled off a list of soldiers and sailors he disliked.

"But I like some men," he continued. "I like Wayne. He's a civilian. I like Tommy Brown."

"You wouldn't mind if he came by to see me a lot?"

"No.

"Mama?"

"Could he stay?"

"What do you mean?"

"I mean like Wayne stays with Penny and Bobo. Like Mr. Brockerton stays with Wanda and Mrs. Brockerton. Like Mr. Cork stays with Ivory and Mrs. Cork. They don't go away. Could he stay? Could he stay like that?"

"Well ... Gabriel. If ... if he stayed like that ... that would mean, that would mean he would be your daddy."

"I know."

Electa closed her eyes.

Gabriel's words seemed to echo like the last notes of a carillon.

I know.
I know.
I know.

Oh, my God. Why didn't I know this earlier? Why didn't I know before it was too late?

22

When Wayne knocked at the door, Electa was awake as she had not been for weeks.

"Who is it?"

"Wayne."

She opened the door a crack and peeked out.

"Hi, Wayne. What is it?"

"I'm here," he said.

"I can see that. What's up?"

What's up? Has she gone crazy?

"I'm h-h-here. I'm here l-l-like y-y-y-you agreed."

She opened the door further. She had on a bathrobe. Wayne could imagine what she had on under that bathrobe. He felt his throat close up.

"I agreed?" She did not remember. "Well, it's late. Gabriel's asleep. Can't it wait until tomorrow?"

What was she talking about? He could smell her. *Woman*. She did not have any perfume on. He could smell her body. Her *woman*.

"G-G-G-Gabriel w-w-w-was s-s-su-su-supposed t-t-to b-b-b-be asleep," he said.

A frown parted her brow. Supposed to be asleep?

"What was I going to see you about, Wayne? I don't remember."

He could not believe his ears. She didn't remember! What kind of fool did she take him for? She must be nothing but a tease. You can't tease me, baby. Uh uh. I'm too much man.

"Y-Y-You, you you d-d-don't re-re-re-remember?"

"That's right. When did we talk?"

"Today! W-w-w-we, we t-t-talk, talked today!"

"No. I just can't remember. I'm sorry. I've had a lot on my mind lately. What - what were we going to talk about tonight?" She could not imagine what it was.

"J-J-J-Just t-t-talk."

Just talk? An incredulous expression swept her face. Oh, no. This can't be what I'm thinking. I haven't been that much off my rocker. I haven't led this man on.

So close yet so far away. Wayne could feel the pulse throbbing in his temple.

Electa dismissed the heretical idea. No. It couldn't be that. It must be something about Gabriel. Wayne had said he was supposed to be asleep. That must be why. We were going to talk about him.

"Wayne, it doesn't sound urgent. I'm tired. Can't it wait until tomorrow?"

If he could just reach out with his big hands, put them around her little waist, and pull her body up against him, she would forget all about this nonsense she was talking.

"Electa," he said.

"Please, Wayne. It'll keep, won't it? It's so late. And I'm so tired. Tomorrow, okay?"

"I c-c-c-caint' w-w-wait —mum-much l-l-l-long-long-longer," he said.

"Tomorrow's not so long. Goodnight, Wayne."

"G-G-G-Good-Good-Goodnight, Electa."

She closed the door.

She turned and walked to her bed. What could he mean, he can't wait much longer? Maybe he has - maybe he has got the wrong idea.

I don't know.

She soon forgot. She could only think about Tommy Brown. Gabriel likes him, she thought. If only he'll come back to me there's a chance. There's a chance.

Wayne stood outside staring at the door. This is not going to happen again! This is not going to happen again! Next time I come in. All the way.

367

23

Bobbing his head up and down the little man sitting on Mrs. McCracken's steps affirmed everything Nice said.

"Yeah, he looked just like that. Lived right here. A giant."

"But the man I'm lookin' for was single," said Nice. "You sure the cat you talkin' about was married?"

"Mmhmm. Well. I don't know about no papers. But they lived together. She called herself Mrs. Hunter and they had a kid about six or seven years old."

"A kid!!"

"Mmhmm. Little boy. Nice kid. Smart as a whip. The man liked to fish. Good fisherman, too."

Nice looked at his fingernails. "He look like him, he just don't sound like him. A wife, a seven year old kid." He shook his head.

"Where he live at now?"

"I don't know. He moved out. All three of 'em. Sudden."

"Out of town?"

"No. Every now and then he come by to talk to Mrs. McCracken. Bring her some fish. Drives a big Buick now."

"How do he dress?"

"Nothin' special."

Nice shook his head. "This cat was a fancy dresser."

"Tell you what," said the man. "I did see him standin' on the porch a couple times in some sharp rags. But he never went nowhere. Just stood on the porch, lookin' sharp, then went inside. Next time I seen him he was dressed the same as ususal."

"Dude sound a little fucked up," said Nice.

"Ain't no two peas in a pod the same," said the man.

Nice nodded. "And you don't know where he moved to?"

"Uh uh."

"When did he move?"

The little man told Nice and Nice straightened up.

"Run that by me one more again."

The little man did.

"Well, I'm at least gon' have t'take a look at this dude."

"Mmhmm. How you gon' do that when you don't know where he lives at?"

"Evanston ain't that big. Somebody got to know where he live at. You say he liked to fish. Where did he go fishin' at?"

"Well, it was one place he wouldn't tell nobody about. He caught the biggest -"

"What about places he did tell somebody about?"

"Yeah, yeah," said the little man. "At the lake - down at the lake. The fishin' piers. That's where he went most of the time."

"Much obliged," said Nice.

He walked straight to his car. He did not know where the fishing piers were, but he was not going to take long to find out.

The soft pile carpet parted and sank for Nice's shoes as he paced back and forth on it.

Camilla followed his every movement voraciously.

He held a glass of scotch on the rocks in his right hand from which he occasionally sipped.

"Evanston's a strange little place," he said.

"Skip the shit, Nice," she said. "I'm tired of telling

369

you - get to the point. What did you find out?"

He laughed, then swilled down some scotch past his tonsils.

"Did you know it's a dry town?"

"Nice!"

"Alright. Alright. Like I was tellin' you, I met this cat named Waterton at the fishin' pier. Ooh, could he talk. He describes this same guy to me. But just like the other old dude he says this cat is married. He's got a wife and a seven-year old little boy."

Camilla's right leg was crossed over her left one. She swung her right foot furiously.

"I axed him if he knowed where this cat lives at. Yeah, he said. Draws me a road map. Says if he's at home it'll be a '37 black Buick Special parked in the alley behind the house right under the bedroom windows.

"It ain't but a couple blocks away from the lake so I drives over there. It's right where the cat said it would be, this funny little colored section. Like a zoo. Like a zoo full o' niggas in the middle of all these rich, white folks. I swear, it'll crack you up. I drives around to the back alley and there's the Buick."

He took a sip of scotch. He watched Camilla. Her right foot rocked back and forth like some kind of metronome. Touch her and she'll explode, he thought.

"So I drives around," he continued, "lookin' for a place to park. It's hard to describe the place I found . It's _"

"I don't give a fuck. Get to the gotdamn point."

"Alright, Mama. Be cool. There's a place down the alley behind this hotel where I can check out this flat and the Buick behind it. I stands there and lights up. I keep lookin' around me to see if anybody notices me 'cause if they does they know I don't live there and I got t'make tracks. But nobody seen me.

"I'm standin' there at least an hour and a half when this big, black cat leaves the flat."

Camilla moved forward crouching off the couch as if she were about to spring. Her mouth opened slightly, showing her teeth.

"I watches the nigger, see. He comes down the steps and around the side of the house going to the Buick. I got a perfect profile of him.

"It's LBN."

She gabbled inarticulately and sprang to the middle of the room. She clenched her hands like talons and she arched her back inwards, her face pointing at the ceiling.

"He's mine," she growled.

Nice watched her. He frowned and sipped his scotch.

"Right. It's just like we agreed. You get first shot. When you through, it's our turn."

"Don't tell nobody else till I'm through," she said, glaring at him. "I don't want nobody fuckin' up my shit."

"You got it, Mama. Hadn't a been for you, who'd o' thought about lookin' for his ass in Evanston?"

Thick, white saliva was building up in Camilla's mouth and coating the edges of her lips.

"Let me use your car, Nice."

"Is you out of your mind!?"

"I ain't got no car and I sure as hell ain't takin' no goddamn el."

Nice pulled a sheaf of bills off a thick wad. He handed it to her. "Take a cab," he said.

24

Wayne finally went out to see who was in the cab parked behind his car. It had been there at least an hour. As be bent over to look in the cab's front window, the back door opened.

"Get in."

He saw Camilla.

He was about to answer, to tell her why he could not get in when he saw the hole in the barrel of the .45 above her purse, pointing directly at him.

He got in.

The cab pulled off.

"Take us to twenty-seventh and Indiana."

"Camilla!"

She bobbed the .45 once.

Wayne closed his mouth.

She was too far across the cab to get her in one motion. She could pull the trigger before he could reach her.

"Put me in the wind. Didn't you?"

"Cami -"

"Didn't tell me you was married.

"Married and got a snot-nosed crumb-snatcher."

"Camilla -"

"Didn't tell me shit.

"Use me, nigga. Use my ass! Use my Black Ass!"

"Look."

"You damn right. I'm gon' look alright. I'm gon' look for damn sure. Pull out yo dick."

"What?"

"You heard me. Pull out yo dick. I want t'see if the bitch done wore it down. Nigga, you heard me, pull it out or I'll shoot it off."

Wayne opened his fly. He reached down and began pulling it out.

"Oh, God! I forgot how big it really is.

"Pull back the foreskin. Pump it up."

She shoved the barrel of the gun under his chin.

"You make one funny move and I'll blow your head off." She hitched up her skirts and climbed up over him.

"Oh, God! Oh, God!"

The cab driver had never heard such a wordless scream as then tore through the cab. But he was familiar with the sloshing sounds that followed.

25

Tommy put on his dress blue uniform. Navy blue, he thought. Coat and pants, pressed to a line. His white shirt was starched, setting off the dark tie. He made sure the row of ribbons over his left breast was straight. He looked at the white, dress hat on his bedside table, the polished bib shiny and black. On his shoulders an eagle and chevrons marked him, as did the red stripes on his sleeve.

Navy. Navy man, he thought. Back to the war.

He picked up his hat as he was going out the door and put it on his head. He had decided to walk the whole way. He needed the time.

He knocked three times on the door.

Electa swung it open.

Lord, Jesus, he thought. How could I forget how beautiful you is?

"Tommy," she said.

Her hand went to her throat. For just an instant she thought she was going to faint. She leaned against the doorjamb.

He could not speak. He stared at her.

I been a fool, he thought. All along. Here she is. The one I loves.

"Would you like to come in," she said. She stepped back from the door.

He nodded and stepped in.

"Where's Gabriel?"

"He's out in the back, playing. Do you want me to get him?"

"Not yet. I ... I would like to talk to you."

"Okay, Tommy."

She walked into the living room.

374

He followed her. She sat down on the couch.

"Please," she said. She patted the couch beside her.

He had his hat in his hands. He sat down. He could not take his eyes off her.

"I missed you," he said.

"Me, too."

"I tried to call. To come by."

"I know. I was rude. I should have explained to you."

"Is it somebody else?"

She looked at him. She put a hand on his.

"No."

She could see relief relaxing him. She smiled.

"No, it was nobody else. It was you."

"What does you mean?"

"I mean ... I was ... falling in love with you, and ... you, you are a sailor, here today and gone tomorrow. I was ... falling in love with you and you were going to go off and leave me the same way I was before you came and I couldn't take it. I couldn't stand the thought of it. I couldn't stand to see you again knowing what would happen because every time I saw you I wanted you more and more. I was wrong for the way I did it, Tommy, I know. But I wasn't thinking. I was just doing what I had to do. I was trying to save myself. I'm sorry. It was wrong the way I did it. If I were stronger I wouldn't have done it that way. I apologize."

He had not taken his eyes off her.

"I wanted to come back t'you, Electa. I didn't want to leave and not come back to you."

"Why didn't you say something?"

"I didn't think you wanted me to come back."

"What?"

"Well. Gabriel. You always kept Gabriel away from me."

375

She laughed.

"I was trying to protect you. I was trying to protect you from Gabriel. Come to find out, I didn't need to protect you at all."

"What is you talkin' about?"

"I was trying to protect you because Gabriel hates men who come around me. I didn't want him to hate you. But come to find out, he was crazy about you all the time. Of course, I found out a little late."

She saw tension easing in him again.

"Electa," he said, "I know I ain't much. I'm a sailor now. Pretty good rank. But I don't want t'stay in no Navy, and when I gets out, I won't have nothin'. I won't be nothin'. Just a man. No education. No trade. I cooks in the Navy, but I couldn't stand t'do it the rest of my life for a livin'. I ain't much. But I love you. I would work hard all my life to do right by you and Gabriel. I would work for us t'build a life together and I wouldn't never let you down. I would do my best by you, Electa. I would always do my best. I love you. I know I ain't much. But I'm askin' if you will marry me."

She leaned back against the couch.

Here it was. Hers to decide. The rest of her life before her and the decision was hers.

She turned to face him. "When are you going back?"

tomorrow.

She felt she'd been shot. She slumped forward, catching her weight with her hand on the cushion in front of her. Her free hand went not to her throat but to her stomach.

tomorrow. She spoke it as he had, as a whisper.

"Yes. I got my orders a little over two weeks ago."

tomorrow.

He put his hand over hers. "I know you could do

376

much better, but we could make a life together. We could make a good life."

"If you're going away - back to the war ...."

"Listen," he said. "I'll get a liberty. We'll do a tour. I don't know. A few months. When we comes back from sea I'll get a liberty. We'll put in at San Diego. I can send you a telegram from Honolulu so's you can get to San Diego about the same time as me. It's places there - Arizona - where you don't have to wait no time to get a license. We could do it then. If you said yes."

She stood up.

So did he.

"Tomorrow," she repeated.

"I love you, Electa."

"Why didn't you come before?"

"Hurt.

"Pride.

"Stubborn.

"Stupid."

He lowered his head.

"It was the biggest mistake I ever made."

"Almost as big as mine." She looked up at him. She put her arms around him and laid her head against his chest. It felt so good to hold him. She wanted never to let go.

"Yes, Tommy, oh, yes oh yes oh yes. I love you so."

377

26

It did not take a full night for Camilla to change her mind. Why should she die when she could keep having him? Living was wonderful. She did not need to kill him if she could have him. That was the main thing - having him, having him. The truth was she could not live without him, but now that she had him, she could live.

Wayne explained that he had to keep his job, that he did have a wife, that he did have a son, that he had to support them and spend time with them. Camilla said she did not care as long as she could see him sometimes. Sometimes. Don't ever leave my life like you done before, she told him. I'll kill you, I swear I'll kill you and kill myself, too.

Wayne said he saw no reason why he couldn't see her sometimes. She said good because that meant they could both keep living but she was going to move to Evanston so she would not have far to go to see him and so she could keep a proper watch on things.

She snuggled against him, humping ceaselessly, her eyes occasionally rolling back in her head.

"But we got a problem," she said.

"What is it?"

"Nice. He gon' kill you."

Wayne held her to keep her from moving.

"Kill me?"

"Uh huh. When I got through with you he was supposed to kill you. Like you killed Light."

"Oh."

"And he knows where you lives at. He's the one what found you."

"You're right. We got a problem."

"There'd be some others, too. 'Cept right now they

378

don't know we done found you."

"My, my, my."

Wayne sighed. He wouldn't run. He wouldn't leave Wimbey's Corner. It was his home. He would never give it up.

"You can take care of Nice," she said. "I know what you can do with your hands."

"I can't. Nice hasn't done anything to me."

"But he will. If you don't do something to him, he will definitely do something t' you."

They lay quietly.

"Uh uh," Wayne said at last. "I just can't. The man has not hurt me."

"He might could hurt your wife and kid."

"But he hasn't."

"I'll take care of Nice," she said.

"What will you do?"

"Kill him."

"No!"

"Look, baby. You don't seem to understand. It's him or us."

"Uh uh. Maybe I should talk to him. I could always talk to Nice. He should understand about Matilda. Maybe if I just talk to him."

"He'll put a hole through you."

"I got to try," said Wayne.

"Alright, but I'm backin' you up." She started moving again.

The big man took up almost half the couch. Nice sat across his living room and watched him.

"You didn't do a thing to me," Wayne said. "That's why I didn't bother you. I tied you up and left you in the closet. I could have killed you. But I wasn't out to

379

kill. Light did me wrong. He did Matilda wrong. He had to pay. That's all it was."

"If he hadn't o' shot the bitch, she would of killed him," said Nice. "I know. I was there."

"Listen to me, Nice. You're not listening. First of all, you and I both know that as strong and quick as Light was, he could have got out of the way and made her drop the razor. You can't bullshit me about that. It's a fact. But, alright - I *wasn't* there - suppose some miracle happened and the only thing he could do was draw and fire, that's still not the point. That's still not the point. Why was she there in the first place? Huh? Why was she there in the first place?

"Cause Light done me wrong. Cause he went after my lady. Why? I hadn't done nothin' to him. I was workin' good for him. I was taking care of righteous business for him. He had a whole stable full of ladies. And he went after mine. It was wrong, Nice. It was wrong. He knew it was wrong. He didn't tell you about it, did he? He didn't have you drive him over there, did he? No. He waited till you were occupied elsewhere. He knew you wouldn't go for it. It was wrong.

"And she couldn't take it. It broke her. She knew she shouldn't o' been with the nigger. She told me - right there in our apartment - to kill him. I should have. I should have done it then. She'd still be alive. But I, like a fool, let him go. Brother Light. My partner. Let him go. After I left her she couldn't take it. That's why she was in the Savoy that night - acting crazy. Because of what Light did to her. That's the point, Nice. And that's why it don't make no difference whether he had to fire then or not. He got put in that position because of what he did, and he had to face the pay-back. It had nothin' t'do with you."

"Light was my main man."

"Let me put it this way. Suppose Matilda had been

380

your lady."

"But Light wouldn't have -"

"He wouldn't have, huh? Because it's wrong. Because it's dead wrong. And what if he had anyway. And then shot her? And then shot her. Did that to her and then shot her. What would you do?"

Nice looked at his shoes.

He looked back up at Wayne. "So you sayin,' call it even?"

Wayne nodded.

Nice leaned back.

He had been after the nigga a long time. He remembered the humiliation of being tied up and thrown into that closet. He had thought a long time about what he would do to the nigga, how he would do it.

Camilla. Camilla had forgiven him. But so what? You cain't trust a bitch no way. A bitch was the cause of all this. Hadn't o' been for a bitch Light would still be alive.

Still, LBN was right. He could of killed me and he didn't. And no doubt about it, what Light done was wrong.

Nice stared at the big man. At last the numbers king stood up and extended his hand. He said one word. "Even."

When Wayne got home he thought he would feel at peace. Instead he was greeted by catastrophe.

She had gone back to the nigger! Wayne could not understand it. The nigger had gone off to California. There was no telling who he would be fucking. All over the West Coast. But she went back to him.

Wayne cursed himself. He knew what he should have done. When she opened the door he should have just stepped in and grabbed her, carried her to the bed. Once she got a look at Mr. Big, once she got her hands on him, once he got inside her, it would have been all over. She would have been his. Camilla had just proved that again. Mr. Big had changed her mind all by himself. She was about to kill him and in a few minutes Mr. Big had her fawning all over him. What a fool I was. I could have fried her brains with him, but I turned around because she said she was tired and now she went back to the nigger. I could have stopped that shit. I could have stopped that shit before it got started. But I didn't. He cursed himself and hated himself.

They ain't married yet, though, he thought.

Plenty of time between now and then. All she needs to do is see it one time. All it needs t'do is get inside her one time. I can melt her brains.

One thing bothered Wayne. Gabriel and his mother slept in the same room. If she resisted at all, which she might for a little while - until she saw Mr. Big, until she felt Mr. Big - the boy might hear her. Wayne did not want that to happen.

Later it would not matter. When she was loving him and wanting him. When she was mad for him and had to have him as Matilda had, when she had to have him as Camilla did, and as Penny did, then it would be alright for Gabriel to see them in bed together. Wayne wanted him to see them in bed together then, so he would know Wayne belonged in his mother's bed. But for the first few minutes of the first night he might be upset by his mother's initial reaction and Wayne did not want that to happen.

Wayne's main concern was to prevent her from getting married. He had to have her before then. Afterwards she would be his and not interested in marrying the grinning sailor. He knew he had some time. The sailor

382

would be at sea a while before he got a liberty. It was Wayne's desire which urged haste. He could resist it. He could resist it to make sure the boy wouldn't be around, as long as he did not have to wait too long.

27

On the ride back from Kankakee, Ruth Wenders was thoughtful. She did not like to visit her brother-in-law. He was another man from what he had been. It was almost more than she could bear. But every now and then, Wynfried, his wife, who was also her best friend, insisted that she go. Ruth understood. Wynfried could take only so much by herself. After that she had to have some support, only for a little while, but she had to have it.

Wynfried, too, was silent. Even though it had been over two years, she was not past crying. She usually cried quietly, briefly, several times on the way home. But for the moment she sat without speaking, staring out the window.

Fends, like Ruth's own husband, Stephen, had been one of the most handsome men Ruth had ever seen. Dashing, cavalier, charming. He had paid for it. The women couldn't leave him alone, nor he them. Now. A madman. What a terrible cost.

But Wynfried had to pay, too, and she had done nothing.

So many victims, blameless, who paid for the crimes of others.

Fends and Wynfried were childless. Ruth wondered how that affected Wynfried's ability to handle the pain. Wynfried was very good to Ruth's children and grandchild. She loved them. They loved her in return. It would be difficult not to. Wynfried Wenders was a touch of light in this war-darkened world.

Ruth shuddered at the thought of war. Her son, Stephen, had been gone almost three years. She did not believe she could stand the strain much longer. Three years and no end in sight. O God.

She tilted her head back and raised her eyes to the

luggage rack above her. She did not see it. She was trying to make a blank of her mind.

So much pain.

So much pain in the world.

She felt Wynfried's hand patting her own.

She looked over at her good friend.

They both cried quietly for a little while.

"You think Electa would mind if Gabriel spent the night with me," asked Wynfried. "I'm a little lonely. It would help to have that young rascal around the house for awhile."

Ruth smiled at the thought of her grandson. "For a hot minute," she said. "She'll mind for a hot minute. Then the rest of the time she'll be thanking you for the peace and you'll be thinking that lonely is not so bad."

They both laughed.

The two women held hands the rest of the way into Twelfth Street Station.

The little boy's hand was enveloped inside the woman's as they walked across the cement patio in front of the Hunter's place and headed towards the stairs which led to the woman's apartment. Wayne's eyes followed them greedily. He had seen them the instant they had exited the boy's front door which was not at the front, but at the side of the house. He had watched them as they took each of the two steps down to the concrete walkway and then followed the walk between the strips of dirt that bordered the Cork house on one side and the Frye-Stuart house on the other. Each step had increased Wayne's gloating and his sense of power. Gabriel proudly held in his right hand a shopping bag which Wayne knew to connote an overnight stay at Aunt Wynfried's. Wayne's pupils grew enormously and his nostrils distended until the skin ached.

Saliva flowed freely in his mouth. Electa was his tonight.

28

Far out in the Pacific Tommy Brown stood on the deck of a fast troop transport, his bare arms hanging over the railing. Blackness surrounded him. Tommy was not able to sleep. A few hours later, just after dawn, he would be piloting a landing craft full of marines onto a beach off the island of Saipan.

One thing you can always count on is the heat, he thought. He was coated with sweat. His clothes stuck to him. His head broiled inside his helmet but he could not take it off. Somehow he felt safer with it on.

One of the reasons Tommy could not sleep was because of the Navy's invasion plan. When he had been piloting at Tarawa the plan had been similar. Planes had bombed the beaches and the gun implacements for a full hour before the ships had opened their barrages. For two and one half hours the ships had rained destruction on the beaches. Tommy and everyone witnessing knew that no one and no thing had survived the bombardment. When the ships' big guns had stopped, the landing craft had sped for the beaches. They had been met by murderous fire, not only small-arms, but also mortars and artillery. Landing craft had been sunk, full of marines. Marines weighted down by heavy packs sank and drowned when their landing craft dropped them out in five and even ten feet of water. Those who had made it to the beaches were pinned down and cut up by deadly cross fire. The slaughter had been horrible before a foothold had been established on the beaches. Many, many landing craft never made it back to the fleet. Tommy had been lucky.

Ever since then an invasion had called for two or even three days of continuous intensive bombing and shelling before the troops hit the beaches. The practice had greatly diminished enemy resistance and marine casualties during the landings.

For Saipan the Navy plan called for a return to landing marines the same morning the shelling began. Tommy did not like it. Maybe the Navy knew something he did not which justified the plan, but he doubted it. The Japanese had controlled the island for twenty-five years. They had all been briefed on that. The defensive installations were all in hardened sites. It would take tons of direct hits by the most powerful explosives to loosen them. That would take days, and here they were going in on the same morning. Maybe they knew something he did not, but he would not want to make book on it. He hung his arms over the railing and shook his head. He did not want to go in.

It also bothered him that his commanding officer on the LCV(P) would be an inexperienced ensign. Tommy had no idea how the kid, he was only a kid, would react under fire.

Tommy thought about the landing area they had been assigned, Able Sector, Red-Y, heading two, thirty-two. He pictured it on the map, he went over in his mind the landmarks he could use when the sky lightened. He was not nervous. He was almost sick.

He thought about Electa. He wondered what she was doing, what she was doing at that very instant. He wished he were with her.

The bombing began before Tommy and the ensign boarded their landing craft. The airplanes roared over like unending rolls of thunder. Then far off Tommy heard dull concussions while directly overhead the aircraft engines still filled the sky with their noise.

There has to be a awful lot of planes, he thought. They got t'be stretchin' out for miles.

Not only was the landing craft in the water but it

was loaded with its full complement of marines when the ships finally opened up their big guns. The shock waves from the giant guns' reports actually drove the landing craft sideways in the water. The sounds, deep and powerful were so loud they stunned the brain. They suppressed thought. They were counterpointed by the screaming whine of rockets.

Tommy kept steering the craft in circles waiting for the command to go in. The longer they waited the better as far as he was concerned. He hoped they kept circling for a couple of days. A couple of weeks would be better, he thought. He watched the ensign. The young officer wore earphones and a headpiece which enabled him to communicate with the commander of their landing sector. He was very impressed by the punishment being visited on the beaches.

He smiled. Then he mouthed to Tommy, "Nothing can live through that."

Tommy shrugged his shoulders. He kept remembering Tarawa, two marines dead before they hit the water out the front of the landing craft, sinking. He remembered the way it felt zigzagging his LCV in and seeing another LCV disintegrate, men and parts of men flying into the air, equipment and pieces of steel vaulting over the ocean, white spray geysering amid the carnage. He remembered the other invasion when he had lost Red Mule. Tommy had been watching Mule's LCV when it had disappeared before his eyes. No part of it was ever found. All hands lost.

Far too soon the order came to go in.

Tommy brought the LCV(P) around and called out, "Able Sector, Red-Y."

The ensign repeated, "Able Sector, Red-Y."

"What's our heading," he asked.

"Two, thirty-two," answered Tommy.

389

"Two, thirty-two, said the ensign, "very well."

Tommy felt a little more comfortable with his commanding officer. Maybe he knew what he was doing.

Ahead, explosions were ripping the beach apart.

A dim visibility had insinuated itself into the air. Tommy could make out streaks of wakes all around him. It was a reassuring sight.

The marines were all huddled together, facing forward. Tommy would have felt sorry for them if he could have spared the effort from worrying about himself. Instead he just looked at them as he wondered whether the LCV would be hit before they got out. If it is, they'll drown, he thought. They'll sink like rocks.

He did not know when the guns stopped. Suddenly he realized a terrible quiet had settled on the sea. He heard only the droning of the LCV engines and the water whomping and sloshing back off its hull.

He kept his eyes riveted on the beaches. He knew what to look for.

O shit.

Flashes of gunfire winked brilliant and incandescent on the slopes above the beaches.

Tommy felt hope drop straight out of him.

He looked over at the ensign.

The officer's face was slack. His jaw hung open. He stared transfixed at the winking batteries.

As the first shots opened holes in the ocean - and created towers of white spray, the noise from the guns' bursts began to reach Tommy's ears. He began to steer the landing craft into evasive action.

The nearer they came to the beach, the more Tommy was able to pick out landmarks. The gun reports that from a mile out seemed indiscriminate developed into clearer patterns as one approached them. Tommy noticed with relief that the water in front of Able Sector, Red-Y was much more devoid of hostile fire than many other beach approaches.

Their beach was clean! What luck. What wild luck!

Throughout his zigzags Tommy kept close track of the two, thirty-two heading. It remained delightfully free of enemy resistance.

Two landing craft assigned to the beach to Tommy's right had already been hit. One had sunk almost immediately. The other was still floundering around in deep water, dead men hanging over the side. Withering fire covered that whole sector. Nobody was going to make it to that beach alive.

Tommy shook his head. He glanced over at the ensign who was listening intently to his headphones. As Tommy's eyes flickered over him the ensign's face turned a ghastly white. After an instant's pause he nodded repeatedly though whoever he was talking to certainly could not see him.

Tommy reached over and touched the ensign. He pointed to the mouthpiece.

"You has to talk," he said.

The ensign stared at the mouthpiece, horror-struck. He looked up at Tommy.

"They want us to go over there," he said, pointing to his right. Before their eyes the surf was filling with death.

29

The night was warm and humid. Wayne wondered what Electa would be wearing. He smiled. He would soon find out.

Penny and Bobo were fast asleep. Wayne looked out of the living room window at the houses in the Corner. All the lights were out. Everyone was asleep. Good.

He was dressed in his darkest shirt and pants, black socks and black shoes. He would be virtually invisible. It was a very dark night. No cloud cover to reflect back the lights from the ground. No moon. Stars in a blackened sky. No one could see him. It was as if the forces of nature had conspired with him.

He stepped out onto his porch and closed the door gently, quietly. He was excited but he felt calmer than he had expected, more deliberate.

His eyes scanned the hotel. A black wall. Not a speck of light.

The street light cast its pole of light down the strip of sidewalk which ran between Electa's house and the Cork's, past Electa's front porch which was on the side of her house.

That was no problem. Wayne would go around the back of the house, along the hotel side, where a row of bushes and mulberry trees would screen him from the hotel. Invisible.

He carried his giant frame quickly and lightly down the stairs and around the back of Electa's house. Once behind the screening line of shrubbery he moved carefully and slowly. He had to avoid noise. No twig snapping. No crunching of dry leaves. He got down on his knees and crawled with utmost care along the side of the house.

When he got even with the bathroom window he

looked up. It was closed. On he went. Electa's bedroom window was open, only the screen between Wayne and the inside. Electa's body lay directly under the window.

Wayne held himself motionless. He tried to still all his senses except his hearing. He listened ... to hear her breathing.

He could not.

He had thought about it for a long time, going in her bedroom window with her asleep directly under the window. How close, how quick, to be on her body immediately. Yet the risk was great. If she heard him tearing open the screen, if the sound should wake her before he got in, she could flee. She could escape. He could be identified before Mr. Big had a chance to do his work. Too dangerous.

But now under the window with her warm, prostrate body so close, he did not know. So quick, so easy. His mouth watered. A roaring began between his ears. Mr. Big rose to attention, thrusting his engorged head against Wayne's pants and pulsating. Now.

Fire burned along Wayne's veins. He stood up. His great head was even with the window. He imagined he could smell her body through the screen. Her *woman*. I could be real quick, the thought, real quick.

No, he told himself. This is too important. I've planned this too carefully to lose it on a sudden impulse. Move. Move. Get away from the window.

He dropped back to his hands and knees and crawled toward the front of the house.

He was breathing heavily. He was sweating profusely. He knew he had almost lost control. He tried to calm himself, to focus on the front of the house.

The streetlight would be shining on the front two windows, but there were bushes directly under them, and if no one were on the street - and at such an hour how could there be anyone - and if everyone across the street were asleep, there would be no witness to his action.

When Wayne reached the front corner of the house he looked across the street. No lights at the Thatch's and the Daws', the families who lived in the part of Wimbey's Corner which was not part of Wimbey's Corner. No lights at the Vermecellis' who lived in the trim white house directly across the street from Electa's. No lights at the Cumbersome apartments which occupied the whole rest of the opposite side of the street.

Wayne released his breath. He had forgotten the giant elm tree on the parkway which blocked the front of Electa's house from the streetlight and almost the whole other side of the street. He chuckled at his good luck.

He wasted no more time. He slipped behind the bush next to the nearest window. He looked up. Yes, the window was raised. Only the screen between him and the inside.

Very quickly he came to his feet and slashed across the whole bottom of the screen with his fishing knife. He dropped the knife into his pocket and with one powerful movement ripped the screen off its frame in one piece. He slipped the screen behind the bush and hoisted himself up and through the window.

Inside, on the living room floor, he was as still as he could be. His body wanted to compensate for his exertion by panting, but he suppressed it. He crouched on the floor in a squatting position trying to recover as he listened. He had to recover slowly because he could not allow himself the luxury of heavy breathing.

He was attuned to the house. He heard no sound.

At last he stood up.

No sound.

He had given a good deal of thought to what he would do next.

Deliberately, slowly, he began to untie his shoes.

When he finished his preparations and at last stood upright again, his huge, powerful body was butt naked.

Swollen and distended, incredible in girth and length, Mr. Big cleaved the air ahead of him.

Wayne Hunter moved on quiet feet into the bedroom.

His eyes had adjusted to the absence of light.

Electa lay on her side, facing the window, her back to him. She wore a long nightgown.

Wayne did not spend much time looking at her, he could see neither her face nor her body and he wanted her.

He had to be careful, though. He did not want her to awaken in fright, but in ecstacy.

He knelt on the floor beside her bed and very, very slowly, very, very gently, began massaging her back.

She must have been sleeping deeply. The massage did not seem to disturb her. If anything it relaxed her further. Wayne heard her breathing deepen.

He massaged her for a long time, the heat from her body flowing into his, and from his into hers. Gradually, almost imperceptibly his hands began to exert more pressure, to become insistent. They began to explore, still impeded by the nightgown, the whole length of her body. Thick drops of saliva fell onto the sheet. Wayne's male member, more like an axe handle than a penis, lay across her right thigh and seeped fluid on the far side of the sheet.

She stirred. She turned onto her back. Her arms were above her head. Her lips were parted. Her eyes were closed.

Wayne bent over and kissed her, sliding his tongue deep into her mouth.

She tensed. Her eyes bolted open.

Now is the time, thought Wayne.

He raised his face from hers.

He knelt over her, reached up and brought her hands down onto his gargantuan sex.

She screamed.

It caught him by surprise, but he jammed his right hand over her mouth.

With his left hand he held her hands onto his surging organ and slid them up and down its length.

"Feel this, baby," he said. "It's all yours. All yours. And soon it's gon' be slidin' up inside you."

Work your magic, Mr. Big, he thought. Work your magic.

She tried to squirm but he had settled his behind on her knees and his weight kept her immobile.

He was in heaven. He was naked astride her. She was stroking her hands up and down his organ and soon Mr. Big's stupendous measurements would incite her passions and she would be all his.

He could not help grinning.

With the hand which imprisoned hers he swung Mr. Big from side to side so that its head rubbed against her breasts. The liquid oozing out of its crack stained her nightgown.

"After you done had me, you won't want nobody else," said Wayne.

The visible parts of her face - her nose, her cheeks, her eyes, her forehead, contorted wildly. She tried to shake her head but Wayne's plank-like hand would not permit it.

Wayne was surprised. He thought by now she would be starting to want him. She could not help having grasped how huge Mr. Big was.

Maybe she'll have to get it inside her, to feel it inside her before she really knows, he thought.

He knelt over her chest, leaving her lower body free to twist and kick, while his huge tool jutted over her face.

"Take a look," he said. "Take a look at what you

396

gon' be gittin'."

Her eyes bucked. Her whole body arched in resistance as if deadly volts of electricity were being pumped through her.

"Oh, well," he said. "The proof of the puddin' is in the eatin'. You gon' find out how good."

He took his left hand and jammed her own hands into her mouth. His freed right hand reached for her lower body.

His eyes were glazed. He grunted now, animal-like. He did not care. It was time. It was time.

His whole being consumed by lust had no awareness of the three shadows darting across the room.

Wellington Cork drove a heavily booted foot directly into Wayne's balls.

Roaring, Wayne stood upright on the bed and bashed his head into the ceiling.

John Brockerton drove a fist into Wayne's adam's apple which both shut him up and dropped him to the floor.

Deftly, Charles Stuart secured a rope around his ankles, then while John and Wellington held his board-like hands together, Charles executed a swift and binding knot around his wrists.

Rebecca Stuart, maneuvering around the trio working over the form prone on the floor, helped Electa off the bed and out of the room.

Charles went into the kitchen and brought out a kitchen chair. They dragged Wayne up and tied him to it.

"Nigger got a big dick," said Wellington.

"Biggest I ever seen," said John.

Wellington and Charles nodded their heads in agreement.

"Look like a horse or a mule dick or something," said Wellington.

The other two nodded.

397

Wayne could not understand what had happened to him. He could not believe it. He looked at the three men.

Them! Them! THEY did *this* to **Me**?

He dropped his head, shaking it.

Charles was sad. "It was just a matter of time," he said.

"We knew you was gon' fall. The only question was when," said Wellington.

John did not say anything.

"You see," said Charles, "We never wanted you in Wimbey's Corner, but once you were here, we hoped," he stopped and looked at Wellington who was exultant, triumph shining in his features, "at least *I* hoped ... that you would see, that you would learn ... that you would live up to the situation into which your overweening pride and ego had untimely thrust you. But you never got straight in your head that this is Wimbey's Corner."

"We takes care of our own," said Wellington.

Wayne could not contain his bitterness. He was reeling with pain. It radiated from a white-hot agony in his groin and shot throughout his body. His throat felt as if it had been stabbed, but he croaked out his disgust anyway.

"You! You! You, assless, phony, chickenshit mothafuckas. Neither one of you is a man! Neither one! You a drunkard," he said, staring at John. "Beat yo wife and daughter. What kind of a man is that?

"You a assless pervert," he said to Wellington. "You ain't half the man I am. Keep yo wife and daughter locked up like they in prison. You ain't nothin' but a common laborer. Ain't got half the job I has, but you keep yo goddman ass up on you shoulders like you owns the goddamn world.

"And you," he said, turning to Charles. "You ain't half a man. Shit, you don't come up to my knee caps. Pipsqueak mothafucka with yo suits and ties, wife leaves

398

yo ass every other weekend. Shit, my boy ain't but eight, and you know what? He's twice the man you is.

"You chickenshit mothafuckas. Everybody knows you let a one hundred year old man scare you to death and run you raggedy - a one hundred year old man! What kind of shit is that? Y'all is dogshit, that's what - dogshit!"

"To this very day you got a eighty-some year old frail ass white woman bossin' you around like you was the dog-doo you is and you take that shit. You take that shit!

"And then you gon' have the nerve - the nerve - to fuck with me. You three assless, chickenshit mothafuckas."

They looked at him.

Silence settled on the room.

They stared at him.

"You through," asked Charles.

Wayne did not reply. He was too furious. He was going to kill them. He was going to kill all three of them.

"Sad, sad, sad," said Charles. "The same problem you have always had. You don't take the time or the effort to observe. What you have to say is all very interesting, but it is also very interesting that you are entirely within our power."

Wellington laughed. "Big nigger. Yeah, big nigger. Be big now." He laughed again.

"I'm going to explain it to you again," said Charles. "You are very stupid so you have a hard time understanding. But they say that repetition will get the job done - get the message across - even through the thickest skulls. You will not believe me, but I genuinely wish you had been able to see this for yourself. I hoped, I earnestly hoped, you would change. You know, we have waited quite a while. Quite a while. But you have not understood, and you do not understand.

"This is Wimbey's Corner."

399

"We takes care of our own," said Wellington.

"And you did not belong," said Charles. "And it is now clear that left on your own you will not belong. There is some deficit, some flaw in you. God knows we gave you the time. God knows, we restrained our hand. But we had to protect our own."

"And we always ready," said Wellington.

"You see," repeated Charles, "this is Wimbey's Corner."

Wayne glanced at John. He had not moved.

"As you have correctly observed," continued Charles, "we all have certain weaknesses. Some of them rather major. And though you might not have identified them correctly - we like to keep our little secrets - your main point is well taken. We are not perfect. On the contrary, we are most imperfect. As individuals. But we do not operate as individuals in the Corner. A fact to which you have remained continually blind. Of course, we live our individual lives. But when it comes to the Corner - not only to our survival, but also to our well-being - we operate as the Corner. Not as Stuart and Cork and Brockerton and Wenders and Hepple. But as the Corner."

"We takes care of our own," said Wellington.

"You have never understood that," said Charles. "You thought we were some kind of exceptional individuals. No. We just know what is necessary for a group of people to thrive in a set of very bad circumstances. Unfortunately, you do not."

"Very unfortunately," said Wellington.

"You have alluded to our kowtowing to Miss Bryce. What you do not understand is that this behavior is a posture of respect, primarily for Eskeridge Wimbey who put together this little collection of buildings and enabled people to come together here and build this little city on a hill. He admired Miss Bryce and left her a legacy. We

400

intend to respect that.

"It is also a posture of respect toward Miss Bryce herself. She worked with Eskeridge while he built his little world, she was of immense service to him. She was - is - a good woman. She has simply grown a bit nutty in her old age.

"But what harm does it do to humor her? She cannot hurt any one of us. She is not malicious. She engages in her flights of fancy. We say, 'Yes, Miss Bryce,' and she goes away.

"Neither her furies nor her declarations have any substance.

"You see, it takes respect, mutual respect, to build anything of continuity. We are not here for the moment. Eskeridge was here before us. And after us will be our children and their children. They may not live in the Corner. But they will have the soil of the Corner to root themselves in. Eskeridge provided for that in his miraculous trust - in perpetuity. We maintain it. We will not let it be destroyed.

"The thought of perpetuity returns me to your allusion to Mackenzie, Mr. Sweet, to you. You are right. He was a very old man, frail. Not as frail as you might imagine, but certainly frail compared to you. He bullied us. But he taught us. And the only way he could retain the vitality to teach us was to bully us.

"Should we not respect what he had learned in over a century of living? Should we not learn from it? Are our egos so frail that we had to shut him up in order to protect them? Please. Many, many times it was Mackenzie who saved the Corner from ruin.

"But you do not understand, Mr. Hunter, because you do not fit."

"You broke the number one rule," said Wellington, "you hurt one of us."

"And would have done much worse," said Charles, "had we not arrived, like the cavalry, in the nick of time. But it was not a miracle. Because, as Mr. Wellington said, in the Corner we are always ready. We are always prepared. We just kept waiting for you not to make a terrible mistake."

"Alcoholic! What do you think about all this," Wayne blurted out at John.

"We cannot turn you over to the police," said Charles.

"Cause you is from the Corner," said Wellington.

"And it would never do to have one of the Corner in the hands of the so-called law. That would make us more vulnerable to attack."

"They could use it t'get us out o' here," said Wellington.

"Because although the trust protects us and though the land and buildings will always remain in the ownership of the trust, it is possible - should there be no resistance - to vacate the buildings and condemn them."

"We's the resistance," said Wellington.

"Yes," said Charles, "so you see, it would be quite impossible to turn you over to the police because although we know you are not one of us, they do not. The unfortunate fact is that you live here. That fact makes them unable to tell the difference between you and us.

"Fortunately for Mrs. Frye, we do not have the same handicap."

"So what you gon' do," said Wayne.

"Notice how under stress the language reverts to type," said Charles, shaking his head in resignation, "though the stutter has quite disappeared."

"Scared it out o' him," said Wellington.

"Perhaps."

Charles stared at Wayne, then walked in a circle

402

around the room, ended up in front of Wayne and stared at him again.

"Deep in your heart you always wanted to belong in the Corner," he said. "Even when ostensibly you resented us and were contemptuous of us, in your innermost being you wanted to belong."

Wellington laughed.

"We really have no option since we can't surrender you to anyone else," said Charles. "We have to accede to your foremost desire. You see, in the end, you win after all."

Wayne lifted his head. He did not understand. Were they going to set him free? Because if they were he was going to kill each one of them. Maybe right here, right now. Maybe he would take his time about it and get them one by one.

Wellington grinned widely. "But we got a problem," he said. "We got to let you become one of us, but you still ain't ready."

That's the truth, thought Wayne. You don't know how much not ready.

"On the other hand, we can't delay," said Charles. "We can't keep you tied up forever. You have a job - there will be inquiries. You have a family."

Cut the mumbo-jumbo, thought Wayne. Get to the point.

"The point, as I said earlier," said Charles, seeming to read Wayne's mind, "is that we have no choice."

"We got t'let you in," said Wellington, beaming incongruously.

"But not as you are," said Charles.

"Uh uh. No way," said Wellington.

"You are too self-centered, too primitive. We have given this careful thought. It is not a spur-of-the-moment decision. We know you, Mr. Hunter. Indeed, we know you too well. Tonight you have given us your final proofs. You have never gained control of your baser instincts. We have to let you in - but," Charles looked directly at Wayne. "There will have to be certain, uh ... alterations."

He nodded to John.

John reached into his pocket and pulled out a dull-looking object. It was dull, at least, until he opened it up and Wayne saw the glistening blade.

"OH NO!"

That was the last thing he said before they jammed the towel into his mouth.

30

Aboard the Monogahela in the Southwest Pacific Tommy Brown twisted in his hammock. He was unable to sleep.

He had refused to take his landing craft into the area death had staked out for his own. He had ferried his marines up to the beach they had been assigned, Able Sector, Red-Y, heading, two, thirty-two.

When he returned to the ship no one had said a word. No court martial was imminent. No reprimand. Nothing.

Good, he thought as he turned over. That's one I won't have to fight.

Because he was going to fight everything he had to. He intended to survive the war. Electa was waiting for him.

He had to get back to her, back to that crazy-ass Wimbey's Corner. He had the feeling they needed another able-bodied man.

List of Featured Characters

Algonquin ....Wayne's fishing mentor
Finnie-Marie Atwater ....Dancing lady
Barbara ....San Francisco nightclub
  denizen
Darla-Anne ....Red Mule's girlfriend
Jersey Blue ....Shoe-shine man
Kenneth Brown ....Sailor
Tommy Brown ....Sailor
Camilla ....Independent prostitute, later
  infatuated with Wayne
Cinnamon ....One of Golden Jones'
  women
Claude Bonfils (Light) ....Pimp
John Brockerton ....Resident of Wimbey's
  Corner
Mabel Brockerton ....Resident of Wimbey's
Corner
Wanda Brockerton ....Wanda and John's daughter
Genuine Cork ....Resident of Wimbey's
  Corner
Ivory Cork ....Genuine and Wellington's
  daughter
Wellington Cork ....Resident of Wimbey's
  Corner
Betty Cutter ....Kenneth Brown's girlfriend
Electa Frye ....Resident of Wimbey's
  Corner
Gabriel Frye ....Resident of Wimbey's
  Corner
Joe Harrison ....A Kentucky villain

Mrs. Hepple ....Resident of Wimbey's Corner

Bobo Hunter ....son of Wayne and Penny

Penny Hunter ....Wayne's wife

Wayne Hunter ....Kentucky Native

Billy Jones ....Sailor

Golden Jones ....Pimp

Matilda ....Wayne's lover

Mrs. McCracken ....landlord

Mr. Mueller ....Kentucky baker

Pearson ....Warrant officer, Tommy Brown's nemesis

Red Mule (George Johnson)...Sailor

Nice ....Light's henchman

Remington .... Wayne's and Penny's reading teacher

Charles Stuart ....Resident of Wimbey's Corner

Rebecca Stuart ....Resident of Wimbey's Corner

Mackenzie Sweet ....Resident of Wimbey's Corner

Delgado Taylor ....Wayne's Chicago apartment neighbor

Theadoshius Williams ....Soldier

Emery Wilson........................Joe Harrison's running buddy

Fends Wenders ....Resident of Wimbey's Corner, hospitalized

Mrs. Wenders ....Resident of Wimbey's Corner

Wynfried Wenders................Resident of Wimbey's Corner

Carol Wimbey ....Niece of Eskeridge Wimbey

Porter Wimbey ....Nephew of Eskeridge Wimbey

Eskeridge Wimbey ....Founder and owner of Wimbey's Corner

About the Author

David Covin and his wife, Judy, have two daughters: Wendy and Holly. They have three grandchildren: Nicola, William, and Claire. They live in Sacramento, with the Akita, Midori